CRIMSON SAND

ALSO BY CHRIS BINNIX

DETECTIVE ROAN SERIES

Crimson Sand

Digital Grave

HANK RITTER SERIES

Give No Quarter

FORTUNE SERIES

Criminal Fortune

Fortune & Forgery - Available Fall 2026

NOVELS

The Interval

NOVELLAS

The Farmhands

CRIMSON SAND

CHRIS BINNIX

25° MEDIA

Identifiers:

LCCN: 2025923237

ISBNs:

979-8-9937336- 0-9 (hardcover),

979-8-9937336-1-6 (trade paperback),

979-8-9937336-2-3 (ebook)

To Dad, I wish you'd seen it.

CRIMSON SAND

The longing sea has eroded me
And I drift abandoned, eternally
The yearning soul taken by another's hand
And I am what remains in the crimson sand

Unknown

CHAPTER

I

THE STREETLIGHT three blocks down had been out for weeks. The cool breeze seeped through the leather of her jacket where the zipper gaped open, and the ocean wind carried the smell of salt and rotting kelp. She shifted her weight, leather creaking, and checked her phone. 10:15. The text she'd sent him—the intersection, typed twice to be sure—stared back at her.

"He said he'd be here." Camila wasn't talking to Jin, but Jin heard anyway.

The darkness stretched longer now, covering more of the cracked sidewalk—fissures spreading like veins through concrete—turning the boarded-up bakery across the street into a hollow shape against the night. Someone had spray-painted MARIA'S across the plywood in faded red letters. Camila's thumb moved to her phone again, the ninth time in five minutes, the screen casting cold light across her face and making her blink. Twenty minutes getting the kohl right, two applications of lipstick, and for what? Where the hell was he?

"Maybe he forgot." Jin's voice came out flat. She stood with her arms crossed over the thin black dress she'd thrown a jacket over, her shoulders hunched against the ocean breeze that pushed between the buildings. The dress had seemed like a good idea earlier—solidarity, she'd said, we're going out, we should look good. "Or maybe he's not coming."

Camila's stomach tightened, a fist of anxiety squeezing just below her ribs. She'd told him where to meet her, had texted the intersection twice to make sure he had it right, had even dropped a pin because men were terrible with directions and worse with promises. But he'd seemed different—his messages careful, asking questions about her day and actually waiting for answers, not like the others who'd blown through her phone with their transparent hunger and bad grammar. This one had felt real.

"He's coming." The words came out too fast, too loud against the empty street. "He just—traffic, maybe. Or he got held up."

Jin made a sound that might have been agreement or skepticism. She stood slightly apart, eyes scanning the street, counting the minutes the way she counted tips—precise, methodical. Camila loved her for that steadiness and resented it in equal measure—loved the careful logic that kept Camila from making truly stupid decisions, resented the silences that felt like judgment.

A car rolled past, a dented sedan with one working taillight, and both of them watched it disappear around the corner. The street felt emptier after it left. More exposed. Camila tugged at the hem of her crop top where it met her jeans—low-rise, studded belt—the outfit she'd spent an hour assembling because she wanted to look good but not desperate, sexy but not trying too hard. The leather jacket helped, gave her an edge, made her feel less like she was waiting for approval and more like she was granting it.

"People are gonna think we're working girls," Jin said, scanning the empty storefronts with their iron gates pulled down, the liquor store two blocks up still open and bleeding yellow light onto the pavement.

Camila laughed, a short bark of sound that surprised them both. "We are working girls." She grinned at Jin's expression, at the alarm that flashed across her face before she caught the joke. "Just not that kind."

"Not funny."

"A little funny."

Jin shook her head, but her mouth twitched, almost smiled, and Camila felt the tightness in her chest ease. They were fine. Everything was fine. He'd be here soon, and they would have a story to tell tomorrow, something good for once, something that didn't involve double shifts and men who stared too long at the restaurant or customers who left Bible verses instead of tips.

Headlights swept across them—a car slowing, pulling toward the curb, and Camila's heart jumped before she registered the shape: a modest sedan, dark blue, not what she was expecting. The window rolled down, and a woman leaned out, fifty-ish with tired eyes and hair pulled back in a practical bun. Scrubs were visible beneath an open jacket.

"You girls okay?" The nurse's voice carried concern, which made Camila feel both grateful and humiliated. "Need a ride somewhere?"

"We're fine," Camila blurted, forcing brightness into her tone, a smile that felt too wide. "Just waiting for someone. But thank you."

The nurse hesitated, her gaze moving between them—taking in Camila's exposed midriff, Jin's uncomfortable stance, the deserted street that probably looked worse from inside a car. "You sure? It's not safe out here this late."

"We're sure." Camila's voice was firm, more final, and after another moment, the nurse nodded and pulled away, her taillights painting the asphalt red before she turned and vanished.

The silence that followed felt heavier. Camila's fingers found her phone before she'd decided to check it. 10:20. The screen's glare made her eyes water—battery at forty-three percent. The anxiety was back, spreading through her chest. Maybe Jin was right. Maybe he wasn't coming. Maybe she'd been stupid to think this time would be different, that a man like him would actually show up for a girl like her, living in a building where the elevator never worked and the hallways smelled like someone else's cooking.

Then she heard it—the low growl of an engine, deeper than the sedan's, more aggressive. Her head snapped up, and there it was—a white sports car, sleek and low to the ground, sliding toward them like something from a music video. Camila's pulse kicked hard against her throat. Her hands smoothed over her jeans. Touched her hair. Dropped to her sides. She forced herself still while her heart hammered, and Jin went rigid beside her.

The car stopped at the curb.

The engine purred, a contained roar that Camila felt in her chest.

Through the windshield, she could make out a shape, a silhouette, but the streetlight was too far and the interior too dark to see details— just a faint outline of shoulders, a hand on the wheel, the glow of the dashboard painting everything in cool blue.

The passenger window slid down with a mechanical whisper.

Relief flooded through her. She moved toward the car, boots clicking on concrete, each step deliberate. She was smiling now, unable to help it, her earlier anxiety burning off. She leaned down, one hand on the door frame—warm metal, expensive—and peered inside. Impressions rather than details: nice clothes, a Rolex catching the dashboard light, cologne that smelled like cedar, and something darker. His face stayed in shadow, angled away, but it didn't matter because he was here, he'd actually shown up, and that was enough.

"Wait." Jin's voice cut through, sharp. "There's no room."

Camila looked. Jin was right—the car was a two-seater, low and fast, built for exactly two people and no more. The bucket seats hugged their occupants, leaving no space for a third. "Oh." The word came out smaller than she had intended. She straightened, turned to face Jin. "I didn't—he didn't mention—"

"It's fine." But Jin's face said it wasn't fine, said this was exactly the thing she'd been worried about, the detail that got overlooked until it was too late. "I'll get a cab."

"Jin—"

"It's fine, Camila." Jin's voice was tight now, controlled. "Go. Have fun. Text me when you get wherever you're going."

Camila's stomach twisted. This wasn't how it was supposed to go. Jin was supposed to come along, to be there, to be the buffer, the witness, and the safety net. Without her, the night felt unmoored, spinning off into possibilities that tilted toward danger as easily as delight. "Are you sure? We could—maybe we could call another—"

"I'm sure." Jin was already stepping back, creating distance. "Go."

Camila looked between Jin and the car, between her friend's closed expression and the open door, the man waiting in shadow who'd driven across the city to find her. She thought about saying no, about choosing Jin over possibility, about being a person who put friendship first. But her hand was still on the door handle, and Jin was still backing away, and the man in the car was still waiting, and Camila was so tired of waiting, of watching other girls get picked while she waited and smiled through her exhaustion and went home to an apartment that smelled like other people's lives.

"I'll be fine," she said, and didn't know if she was reassuring Jin or herself. "I'll text you. Promise."

Jin took a step back. "Don't promise me. Just—be careful."

She slid into the car before she could change her mind. The seat cradled her, leather cool against her back. The door closed with a solid thud, sealing her inside, and through the window, she watched Jin standing on the curb, growing smaller as the car pulled away, her arms wrapped around herself, backlit by the liquor store's yellow glow.

Then they turned the corner, and Jin was gone, and Camila was alone with a man whose face she still couldn't see clearly, whose hand was steady on the gearshift, whose cologne filled the small space between them.

Jin stood on the curb for thirty seconds after the taillights disappeared. Her arms stayed wrapped around herself. The street was empty again —just her and the dark and the distant sound of traffic on the main road. She counted to ten. Checked her phone. Dead battery warning: eight percent. She looked in the direction the car had gone, as if it might reappear, as if Camila might change her mind and tell him to turn around.

Nothing.

She walked.

The fluorescents in the gas station made Jin squint after the dark street. The lights exposed everything—the cracks in the sidewalk spreading like a shattered mirror, the oil stains in iridescent swirls, the trash collected against the building's concrete base. Inside, it was cooler and smelled like burnt coffee and pine-scented cleaning solution that didn't quite cover the stale cigarette odor. The floor was sticky under her heels. She called for a cab from the number taped to the wall because her phone was nearly dead and she didn't trust it to last the ride home.

Her heels clicked against concrete—too loud, too sharp—as she waited outside under the fluorescent overhang. She kept checking her phone, thumb moving automatically to the screen. Nothing. No text from Camila. The scenarios her mind kept creating made her stomach twist. Camila was smart. She knew how to handle herself. She'd promised to text.

Fifteen minutes later, she was in the back of a sedan that smelled like synthetic vanilla air freshener and old cigarettes, watching the city slide past outside her window—blocks of dark buildings punctuated by convenience stores and fast-food joints still open, their lights harsh against the night. The driver didn't speak, which Jin appreciated. She needed silence, needed not to explain why she'd been standing alone on a dark street in a dress and jacket, why her friend had left without her, why this knot of dread sat in her stomach.

The apartment building loomed in the dark—four stories of crumbling brick and rusted fire escapes, the metal slick with ocean damp. Jin paid the driver with bills she'd folded into her jacket pocket, climbed the three flights of stairs that smelled like decades of cooking grease and mildew, and let herself into the apartment that was too small and too warm. The television flickered with a blue light across her mother, asleep in the recliner, her mouth open, her hands folded over her stomach.

Jin stood in the doorway, and something shifted in her chest. She crossed to the closet, the floorboards creaking under her weight, pulled down the worn blanket from the shelf—threadbare fleece that had been soft once—and draped it over her mother's shoulders and lap, tucking it around her sides. The fabric caught on her mother's wedding ring. Her mother didn't wake, just kept breathing those slow, steady breaths.

In the bathroom, Jin peeled off the black dress, letting it pool on the tile floor. She turned the shower on hot and stepped under the spray, letting the water pound against her shoulders, scalding at first, then just hot enough to hurt. The memory of Camila's face as the car pulled away wouldn't leave her alone. She stood there, hands pressed against the tile—cold and slick under her palms—watching water spiral down the drain, and tried not to think about her own voice saying, 'It's fine, go,' giving permission for something that felt increasingly wrong.

She dried off with a thin towel that smelled like detergent, pulled on an oversized t-shirt and cotton shorts, and climbed into bed with her phone clutched in one hand. The screen stayed dark. No texts. No missed calls. Just the time, 11:30, battery indicator down to five percent, the red warning bar pulsing. Jin plugged it in, set it on the nightstand where she could see it if it lit up, and lay on her back staring at the ceiling where water stains made shapes in the dark.

Sleep wouldn't come. Her mind kept circling back—the white sports car, Camila's eager face, Jin's own failure to insist harder, to pull Camila back, to be the friend who said no. Outside, sirens wailed past. A dog barked. Someone's television murmured through the thin walls. Jin checked her phone—11:40—and still nothing. The dread that had been sitting in her stomach all night spread, reaching up into her chest, tightening around her lungs.

She should call, should text, should do something other than lie here frozen.

But her phone stayed silent, and the ceiling stayed dark, and Jin stayed caught between action and inaction, until exhaustion pulled her under into shallow, fitful sleep.

CHAPTER

2

Marge wiped the same spot on the bar for the third time, the rag catching on a groove worn smooth by decades of elbows. Her wedding band clicked against the wood—she still wore it, though Rick had been gone eight years. The college kids in the corner worked their way toward sloppy. The boy's Red Sox cap sat crooked, the girl's laugh sharp enough to cut through "Margaritaville" on the jukebox. They'd been at it for an hour—vodka cranberries instead of beer, touching too much, talking too loud. Palm Beach State, maybe FAU, or out-of-towners. The kind who'd stumble out soon and become someone else's problem. She'd seen a thousand versions of them, and they always ended the same way.

The Oceanside Pub smelled like spilled beer soaked into the wood, fryer oil that never left, and cigarette smoke from before the ban— residue that had worked itself into the grain decades ago and refused to let go. The boards underfoot sagged in places, tacky where the mop missed. The walls wore layers of paint like scar tissue, each coat covering the damage from the last hurricane or the last bar fight or just the slow rot that came from being twenty yards from saltwater for forty years.

Outside, neon signs flickered above the pier. The ocean crashed against the pylons, and somewhere down A1A, a car's bass rattled windows. But inside was her domain. She moved behind the bar with the economy of someone who'd worked the same ten feet for two decades—reaching for bottles without looking, sliding coasters under glasses before they touched wood, catching the eye of anyone who needed another round. Her hands stayed busy. Wipe the counter.

Stack the empties. Check the register. Her eyes stayed busier. Counting faces, measuring moods.

The regulars owned their corners. Old fishermen with sunburned necks nursed Budweisers, talking about kingfish they'd caught twenty years ago. A roofer and his crew sat in the back, laughing, dust still in their hair and under their nails, the logo for Martinez Roofing faded on their shirts. Two bikers leaned at the rail near the TV, eyes glued to a Marlins game, shoulders tense every time Miami struck out. The jukebox kept cycling Buffett—steel drums clattering against voices, laughter, and the crack of pool balls breaking.

Near the back, the college kids—Mason and Brittany, she'd heard them call each other—broke the rhythm. The boy slammed his glass down after another shot, leaned close, and shouted something in the girl's ear. She threw her head back and laughed, tossing her hair and leaning into him. Their kiss landed messy, all tongue and teeth, giggles spilling between.

Marge poured another draft for a biker, watching them from the corner of her eye. The girl's white tube top barely contained her; her mini skirt was riding up. Fake tan lines were visible where her straps should be. The boy's polo shirt was untucked, cheeks flushed whiskey red.

The room carried its usual rhythm. Boots thudding. Glass clinking. Someone's laugh cut through the air, then faded back into the mix. When the noise built too high, Marge shut it down with a look, a word, sometimes just her presence at the end of the bar, arms crossed.

Then Mason leaned too hard into Brittany, nearly toppling the table. She caught him. Kissed him. Laughed through it. They ordered another round, voices slurred now, words bleeding together.

Marge poured and slid the glasses over. The girl's laugh cut the air —bright, brittle. The boy kept looking at the door, then back at her, restless.

At a quarter past midnight, Brittany tugged him up by the hand.

He stumbled. Caught himself on the back of a chair. Laughed.

She pulled harder, dragging him toward the door, their bodies pressed together, his hands already reaching.

They kissed in the doorway, blocking a regular on his way in from a smoke break.

The fisherman grunted a curse, pushing past them. The door swung shut behind him, and through the window, Marge watched the two kids stumble across toward the beach, the girl's white outfit glowing under the streetlights, the boy chasing after her.

Marge shook her head and returned to tending the bar. Someone needed a refill. The Marlins popped out again. Buffett sang about wasting away.

Outside, the air hung humid and thick, salt-heavy enough to taste. The parking lot stretched along the pub and the beach, cracked asphalt scattered with crushed Bud Light cans and Marlboro butts. Overhead, lights buzzed a sickly orange, painting everything in a similar hue. The temperature had dropped ten degrees since they'd gone inside, enough to raise goosebumps but not enough to sober anyone up.

"You're so slow," Brittany said, giggling, spinning on her heels. Her blonde hair caught the light, spun gold for a second before falling back into shadow. She walked backward, arms out for balance, mini skirt riding higher with each step.

"I'm drunk," Mason said, laughing, stumbling after her. His Red Sox cap sat crooked on his head now, the broccoli-textured curls beneath it damp with sweat. "You're drunk."

"I'm perfect." She spun again, nearly fell, and caught herself. "Come on, Mason. Beach. Now."

"I'm going. We're going."

Brittany stopped, turned, and waited for him to catch up. When he did, she grabbed his face with both hands and kissed him hard, messy, tasting like vodka and cranberry and lip gloss. His hands found her waist, slid lower, and grabbed.

She pulled back, grinning. "Race you."

She was already running—heels in her hand now, bare feet slapping the pavement, white outfit glowing. Mason swore, laughed, chased after her, legs unsteady.

They hit the sand at the edge.

The beach opened up before them—wide and dark, the ocean a black wall beyond. The pier stretched off to their left, lights strung along its length. Waves crashed in sets of three, the rhythm hypnotic, foam hissing as it dragged back across packed sand.

Brittany stopped at the edge of the dunes, breathing hard, grinning back at him. Mason caught up, hands on his knees, chest heaving.

"You're—crazy," he gasped.

"You love it."

"Yeah."

She straightened and looked at him. Her grin shifted into something else—something sharper. She reached down, grabbed the hem of her tube top, and pulled it up over her head in one quick motion.

Her breasts spilled free, pale and full, nipples hard in the night air.

Mason's mouth opened, closed, opened again.

"Well?" she said, laughing at his expression. "You coming or what?"

She turned and ran again, topless now, her bare skin catching moonlight, and Mason followed—stumbling through the sand, heart pounding, every thought gone.

They ran past the pier's reach, into the darker stretch where the streetlights didn't touch. The dunes rose on their right, sea oats whispering in the wind. The waves crashed louder here, white foam visible against black water. The sand changed texture—softer here, looser, giving way under their feet with each step.

Brittany stopped, turned, and Mason crashed into her. They went down together into the sand, laughing, limbs tangled, her hair in his face. She kissed him again, harder this time, hands pulling at his shirt. He kissed back, hands everywhere, breath coming fast.

The sand was cold and gritty beneath them. It got into everything—hair, mouth, under fingernails—but neither of them cared. Mason's hand found her breast and squeezed. She arched into him, making a sound low in her throat.

Then his hand slid lower, past her waist, and touched something wet.

Not skin wet. Not sweat wet.

Sticky wet.

Warm.

Thick between his fingers.

Slick in a way that made his drunk brain hesitate, confusion cutting through the haze before understanding could form. His palm pressed flat against fabric that should have been dry, and the wetness spread, soaking into the creases of his hand, getting under his nails.

He pulled his hand back.

Looked at it in the moonlight.

Dark. Glistening. Too dark. The liquid caught the moon's light in a way that made his stomach drop before his mind could name what he was seeing.

"What the—"

Brittany sat up, looked down at her stomach, at the dark smear across her white mini-skirt, at Mason's hand, covered in something black and viscous.

Her scream started small. Then built. Then became something that ripped the night open.

Mason scrambled backward through the sand, and then he saw it —the thing they'd been lying on.

A body.

Half-buried in the sand between the dunes, positioned on its back with one pale arm flung outward, fingers curled. White crop top beneath a black leather jacket slick with something that had soaked through to the sand beneath, creating a dark halo. Jeans clung to the hips, low-slung, the studded belt cinched tight. Sand had already begun to drift across the legs, collecting in the folds of denim. Dark hair fanned out around the head in a corona, individual strands visible where moonlight touched them. Face upturned, catching the moonlight full-on, eyes wide open and vacant, reflecting nothing. Makeup streaked beneath the lashes—black kohl dissolved by tears or seawater. Mouth parted as if caught mid-breath.

The wounds across her stomach gaped where the jacket had fallen open—deep slashes, edges ragged, black in the moonlight but unmistakably wet. Her neck bore a similar wound, a line that ran from beneath her ear toward her collarbone. Blood had pooled in the surrounding sand, still tacky to the touch, oxidizing at the edges to rust but fresh enough at the center to be nearly black, mixing with sand grains to form a dark paste.

Brittany's screaming didn't stop.

Mason's stomach lurched. He rolled onto his hands and knees and vomited into the sand—vodka and cranberry and bar chips, everything coming up in hot waves while his body shook. His mind tried to process what he was seeing and couldn't, just kept circling back to those open eyes, that dark blood, the way they'd been lying on her, touching her. The first heave burned his throat. The second brought up mostly liquid, spattering the sand. The third was dry, his body convulsing, trying to expel something that wasn't there, ribs aching with the effort.

Brittany had stopped screaming. She sat in the sand now, knees pulled to her chest, blood on her legs and stomach, staring at the body with an expression that had gone past horror into something blank and distant. Her fingers picked at the blood on her skin, scraping without purpose, the motion automatic, robotic.

Mason wiped his mouth with the back of his hand. Looked at it. Blood covered his hand from where he'd touched her. From where they'd—his stomach heaved again, but nothing came up, just bile burning the back of his throat.

Waves pounded the shore. Moonlight cast long shadows. Sea oats swayed in the sand around what had once been a woman.

Mason's hands shook as he pulled his phone from his pocket. His fingers, slick with blood, wouldn't work right. He dropped it. Picked it up. Tried again.

The screen wouldn't unlock. Blood smeared across the glass in rust-colored streaks, his fingers sliding over the sensor, leaving prints. The phone's Face ID rejected him—his features were too distorted, too panicked, and the low light confused the camera. He wiped his hand on his jeans, smearing more blood, creating sticky patches on the denim. Tried again. The phone buzzed, and it rejected him. His hands shook too hard to hold it steady. The screen's harsh white light illuminated the blood coating his palm, making it look almost purple.

Brittany still hadn't moved, still hadn't spoken, and just sat there covered in someone else's blood, staring at the dead girl's face, at those eyes that stared at nothing.

In the distance, the Oceanside Pub pulsed—music and laughter spilling out into the night, Buffett still singing about cheeseburgers in paradise, Marge still pouring drinks, the regulars still telling their stories. The city's heart kept beating, but here in the crimson sand, a girl's had stopped.

CHAPTER

3

His phone buzzed against the nightstand at a quarter to one. Daniel Evans had been in Lake Worth a month, still waking to the smell of burnt garlic and cumin—the last tenant's cooking still seeping through the rental house vents. Body on the beach. Oceanside Pub. Homicide.

He grabbed his jacket, keys, and badge. Six minutes later, his unmarked Ford Explorer Police Interceptor rolled into the beach parking lot.

Two cruisers angled near the beach access, light bars throwing blue and red strobes across the Casino Building's coral arches. The strobes turned faces in the crowd ghost-pale, then blood-red, then ghost-pale again, shadows jerking with each rotation. Yellow tape flapped between pylons in the salt wind. A small crowd pressed against the perimeter—late-night stragglers, bar patrons who'd wandered out to watch. Uniforms kept them back, hands on their belts. A radio crackled somewhere, a dispatcher's voice cutting through the crash of waves against the pier pylons.

Evans cut the engine. The air hung thick when he opened the door, tasting of salt and gasoline and something metallic underneath.

He ducked under the tape. A tech in gloves knelt near the dunes, planting evidence markers. Another one photographed tire tracks in the sand. Near the pub's entrance, a blonde girl sat wrapped in a shock blanket, mascara streaked down her face. A uniformed officer stood beside her, notepad in hand.

"Detective Evans?"

He turned. A woman in uniform stepped forward—black hair pulled so tight it gleamed, not a strand out of place. A precise line of eyeliner made her gaze cut through him. The badge on her chest read: C. PEREZ.

"Officer Pérez." She handed him a clipboard. "The body's in the dunes, forty yards down from the pier. Two college kids found her around twelve-thirty. The male vomited at the scene, and the female went into shock. Both held for statements."

Evans took the clipboard and scanned the initial incident log. Nichols had filled it out—sloppy handwriting, one time stamp already scratched out and corrected.

"Nichols on scene?" Evans said.

"Yeah." Pérez's tone carried resignation. "He's working perimeter. Or supposed to be."

Evans nodded. "Victim ID'd?"

"Not yet. No wallet, no phone on the body. We're checking the bar."

"Cause of death?"

"Stabbed. Multiple times. Avery's coming."

Evans clicked his pen and made a note. His hand stayed steady—first homicide. Wellington had property crimes, domestics, and the occasional overdose. This was different. This was what he'd transferred for, what he'd spent six years working toward, and now that it was here, his stomach felt tight and his mouth tasted like copper.

"Show me," he said.

Pérez led him down the beach. The sand shifted underfoot, harder to walk on than asphalt, giving way with each step and filling his shoes with grit. The pier lights buzzed overhead, casting weak circles that barely reached the surf. Waves crashed in sets, indifferent.

They reached the dunes.

The body lay half-buried in sand between two rises of sea oats. White crop top. Black leather jacket. Dark jeans. Dark hair spread like seaweed. Face turned toward the moon, eyes open, lifeless.

Evans stopped. Made himself look. His eyes wanted to skitter away, to focus on the sand, the sea oats, anything else. He forced them back to her face. Then her neck. Then her torso. Building the picture piece by piece because that was the job.

She was young. Maybe twenty, twenty-one. Skin pale in the floodlights—harsh white light that washed out color and made the blood look black—lips parted. Blood pooled beneath her torso, mixing with sand to form a dark paste that spread in a rough halo. The crop top showed tears—two punctures across the stomach, fabric stained dark and stiff. Another wound at the neck, deeper, ragged at the edges where the blade had caught and torn.

Evans wrote: Three visible wounds—two abdominal, one neck. Extensive blood loss.

A tech glanced up. "Detective."

"Yeah."

"We've got footprints—two sets leading in, same two staggering back out. Probably the kids who found her. There's another set here, heavier, leading toward the parking lot. Could be older."

Evans nodded. "Mark them. Get casts if you can."

"Already on it."

Pérez handed him gloves. "Dr. Avery should be here in five."

Evans pulled them on, latex snapping against his wrists. He crouched near the body, careful not to disturb the sand. The smell hit him harder down here—copper and seaweed and the sweet-rot smell of blood in salt air, something that made his throat want to close. He leaned closer, breathing through his mouth.

Her hands showed scuffs across the palms, skin abraded—defensive wounds. No dirt under the nails, but she'd fought, tried to push the blade away.

"Detective Evans."

He stood, turned.

A man approached from the pub—tall with stooped shoulders, skin pale and veined grey, hair iron-black streaked with silver. Round wire-rimmed glasses sat low on his nose, catching the floodlight. He carried a black bag in one hand, a clipboard pressed tight in the other, and moved with the careful economy of someone used to working around the dead.

"Dr. Avery," Evans said.

Avery nodded. No handshake, no greeting. He set his bag down with care, the metal clasps clicking. Gloves went on, practiced, then he knelt beside the body, moving with the impersonal neatness of habit.

For a long moment, he didn't speak. His eyes moved—face, neck, torso, hands, legs—cataloging without comment. His fingers pushed his glasses higher, an automatic gesture.

He leaned closer. Lifted the victim's chin a fraction, supporting the head with his palm. Examined the neck wound, tilting his head to catch the light.

"Single-edged blade. Nine to ten inches. Puncture of the carotid. That's the probable cause of death. Wounds to the abdomen are deep."

Evans' pen scratched against paper.

Avery straightened, nudged his glasses higher again—the same unconscious adjustment. "Lividity puts her here for about an hour. Rigor hasn't set. Time of death, between eleven and eleven-thirty."

"Any signs of sexual assault?"

"Need to get her on the table first. No obvious tearing of clothing other than the stabs. No visible bruising on the thighs. Doesn't rule anything out, but nothing apparent."

Evans nodded, writing.

Avery's gaze flicked up. "You're new."

"About a month now."

"From Wellington?"

"Yeah."

"This isn't Wellington."

"I know."

"Good." Already focused on his work, hands moving over the body with clinical precision, checking lividity patterns along her back and shoulders where blood had settled.

Evans stepped back. The crowd at the perimeter had grown—thirty, maybe forty people. A news van pulled up. A reporter with a microphone pushed toward the tape. A patrolman moved to intercept.

Evans looked at Pérez. "Let's start with the bar. Someone inside might know her."

"Already cleared the interior," Pérez said. "Marge—the owner—she's waiting."

They walked back toward the Oceanside. The music had stopped. The jukebox sat dark. A few patrons lingered near the back—old fishermen nursing drafts, bikers watching through the window.

Marge stood behind the bar, arms crossed. Hair still piled high, lipstick still red. The fatigue on her face came from seeing too much, knowing more was coming. A cigarette burned in an ashtray beside the register, smoke curling up toward the ceiling fan that turned too slowly to do any good.

Evans approached. "Ma'am. Detective Evans, Palm Beach Sheriff's Office."

Marge nodded. "Marge Lecomte. I run the place."

"I understand you were working tonight when the body was discovered."

"I was." Her voice stayed steady with an edge underneath. "Heard the screaming from the beach. Called it in when I knew what it was."

"Did you see the victim earlier tonight?"

Marge hesitated. Then nodded. "Yeah. She was here."

Evans' pen stopped moving. "You're sure?"

"Positive." Marge reached under the bar, pulled out a plastic ID. "She left this behind."

Evans took it. Turned it over.

Florida driver's license. Photo of a young woman—brown hair, kohl-lined eyes. Camila Morales.

Evans stared at the photo. Then looked through the window at the body on the beach—same girl.

"When was she here?"

"Came in around quarter to eleven with a guy." She tapped the bar top. "They sat up here. Had a couple of drinks. He left, maybe at quarter past eleven. Eleven-twenty tops. She hung around. Knocked back two more rounds solo, then took off herself, maybe fifteen minutes after he did."

"Can you describe the guy?"

Marge's eyes went to the ceiling, thinking. "Tall. Dark hair—not much grey. Late thirties, I guess. Linen shirt, if I'm remembering right. I didn't get a good look at his face. He didn't say much. Paid cash."

"Did they argue?"

"Started off all over each other." Her eyebrows showed distaste. "But it soured quickly. Little spat, sharp words. He signaled for the check right after."

Evans wrote it down. "Anyone else see them?"

"Probably. The place was busy. But most folks were minding their own business."

Evans glanced at Pérez. She nodded, already pulling out her notebook.

The door swung open.

A man stepped inside.

The fisherman's glass stopped halfway to his mouth. One of the bikers straightened, boot scraping against the floor. Marge set down the glass she'd been polishing.

The man was in his late forties or early fifties, of average build, wearing a grey suit without a tie. Salt-and-pepper hair combed back but not fussy. Pale grey eyes that missed nothing. A thin scar ran along the left side of his neck, almost invisible unless the light caught it right.

He moved with purpose—each step, measured.

His gaze swept the room—counted faces, noted positions, cataloged exits—then landed on Evans.

Evans straightened.

The man walked over. Stopped two feet away.

"Detective Roan. You must be Evans."

Evans nodded. "Yes, sir."

Roan extended a hand. Evans shook it. Firm grip, brief.

"Heard you transferred in from Wellington," Roan said.

"That's right. Took the promotion a month ago."

Roan nodded. "Good timing." Matter-of-fact. "What do we have?"

Evans gave him the rundown—body on the beach, multiple stab wounds, victim identified as Camila Morales, last seen here with an unidentified male around eleven-thirty.

Roan listened without interrupting. When Evans finished, Roan glanced at Marge.

"Marge."

"Roan." Her voice warmed.

"Never thought I'd find your place dressed up in crime-scene tape."

Marge cocked an eyebrow. "Oceanside hasn't seen this much excitement since the health inspector threatened to shut me down."

She gestured toward the beer taps—three standard handles, and at the end, a bright pink plastic flamingo mounted sideways like a fourth tap. Behind it, a faded Polaroid was thumb-tacked to the wall: Marge, twenty years younger, holding the flamingo like a trophy.

"Told him the flamingo was structural. He didn't buy it."

A corner of Roan's mouth lifted. "And yet, here you are, still pouring the coldest beer in Lake Worth."

"That's because I bribed him with conch fritters." A wink tucked in.

"Busy night?"

"Was." She gestured toward the window. "Less so now."

Roan's mouth twitched. "I'll need a statement."

"Figured."

He turned to Evans. "Dr. Avery here?"

"On the beach with the body."

"Good. Let's have a look."

They walked back outside. The crowd had swelled—flashbulbs popping, a reporter shouting questions. Roan ignored it.

Pérez fell into step beside them. She handed Roan a clipboard without being asked. He scanned it as they walked, eyes moving fast.

They reached the dunes.

Dr. Avery glanced up. "Roan."

"Martin."

Avery gestured at the body. "Three wounds. Blade's single-edged, nine, maybe ten inches. Carotid puncture—that's what did it. Abdominal wounds are deep, quick strikes." He looked down again. "Time of death between eleven and eleven thirty. Lividity's one to two hours post-mortem, which fits."

Roan crouched beside the body. Controlled movements—one knee down, the other bent, weight balanced. He didn't touch anything, just looked. His gaze traveled—face, neck, torso, hands—slower than Avery's, reading something only he could see. Twenty years of homicides had taught him to notice what others missed: the angle of a hand, the pattern in blood spatter, the small disruptions in sand that told a story.

He stopped. Leaned closer, head tilting to catch the light on the wounds.

"You smell that?" Roan's voice came low.

Evans nodded. "Blood, sir."

Roan tilted his head. "Not just blood. There's liquor in it. She'd been drinking." No judgment, just fact. He'd learned long ago that victims came as they were—drunk, sober, careful, reckless—and it all mattered.

Evans tightened his grip on the notebook.

Roan's eyes moved to Camila's hands against the dark sand.

"Defensive wounds."

"Yes, sir," Avery said. "Scuffed hands but no tissue under the nails."

Roan examined the angle of the neck wound, his own hand moving in the air to trace the blade's path without touching. "This one's different from the others."

Avery pushed his glasses up. "How so?"

"Abdominal wounds are straight in, perpendicular to the body. Efficient. No hesitation." Roan's finger traced the air above the wounds, demonstrating the downward angle. "But the neck—" He paused, his hand shifting to mimic a horizontal slash. "That's a slash, not a stab. Different motion. Different intent."

Avery leaned in, looked again. Evans saw the moment he registered what Roan was seeing.

"Two separate actions," Avery said.

"Two separate moments," Roan corrected. He stood, eyes still on the body, mind piecing together the sequence. "He stabbed her twice in the stomach. She went down. Then he cut her throat." He looked at Evans. "Why?"

Evans blinked. "Sir?"

"The abdominal wounds were enough. Most likely fatal. So why the throat?"

Evans thought. "To make sure she was dead?"

"Maybe." Roan didn't sound convinced. "Or he knew what he was doing."

Roan turned and scanned the surrounding sand. His gaze moved in a pattern—footprints, blood spatter, Camila's position relative to the parking lot. He crouched again, this time near her feet.

"She was facing him when he stabbed her."

"How do you know?" Evans said.

Roan pointed at the blood spatter, droplets visible in the floodlight's glare. "Pattern moves backward, toward the dunes. If she'd been turned away, it would spray forward. She saw him coming."

He crouched again, studying the sand near Camila's feet. "Drag marks here. Faint, but there. Her heels dug in." He looked up at Evans. "She tried to move backward. Tried to get away."

Evans wrote fast, his hand cramping.

Roan stood and brushed sand from his knee. Turned and lowered his voice so only Evans could hear. "One more thing. When we question the patrons—look at their hands."

Evans frowned. "Their hands?"

Roan's stare was granite. "Nothing's clean about knife work. Blood makes everything slippery—handle, fingers, everything. Half the time, the killer walks away wearing their own cut. You find someone with a fresh slice on their hand, you write it down."

Evans committed it to memory—hands, always the hands.

Roan straightened, scanned the scene once more. Committing it to memory. Then headed back toward the pub.

"Let's get statements."

The bar's energy had drained. The remaining crowd huddled in corners, ice melting in tumblers, voices barely carrying. The fisherman's hand trembled as he lifted his glass, beer sloshing against the rim. Others stared at nothing.

Behind the counter, Marge polished the same glass for the third time, the rag moving in circles.

Roan walked up and leaned on the rail. "Marge."

She set the glass down. "Miller Lite?"

"Please."

She pulled a frosted glass from the cooler, poured, and slid it across. Roan caught it, took a sip, and set it down.

She looked at Evans. "Would you like a drink—?"

"Detective Evans is on duty, Marge."

Marge's mouth quirked. "Right."

Heat crawled up Evans' neck. He kept his expression neutral.

Roan took another sip and set the bottle down. Looked at Pérez. "Start with the regulars. Evans, you lead. Pérez, you assist."

"Yes, sir," Pérez said.

Evans nodded.

They moved to the first table—two fishermen, both in their sixties, sunburned and weathered.

"Evening, gentlemen. Detective Evans, PBSO. I need to ask you a few questions about tonight."

The first fisherman shrugged. "Don't know nothin'. Was drinking, minding my business."

"Did you see this woman?" Evans showed him Camila's ID photo.

The man squinted. "Maybe. Lotta people in here tonight."

"She was at the bar around ten-thirty with a man. Tall, dark hair, linen shirt."

The second fisherman grunted. "Saw a girl at the bar. Didn't pay attention. Marge runs a good place—you don't stare."

Evans noted it. Checked their hands—thick calluses across the palms from rope and fishing line, a healing cut on one man's thumb that looked days old, edges already scabbed. Clean otherwise—no fresh cuts.

"Thank you."

They moved on. Interviewed the bikers—same story. Saw nothing, heard nothing. Evans checked their hands: motor oil under the nails, knuckles scarred from old fights—no fresh wounds. The roofers in the back gave identical answers. Evans noted tar stains on their fingers, one man's palm wrapped in gauze from a job site injury, but nothing recent enough to matter.

Then they reached Mason and Brittany.

Mason sat hunched forward, elbows on his knees, Red Sox cap still backward. Green around the edges, ready to vomit again. The smell of sick clung to him, sour and sharp. Brittany sat beside him, shock blanket pulled tight, eyes red from crying. Black mascara smeared the edge of the blanket where she'd pressed her face.

Evans sat across from them. "I'm Detective Evans. I know this has been a rough night, but I need you to walk me through what happened."

Mason swallowed. "We—ah—we were just…"

"We were drunk," Brittany said, voice hoarse. "We left the bar and went to the beach. We were just—" She broke off, face flushing.

"We were making out," Mason finished, miserable. "In the sand. And then—" His throat worked. "We rolled over and—she was just—there."

Brittany started crying again.

Evans kept his voice gentle. "Did you see anyone else on the beach? Hear anything?"

"No. Just—just us. And then—her."

"Did you touch the body?"

"I—yeah. I mean, not on purpose. We—" Mason's face went pale. "There was blood. On my hands. I didn't know until—"

"It's okay. Did you see anyone leaving the area? Hear a car?"

Both shook their heads.

Evans checked their hands. Blood under Mason's nails, still visible despite his attempts to wipe it off, rust-colored crescents trapped beneath the quick. More blood had smeared on Brittany's legs where she'd tried to scrape it away. But no cuts. No fresh wounds.

"Thank you. Officer Pérez will take your contact information. We'll be in touch."

They moved on. Questioned the last few patrons. Nothing useful. No one saw Camila leave. No one remembered the man she was with —no cuts on anyone's hands.

Evans returned to the bar. Roan was still there, second Miller Lite half-full. Marge stood across from him, arms folded, expression thoughtful.

"Anything?" Roan said.

"No, sir. No one saw anything after she left the bar. All hands clean."

Roan drained his beer, then set it down. Looked at Marge. "Thanks."

"Anytime."

He turned to Evans. "We need to notify the family. You have her address?"

Evans checked the ID. "709 South Federal Highway, Lake Worth."

"Let's go."

They walked toward the door. Evans' chest tightened—his first death notification in Lake Worth. Once before, in Wellington, a car accident. He remembered the particular nausea of it, the mother's face when he'd said the words, the way she'd folded in on herself like something collapsing.

Outside, the crowd had thinned. The news van lingered, its lens fixed like an unblinking eye. Roan passed by as though it didn't exist.

Nichols approached, forensic suit creaking. "You want me back here, Detective? To keep the tape?"

Roan's lips twitched. "Evans, you drive. Nichols, hold the tape. Try not to hang yourself with it."

Evans found his Explorer. Roan took the passenger seat, settling in without comment. Evans settled behind the wheel, his hands finding their usual position at ten and two. For a moment, neither spoke. Then Roan's voice came level.

"Good work tonight."

Evans turned. "Sir?"

"You kept your head. Asked the right questions. Followed procedure." Roan's gaze was direct, lines at his eyes revealing nothing. "That's half the job."

Evans swallowed, sat straighter. "Thank you, sir."

One nod from Roan, slow and final. "Let's go tell her family."

Evans started the engine and pulled out of the lot. Behind them, the crime scene tape fluttered in the wind.

CHAPTER

4

ROAN STOPPED at the bedroom doorway. A patrol car idled outside. The ceiling fan ticked overhead, wobbling with each rotation, shadows shifting across faded wallpaper.

He breathed in the air. Coconut lotion, drugstore vanilla body spray, the faint coffee-and-grease smell clinging to the diner mug on the desk—all of it trying to mask what bled through: old cigarette smoke seeping from the hallway, damp mildew crawling from the walls. But underneath, faint—Chanel. Not a knockoff. The real thing. A single bottle on the dresser, half-empty, dust-free in a perfect circle where she'd moved it daily. The room tried to be young, hopeful, but was already losing ground to the surrounding apartment.

Evans stood just inside the doorway, shoulders squared, notepad open. His eyes swept the room too quickly, like he didn't want to see too much at once.

"First time in a victim's home?" Roan said.

Evans swallowed. "No, sir. Had a traffic fatality in Wellington. Went to notify the next of kin."

"That's not the same." Roan stepped inside. "Death notifications are about delivering news. This is about reading a life backward."

He moved to the bed first—sheets still tangled from this morning, the impression of her body still visible in the mattress. Then to the laundry basket—clothes from yesterday's shift, maybe the day before. Then to the desk—textbooks open to chapters she'd been studying, notes dated two days ago. Working backward through her routine, reconstructing the hours before someone ended them.

Evans nodded, pen poised, watching Roan's pattern.

The bed pressed against the wall, sagging with use. Tangled sheets, sunflower quilt faded at the seams. A pink velvet throw pillow on the floor carried a smear of mascara, the fabric worn smooth in the center where she'd held it, matted at the edges. White sneakers slumped nearby, laces mismatched and trailing. Over the headboard, posters sagged in the humidity—pop stars with perfect smiles, a Frida Kahlo print bent at the corners, edges curling away from the wall, thumbtacks straining.

The desk under the window leaned to one side. Textbooks tottered beside palettes of makeup dusted across the surface, pages beginning to ripple from the moisture in the air. A mug advertising the Nifty Fifty Diner held pens and highlighters, the logo worn. A curling iron with stripped insulation perched too close to yesterday's notes. Over the chair hung a denim jacket with embroidered roses, pockets heavy with receipts and coins.

Evans, already gloved, crouched by the nightstand. He opened the drawers a fraction of an inch at a time. Empty. He slid his hand under the edge of the mattress, smoothing the sheet back into place with the same careful precision he'd used sealing the evidence bag earlier. His notepad lay across the quilt, pen lined beside it, perfectly parallel.

Roan scanned the rest: laundry basket toppled with clothes—denim worn thin, a sequined dress, diner apron blotched with grease—the dresser top: hollow hoop earrings, a snapped charm bracelet, cheap jewelry.

But it was what wasn't here that caught him.

No purse on the hook by the door. He moved closer, touched the wall beneath it—paint worn lighter in an arc where a strap had rubbed against it daily. The hook itself was sturdy, screwed tight into the stud. She'd used it every day. He pulled out his phone, photographed the empty hook, the wear pattern on the wall.

No phone charging on the nightstand. He crouched where Evans had been, noting the outlet and the dust pattern on the surface where a charging cable would have rested—another photo.

Evans glanced up from the nightstand, frown deepening. "Sir, there's nothing here. No wallet, no phone."

"Exactly." Roan straightened, eyes on the empty hook by the door. "She left with them. Or someone took them after."

Evans made a note, then positioned himself where Roan had stood, looking at the same angle, learning the methodology.

Roan moved to the desk, fingers hovering over the textbooks without touching. Introduction to Psychology. English Composition II. Palm Beach State course codes scrawled on the inside covers. She was trying hard. In homicides, victims weren't bodies first—they were people with routines, ambitions, futures they'd never reach—understanding who they'd been meant understanding who might have wanted them gone.

"Look at this room, Evans. What do you see?"

Evans straightened and studied the space. "Student. Working class. She wanted out. Wanted more."

"Good. Now look closer. What's she fighting against?"

Evans' gaze drifted to the mildew creeping at the window frame, the peeling wallpaper. "Poverty."

"Poverty. But not just that. Look at how hard she's trying. The textbooks. The diner mug. The jacket she probably saved for. She's clawing her way out of something." He paused. "And then someone stopped her."

Evans returned to the desk, rifling through notebooks. His hand paused on a small, spiral-bound diary, cover softened with use, a rose sticker peeling at the edge.

"Sir." He held it up.

Roan didn't reach for it. "Bag it." His eyes caught the date scrawled across the open page: three days ago. "We'll read it at the station. Right now, we need to understand the family."

Evans slipped the diary into an evidence bag, sealed it, and marked it with the same meticulous care he'd shown before. Date, time, location, item description—his handwriting was small and precise.

Roan took one last look at the room. The ceiling fan kept ticking, shadows twitching on the walls.

"Negative space," Roan said.

Evans looked up.

Roan gestured to the hook, then the nightstand, demonstrating the concept with his hand tracing the absent shapes. "The real story's in what's missing. Hold on to that."

Evans wrote it down. The real story's in what's missing.

The hallway outside Camila's room was dim, the drywall sweating in patches where pipes leaked. The tick of the ceiling fan faded behind them, replaced by the heavier silence of an apartment that had given up. The carpet underfoot was threadbare, every step sighing dust into the air.

Evans walked close behind Roan, pen clipped to his notepad.

The living room opened before them. A lamp with a jagged shade spilled light across a sagging sofa. Cigarette burns charred the cushions, springs showing through the seams. The air carried cheap vodka, fried food, and nicotine baked into the walls.

Maria Morales sat in the armchair beneath the lamp, crumpled in on herself, hands clenched around a tissue dissolved to pulp. Bruises of exhaustion pooled under her eyes, skin blotched red. Her blouse, once floral, now carried wine stains. Hair unwashed, pulled back in a loose knot, sagging at her neck.

On the coffee table, empty bottles leaned against each other. Dollar bills were scattered between them. The kitchen beyond showed worse—dishes floating in grey water, a skillet rusting on the stove, trash overflowing onto the floor.

Evans slowed, hesitation in his shoulders. His throat tightened. The bottles reminded him of his uncle's apartment in Wellington, with the same smell of surrender. He shifted his weight, pen gripped harder than necessary.

Roan didn't break stride. He pulled a chair from the table, set it opposite Maria, and sat. Distance enough not to crowd her. Distance enough to read her.

"Mrs. Morales. Detective Roan. This is Detective Evans."

Maria looked up once, then dropped her gaze back to the tissue.

"We need to ask some questions while the details are fresh. Even if they don't seem important now, they help us see the pattern."

She gave the faintest nod.

"Your daughter's name."

"Camila." The word trembled, breaking on the second syllable. "Camila Morales."

"Age?"

"Twenty-one."

"This address?"

She murmured it in fragments. Roan repeated it whole. "1709 South Federal Highway. Apartment 2B."

"Was Camila working?"

Her lips parted, closed, opened again. "Nifty Fifty Diner. Any shift they'd give her. Mornings, nights. Doubles when she could."

"And studying?"

A swallow. "Palm Beach State. She wanted—" Her voice cracked, dropping to a whisper. "She wanted to be the first in the family to graduate."

Roan let that settle. "Tell me about her week. What did it look like?"

"Work. School. Studying late. Sometimes at the diner after closing. She'd sit in a booth with her books." Maria's hands twisted the tissue. "She barely slept."

"Conflicts? Trouble with anybody?"

Maria shook her head. "She didn't like to talk about problems. Not with me."

"At work?"

"No. She just worked. Kept her head down."

"Debt?"

"She got by. If she owed—she didn't tell me."

Roan leaned forward. "Relationships? Boyfriends?"

Her mouth twisted. "Boys. Sometimes. Nothing serious. Not that I knew."

"Did she bring anybody here?"

Maria's eyes lifted, hollow. "No. Never. She kept that part of her life away."

Evans made a note. Camila didn't bring people home because home was this—bottles, decay.

"Any friends you distrusted?" Roan said.

"She kept them all away from the apartment. I didn't know most of their names."

"Threats? Anyone making her afraid?"

"No," Maria whispered.

Roan paused. "When did you last see her?"

"Yesterday. Before her shift. She left around seven in the morning. Said she'd be back late."

"And tonight?"

Her eyes drifted to the bottles. "Here. Drinking. Alone almost all night. I think Ariel was in his room, but he doesn't talk, doesn't come out much."

"Anything missing from her room?"

Maria's gaze shifted. "Her phone. Purse. She went nowhere without them."

Roan placed a card on the table. "Call us if you remember more."

She didn't respond, just squeezed the tissue until it unraveled.

Roan stood. His eyes flicked to the hallway, where another door waited.

He was already moving.

The hallway constricted around them. At the far end, a door hung open, casting yellow light over the dust. Roan pushed the door the rest of the way.

Ariel Morales perched at the edge of the bed, shoulders hunched, knees jutting through thin denim. Long sleeves, despite the heat, black fingerless gloves frayed at the seams. White bandages were visible on his wrists, wound tight.

The room: sketches everywhere. Scattered over the carpet, taped to the walls, stuffed beneath the mattress. Charcoal streaks blackened Ariel's fingertips, staining his shirt collar. The air smelled of charcoal and paper and something more acrid—sweat and close quarters and unwashed clothes.

The drawings: angels with swords, crosses consumed by fire, contorted figures screaming. The paper felt brittle under the A/C's dry breath, edges curling, charcoal dust coating everything. And phrases repeated in block letters:

THE WAGES OF SIN IS DEATH
REPENT OR BURN
GOD SEES ALL

On the desk: an open sketchbook half-hidden beneath textbooks —Leviticus: A Commentary, Romans and Redemption, Living in God's Grace. Well-thumbed, creased spines. Just visible below, softer sketches in pencil—two male figures, hands knotted together.

Roan took it in. His face stayed neutral, professional. Evans stood behind him, watching Roan's poker face, trying to learn it.

A photograph on the dresser, facedown. Through the backing paper, formal vestments—a church photo, an altar boy.

Over the bed, a crucifix hung crooked. Rosary slung from one arm, beads tangled.

In the trash: empty prescription bottles. Maria's name on the labels. Oxycodone. Xanax. Painkillers.

Evans stopped at the doorway. The air pressed in, suffocating, several degrees warmer than the hallway.

Ariel looked up, eyes bright and unblinking, pupils slightly dilated. The Bible was open on his lap. Both hands splayed across the pages. The thin paper rustled when he shifted his weight. Face gaunt, cheekbones sharp, skin pale. Dark circles under his eyes.

"Ariel Morales?" Roan said.

"Yes." Quick reply, no warmth or hostility.

Roan stepped further in, checking corners first—a habit from twenty years of not knowing what waited in a suspect's room. Evans kept behind, notebook ready, mimicking Roan's positioning.

"We have some questions about your sister."

"I already know what happened." Ariel's gaze slid to a shadowed corner. "She was my sister. But she didn't live right."

Evans' pen hesitated.

"Your sister was murdered," Roan said.

"She met her reckoning." Like reciting a prayer. His hands pressed harder into the Bible, bandages shifting. "She didn't live right. She dressed indecently. Went out at night."

Pause.

"God punishes that."

"Explain."

Ariel's mouth curled. "She went out. Dressed like a whore. Whore clothes. Whore ways. Tight jeans, low tops, makeup thick as paint. She looked like she was selling herself." His glance flickered from Roan to Evans, tracking their reactions, pupils contracting slightly in the light. "God punishes that."

The final word snapped, thin and splintered.

"Did you know her routine?" Roan said.

"She worked at the diner. Studied Tuesdays and Thursdays. The rest?" A hollow laugh. "She came home late, smelling like men's cologne. She got to do whatever she wanted. Wear whatever she wanted. Be whoever she wanted." Ariel's knuckles whitened against the Bible. "Don't ask me which men. I didn't care to know."

"Did she ever get in any fights with anyone?"

"She fought every time I told her the truth." His grip tightened. The bandages strained. "But I wasn't the one who needed forgiving."

"Any issues at her work that you know of?"

"Customers tipped too much. She always said so. Men tipped her because she looked the way she did. Because she was free."

Beat.

"That's how sin pays."

"Any Debts?"

"If she owed anything, it was to herself and to God. She got everything. Got to leave. Got to be—" A pause. Swallow. "I'm the one who stays. I'm the one who has to atone."

"Relationships you know of?"

"Always. None of them was worth God's mercy. She could pick anyone. Do anything." His jaw clamped. "While I have to be righteous."

"Any friends you disliked?"

"All of them. Every single one. They dressed like her, acted like her."

Short breath.

"Godless. Free."

"Threats?"

"Every day. The world is nothing but threats. The weak. The faithless. The sinful." His stare was steady, unblinking. "She didn't protect herself. So God didn't protect her. She got to be free for a while."

Pause.

"But freedom has a price."

"When did you last see her?"

"Yesterday morning. Before she left for her shift, before she walked out, dressed how she pleased, living the life she picked."

"And tonight?"

"I was here. Reading the Word." Ariel lifted his chin. "Mother passed out before nine. But God saw me. God always sees. God sees everything." A pause. "I can't hide."

Lower, almost to himself. Roan noted it. Evans underlined the phrase. God sees everything. I can't hide.

"Did you and Camila argue?"

"Every time she left dressed like that. Every time she reminded me of what I can't—what I'm not allowed—" He caught himself, exhaled sharply. "But that isn't what kills. Sin does. She chose her path. I chose mine. She got to choose." A glance at the Bible. "Maybe someday God will let me choose too." Pause. "I sinned once. I don't sin twice. I can't afford to."

"What sin?"

Ariel's ghost of a smile, hand drifting to his taped wrist. "That's between me and God."

The wall drawings seemed to lean in, the crucifix canted, rosary twitching in the air from the A/C.

Evans capped his pen.

Roan stood. "If anything comes back to you, call. We'll have patrols out front. Don't leave."

Ariel inclined his head, hands unmoving on the Bible.

"God's will be done."

Roan exited. Evans pulled the door shut.

In the hall, Evans let out a breath. "Sir, that kid—"

"Scares you?"

"Yeah."

"Good. He should. Tears are human, Evans. Anger, denial, silence, even. But righteous certainty? That's something else. That's someone who's already written the end of the story in their own head. People like that are capable of anything."

Evans swallowed. "You think he did it?"

"I think he's a suspect." Roan glanced back at the closed door. "But more than that, he believes she deserved it. And a belief like that? Means, motive, opportunity. All wrapped up with a Bible verse."

They walked back through the hall.

The front room looked worse. Maria slouched in the chair, snoring, tissue unraveled on her lap. A bottle was angled against her ankle, rocking with her breathing.

Roan crossed to the crooked school portrait of Camila on the wall. Glass split down the center of her smile. He lifted the frame—cheap plastic, lighter than it looked, dust thick enough to smell, old and papery. He brushed the dust away and looked into her face—recent picture: hair combed, ambition in her expression.

"Better the world remembers her like this, not the way we found her."

Evans' gaze drifted to the room's debris—bottles, a crooked lamp, crumpled bills. He understood.

Camila had fought to rise above this. And then someone stopped her.

Roan slipped the frame inside his jacket, drew his phone. "Send a Unit to 1709 South Federal Highway, Apartment 2B. Keep the apartment secure. Mother's intoxicated; son's unstable. Don't let either wander."

He pocketed the phone. Evans tugged at his tie, then hesitated, fingers on the knot. His hand dropped.

"Ditch the tie, Evans."

"Sir?"

"You're in Florida. A tie makes you sweat. Or gives someone something to grab if things go sideways. Get used to the heat. It doesn't care about your dress code."

Evans' fingers fumbled at his collar, loosening the knot, pulling the silk free. He folded it carefully and slipped it into his jacket pocket. The gesture felt significant—shedding Wellington, becoming something else.

Roan headed for the exit. At the door, he looked back at Maria, then at Evans.

"Diner next. That's where she spent her days. That's where you find the parts that matter."

Evans followed. The apartment door scraped open, dawn leaking under the threshold in pale strips.

Outside, the Explorer idled, exhaust hanging close to the ground.

Down the metal stairs, Evans glanced up at the window, the tired curtain, the battered paint. He thought of Camila's textbooks, her embroidered jacket. Her mother passed out—her brother, wrapped in scripture and judgment.

Ariel's words echoed. God's will be done.

At the Explorer, Roan got into the passenger seat. Evans took the wheel and started the engine.

They sat in silence. Through the windshield, Evans watched the apartment building and caught a movement—a figure at the window. Ariel, watching them leave.

CHAPTER

5

EVANS SAT rigid at the wheel, both hands clamped at ten-and-two, knuckles pale under the dash's green glow. The Explorer rolled north along Dixie Highway, tires humming over patched asphalt, then thumping across expansion joints in a rhythm that matched his pulse —headlights carved through the last threads of mist. The A/C howled at full blast, but sweat still pooled under his collar. Inside smelled like old coffee and the pine air freshener dangling from the mirror, trying and failing to cover the scent of stale takeout.

Roan didn't speak for a while. He just leaned in the passenger seat, elbow propped, gaze glued to the windshield as though the road owed him an explanation and might cough one up if he stared long enough. It was that chess-player stillness: Roan didn't have to look at Evans to make him feel scrutinized.

"You drive like a rookie," Roan said, voice dry as old leather. "Ease up. Unless you're trying to peel the rim off the wheel."

Evans loosened his grip by a fraction—not enough to look sloppy. "Just keeping it straight."

"Steady's good. Stiff isn't. This isn't a senator's limo; it's a detective's car." Roan's eyes never wavered from the road ahead.

Evans risked a sideways glance. "You always critique your drivers?"

Roan almost smiled—the suggestion of it, nothing more. "Just the ones about to pick a fight with the steering column." Eyes back on the road. "You held your ground with the crowd last night. That matters."

Evans let out a breath, tension draining in increments. "Didn't feel like it helped. Nobody wanted to talk. Most wouldn't even look at me."

"You'll get used to that. Death makes people clam up. It could be nerves, guilt, or self-preservation. Could be all three. You watch for the edges. Who talks too much, who says nothing, who watches the clock. People hang themselves with their own rope."

Evans kept his eyes on the centerline. "Ariel. The brother. What's your read?"

Roan's jaw twitched, barely visible. "More outrage than grief. Religious, maybe, or something wearing that mask. Didn't like how quickly he threw his sister under the bus, even when she was already dead."

"You think he did it?"

"I think he's worth keeping an eye on. Zealots don't always swing the knife themselves. Sometimes they just leave the door open."

The highway went on. The morning mist burned away. And then the diner's neon hit, all bruised pink and chrome, fighting dawn.

Roan nodded at it. "That's us."

The Nifty Fifty Diner looked like it had washed ashore from a decade that didn't survive, left to rust on the shoulder of Dixie Highway. Neon missing teeth buzzed Nify Fify for anyone still awake to read it—a low, electrical hum punctuated by a stutter every few seconds. Locals just called it Nifty. A fake Cadillac hood ornament on the signpost leaned sideways, chrome eaten dull by salt and time.

Round back, semis idled with their noses to the wall, diesel engines rumbling in a chorus of different pitches, headlights slicing patterns over gravel. The drivers inside clung to their coffee cups as if they were lifelines.

Evans flicked the indicator and turned in. Gravel crunched under the tires, loud in the morning air.

Roan laced his fingers together; his gaze locked on the diner. "Two things, Evans. Talk less, listen more. Diners run on rumor. There's a thread in there somewhere. Someone's seen it."

Evans cut him a glance. "And if they haven't?"

Roan looked over, flat as a parking lot. "Then we missed it."

He opened the door, letting in a rush of Florida heat thick with the scent of fryer grease.

"Up and at 'em," Roan said, almost to himself. "Let's see who's left standing."

Inside, the Nifty Fifty looked less like a shrine to nostalgia and more like a battle zone where time had been losing for decades. Chrome washed to pewter, neon buzzing and stuttering, the siding pocked by storms. The place didn't stay open to remember anything. It stayed open because it wouldn't give up.

As soon as Evans and Roan stepped in, the air hit: fried bacon gone stale, coffee thick as tar on the burners, mop water and old grease oozing from seams in the floor. The linoleum, once black and white, had mostly given way; what was left was a checkerboard of greys, squares missing, replaced by blunt scars of concrete. The fluorescents overhead hummed in two different keys, one fixture flickering every few seconds like Morse code.

Booths sagged, duct tape patchworks holding together vinyl that bled stuffing. The vinyl stuck to skin in the humidity, tacky and unpleasant. Every table carried the same shrine: a ketchup bottle scabbed dry at the ring, a sugar shaker welded into a crust by humidity, and a napkin dispenser with a bent hinge.

The jukebox blinked in the corner, lights dead but still taking up space like a retired fighter who refused to leave the ring.

Patrons played roles: Two truckers with eyes like gravel pits ate eggs slowly, mugs welded to their hands. A couple whispered across a shared plate, glances darting to the detectives before sliding away. An old-timer sank into a booth alone, newspaper held high, hearing aid cranked so the whole room caught the ghost of a ballgame broadcast.

No one stopped them; no one welcomed them. There was silence, dropping a notch and then resuming in the careful way people use when they know cops are listening.

Behind the counter, the man running the place might as well have been bolted down with the stools. A white shirt worn thin, an apron streaked like an oil rag, hair flat under years of grease and heat. He watched Roan and Evans cross the tile, weighed them with a squint, and returned to spinning the ticket wheel.

Roan logged him, already knowing the type: an owner, a local baron, not interested in trouble unless it started touching his bottom line.

"Morning," Roan said, badge out, tone flat.

The man scowled as if it cost him money. "Cops?"

Evans flashed his ID, a tick behind Roan.

The man read it, jaw tightening. Rag hit the counter. "Figures. About damn time. You heard about Camila?"

Evans felt a twist in his ribs. Roan gave the nod. "We need somewhere private."

That got a laugh, flat as griddle burn. "Private? Ain't nothing private in Nifty. Everybody already knows. The girl doesn't show, throws the whole day sideways. Should've cut her weeks ago. Gave me nothing but grief. Drugs, maybe worse." He said it loud enough to carry. A couple of heads turned, then ducked down again.

Roan didn't rise, didn't blink. Just kept his eyes locked. "Is there an office we could go to?"

The man chewed on it, then jerked a thumb toward the shadowed hallway at the back. "In the back. Five minutes. I run a business here."

Roan didn't move until the room had let the words settle. Then: "That'll do." He gestured for Evans to follow.

They passed the booths, the jukebox, the coffee steam, leaving behind the hush that always followed cops when they went somewhere private.

The back office was a closet masquerading as a room. Paint peeled from the cinderblock walls in strips, the color of old bile. Grime had sunk too deep into the corners, sweating back out no matter how much degreaser you threw at it. The air carried the fatigue of twenty years' worth of fryer smoke and unpaid bills. It was ten degrees hotter here than in the dining room, the fan in the corner doing nothing but rearranging the sweat.

A desk sagged in the middle, cardboard wedged under one leg to keep it upright. The surface was sticky under the fingers, years of spilled coffee and grease forming a lacquer. On top: a tide of invoices, order slips, battered mugs, and coffee rings that went down in layers like archaeology. The fan wheezed in the corner, blades ticking against the cage with each rotation.

Frank DeAngelo dropped into the chair behind the desk, elbows spreading to claim what little space the office had. Shirt clung to him, apron streaked with stains, face set in the permanent scowl of a man who'd been losing the same fight for years.

Roan stayed by the door, blocking the only exit without appearing to do so. Evans pulled up a folding chair that groaned under his weight, his notepad already open, and his pen cocked at the page.

Roan started it clean. "Name for the record."

"Frank DeAngelo. Owner. Twenty-two years." The words shot out clipped, practiced.

"Does Camila Morales work here?"

"Yeah. Waitress. Mornings. Sometimes later, if she didn't flake." DeAngelo's gaze jumped between them, as if he hurried through his answers, the cops might vanish into the morning rush.

"How long on the payroll?" Roan's voice didn't rise above monotone.

"Close to a year. Staff turns faster than the grill. But she stuck. I'll give her that."

Evans leaned in a notch. "Trouble between you two?"

"Sure." DeAngelo scratched at his jaw, leaving a streak of oil. "She's got a mouth on her. Bosses the rookies, smirks when I call her out on it. Customers like her, though. That type. Got more tips than the others. Sometimes too many."

Roan: "Reliable?"

DeAngelo's laugh came harshly. "Reliable? Hell no. Late half the time. Like today, supposed to be here at seven—no show, no call. I could've told you she'd run off, eventually. Probably chasing a man or chasing a high. Wouldn't have shocked me."

Roan let the silence spread, eyes steady, voice flat when it came. "She didn't run off. She's dead. Found on the beach last night."

The pen in DeAngelo's hand stopped mid-spin.

Clattered once on the desk.

Rolled toward the edge.

His hand shot out, fumbling, and missed. The pen hit the floor with a plastic crack. He caught his jaw with one hand, as if he needed to hold it up, the other frozen halfway to where the pen had been. "Jesus. You're sure? Camila?"

"No mistake."

DeAngelo sank lower, elbows grinding into the desk. His scowl buckled into something sourer, the look of a man realizing the words he'd just thrown around the counter now hung like a noose. His face went grey under the fluorescent light. "Thought she'd just skipped out. Maybe chasing some guy. Didn't expect—" He stopped himself, couldn't finish.

Roan gave him nothing. "We need her schedule. Habits. That's on you."

Evans kept his pen moving. "She usually worked from seven to three?"

"That was her shift. Clocked out on the dot. Never lingered. Sometimes nights, but not often. Seven to three, always."

"Yesterday?" Roan pressed.

"Yeah. Left at three. Didn't come back."

Roan pointed at the drawer. "Her file."

DeAngelo pulled it fast, like he couldn't wait to get it out of his possession. A thin folder, barely an inch thick: job application, photocopy of her ID, a couple of payroll slips. Nothing else. He shoved it across the desk.

Evans bagged it, sealed it, marked the evidence label with the same meticulous handwriting he'd used at the apartment—date, time, location, contents. He clipped the folder shut with the reflex of a man who'd done it a hundred times already.

"That covers it," Roan said in a flat tone.

DeAngelo sagged back, ran both hands over his face, then let the anger come back—anger was easier than fear. "She was bad news. Always said it. The world's full of girls like her. You can see the ending a mile away."

Roan's grey eyes cut across him, voice colder than the A/C vent. "Nobody stabs themselves in the gut, Mr. DeAngelo."

That landed. DeAngelo looked away, lip caught between his teeth, all fight gone.

Roan tipped his chin at Evans. "We'll talk to the staff now."

Evans capped his pen with a click and rose out of the folding chair. The sound of the diner rushed back in as Roan opened the door—the scrape of forks, the drone of fluorescents, and the hum of a rumor mill already spinning.

The diner's resonance had shifted while they'd been locked in back. Forks scraped more softly, voices lowered, the smell of burnt coffee and grease clinging more heavily than before. News traveled faster than orders in a place like this. By the time Roan and Evans stepped out of the office, every trucker, every server, every lingering regular knew the girl wasn't just missing anymore.

Roan moved to the counter. A waitress stood behind it, dark hair tied back, lines around her mouth that spoke of years on her feet. She didn't flinch when he showed the badge. Her hands rested on the counter, knuckles slightly swollen, nails cut short—working hands.

"Name."

"Ana Jiménez. Eight years here."

"Camila Morales worked with you."

Ana's face softened, just slightly. Her hand moved to the coffee pot, gripped the handle, but didn't lift it. "Yeah. Sweet kid. Worked hard when she made it in. Had a lot on her plate."

"Fights?"

She shook her head. "Not with me. Frank rode her for being late, but Frank rides everybody. Camila took it better than most."

"Did she confide in you?"

"No. Kept her business close. She did her shift and left right after. At three o'clock, she was gone like clockwork."

Roan marked it. Evans noted the warmth in Ana's voice—the first they'd heard all morning. He underlined it in his notes, drawing a bracket around the observation.

"Anything unusual about yesterday?"

Ana paused, thinking. Her eyes went to the window, to the parking lot beyond. "No. Same as always. She clocked in at seven, worked through the lunch rush, and clocked out at three. Didn't seem upset or scared. Just... Camila."

"Thank you," Roan said, genuinely.

Ana nodded, reached for the next coffee pot, but her hand hesitated. "She was trying, you know? Really trying. Wanted something better than this place."

Evans felt something catch in his chest. He wrote it down, the words taking up more space in his notebook than they should have.

They moved to the soda fountain. Younger waitress, pixie cut, chipped polish, eyes sharp as knives. She poured coffee for three truckers in one swift motion, then gave Roan a look that said, "Make it quick." Her shoulders stayed squared, defensive, but her eyes kept sliding to the kitchen door.

"Jessica Williams," Roan said, not a question.

"Jess," she corrected.

"You worked shifts with Camila."

"Sometimes. She was the morning; I was the night. We overlapped maybe for an hour." Jess popped her gum and poured another refill with quick, efficient movements. "Customers liked her. Sarcastic. Could be funny if she felt like it."

"Reliable?"

Jess snorted. "No worse than the rest of us. Frank just rode her harder. He's got a talent for that."

"Friends?" Evans cut in, finding his footing.

Jess shook her head, eyes fixed on the coffee pot as she topped off another mug. "Didn't bring her personal life here. If she was seeing somebody, I never heard about it. She kept everything separate—work, school, home. Like she had different versions of herself and didn't want them touching."

"Conflicts?"

"Just Frank. Everybody fights Frank eventually." Jess turned away and refilled another cup. "But she didn't deserve what happened. Nobody does."

Evans noted the shift—beneath the sarcasm, real grief. He wrote it down, underlined it, and added a note: Jess—defensive but genuinely upset.

Roan let her go. Sometimes what someone didn't say was louder than what they did. He'd learned to read the spaces between words, the gestures that contradicted statements, the way people's bodies told truths their mouths wouldn't.

Last was the dishwasher in the back. Skinny kid, maybe nineteen, acne-scarred, arms raw from bleach and water. He looked like he'd been caught stealing when Roan walked in, eyes wide, rag twisting in his hands. His other hand kept scrubbing at a spot on the counter that was already clean, the motion automatic, nervous.

"Luis Ortega," Roan said, voice gentler now.

Luis bobbed his head fast. "Yeah. I—I knew her. Camila. She was nice. Gave me muffins if the customers left them."

Evans felt a pang—a small kindness in a hard place.

"Anything odd about her?" Roan asked.

Luis thought hard, eyes flicking to the floor, to the sinks, anywhere but the detective's stare. His hand kept moving on the counter—scrub, scrub, scrub. "She left quickly—every day. As soon as her shift ended, she was gone. Didn't smoke a joint, didn't hang out with the other waitresses. Just... gone."

"Scared?"

Luis bit his lip and finally stopped scrubbing. His hand gripped the edge of his apron instead. "Not scared. More like... in a hurry. Like somebody was waiting on her."

Evans' pen scratched fast across the pad. Roan gave a single nod.

"You did well, Luis. Thank you."

The kid's shoulders dropped, relief washing over him.

When they came back through the kitchen, the lunch rush was building—more bodies filling booths, the clatter of dishes louder, sunlight streaming through the front windows at a steeper angle. Coffee in abandoned mugs had gone cold, cream forming a skin on top. Patrons whispering, forks clinking too loud, the jukebox's dead silence pressing at the walls. Everyone knew something had shifted.

Roan and Evans didn't linger. They'd taken what they could from the place. The rest would come later, from the blanks in the notebooks.

Outside, the morning had fully arrived, the heat already climbing, the sun bleaching the color from the asphalt. The neon sign buzzed Nify Fify, stubborn against daylight.

Roan pulled his phone and dialed with muscle memory. He spoke low, but Evans caught every word.

"Roan. Badge eleven-thirty-eight. I want a press conference to be called for 4 p.m. today. Murder last night, female victim, twenty-one years old. We go public—ask for tips, sightings, anything." He listened, short pause. "Yes. Priority."

He ended the call with a finality that made Evans feel the clock start ticking.

Evans frowned. "Press already?"

Roan's eyes stayed on the parking lot, on the gravel crushing under a semi's tires, on the neon sign buzzing its broken syllables. "Camila's mother thinks she worked double shifts—nights, coming home late. Here, everyone says she clocked out at three, gone on the dot. Brother swears she came home late smelling like cologne." He looked at his watch from his waist—Omega Seamaster—and tapped the face. "That means there's a missing stretch. Three p.m. until whenever she showed up at that pub. Hours she spent somewhere nobody's talking about."

Evans tucked his notebook against his chest, the pieces clicking. "A gap."

"Big one. Between three p.m. and whenever she ended up at the pub and then the beach." Roan's jaw set. "I don't like holes that size. Someone out there fills it. Press shakes loose what the diner won't."

Evans understood now—Roan wasn't guessing. He was playing chess, forcing moves, waiting to see what fell.

When Evans shifted his notebook to his left hand, sunlight caught the band on his ring finger—simple gold, slightly worn. Roan's eyes registered it, filed it away without comment. Married. Another piece of who Evans was, another reason he'd left Wellington for a promotion that meant longer hours and harder cases.

Roan started for the Explorer, voice just for Evans. "You drop me at the station. Then you go home, type those notes. On my desk by eight a.m. tomorrow. No gaps. No excuses."

Evans nodded, jaw tight. "Yes, sir."

They climbed into the Explorer. With Evans behind the wheel, Roan in the passenger seat. The engine caught, rumbling steadily beneath the weight of a day that had only just started.

Evans pulled out of the lot, tires crunching gravel one last time. In the rearview, the Nifty Fifty Diner shrank—a tired landmark swallowed by heat and memory, Camila's absence still hanging in the air like grease that wouldn't wash out.

Roan stared ahead, silent, already three moves into the next game.

Evans gripped the wheel—looser this time, steadier—and drove.

CHAPTER

6

EVANS PARKED in the driveway under the battered banyans, engine ticking as heat bled from the hood—metal pinging in slow intervals, the sound stretching out between each click like a dying heartbeat. Inside the car, the smell of old coffee grounds lingered in the cup holder, and his own sweat had soaked into the upholstery.

He saw Camila Morales on the beach behind his eyelids—her body sprawled in the dunes, floodlights turning sand to bone-white powder, blood dried to rust. He blinked it away, but it lingered.

Through the windshield, the neighborhood stretched quietly. Small houses pressed close together—single-story, stucco, driveways cracked and weeded over. Porch lights glowed through the humidity while moths circled, and a dog barked three houses down.

Evans climbed out. Florida evenings never cooled, only shifted from unbearable to oppressive. The air smelled of cut grass and charcoal, almost sweet, mixed with lighter-fluid residue still clinging.

The kids' evidence covered the yard. Chalk hopscotch boxes had faded on the concrete, their numbers smudged. A tricycle lay on its side, training wheels pointed skyward. The basketball hoop above the garage sagged; the backboard was yellowed, and the net shredded.

Evans paused at the door, hand on the handle. Inside, voices murmured—Clara's laugh low, Emily's higher pitch—and the television hummed through the walls. This was what he came home to— warmth and noise and ordinary life—while Camila's apartment had reeked of cigarette smoke and mildew; her mother had passed out drunk in her chair, and Ariel's room was papered with scripture.

He opened the door and stepped inside.

Clara met him in the hallway, hair pulled back loosely, strands falling across her face. Faded jeans, an old tee, flour dusted on one sleeve—she brushed at it absently with her other hand, leaving a white streak. Her eyes found his—worry smoothing to relief. Dark hair with lighter streaks caught the lamplight; her skin was warm, even in the dim hallway. She moved toward him, and something in his chest eased.

"Hey, stranger," she said.

Evans tried for a smile. The house smelled like dinner—onions and garlic simmering, something baking beneath. Ordinary life. Another planet from where he'd been.

"Long day?" Clara said.

"Yeah." He set his keys down and loosened his collar. "Real long."

She squeezed his hand and kept hold of it for a second longer than usual, her thumb pressing against his pulse point. That was Clara—knowing when to ask and when just to be there.

The living room opened, small and cluttered: toys across the carpet, library books teetering on the coffee table, Emily's backpack against the couch, framed photos on the walls—wedding day, the kids as babies, the Keys three summers ago.

From the back—laughter, small feet racing over tile, then muffled on carpet. Emily's voice: "Is that Daddy?"

She barreled around the corner, pajamas bright with cartoon clouds, arms out. "Daddy!"

Evans knelt, caught her, lifted her. She wrapped her arms around his neck, hair tickling, cheeks flushed. Bubblegum shampoo and marker ink. She was heavier than she had been last month, solid and warm and alive in his arms, her heartbeat quick against his chest.

"Hey, kiddo." He set her down and brushed her hair back—the gesture automatic, something he'd done since she was a baby. "Have you been good?"

"I got a hundred on my spelling test! Mrs. Parker said I was the only one who got 'necessary' right. One C's and two S's, but people always mess it up."

"A hundred? That's my girl." He tapped her nose. She giggled. "What else?"

"And I drew a unicorn in art class, and Miss Rodriguez put it on the board, and Tommy said it looked like a horse with a stick on its head, but I told him unicorns are supposed to look like horses, that's the whole point."

Evans laughed—the first genuine laugh today. "Tommy doesn't know what he's talking about."

"That's what I said!"

Matthew lingered in the hallway, taller every time, limbs awkward. Golf bag against the wall. Faded tournament polo, sleeves too short, hair sticking up.

Evans straightened. "Good practice today?"

Matthew shrugged. "It was all right." Pride tugged at the corner of his mouth. "Coach said I'm getting better. Hit past the 150 yards today."

"That's huge. At this rate, you'll beat me by next week."

Matthew ducked his head, a smile breaking through. "You don't even play golf, Dad."

"Exactly. Makes it even more embarrassing when you beat me."

That got a snort. Matthew shifted, glanced at the golf bag. "You missed it. Practice."

Evans' gut tightened. "I know. I'm sorry, bud. Work ran long."

"It's fine." The tone said it wasn't.

Evans clapped his shoulder—felt the tension there, the disappointment Matthew was trying to hide. "Next one, I'm there. Promise."

Matthew nodded, eyes dropping. The smile lingered, but barely.

Clara gestured toward the kitchen. "Dinner's ready. Wash up."

Clara had set the table: ropa vieja with white rice, black beans, and sweet plantains. She poured iced tea while the kids settled in.

Evans sat. The chair creaked—the same creak for two years. Emily picked out onions; her tongue pressed against her upper lip. Matthew reached for the salt before tasting. Clara served herself last, with a portion smaller than everyone's.

"So," Clara said, passing the bowl. "Routine investigation?"

He nodded and chewed. "Just covering ground. Following leads."

Emily piped up. "Did you catch any bad guys?"

Evans glanced at her and forced a smile. "Not yet, kiddo. But we're working on it."

Matthew frowned, fork paused. "Is it dangerous?"

Clara's eyes met Evans'. She set her glass down carefully, her hand finding the edge of the table, knuckles white. Waiting.

"Sometimes," Evans said. "But I'm careful, always."

"That's what Uncle Mike said before he got shot," Matthew said.

Clara stiffened, reaching for her glass, remembering when her brother had been in the hospital for a month; her fingers trembled slightly before she steadied them. "Matthew—"

"It's okay." Evans held his son's eyes, choosing his words with the same care he'd use testifying in court, protecting Matthew from the truth while not quite lying. "Uncle Mike made a mistake. Went in without backup. I work with a partner. We watch each other's backs. That's how you stay safe."

Matthew nodded, satisfied, and returned to his plate.

Emily launched into another story—recess, a girl named Sophie with dinosaur gummy bears. Clara asked questions and kept the conversation moving.

They ate at a comfortable rhythm. Clara asked about Roan. Evans described him—experienced, methodical, tough but fair—without mentioning the gruffness, the way Roan could strip a scene down with one look.

Clara smiled. "Sounds like someone I'd want watching your back."

"He is."

Clara's ropa vieja was her mother's recipe, comfort food, but Camila's face kept creeping back—her DMV photo, her body on the sand. Her brother: *She didn't live right.*

Then my image of Emily's arms around his neck. Matthew proud. Clara steady. Camila had been somebody's daughter, too.

Clara's hand brushed his under the table—a quiet anchor. The refrigerator hummed steadily—a low drone with a slight rattle when the compressor kicked in.

After dinner, Clara cleared the plates. Evans helped Matthew with homework. Fractions.

"Okay," Evans said, leaning over. "Three-eighths plus five-eighths. First thing?"

"Add the tops?"

"The numerators, yeah. And the bottom?"

"Stays the same. Eight."

"Right. So?"

Matthew scribbled, erased, scribbled. "Eight-eighths."

"Which is?"

"One." Matthew grinned. "That's it?"

"That's it. See? Not so bad."

Matthew worked through problems, building confidence. Evans guided him patiently.

He thought about the diner. Ana Jimenez: *Camila left at three, always.* Frank DeAngelo: *She was bad news.* There was a gap—seven hours. Three to ten. Luis Ortega: *Like somebody was waiting for her.*

"Dad?"

Evans refocused. Matthew watched him, brow furrowed.

"Did I get it wrong?"

Evans checked, leaning closer, touching Matthew's shoulder to pull him back from wherever his mind had gone. "No, you got it. Good job."

Matthew refocused, movements slower. He could tell.

Emily colored a mermaid on the floor, humming. Crayons scattered—purple tail, blue ocean, yellow hair. A cartoon song with a high, off-key voice. Her tongue stuck out the side of her mouth when she concentrated, the same way Clara did when she was focused.

Clara came back, dish towel over her shoulder, and leaned against the counter. She watched Evans—hunched over homework, shoulders tense.

"News is on soon," she said. "Anything you need to catch?"

Evans shook his head. "Not really."

But Clara was already moving, flipping through the TV channels, stopping on News 5. The broadcast went through systematically, covering traffic, weather, and a new park downtown.

Matthew finished. "Done."

Evans checked. "Good job. Go get ready for bed."

Matthew grabbed his bag. "Can I read for ten minutes?"

"Sure."

Emily stayed, crayons everywhere, as the mermaid took shape.

Evans stood and stretched, joints popping. He walked into the living room as the anchor's tone shifted.

"Breaking news tonight: The Palm Beach Sheriff's Office is asking for the public's help in a murder investigation."

Evans froze.

Clara glanced at him, then at the screen.

"Twenty-one-year-old Camila Morales was found dead early this morning on Lake Worth Beach. Detectives held a press conference this afternoon."

The screen cut to Roan behind the podium, badge clipped, face stone. Behind him—Camila's photo.

Smiling, bright, alive.

Her hair was pulled back in a ponytail, a silver necklace just visible at her collar; her lipstick was perfectly applied, and her eyes caught the camera with something like hope.

Evans' chest tightened.

Roan's voice, flat: "Camila Morales was murdered late last night or early this morning. Twenty-one years old, a Palm Beach State student, worked at the Nifty Fifty Diner. We ask anyone who saw her yesterday evening to contact the Department."

The camera zoomed in on Camila's photo—her smile wide and hopeful, her hair brushed smooth, her eyes bright.

Emily looked up. "She looks pretty."

Evans couldn't speak.

The girl from the beach—blood soaking into sand, floodlights turning her skin grey, eyes vacant—was smiling on TV like she had her whole life ahead of her, which she had until someone took it.

Roan continued: "Last seen leaving the Nifty Fifty at approximately three p.m. yesterday. May have been at the Oceanside Pub later. If anyone saw Camila between three and ten p.m., please come forward."

Reporter: "Do you have suspects?"

Roan: "Following multiple leads."

"Random attack?"

"We don't believe so."

"Are residents in danger?"

Roan leaned in. "Remain vigilant. Report suspicious activity. But no ongoing threat to the community."

The camera lingered on Camila's photo, then went back to the studio. Tip line. Weather. Rain midweek.

Clara clicked off.

Quiet filled the room. Emily continued coloring. Matthew called for a towel.

Clara studied Evans. "That's your case."

He nodded.

"You saw her."

Another nod.

Clara's hand found his, the grip tighter than usual.

Evans looked at Emily coloring and then at Camila's smile on the screen, still echoing in his mind. The gap—seven hours. Emily at twenty-one—same age, same future, same vulnerability.

His stomach turned.

Clara touched his arm. "Come on. Let's get the kids to bed."

Bedtime—teeth, pajamas, stories. Evans sat on Emily's bed edge, reading Princess and Dragon, his mind drifting.

Emily's room was filled with purple everything, complete with stuffed animals on the shelves. A unicorn poster hung on the wall, one corner peeling.

Emily lay under the covers, clutching a worn rabbit—the fur rubbed smooth on its ears from years of holding, one eye missing— fighting sleep.

"Daddy," a small voice. "That lady on the news. What happened?"

Evans closed the book. He saw Camila's neck wound—ragged, deep, the carotid severed. Blood pooled in the sand. Her eyes reflected nothing. He swallowed hard, forced the image down, and chose words that would let Emily sleep tonight. "Something bad, sweetheart. That's why Daddy's working hard to figure it out."

"Did it hurt?"

He let the lie come more easily than the truth. "I don't know, baby. Hope not."

Quiet. Then: "Will you catch the bad person?"

He kissed her forehead. "That's the plan."

"Good. Bad people should go to jail."

"They should."

She yawned, eyes closing. Minutes later, her breathing evened. Evans watched as the night-light turned the walls lavender, casting shadows that shifted with each breath. Emily was safe in bed. Camila was dead in the sand.

He pulled the door shut.

Matthew's room held golf posters, with clubs in the corner. The bed was neat, military-tight. A signed Tiger Woods poster hung above the desk.

Matthew sat cross-legged with Golf Magazine in his hands, the glossy pages making soft sounds as he turned them. He looked up and set it aside.

"Lights out soon?"

"Yeah. Ten minutes."

Evans sat on the bed's edge, the mattress dipping under his weight. "You did well today. Homework. Practice."

Matthew shrugged. "Just fractions."

"Still counts."

Silence. Matthew picked at a blanket thread.

"The woman on TV... Is that your case?"

Evans nodded.

"So... murdered?"

"Yeah."

Quiet. "Are you scared? Working cases like that?"

Evans considered. "Sometimes. But not of getting hurt. More... not figuring it out. Letting someone down."

Matthew looked up. "You won't."

"How do you know?"

"Because you're good at your job. And you care."

Something caught in Evans' chest. He ruffled Matthew's hair—the same gesture he'd made since Matthew was small enough to fit in the crook of his arm.

"Lights out. Dream of birdies."

Matthew grinned. "Eagles are better."

"Whatever you say, Tiger."

Evans stood, lingered, and stepped into the hallway. The house settled; Emily's night-light glowed; Matthew's bed creaked as he shifted.

Camila Morales had left no sign of having left. She had slipped out of her day and landed in the morgue.

Clara sat in bed, propped against pillows, paperback in her lap. She looked up and set the book aside.

"You okay?"

Evans changed into sweats and sat on the mattress. "No."

She waited.

"She was twenty-one. Your cousin Rosa's age when she married. Same as my sister when she graduated. Whole life ahead. School. Work. Dreams. Now... gone."

Clara's hand rested warmly on his back, her fingers tracing small circles. "You'll find who did it."

"Maybe." He rubbed his face. "There's a gap. Seven hours unaccounted for. Left work at three, dead after midnight. Nobody knows where. What? Who with?"

"You'll figure it out. You and Roan."

Evans wanted to believe her. He lay down, Clara curling against him, but sleep wouldn't come. Camila's smile. Body on sand. Emily's face where Camila's had been—thirteen years until twenty-one—out in the world, vulnerable.

His gut twisted.

He sat up and slipped out.

The kitchen was dark, the house silent except for the refrigerator hum —that steady drone punctuated by the compressor's click every few minutes. Evans poured water, stood by the sink, and stared at the backyard in the moonlight. The grass was silver-grey; the fence shadows long. The water was icy enough to make his teeth ache, tasting faintly of a filter that needed to be changed. Through the bedroom door, Clara's breathing came slow and even—the rhythm of someone deeply asleep.

Somewhere in those seven hours, Camila met her killer.

Clara kept a gun locked away in the closet, a Glock loaded after a suspect found a detective's home, six months of range time. The combination was muscle memory: six-two-four-one.

The diner, the apartment, the bar—the spaces between, the gaps where life slips through. He heard Roan's voice: What's missing is the real story.

Evans pulled his notebook, flipped it open, and clicked a pen. In the dim light, he wrote center page:

Find the gap.

He underlined it twice, pressing hard enough that the pen tip nearly tore the paper. He stared until it burned in.

Tomorrow he would follow leads, press witnesses, work until the gap was closed—until Camila got justice. Tonight, in his quiet kitchen, with his family asleep, he carried the weight.

Evans closed the notebook, finished the water, and stood listening. The fridge hummed, a dog barked, and wind moved through the trees.

He went back to bed.

Clara stirred and reached out an arm to him, and he let her pull him close. Her breath was warm on his neck. He stared at the ceiling —shadows from the streetlight moving as branches swayed outside— his mind cycling through statements and photos, Roan's questions, the wrong timeline.

From three to ten—seven hours—somewhere in there was the answer.

He shut his eyes. Camila's smile waited behind his lids. The digital clock on the nightstand read 11:30 in bright red numbers. Sleep would come, but not quietly.

CHAPTER

7

The girl on the TV was dead.

Ellen knew that face.

She set her coffee down on the nurse's station counter—a hospital cafeteria mug, still warm, with bitter dregs at the bottom—and moved closer to the mounted screen in Good Samaritan's ER waiting area. The air smelled of antiseptic and burnt coffee and the particular sweetness of illness, a combination that after fifteen years she barely noticed anymore. A monitor beeped steadily somewhere behind her. The elevator dinged at the far end of the hall. The closed captions scrolled across the bottom: Camila Morales, 21, found dead on Lake Worth Beach early Friday morning.

Ellen's throat tightened. The coffee mug rattled against the laminate counter.

She'd seen her. Last night. Not at the hospital. On Dixie Highway, near the corner of Southern Boulevard.

The screen cut to a press conference. A detective stood behind a podium—older, with a grey suit and a face carved from stone. The caption identified him:

Detective Robert Roan
Palm Beach County Sheriff's Office

His voice came flat through the tinny speaker: "Camila Morales was last seen leaving her place of employment at approximately three p.m. on Thursday. We believe she may have been at the Oceanside Pub later that evening. We are asking anyone who saw Camila between the hours of three p.m. and eleven p.m. to come forward."

Three to eleven. The gap Roan was trying to fill. Ellen's hands gripped the counter edge, knuckles going white.

The phone at the nurse's station rang. Ellen didn't move.

She'd seen her. Not at three. Not at eleven. At 10:15 p.m. on Dixie Highway. With another girl.

Ellen had clocked out at ten on Thursday night after a twelve-hour shift. Her feet had been throbbing in her Danskos, scrubs damp with sweat down her spine, the particular bone-deep exhaustion that came from standing for twelve hours settling into her lower back. She'd walked to her car in the employee lot, keys already out, mind already home—shower, leftover pasta, bed.

Two girls on the sidewalk along Dixie Highway, a few miles south of the hospital. Under a streetlight near Southern Boulevard—harsh sodium orange. Traffic was light at that hour, just the occasional semi rumbling past toward I-95. One was Latina—Camila, although Ellen hadn't known her name at the time. Black leather jacket over a white crop top, dark jeans, and heeled boots. The other was Asian, shorter by four or five inches, maybe five-two, with dark hair pulled back in a sleek ponytail. Wearing a fitted black dress with a denim jacket and strappy sandals, despite the late hour. Early twenties, both of them—Ellen's nursing eye caught the details automatically: smooth skin, no sun damage yet, the particular carriage of youth, confident despite the late hour and empty street.

They stood still. Not walking, not sitting at the bus stop, just standing there, talking low, looking down the empty street toward the intersection as if expecting someone.

Ellen had slowed her car and rolled down the window. The steering wheel was slick with condensation from the air conditioning, as warm night air rushed in.

"Need a ride somewhere?"

Camila had turned—polite smile, the kind you gave strangers when you wanted them gone. Confident, not dismissive. "We're good, thanks."

Ellen had hesitated. Two young women, alone, on Dixie at night.

She'd seen what came through the ER—assault victims, overdoses, the ones who didn't make it. "You sure? It's late."

"Someone's coming for us," Camila had said, firmer but with politeness.

Ellen nodded, rolled the window up, and drove away. She'd checked the rearview once. They were still there, still waiting under that sickly orange glow.

She'd gone home. Slept. Worked Friday morning until now.

Ellen pulled out her phone. The tip line number scrolled across the TV screen. Her fingers fumbled with the numbers. She had to try twice.

Two rings. "Palm Beach County Sheriff's Office, tip line."

"I saw Camila Morales. Last night. Thursday night, around 10:15 p.m., on Dixie Highway, near Southern Boulevard."

Keyboard clicks. "Can you describe what you saw?"

"She was with another girl. Asian, early twenties—I'd assess mid-twenties based on presentation. Dark hair in a ponytail—sleek, pulled back tight. Wearing a black fitted dress with a denim jacket. Strappy sandals. About five-two. They were standing on the sidewalk under the streetlight at Southern and Dixie, waiting for someone. Not at the bus stop—just standing there on the sidewalk."

Ellen's nursing brain cataloged the details automatically: height differential, clothing specifics, posture, the way Camila had shifted her weight onto one hip when she'd turned to answer.

"Did you speak to them?"

"Yes. I asked if they needed a ride. They said no. Camila did the talking—she seemed confident, not nervous."

"Did they say where they were going?"

"No. Just that someone was coming for them."

"Did you see them leave?"

"No. I drove away. They were still standing there when I checked my mirror."

The operator took Ellen's name and her number. Said a detective might follow up. Ellen hung up and stood there in the break room, phone still in her hand.

She'd offered them a ride. They'd said no, and now one of them was dead.

At five-thirty, a domestic case rolled in. A woman in her thirties, bruises blooming purple-black on her ribs, wrist swollen, the pattern of finger marks visible on her upper arm. Ellen wrapped the wrist, prepped the IV site, and inserted the catheter. Missed the vein. The woman flinched. Ellen withdrew, applied pressure, and tried again on the other arm. Missed. Her hands wouldn't steady.

Two girls under a streetlight. Camila's polite smile. Someone's coming for us.

"You *okay?*" Dr. Patel asked, glancing over from the computer station.

Ellen nodded, steadied her breathing the way she'd learned in nursing school—triage your reactions, compartmentalize, function first—and got the IV on the third try. The woman was young, vulnerable, and making choices that would get her hurt. Just like Camila. Just like the other girl, whoever she was.

The woman walked back out to the parking lot, where her husband waited in the car. Ellen watched her go through the ER entrance doors. You couldn't save people who didn't want to be saved. Just like you couldn't save people who said they were fine when they weren't.

The rest of the shift blurred—an overdose—twenty-one years old, the same age as Camila. Ellen registered the age as she pulled the naloxone from the crash cart, hesitated for a fraction of a second— Camila was twenty-one, Camila won't wake up—then pushed the naloxone, watched the girl gasp back to life, pupils contracting as consciousness returned. Through it all, the image stayed: two girls under a streetlight, waiting.

At ten o'clock, Ellen clocked out. At the same time, she'd left Thursday night. She walked to her car through the same employee lot and took the same route home.

She drove south on Dixie Highway, slowed at Southern Boulevard.

The streetlight still hummed overhead, that harsh sodium orange turning the sidewalk the color of old bruises. The sidewalk looked the same—cracked concrete with grass forcing through, cigarette butts scattered in the gutter, the bus bench tagged with fresh graffiti.

Empty now. Just pavement and shadows and the hum of that failing light.

But Ellen could still see them. Camila and the other girl were standing under the light. Waiting. The way Camila had shifted her weight. The Asian girl's ponytail caught that orange glow. Their postures were loose, confident, and expecting someone they knew.

Ellen pulled into the parking lot of the closed gas station across the street. Put the car in park. Stared at the empty sidewalk. Ten forty-five by the dashboard clock. She sat there for fifteen minutes, maybe twenty, watching the spot where they'd stood.

For what? For whom?

Ellen didn't know. Now she never would.

She drove home, parked in her driveway, and cut the engine. Sat in her car in the dark. Behind her closed eyes, two girls stood under a streetlight, waiting—Camila with a polite smile. Someone's coming for us.

Ellen had believed her.

The streetlight had believed her, too, holding them in its circle of orange light, as if it could keep them safe.

They'd both been wrong.

CHAPTER

8

Evans backspaced through the same sentence for the third time. The keyboard clicked—cheap, hollow plastic that echoed across the bullpen. The cursor blinked—

Camila Morales, 21.

The words looked wrong no matter how he typed them.

Sweat pooled under his collar despite the grinding A/C. District 14's bullpen—twelve metal desks arranged in facing rows, wanted posters curling on beige walls, a coffeemaker burbling something that tasted like burnt rubber. The air smelled of floor cleaner, with an undertone of holding cell sweat that never quite left the ventilation system. Fluorescent tubes overhead hummed at two different frequencies, one flickering every few seconds. His computer wheezed through every keystroke, the screen flickering slightly when the cursor moved.

Thirty-two days in the detective slot. Thirty-two days of writing reports that sounded like they were borrowed from crime shows. The desk still smelled like someone else—old cologne, something woody and sharp, and the staleness of desperation.

Martinez argued with someone on the phone, volume climbing: "You told the officer you saw everything. Now you saw nothing? Which is it?"

The ancient printer wheezed out warrants. Someone had kicked it three times already.

Evans typed:

Victim: Camila Morales, age 21, Hispanic female. Found deceased at 0045 hours on Friday on Lake Worth Beach. Preliminary cause of death: multiple stab wounds to the torso and neck.

He stared at "preliminary." Was that the correct term? "Apparent cause"? His eyes burned from the screen. He rubbed them, blinked hard.

The pier security camera had been out of order for three weeks. Her mother was too drunk to remember her daughter's name. Her brother, quoting scripture, calls her a whore. The manager at the Nifty Fifty was barely looking up from his receipts.

He backspaced again. The click-click-click filled the two feet around his desk.

"Detective Evans."

He turned.

Carmen Pérez stood near his desk. Dark hair pulled tight, uniform squared. A faint line of ink showed above her collar—botanical curve disappearing under fabric. She moved with the economy of someone who'd spent years on patrol—weight balanced, ready to shift.

"You're on Morales?" she said. She stepped closer, eyes scanning his screen. "First time working with Roan?"

"Yeah. How'd you guess?"

"You look like you're trying to solve a math problem with your forehead." She leaned against the partition. "He's a storm that knows where it's going."

"Good thing?"

"Depends on whether you're facing the wind or running with it."

"Evans. Pérez."

Trent Rocca emerged from the break room with coffee. Six-three, two-sixty, deep tan, beard trimmed precisely. He moved down the aisle —shoulders turned slightly to navigate between desks, other detectives unconsciously leaning back to give him room.

"Roan had this place running all night," Rocca said. "Patrol on reports till two. Call lists until four. Cross-district canvass for cameras by five. He wants everything stacked on his desk by eight."

Evans' ears burned. He'd gone home, kissed his wife. Put his kids to bed. Slept in clean sheets while Roan turned District 14 into a war room.

His coffee turned acidic in his stomach. His jaw ached—he'd been clenching it since he sat down.

"Didn't mind," Pérez said.

"You didn't?" Evans said.

She kept her eyes on Rocca's shoulder. "Home's not my favorite place this week. Work's better."

Rocca stopped at Evans' desk, leaned against it. "She wanted the slot you got. Filed the packet, aced the board. Timing was lousy."

Evans' stomach dropped. "I didn't know."

"Why would you? Captain made the call. Said I needed more experience, more time on patrol. Said you had five years at Wellington and that counted for something."

"I'm sorry."

"Don't be. It's not your fault." Pérez shrugged. "Detective isn't a lottery ticket. You chase it until it stops running."

Evans studied her face, looking for resentment, finding none. Curiosity flared—what made home worse than working an all-nighter on someone else's case?—but her expression closed the door. He recognized the boundary. Respected it.

Evans dug into his report. Victim identified, wounds cataloged, witness statements logged. Pérez slid a folder across his desk—the motion precise, aligned with the edge of the desk.

"Camera pulls," she said.

Photos stapled to reports: the Oceanside Pub's grainy corner feed. The lens was aimed crooked; all glare from a neon sign was bleeding white across the frame. Headlights washing out everything—overexposed halos where faces should be, motion blur turning bodies into ghosts. No people, no detail. The angle caught mostly the sidewalk and sky.

"Dead?" Evans said.

Pérez nodded. "Every angle. The south door cam hasn't worked in six months. A dumpster blocked the view of the North parking lot camera. West lens cracked—someone threw a bottle three weeks ago, never got fixed."

Evans marked it. Roan's voice in his head: *What's missing is the story.*

Rocca dropped a thumb drive on the desk. "Phone logs. Morales' last twenty-four hours."

Evans opened it. Texts to coworkers, calls to her mother. One number stood out: **Unknown. Outgoing at 5:12 p.m., 9 minutes. Incoming from the same number at 6:01.**

His pulse kicked up. Nine minutes. People didn't chat for nine minutes unless they knew each other. Was this the gap? The person she'd been waiting for?

"That stands out to you?" Evans said.

"Always the ones with no names," Rocca said.

Pérez leaned over. "We can subpoena the subscriber info."

Evans scrolled: **7:43 a.m., incoming call from the Nifty Fifty. 56 seconds.**

"Employer check-in?"

"Or her calling back," Pérez said. "Frank probably leaned on her for being late."

Evans logged both. Tried to picture her: apron on, phone pressed to her ear, fighting with her boss.

"Socials?" he asked.

Pérez pulled out a tablet and unlocked it with a swipe. Camila's Facebook glowed blue. Last post: a filtered selfie with a coworker, two weeks ago. Comments full of emojis and hearts. Then nothing. Instagram the same—smiles, pics from the diner, a shot of textbooks with a mug. Digital life, curated, all surface.

"Any DMs?" Evans asked.

"The request for metadata is in," Pérez said. "But it'll crawl. Zuck's people don't sprint for subpoenas."

Rocca sipped coffee, smirked. "Sometimes they sprint if you embarrass them in the press. If the kid's face is on the ten o'clock news, they don't want to look like the platform of choice for murderers."

Evans rubbed his temple. "So far we've got broken cameras, phantom calls, social silence."

"That's half the job," Pérez said. "You learn more from what's missing."

Evans thought of Roan's words at the Morales house: *The real story's in what's missing.*

"What about the Good Samaritan nurse?" Evans said.

"Ellen Mills. Called the tip line." Pérez dropped a pink slip on his desk.

Name: Ellen Mills.

Time: 10:15 p.m.

Location: Southern and Dixie. With a companion.

With a companion. Evans' mind caught on it. The Asian girl. Another witness. Another piece of the gap.

"You should call her back," Pérez said.

"I want the report clean first."

"Don't let *'clean'* make you late. People change their minds when the sun hits them."

The bullpen door opened. Detective Robert Roan walked in.

Conversations tightened.

Typing got precise.

Martinez straightened the stack of files he'd been ignoring.

Freshly shaven, with damp dark hair, and in a suit. No tie. He'd been up all night but went home and cleaned up.

Roan stopped at Evans' desk.

Set down a Starbucks cup.

"Report on my desk when you're done," Roan said. "I'll be with the captain."

Evans looked at the coffee cup, then at Roan. "Yes, sir."

Roan walked to the captain's office, knocked once, and disappeared inside.

The door closed.

Evans stared at the coffee.

Still warm.

Roan had worked all night.

Gone home.

Cleaned up.

Stopped at Starbucks.

Brought him coffee.

"Holy shit," he said.

Pérez let out a breath. "He does that."

"Walks?"

"Puts air back in the room. After he's taken some out."

Rocca stretched. "Man doesn't sleep. Runs on coffee and spits out wins."

Pérez grinned. "He brought you coffee. After working all night, he went home, cleaned up, stopped at Starbucks, and brought you coffee."

"What does that mean?"

"It means he thinks you're worth teaching."

"You said you don't like to go home," Evans said.

Pérez kept her eyes on the door. "Not this week."

"Bad landlord?"

"Bad everything." Her smile didn't reach her eyes—told him that was all he'd get.

"Okay," he said.

Evans typed. The nurse's hotline tip—he marked it in his notebook, underlining.

Call Ellen Mills

Rocca pushed off the desk. "If we're done with feelings, I'm trying to find out why the canvass report from Oceanside jumps from page two to four."

"Because Nichols used page three to write down a phone number," Pérez said. "He hid it in his sock when I walked up."

"You scare them," Rocca said.

"I give them rules. They scare themselves."

Evans sipped his coffee—strong, exactly how he needed it. He typed:

**Call Mrs. Morales. Ask about friends, routines, and
anyone new.**

Numbered them. One. Two. Priorities.

"Evans," Pérez said. "If you had to rank the worst things you've told a mother, where does 'I'll call after I finish a report' land?"

He closed his eyes. "Above 'we're doing everything we can,' below 'tell me again about her last day.'"

She nodded. "Do it now. The report will be better after."

"I will. Thanks."

"Don't thank me. Just get it right."

Rocca came back with a folder. "Found page three. Phone number, hearts around it. Nichols can't spell Julissa."

"Two S'," Pérez said. "He'll learn."

"You're serious about leaving?" Evans said to Rocca.

"Month, maybe less. Got three wives tired of guessing where their husbands spend Thursdays. I point a camera. They write checks."

"Glamorous," Pérez said.

"Rocca," Evans said, typing, "you really taking pictures of guys with no pants?"

"You say it like it's a dream of mine," Rocca said. "It's not art, but checks clear. People don't haggle when they want the truth that hurts."

"Truth doesn't care what it costs," Pérez said.

"Truth costs exactly what you can afford," Rocca said, pleased. "Also, I bought a camera."

"What kind?" Evans asked.

"The expensive kind," Rocca said, which meant the salesman sold him everything with a strap.

"You tell the Captain you're leaving?" Pérez asked.

"I'll tell him when my office plant dies. It's a cactus. So—never."

Evans smirked. "You have a plant?"

"It came with the desk."

"Two occupants ago," Pérez said. "You just started watering it last month."

"I'm practicing commitment. PIs need to look reliable."

"Your tie's on your chair," Pérez said.

Rocca looked down as if he'd caught himself undressed. "I wore one last night. Its job is over now."

Evans moved it aside. "A month, huh?"

"As soon as the retainer is clear. And I get a fedora."

"No," Pérez said. "Absolutely not."

"What, I can't have a fedora?" Rocca asked, wounded.

"You can have a camera," Pérez said. "You wear a fedora, and I write you up."

Pérez flicked a glance at Evans' screen. "You spelled 'Oceanside' right. That'll impress him."

"I Googled it," Evans said.

"You did not," she said, amused.

"Okay. I didn't."

"You should call Mrs. Morales," Pérez said. "And Ellen Mills."

She looked over her shoulder. "You're not the wrong guy because you came from Wellington. You're only the wrong guy if you won't learn this place."

"I'll learn it," he said.

"Good."

Rocca watched her go. "She's better at this than most people with bars on their shoulders."

"I think she knows," Evans said.

"You think she knows everything," Rocca said. "You're not wrong."

Evans picked up the Starbucks cup. Strong coffee. Coffee that said someone understood exhaustion and wanted to help.

He glanced at the wall clock—7:52. Eight minutes until Roan's deadline. His neck ached from hunching over the keyboard. The fluorescent flickered overhead.

He got back to work, the District 14 bullpen churning around him, the morning sun cutting through tall windows, the investigation grinding forward one piece at a time.

CHAPTER

9

ROAN STOOD at the captain's window, hands clasped behind his back, watching Evans type in the bullpen below. The kid hunched over his keyboard, shoulders tight, hammering at his report like every word was trial evidence. In the same way, Roan used to sit—twenty years ago, when cases still felt like puzzles instead of epitaphs.

Captain Norris' office smelled different from the bullpen—old wood polish and stale cigar smoke, not the burnt coffee and holding cell sweat that permeated everything downstairs. Warmer, too. Norris kept the thermostat at seventy-two. Sound was dampened in here, muffled by the closed door and the carpet that didn't exist anywhere else in District 14.

"You brought him coffee," Norris said from behind his desk, tone somewhere between amused and concerned.

Roan didn't turn. "He's steady."

"Steady." Norris pulled the Morales file across his desk and opened it. "That's all?"

"He shows up. Does the work. Doesn't ask stupid questions."

"Doesn't ask questions at all, from what I've seen."

Roan's jaw tightened. Norris leaned back in his chair—the springs creaking under his weight—waiting.

"He's learning," Roan said.

"Learning what? How to stand in your shadow?" Norris tapped the file. "He's got a family, Roan. Wife, kids. You see that ring on his hand?"

"I saw it." Roan's reflection shifted in the window—a grey ghost superimposed over the bullpen below. For a moment, he remembered his own ring, the weight, the groove it had left on his finger for months after he'd stopped wearing it. "That's why I sent him home early. He's got people waiting for him."

"Since when do you play guardian?" Norris said, belly against the desk edge. Sixty-two years old, grey threading through what was left of his hair, tie loosened at the collar. "You worked him all night. The kid went home to his family thinking he had failed."

"Not sentimental." Roan's gaze dropped to Evans. "Practical. A man with a family either breaks faster or lasts longer. Depends on how he learns to balance it."

"Balance." Norris pulled a pack of cigarettes from his drawer, rolled one between his fingers without lighting it—a habit from the year he'd quit, fifteen years ago, when his doctor had shown him the X-rays. "Funny word coming from you."

Roan let the jab fall.

"You think I'm turning him into me," Roan said.

"I think you see yourself in him." Norris dropped the unlit cigarette back into the drawer. "And you're trying to save him from your mistakes."

Roan turned to face him. "He goes home. He's got something waiting for him that isn't just this job."

"For now." Norris scanned the Morales file. "Pub scene, Oceanside. Witness statements all over the place. Bartender says the male she was with left before her." He flipped a page. "Nurse—Ellen Mills—called in a sighting. Southern and Dixie, around ten-fifteen. Says she saw a girl matching Morales' description with another female, Asian, early twenties."

"I'm following up."

"When?"

"When I'm done here."

Norris kept reading. "Phone records. Nine-minute call to an unlisted number, outgoing at 5:12 p.m. Callback from the same number at 6:01. Both clean disconnects."

"Telemarketer."

"Probably." Norris closed the file. "You've got fog and ghosts, Roan. Nothing solid. Nothing that holds."

"It'll clear."

"You always say that." Norris folded his hands across his stomach. "But this one feels different."

"We've got the gap. Seven hours. Three to ten. Someone knows where she was."

"Evans gonna figure that out?"

"He's getting there."

Norris studied him, the way a man studies something he's watched deteriorate over decades. "You're teaching him. Whether you mean to or not, he watches you. Pretty soon, he's gonna start thinking like you."

"Maybe he won't," Roan said. "Maybe he'll figure out how to do this without losing everything."

"There's no other way."

Norris unwrapped a piece of gum and chewed it slowly—the spearmint smell cut through the cigar residue.

"We all break, Robert. Some break slowly. Some break clean. But we all break."

Norris leaned back into his squeaking chair.

"Why do you do it?" Norris asked.

"Do what?"

"Keep chasing. You've got a pension waiting. You've cleared more cases than anyone else in this building."

Roan's reflection stared back from the window—the lines around his eyes deeper than they'd been five years ago, the grey in his hair more pronounced, posture still military-straight, but the cost of maintaining it visible in the set of his shoulders. "And do what? Sit on a dock and wait to die?"

"Live, maybe."

"I wouldn't know how."

Norris sighed. "That's why I still let you run the way you do. You get results. You close cases nobody else can close."

"I'm fine."

"You're not. But you're functional. And functional's all I need."

Roan faced Norris head-on, stepping away from the window. "You didn't call me in here to talk about Evans."

"No."

"You called me in here to tell me to back off."

"I called you in here to tell you to be careful." Norris stood, walked around the desk—his gait slower than it used to be, arthritis in the left knee he never mentioned. "Evans is good. He's got potential. But he's soft. Still got a family. He still goes home to a wife who loves him. You start pulling him into your orbit, that's all gonna fall apart."

"That's why I'm teaching him balance," Roan said.

"You can't teach what you don't have." Norris' jaw worked, chewing the gum with deliberate slowness. "I was there, Robert. Saw you lose everything that wasn't a case file."

The memory hung in the air between them.

"It still matters," Roan said.

"Not at the cost of everything else." Norris stepped closer, close enough that Roan could smell the spearmint and the coffee on his breath. "You worked, Evans, all night. You burn everything you touch. Don't burn that kid, too."

"Not if I teach him how to survive it."

"You can't teach him that," Norris said. "Because you never learned it yourself."

The words hung between them.

Roan picked up the Morales file from the desk. "I need to work this case."

"Robert—"

"I need to work this case," Roan said, colder. "Unless you're telling me, I can't."

Norris stared at him, jaw tight. "No. I'm not telling you that."

"Good."

Roan walked to the door and pulled it open. The bullpen noise rushed in—phones, voices, the printer wheezing.

"You'll drown him if you're not careful," Norris said.

Roan stopped in the doorway, didn't turn. "He'll either swim or he won't."

He stepped through and pulled the door shut behind him—not a slam, but firm enough to be final.

The bullpen quieted as Roan moved through it. Phones still rang, keyboards still clacked, but conversations paused mid-sentence.

Evans looked up as Roan passed. They nodded to each other. Evans returned to his report.

Pérez watched from near the break room, arms crossed. She'd seen men walk out of that office carrying weight they hadn't stepped in with.

Rocca glanced up, caught Roan's eye. The look was enough acknowledgement, the silent language of men who'd survived long enough to recognize storms.

The door at the far end of the bullpen swung shut behind Roan, the pneumatic hinge hissing.

Inside the captain's office, Norris stood at the window, watching Roan disappear down the hall. The blinds rattled when the A/C kicked on, a metallic flutter that filled the silence.

He walked back to his desk, opened the bottom drawer, and pulled out a bottle wrapped in an evidence bag. Wild Turkey, the label faded. The case number on the bag had smeared into illegibility years ago—a domestic from 1998, the bottle confiscated and never returned to evidence, migrating instead to Norris' drawer after the case closed.

He poured two fingers of whiskey into a coffee mug. The bourbon caught the light streaming through the window, amber shot through with gold, older than it had any right to be.

He sipped; the burn was familiar.

Set the mug down.

The phones kept ringing. The cases kept coming.

Norris wondered—not for the first time—whether Roan was trying to save Evans or create a better version of himself. A version that learned balance. A version that didn't trade everything for the job. A version that kept the ring on his finger, the photos on his desk, and the family waiting at home.

He poured another drink, the bourbon glugging into the mug.

CHAPTER

10

Roan pressed the pen hard enough to indent three sheets of paper. The scratch of a ballpoint on paper filled the single-window office. His coffee had gone cold twenty minutes ago—tried once, grimaced at the bitter chill, set it back down.

The office at the end of the corridor had one window, four walls, a desk, two chairs, and a file cabinet that never closed properly. The air smelled of old case files and stale paper, unlike the cigar smoke and wood polish in Norris' office. Cooler here, too. The thermostat had been broken for six months, stuck at sixty-eight.

Commendations covered the walls. Framed certificates for cases closed, suspects caught, and bodies given names. Dates going back fifteen years. Not a single photo. No family snapshots, no vacation postcards. Plaques told stories in shorthand:

Outstanding Service 2008.
Meritorious Conduct 2011.
Distinguished Investigation 2015.

Years stacked like layers of sediment.

The fluorescent overhead buzzed—a high-pitched whine that never quite stopped, the tube flickering every thirty seconds.

Roan tapped the pen against the legal pad. Once. Twice. His lower back ached from sitting hunched for two hours straight. He wrote Second girl—key. Find her, find the killer.

The second girl had stood on that corner with Camila, waiting. People who stand on street corners with murder victims know things. Either they're witnesses, or they're involved.

A knock.

"Come."

Evans pushed the door open, folder in hand. Collar wrinkled, tie loosened, eyes red from staring at a screen. The folder shook in his grip. Roan noticed. Fear or exhaustion—it didn't matter. What mattered was whether Evans would push through it.

"Report," Evans said, setting it on the desk.

Roan didn't open it. Kept his eyes on Evans.

"Have you talked to Ellen Mills yet?"

Evans blinked.

"The nurse? I was going to call her this afternoon—"

"She's coming in. Eleven-thirty."

Evans' jaw clenched, released. His hand stayed on the folder, frozen halfway between pulling it back and letting it go.

"You already contacted her."

"Two hours ago."

Evans nodded slowly. His fingers drummed once on the folder, then stilled. His gaze flicked to the legal pad, trying to read the timeline upside down.

"What do you need from me?"

"Sit in on the interview. Take notes. Listen." Roan tapped the folder. "This stays here. I'll read it after."

"After."

"After we know what Ellen saw."

Evans stood there a second too long. Then nodded.

"Eleven-thirty. Conference room. Pérez will bring her."

"Got it."

Evans turned to leave.

"Evans."

He stopped. Hand on the doorframe, shoulders rigid.

Roan leaned back in his chair, choosing his words the way his own training officer had—not lecturing, but planting seeds.

"You did good work last night," Roan said. "But reports don't solve cases. Witnesses do. You can write a perfect timeline and miss the one detail that breaks it open. That's why we talk to people. That's why we listen."

Evans met his eyes. Nodded, shoulders loosening fractionally. "Understood."

"Good. Be ready."

Evans left. The door clicked shut.

Roan went back to the legal pad. Drew another line.

Second girl. Asian. Black dress. Who?

Find her, and the rest would fall.

The conference room table bore scars from years of elbows and coffee rings. Chairs creaked no matter how still you sat. A whiteboard on one wall still had someone's timeline from a case two months old, half-erased, ghosting through. The air carried the scent of dry-erase marker, warmer than the hallway by five degrees. Overhead, fluorescent lights buzzed with insect persistence, one flickering in the periphery.

Roan sat at the head of the table. Evans, to his right, with a legal pad open and a pen ready. Pérez stood by the door, arms crossed.

She knocked twice and then opened it.

"Detective Roan, this is Ellen Mills."

Ellen Mills' scrubs hung wrinkled, hair pulled back in a ponytail that had started neat twelve hours ago. Dark circles shadowed her eyes. Her hands clutched her purse strap, knuckles pale. But her gaze held steady. The faint smell of hospital—antiseptic and hand sanitizer—came with her into the room. A hospital ID badge hung from her waistband. Ellen Mills, RN, Good Samaritan Medical Center. The lanyard frayed at the edges.

Roan stood. Gestured to the chair across from him.

"Ms. Mills, thank you for coming."

She sat facing him, her back to the door. Pérez angled to her left and set her purse on the floor.

"I should've called sooner."

"You called when you could. That's what matters."

Pérez took the seat beside Ellen, angled to watch both her and Roan. Evans' pen hovered over the paper.

Roan sat. Folded his hands on the table. No notebook. No recording device visible.

"Thursday night. You left at ten?"

"I clocked out, walked to my car in the lot, and left."

"You drove south on Dixie?"

"No. I cut through the side streets to Dixie. Faster that way. Less traffic."

"What time did you reach Dixie?"

"Maybe ten-ten. Ten-fifteen. I wasn't checking. I just wanted to get home."

"And that's when you saw them."

Ellen nodded. Swallowed.

"Yeah. The two girls."

"Where were they standing?"

She took a breath. Her hands gripped the table edge—not shaking, but white-knuckled. Roan noted it—nerves, not deception.

"Southern and Dixie, southwest corner. Right under the streetlamp."

"Describe them."

"One had... brown hair, maybe shoulder-length, a white crop top, a leather jacket. But the jacket was only halfway on, like she'd thrown it on in a hurry. Gold hoop earrings. I remember because they caught the light."

"What else?"

Roan waited.

"She had a bracelet," Ellen continued. "Gold. Thin. I heard it jingle when she moved her arm. She was gesturing. Talking. Not loud, but... animated."

"To the second girl?"

"No. Just... talking. Like she was nervous. Or excited. I couldn't tell."

"And the second girl?"

Ellen's gaze dropped.

"Asian. Early twenties. Black dress, short. Jacket over it. Strappy sandals, shoes that aren't good for standing on a street corner that long."

"How do you mean?"

"She kept shifting her weight. Like her feet hurt. But she didn't sit. Didn't lean against anything. Just stood there. Straight. Still."

"Did she look afraid?"

"No."

"Nervous?"

"No."

Ellen looked up.

"She looked like she didn't want to be there. But not afraid... more like she was waiting for something to be over. Like she'd made a decision and was going through with it."

Roan made a note. His face stayed neutral.

"Like she'd decided and was just going through with it," he repeated quietly, confirming he'd heard correctly.

"Yes."

"What happened next?"

"I pulled over. Rolled down my window. Asked if they needed a ride."

"What did they say?"

"The one in the crop top—Camila—she looked at me and said they were waiting for someone. She smiled. Said thanks, but they were good."

"How did she say it?"

Ellen frowned.

"What do you mean?"

"Her tone."

Ellen thought.

"Polite. Maybe a little... eager? Like she wanted me to leave so whoever they were waiting for would show up."

"And the second girl?"

"She didn't say anything. Just stood there. Watching me. Not hostile. Just... blank."

"Did either of them seem intoxicated? Impaired?"

"No. Steady. Camila was... energetic. But steady. The other one was calm. Too calm, maybe."

"What did you do?"

"I said OK, be safe, and drove off."

Ellen's voice cracked.

"I should've stayed. I should've—"

"You couldn't have known," Roan said. "What happened after you drove away?"

"I went home. Showered. Made dinner. Watched TV. I didn't think about it until I saw the news the next day. Her face was on the screen. The girl in the crop top. Camila. And I just... I knew."

"You called right away?"

"As soon as I saw it."

"Did you see a car pull up while you were there?"

"No. I left before that."

"Did you see anyone else? Other pedestrians? Other cars?"

"A few cars passed. Normal traffic. Nobody stood out."

Roan set the pen down. Looked at Ellen. Her hands trembled against the table.

"Ms. Mills," he said, "you did what you were supposed to do. You called. You told us what you saw. That's more than most people do."

Her eyes welled. She blinked it back.

"I should've made them get in the car. I should've—"

"You couldn't have known."

"But if I had—"

"We'll try," Roan said. "That's all I can tell you. We'll try."

Ellen nodded, wiping her eyes with the back of her hand. Pérez handed her a tissue.

Roan stood.

"If you remember anything else—car details, anything more on the second girl, any sounds—call me directly." He slid a card across the table. "Day or night."

Ellen took it. Folded it carefully into her pocket.

"Thank you."

Pérez walked her to the door. Ellen paused at the threshold and looked back.

"Find her," she said. "The other girl. She's still out there. And she knows something."

"We will."

The door closed.

Roan turned to Evans.

"What did you hear?"

Evans looked at his notes.

"Two girls on a corner. Ellen offered a ride. Camila said they were waiting for someone—polite, eager. The second girl said nothing. Ellen drove off."

"What else?"

Evans hesitated.

"The second girl didn't want to be there."

"Why?"

"She didn't move. Didn't speak. Just waited. Like she'd made a decision and was going through with it."

"And?"

"If she didn't want to be there but stayed anyway, that means something. Either she was obligated, or scared, or... involved."

Roan nodded.

"Names are just time, Evans. Right now, we don't have hers. But we will."

He walked to the whiteboard and grabbed a marker. The cap came off with a pop, the chemical smell sharp.

Timeline:

3:00 p.m. – Left Nifty Fifty.

5:12 p.m. – Phone call, unlisted number, 9 min.

6:01 p.m. – Callback, same number.

10:15 p.m. – Southern & Dixie. Two girls. Waiting.

11:15 p.m. – Oceanside. Argued. Male. Linen shirt.

12:45 a.m. – Beach. Body found.

The marker squeaked against the board—high-pitched, rhythmic—as he drew arrows between points. Circled the gaps.

3:00–10:15: - 7 hrs. 15 min – WHERE?
10:15–11:45: - 1 hr. 30 min – STREET TO PUB,
WITH GUY IN LINEN SHIRT?
11:45–12:45: - 2 hrs. – PUB TO BEACH.
CAMILA LEAVES AFTER GUY.

"It's not just a man," Roan said. "It's a man and a second girl. That changes the hunt."

Evans stared at the board.

"You think she's involved?"

"She was there. People who are there know things. Either she's a witness who can help us, or she's involved and doesn't want to be found. Either way, we need her."

"How do we find her if nobody knows who she is?"

"Someone knows. College-aged, Asian, wearing a black dress with sandals. Someone saw her with Camila before Thursday night. Someone knows her name."

Pérez stepped back into the room.

Roan turned.

"Pérez."

She straightened.

"Sir."

"Canvass Palm Beach State. See if you can find information on the second girl matching her description, show Camila's photo, and ask if anyone saw them together. Check dorms, study groups, late-night hangouts."

"Yes, sir. When do you want me to start?"

"Now. And Pérez—if you get a name, call me. Don't wait for confirmation."

"Understood."

She left.

Roan capped the marker. Turned to Evans.

"Check rideshare logs, cab companies, Uber, Lyft—anything that picked up two females from Southern and Dixie Thursday night between ten-fifteen and eleven—cross-reference with drop-offs at

Oceanside Pub or Lake Worth Beach. Check cell tower pings. Anything that puts a phone in that location during that window."

Evans jotted it down.

"Got it. See if anyone else stopped. Get a plate number on whatever car picked them up after Ellen left."

"On it."

Roan lifted his jacket from the chair.

"Now we go see where she died."

Evans blinked.

"The beach?"

Roan was already at the door.

"You want to see the truth; you stand where it happened. Reports won't teach you that."

Evans pushed back his chair and gathered his notes.

"Who's driving?"

Roan's hand was on the door handle.

"You are."

Evans nodded once and followed him out.

CHAPTER

II

PÉREZ PULLED into the Lake Worth campus lot and killed the engine. The A/C died with a rattle. She sat behind the wheel, watching students cross the asphalt—backpacks slung, earbuds in, iced coffees dripping condensation. They laughed, swerved around each other.

Her phone buzzed. Jacob. Again.

She let it ring out, not glancing at the screen. Her shoulders tensed, a knot forming between her shoulder blades where the vest sat heaviest. Last night's fight was still fresh—his voice rising, hers staying flat, an argument where nobody wins because nobody's actually talking about what they're fighting about. He wanted answers she didn't have. She wanted space; he wouldn't give. (Not now. Not today.)

She stepped out. Heat climbed her uniform sleeves before she'd made it to the curb, the polyester trapping humidity against her skin. Palms lined the walkways in even ranks, shadows striping damp concrete where sprinklers had just shut off. Stucco fronts gleamed white, green banners shouting futures in block letters. The humidity pressed down like a hand, thick enough to taste.

She walked the campus slowly, gold badge clipped at her chest where the sun caught it—the weight familiar but heavier today, every ounce a reminder. The air smelled of fresh-cut grass and baking asphalt, the faint chemical tang of fertilizer underneath. Sprinklers ticked in the distance, automated, indifferent. Someone had dropped a textbook near the bike racks—pages splayed open, already warping in the humidity.

Students passed her in loose clusters. A girl in yoga pants carrying a Starbucks cup, oversized sunglasses pushed up into bleached hair, phone pressed to her ear mid-laugh. Two guys in basketball shorts were arguing about a professor, one gesturing with a vape pen. A kid on a skateboard was weaving through the foot traffic, wheels clicking over pavement cracks. Nobody looked at her badge. Nobody made eye contact.

Bulletin boards lined the covered walkways. Flyers layered three deep—yoga classes, tutoring services, club tryouts, lost pets, roommates wanted. A flyer for a poetry slam, half torn down. One advertising guitar lessons with phone number tabs ripped away except for two. A missing cat poster faded in the sun.

She passed a bench where a kid sat alone, laptop open, headphones blocking out the world. His screen showed spreadsheets. Numbers. The focus that came when a man needed things to work.

Pérez wondered when Camila Morales had first walked these sidewalks—if she'd carried the same easy air, or if she'd already had the weight then. Community college wasn't the dream. It was the fallback. The second chance. The place you went when the first plan didn't work out.

The student union smelled of industrial cleaner. Vending machines lined one wall, humming. Tables were scattered across the cheap linoleum. A bulletin board covered in flyers for clubs nobody joined and events nobody attended.

Pérez approached a table where three girls sat, laptops open, notebooks spread, and energy drinks sweating condensation onto the table.

"Excuse me. Officer Pérez, PBSO. Can I ask you a quick question?"

They looked up. One blonde, two brunettes. All three were under twenty-five and immediately wary.

"Is something wrong?" the blonde asked.

"No. I'm looking for information about someone who attended here." Pérez set Camila's photo on the table. "Do you recognize her?"

The blonde leaned in. Squinted. "Maybe? I don't know."

The brunette shook her head. "Never seen her."

The other brunette hesitated. "She looks familiar. I think I've seen her around."

Pérez nodded. "Did you ever see her with another girl? Asian, early twenties, maybe?"

They exchanged glances. Shook their heads.

"Sorry," the blonde said. "We can't help you."

Pérez thanked them. Moved on.

She hit another table. Same approach. Same response. Then another. By the fourth table, she'd adjusted her pitch—less formal, more conversational. Asked if they'd seen Camila at parties, study groups, anywhere off-campus. Still nothing. One girl thought maybe she'd seen her at the library. Another swore she'd never been on this campus before, though she had a student ID hanging from her lanyard.

Fifth table. A guy with headphones around his neck, economics textbook open. "Yeah, I remember her. She sat in the back row in Intro Psych. Always on time. Never said much." He shrugged. "That's all I got."

Sixth table. Seventh.

Same result. A few students recognized Camila's face—maybe from a class, maybe from passing her in the hall—but nobody knew her. Nobody remembered her in connection with anyone specific. Nobody had seen the second girl.

Large classes. Rotating adjuncts. No cohort. No community. Just bodies moving through a system.

Her breathing went shallow. The frustration built low, steady. It didn't show on her face.

Her phone buzzed. Jacob:

> You can't ignore me forever.

She silenced it. Shoved it back in her pocket.

The registrar's office sat behind glass doors etched with the school seal. Inside, the hum dropped a notch—cooler air hitting her face like a slap, the temperature shift immediate after the outdoor sauna. Fluorescents buzzed over a counter stacked with forms no one wanted to fill out, printers coughed out tuition receipts, and the sharp clack of keyboards behind partition walls: toner and floor wax mixed in the sterile air.

Three students sat on plastic chairs along the wall. One scrolled through his phone. One filled out a form, the pen moving slowly and deliberately. The third stared at nothing, jaw tight, calculating costs.

Pérez watched them. Wondered if Camila had sat in one of those chairs. Wondered if she'd filled out the same forms, checked the same boxes, and handed over cash.

The counterwoman looked up. Mid-forties, wearing a floral blouse, and with reading glasses perched low. Her name tag said Linda.

Pérez flashed her badge. "Officer Pérez, PBSO. Looking for records on a student. Camila Morales."

Linda's posture changed. Less bored, more guarded. "We don't usually give out private information without a subpoena."

"Not asking for her Social Security number," Pérez said. "Classes. Enrolment history. Who she sat in rooms with. Morales was found dead two nights ago."

Linda's lips parted, shut, then pressed tight. She reached for the phone, dialed an extension, and murmured low. After a pause, she hung up. "Registrar will see you. Back office. Through there."

Pérez walked down a hall lined with framed photos of past graduating classes. Smiling faces in caps and gowns, printed slogans underneath: Your Future Starts Here. She kept her hands loose at her sides, jaw tight.

The registrar's office door opened before she had a chance to knock. A man in shirtsleeves and a tie too narrow stepped out, folder in hand. "Officer Pérez?"

"That's me."

"I pulled what you asked." He lifted the folder. "Come in."

The registrar's office was smaller than she expected. One window, blinds half-crooked, light falling across stacks of binders balanced on the credenza. The man in the narrow tie—his nameplate read D. Carson—motioned her toward the chair opposite his desk. A coffee mug sat half-full, and a framed degree from Florida Atlantic hung slightly crooked behind him.

Pérez sat, badge resting against her chest, her posture just formal enough to remind him why she was here. He opened the folder with care, pages clipped neatly.

"Camila Morales," Carson said. "Enrolled here on and off for the last two years. Mostly general education—Intro to Psychology, College Algebra, English Comp. Standard track." He flipped a page. "She also completed a massage therapy certificate program last spring."

Pérez lifted a brow. "Here?"

"Continuing Ed. Night program. Not unusual. Students looking for some quick credentials to get into the workforce."

She jotted notes on the small pad she carried, shorthand looping quickly, numbers circled, key facts underlined. "Is she on financial aid?"

Carson shook his head. "No FAFSA. No Pell. She paid cash or card every semester. No loans in her file. Everything cleared."

Pérez's pen stopped moving.

No aid.

No loans.

Diner wages—minimum plus tips. Maybe $25,000 a year, if she worked full-time, which the hours showed she didn't. Tuition ran about $3,800 to $4,200 per semester. Call it $8,000 a year. Rent, food, phone, car—call it another $15,000 conservative. That left $2,000 for everything else. Clothes, emergencies, books, gas. It didn't work. The math didn't close.

Tuition for a community college wasn't Ivy League, but it stacked. Semester after semester, no aid, no loans, just cash up front. She thought of Camila working days at the diner, tips, and minimum wage. That didn't square.

"She had a scholarship from anywhere? Private donor?" Pérez asked.

"Not here," Carson said. "We keep track. Nothing like that attached to her record."

"How much per semester?"

Carson glanced at the screen. "Varies by credit load. Last spring, $4,200. This fall, $3,800."

Pérez stopped writing. $4,200. $3,800. Diner wages didn't cover that. Not even close.

"Payment methods?"

"Cash for last fall and spring. Debit card for this spring and fall."

"Name on the card?"

"System doesn't track that. Just payment type."

Pérez's pen hovered over the page, then stopped. She let her eyes drift to the walls. A corkboard held the usual clutter—flyers for résumé workshops, deadlines for withdrawing without penalty, glossy posters of smiling students underlined with tuition slogans. She thought of Camila: crop top under a jacket, hoops catching the streetlight, smiling at a stranger's car.

"Who'd she take classes with? Any group projects, lab partners, clubs?"

Carson glanced at the roster sheets. "Psych and algebra are typically 30 seats—lots of turnover. Professors rotate adjuncts in and out. No stable cohorts." He spread his hands. "We don't track friendships."

Pérez leaned in, voice quiet but pointed. "Anyone ever see her on campus with an Asian girl? Dark hair, early twenties, black jacket. That ring a bell?"

Carson thought, shook his head. "Not in these records. I could ask a few of the faculty, but if she wasn't disruptive, she'd just be another face."

Pérez sat back, jaw tight, pen pressed flat against the page—another dead end. The second girl hadn't walked these halls—or if she had, she hadn't left a footprint.

She closed her notebook. "All right. That's enough for now."

Carson slid the folder back across the desk. "If you need anything more official, you'll have to come through channels."

Pérez stood and left.

She stepped out into the heat. The glass doors closed behind her with a hiss, cutting off the air-conditioned drone of campus life.

Palm Beach State, in the late morning, was filled with students cutting across the walkways in knots of two and three, earbuds wired in, laptops hugged tightly. A cluster of smokers claimed the benches by the lake, the breeze pushing their chatter sideways. The sun bounced hard off the asphalt of the lot, turning every car roof into a mirror.

She walked slowly, giving herself the rhythm to think. Camila's classes—psych, algebra, English. Massage therapy certificate. Paid cash, no aid. Cash meant freedom, but it also meant questions. Pérez pictured the girl sliding diner checks into a pocket, counting tips in crumpled bills, then walking into the registrar's office to hand over tuition. No scholarships, no loans. Where was the extra coming from?

She reached her cruiser, unlocked it, but didn't get in. She leaned on the door, notebook still in her hand, pen tapping the cover.

Last year. She took the detective exam and got 92 percent. Top fifteen percent. The interview went clean—three captains, two lieutenants, all nodding in the right places. She'd answered every scenario question with precision. One captain had asked about a domestic with a weapon present and conflicting statements. She'd walked him through de-escalation, evidence preservation, and witness separation. He'd nodded, made a note. Talked about clearance rates, community relations, and case management. Walked out feeling solid.

Two weeks later:

At this time, we have decided to pursue other candidates for this position.

Then, Evans transferred in from Wellington a month ago. Good cop. Solid instincts. But greener than she was by eighteen months. And he got the shield.

She told herself it didn't matter. Told herself the work was still the work, badge or not. But it stung every time she introduced herself as "Officer Pérez, PBSO," when what she should be saying was "Detective Pérez." The title she'd earned but would never wear.

Evans had something she didn't. And it wasn't test scores. Wasn't the experience.

She shoved the notebook into her vest, jaw tight.

Her phone buzzed once in her pocket. She pulled it out. Jacob again.

I'm not the enemy.

She stared at the message. Then another came through.

You're always working. Even when you're home.

Then a third.

Just tell me what you need.

Her thumb hovered over the keyboard. Part of her wanted to type back—*I need you to stop asking me to choose.* But she didn't. Because that wasn't fair either, he wasn't asking her to choose. He was asking her to show up. And she couldn't. Not right now. Not when Camila Morales was dead, and the answers were somewhere in the gaps.

She locked the phone without answering. Last night's fight still sat between them like glass. He'd said she lived more at the station than at home. She'd said the station didn't lie. Neither of them had been wrong.

Pérez slid into the driver's seat, the interior hot enough to sting her hand on the wheel. She started the engine, the A/C coughing awake, and sat there for a long minute with the phone in her lap.

She thought of Evans hunched over his desk, trying to make the report look clean. She thought of Roan, grey-eyed, watching everything without blinking. She thought of Camila Morales—twenty-one, smiling too politely on a dark street.

Dead ends at Palm Beach State. No Asian girl, no second lead. Just tuition paid in cash and classes that went nowhere.

But the money trail was real. And if it mattered, Roan needed to know.

She thumbed through her contacts, hovered on Evans. Hit call. Once. Twice. Voicemail.

"It's Pérez. The campus was a dead end for the second girl, but I found something on Camila's tuition payments. Call me back."

She hung up. Waited. Stared at the phone.

Nothing.
Then the phone buzzed. She exhaled when she looked.
Jacob:

> We need to talk.

The message sat there.
Not now.
She deleted the notification. Put the car in gear.
The campus shrank in the rearview mirror.
And somewhere in the gap between what Camila earned and what she paid, someone had filled the space with cash.
She hit Roan's number. Two rings.
"Go." His voice was flat, focused.
"I found something," she said.

CHAPTER

12

SUNSHINE HAMMERED down white and mercilessly on Lake Worth Beach. Jet skis carved the water in tight arcs, engines screaming, throwing up spray that caught the light. Volleyball nets sagged between poles stuck in the sand, bodies diving and shouting. Music thumped from a Bluetooth speaker propped on a cooler—reggaeton, something with too much bass. The smell of coconut sunscreen and salt air, mixed with the scent of barbecue drifting from a smoker stand near the parking lot.

Girls in micro bikinis stretched out on towels, skin oiled and bronze. A few wore thongs, turning over every twenty minutes, bodies shifting positions in the relentless sun. Guys threw footballs. Kids screamed in the shallows. Fishermen lined the pier with rods propped against the rail, lines hanging slack in the current, waiting for something to bite.

Evans pulled the Explorer into the lot. Roan was out before the A/C stopped blowing.

"Walk first," Roan said. "Then questions."

Evans followed, tie already loosened, jacket slung over one arm. The heat pressed against them. His shirt stuck to his back; the collar was damp with sweat.

They stood near the boundary of the crime scene tape, still up from the night before, fluttering in the breeze—yellow plastic against neon umbrellas.

"Walk it," Roan said.

Evans hesitated. "What am I looking for?"

"Everything." Roan stepped under the tape. "Ground tells you things paper can't. Walk it until you see what happened."

The sand was pale, fine, tracked with footprints from beachgoers who'd walked too close before the tape went up. The area where they found Camila was marked by stakes driven into the ground, numbered placards still in place. Blood soaked into the sand, darkening it, then tide and time washed it clean. Now it just looked like wet sand drying in the sun.

Evans walked slowly, eyes scanning the ground. Roan watched him, measuring his focus.

"What do you see?" Roan asked.

"Sand. Stakes. Where they found her."

"What else?"

Evans looked around. The pier stretched out over the water to the north, old wood creaking under the weight of fishermen and tourists taking photos. The parking lot sat thirty yards to the west. The dunes rolled low to the south, sea oats bending in the wind.

"Access points," Evans said. "Lot to the west. Dunes to the south. Pier to the north."

"Good. What else?"

Evans frowned. "I don't—"

"Light," Roan said. "Wind, shade, factors. This beach at midnight looks different from how it does now. Stand where they found her. Feel it."

Evans moved to the center of the taped area. Stood where the body had been. The sun hit him full, no shade, nothing between him and the water except twenty yards of open sand.

"At night," Roan said, "this is dark. Pier lights don't reach here. Parking lot lights don't reach here—just the moon and stars. Wind carries sound away from the pier, not toward it. Waves drown voices. You could scream here, and nobody on the pier would hear you. Nobody in the lot would see you."

Evans turned, slow, taking it in. His gaze swept the parking lot, the pier, the dunes. Calculating angles, distances, and visibility.

"So whoever did this to her here knew that," Evans said.

"Or got lucky."

"You don't believe in luck."

"No." Roan walked to the pier side and gestured up. "Pier's got foot traffic until eleven, maybe midnight on weekends. After that, only the obsessed fisherman. They're looking at the water, not the beach. Someone walks a girl out here near one a.m.; nobody's watching. The waves are loud. The wind moves offshore. Everything that happens here stays here."

Evans nodded. "About ten or fifteen minutes from the time she left the pub until she died, according to Doctor Avery. What happened in between?"

"That's the question." Roan checked the time on his phone. "About ten or fifteen minutes, long enough to argue, stab her, drag her here, let her bleed out, and wait."

"Why wait?"

"Maybe he had to. Maybe he wanted to make sure she was dead. Maybe he was watching to see if anyone came."

Evans walked the perimeter and stopped at the tape closest to the parking lot. "If I'm doing it here, I'd park close. Walk her out. Do it fast. Leave."

"Unless you're not worried about being seen."

"Why wouldn't you be worried?"

Roan didn't answer. Just stared at the sand in thought.

Evans looked back at the spot where the body had been and tried to imagine it at night. Dark. Empty. Waves crashing. Wind pushes sound away from civilization.

Seven hours between the diner and here. For seven hours, Camila Morales was somewhere, with someone, doing something that ended with her in the sand.

Evan's breathing went shallow. Not pity—not anything as gentle as that. Just the weight of hours, time, and violence stacking up. Seven hours: enough for anything. Enough to drive to Orlando and back, if you wanted. Enough to argue, to plead, to beg. Enough to feel it finally sinking in that nobody would come. Nobody. In the end, that's what seven hours really meant.

Evans walked the perimeter one more time, trying to see it the way Roan did. The barbecue smell drifted stronger now—hickory, mesquite, something sweet underneath. His stomach growled. He ignored it.

"Let's move," Roan said.

They saw Ariel before he saw them.

Tall, thin, shoulders hunched under a backpack. He carried a staple gun in one hand, a stack of flyers in the other. Moving along the pier posts like a man on a mission, nobody had asked him.

Evans spotted him first. "That's the brother."

"Yeah."

They kept their distance. Watched from the parking lot side, fifty feet back, Roan leaned against a piling, arms crossed. Evans stood beside him.

Ariel approached a post near the pier entrance, pressed a flyer flat against the wood, and drove three staples through it. Metallic clicks carried across the sand. He moved to the next post. Same motion. Staple, staple, staple. Mechanical. Compulsive.

The flyers showed simple black text on white paper. In bold print, they couldn't quite read from here, but Evans had seen one already. Scripture:

The Wages of Sin is Death — ROMANS 6:23

Ariel worked his way down the pier posts, one after another. His hands moved with precision born from repetition. Fingernails ragged, bitten down. His lips moved, muttering something they couldn't hear. Prayer, maybe. Or curses. Hard to tell from here.

"Should we talk to him?" Evans asked quietly.

"No." Roan's voice was flat. "Let him have this."

They watched in silence. Ariel stapled another flyer. And another. Moving down the line like he was baptizing wood with grief. Post after post—flyer after flyer. Scripture against spring break posters, lost dog signs, and yoga class advertisements.

The beach roared around him. Jet skis screamed. Music thumped. Girls laughed. Kids splashed. Nobody noticed the thin boy stapling his grief to every surface he could reach.

Ariel finished his circuit. Stood at the last post for a long moment, staple gun hanging limp at his side. Then he turned, walked back toward the parking lot, shoulders rounder now.

He passed within thirty feet of them. Didn't look up. Didn't see them. Lost in whatever space he'd made for himself.

They watched him reach a battered white sedan—Maria Morales' car, Evans recognized it from the home visit. Ariel tossed the backpack in the back seat, climbed in, and sat behind the wheel for a full minute. Just sitting. Hands gripping the wheel. Head down.

Then, the engine turned over. Rattled. Coughed. Started.

The sedan rolled out of the lot, brake lights flashing once at the exit, then gone.

"He's losing it," Evans said quietly.

"Grief does that."

"Those flyers aren't helping anyone."

"They're helping him, maybe." Roan pushed off the piling. "He's trying to make sense of something that doesn't make sense. Scripture gives him structure. Purpose, maybe."

Evans looked back at the pier. The flyers fluttered in the breeze. Roan took a quick snapshot of them with his phone.

Roan started walking toward the pub.

A barbecue trailer sat near the entrance—Brandon's BBQ, hand-painted letters in orange across the side. Smoke poured from the chimney. A large man in a white apron worked the pit, flipping ribs and talking to customers lined up three deep. He had a deep laugh that carried, gold chain catching sunlight, tongs moving like a conductor's baton. Every customer got a smile and a story.

Evan's stomach growled again.

"You hungry?" Roan asked without looking at him.

"Starving."

They kept walking. Evans glanced back once. The man at the grill caught his eye, nodded—friendly, easy—then let his gaze return to the pit.

The Oceanside Pub looked different in daylight.

The neon sign was off. The windows were open, letting in air that smelled like ocean and old beer—decades of spills soaked into wood, never quite coming clean. The stools at the bar were empty except for one—a woman in her fifties with dyed red hair piled high and a cigarette dangling from her lips, even though smoking indoors was illegal in Florida and had been for years.

Marge.

Roan pushed through the door. Evans followed, eyes adjusting to the dim interior after the glare outside.

Marge looked up, took a drag, and exhaled through her nose like a dragon. Smoke curled toward the ceiling fan, spinning slowly overhead. "Detectives."

"Marge." Roan took a seat at the bar. Evans sat beside him, notebook already out.

"I saw the news about the girl." Already pouring a pint of Miller Lite and setting it down in front of Roan. She didn't ask Evans.

"Yeah."

Marge stubbed out the cigarette in an ashtray shaped like a palm tree, half its fronds broken off. "Figured you'd be back. Cops always come back."

"You remember last night?"

"I remember every night. Part of the job." Marge pulled a rag from under the bar and started wiping down the wood even though it was already clean. Muscle memory. "What do you want to know?"

"The man she was with. Tell me more about him."

Marge leaned back, arms crossed over her chest. "Forties, maybe. White. Average height, average build. The sort of guy you forget five minutes after he walks out the door."

"What was he wearing?"

"Linen shirt. Looked expensive. Pressed. Tucked in. Slacks, not jeans. Leather belt. The clothes you wear when you want people to know you've got money but you're not trying too hard."

"Clean?"

"Oh yeah. Too clean for this place. Hair combed. Nails trimmed. No wedding ring, but there was a tan line." Marge tapped the bar. "My ex had the same thing. Took his ring off every time he came through that door. Thought I wouldn't notice." She exhaled smoke toward the ceiling. "You learn to spot it."

"What'd he order?"

"Vodka tonic. Tito's, specifically. Paid cash."

"Big bills?"

"Twenties. Had a money clip. Silver. Pulled it out like he was counting cards." Marge shook her head. "Cheap tipper. One of those guys who calculates everything down to the penny. Left exactly what he owed, nothing extra. Kinda guy who likes to make you work for every dime."

Roan nodded. "What were they arguing about?"

"Couldn't hear most of it. Music was loud. Thursday's karaoke night—a bunch of drunk idiots singing Journey. But I caught pieces when they got loud."

"What pieces?"

"'You said this. I said that.' Back and forth like that. She got pissy. Voice rising. Finger pointing. He got loud but in a more defensive manner. Like he was trying to explain himself, but she wasn't listening."

"Did he threaten her?"

"Not in words. But his body language, yeah. Leaning in. Crowding her space. The way men do when they want you to know they're bigger."

"What did she do?"

"Stood her ground. Didn't back down. The girl had a spine." Marge's expression softened. Just a fraction. "She finished her drink. Told him to go to hell. He threw down cash and walked out."

"Did she leave with him?"

"No, he left first. She stayed maybe fifteen more minutes. Got another drink. Downed it. Sat there staring at her empty glass, teary-eyed. Then she got up and walked out, too."

"Alone?"

"Yeah."

"Did you see anyone else with her last night? Before or after? Another girl? An Asian girl in a black dress?"

Marge shook her head. "Just her and Mr. Linen. Nobody else came up to her except for a couple of drunk guys trying their luck. She shut them down fast."

"Did she seem scared?"

"No. Sad. But not scared."

"What time did she leave?"

"Eleven-fifteen or eleven-thirty, maybe. I remember because Fallon just came on at and she was already gone."

Roan made a note. Looked up. "Anything else stand out?"

"Yeah. The way he left. Most guys, when they're pissed, they storm out. Slam the door. Make a scene. He didn't. He just... left. Calm. Controlled. Like flipping a switch." Marge lit another cigarette and drew deeply. "That stuck with me. The control."

Roan drained the beer. "If you remember anything else—"

"I'll call." Marge exhaled smoke toward the ceiling. "You find him, you let me know. The girl didn't deserve that."

"No," Roan said. "She didn't."

Outside, the heat pressed down like a hand. The beach roared with life —jet skis, laughter, music, the crash of waves folding over and over into themselves. Somewhere, a dog barked. A kid screamed, either delighted or terrified; it was impossible to tell.

Roan's phone buzzed. Pérez.

He answered. "Go."

"Campus was a dead end." Traffic noise behind her voice. "No one remembers seeing Camila with an Asian girl. I visited the student union, registrar, and the library... everywhere. Showed her photo to maybe thirty people. Nothing."

"What'd the registrar give you?"

"General education courses. Intro Psych, College Algebra, English Comp. Nothing fancy. She also completed a massage therapy certificate last spring. Night program. Continuing Ed."

"Financial aid?"

"None. No FAFSA. No Pell Grant. No loans. She paid cash and debit card lump sums every semester."

Roan stopped walking. Evans stopped beside him, listening.

"How much?" Roan asked.

"Four thousand two hundred last spring. Thirty-eight hundred this fall."

Roan's jaw tightened. "Say that again."

"Four thousand two hundred. Thirty-eight hundred. Eight grand total over two semesters. Registrar confirmed it. Cash for fall and spring last year. Debit card this fall. No name on the card was tracked in the system. Just payment type."

"Where's a diner waitress getting eight thousand dollars?"

"That's what I'm asking."

Roan pulled out his notebook, flipped to a blank page, and started writing. Numbers. Dates. Questions.

"Check with the adjuncts," Roan said. "Night program instructors. Massage therapy faculty. Community colleges rotate adjuncts in and out like temp workers. But someone taught her. Someone saw her face two nights a week. Someone might remember if she was close to another student. Asian girl, black dress, early twenties."

"On it."

"Good work, Pérez."

"Thanks." A moment. Static, then: "Evans with you?"

"Yeah."

Another pause. Longer this time. "Has he checked his voicemail yet?"

Roan glanced at Evans, who was staring at the water as if it held answers he couldn't reach. "Hold on." He lowered the phone. "Evans. Where's your phone?"

Evans blinked. Patted his pockets—chest, hips, back. His face shifted. Realization. Frustration. "Shit. Desk."

Roan lifted the phone back to his ear. "Desk."

"Figures." Pérez's voice carried something—resignation, maybe. Or the exhaustion of trying not to care. "Tell him I called."

"I will."

The line went dead.

Roan pocketed his phone and turned to Evans. "You forgot your phone."

"I know."

"Pérez called earlier. You didn't answer."

Evan's jaw tightened. "I'll grab it when we get back."

"You'll carry it from now on."

"Yes, sir."

"And lose the 'sir.'"

Evans blinked. "What?"

"We're not in the army. You call me Roan or Detective. 'Sir' makes you sound like a rookie."

"I am a rookie."

"Then stop acting like one." Roan started walking toward the parking lot. "And lose the tie. You're making yourself a target for heatstroke."

Evans tugged at his tie. "You really hate this?"

"I hate anything that gives a stranger a handle on your neck," Roan said. "And you calling me 'sir'."

Evans pulled the tie loose and shoved it in his pocket. "Anything else?"

"Yeah. Carry your phone. It's not decorative."

"Got it."

They walked in silence for a few yards. The sand crunched under their shoes. A frisbee sailed past, chased by a golden retriever.

"Walk the ground," Roan said, dropping his voice. "Every time. Sometimes twice. Reports tell you what people want you to know. Ground tells you what happened. Learn the difference."

Evans nodded. Wrote nothing down. Just listened.

Evans sat behind the wheel, Roan in the passenger seat. The A/C rattled, barely keeping up with the heat bleeding through the windshield. Roan stared out at the road, hands loose in his lap, shoulders set.

Through the windshield, Evans could see the barbecue trailer in the rearview, smoke still curling. The line hadn't gotten any shorter.

"That place does good business," Evans said.

Roan said nothing. Stared out the window.

Evans kept his eyes forward. Didn't push. Didn't ask.

After a long silence, Evans spoke. "The brother bothers me."

"Me too."

"Those flyers aren't helping anyone."

"Not a search, but a sermon." Roan's voice was flat, matter-of-fact. "Grief takes many shapes. Sometimes it builds altars. Sometimes it builds noise."

"It doesn't make sense."

"Doesn't have to," Roan said. "Just has to make him feel something."

Evans nodded. "What about the man at the pub? Mr. Linen?"

"We'll find him. Marge gave us enough—forties, a linen shirt, a money clip, and Tito's vodka. Someone knows him. Someone's seen him. Men like that leave patterns."

"And the money? Eight grand in tuition?"

"That's the thread." Roan turned and looked at Evans. "Pull it. Don't let go. Waitress wages don't cover $4,000 a semester. Someone was paying her. Or she was working somewhere else. Or she had something someone wanted bad enough to pay for."

Evan's hands tightened on the wheel. "You think she was involved in something?"

"I think everyone's involved in something. Question is what, and whether it got her killed."

The sun hung lower now, orange bleeding into the horizon. Shadows stretched long across the road.

Finally, Roan spoke again. "You've got a family. Wife. Kids."

Evans glanced at him. "Yeah."

"That makes this harder. And easier."

"How's that?"

"Harder because you've got something to lose. Every case, every body, every hour you spend here is an hour you're not home. That weight builds. You feel it yet?"

Evans thought about Clara, about dinner table conversations he'd missed, about bedtime stories skipped. "Yeah. I feel it."

"Good. Don't ignore it. The job'll eat you if you let it. Family keeps you balanced. Use it. Don't let the work become the only thing."

Evans nodded. "And the easier part?"

"You've got something to go home to. Not everyone does." Roan dropped his voice. "That matters. Don't forget it."

Evans looked at Roan, studying his profile. No wedding ring. No photos in his office. No personal calls. Just the work. Just the cases.

"What about you?" Evans asked.

"What about me?"

"You got someone to go home to?"

Roan didn't answer for a long minute. Evans started the car.

"Drive," Roan said finally.

Evans let it go.

The beach shrank in the rearview. Jet skis still carved the water. Girls still stretched out on towels, bronze skin catching the last of the sun. Music still thumped from speakers. Ariel's flyers still flapped in the wind, stapled to posts, scripture bleeding into sunlight.

Brandon's barbecue trailer still smoked, the big man still working the pit, still smiling at customers, still moving through the world like he belonged.

Evans drove. Roan stared out the window.

"Where to?" Evans asked.

Roan was quiet for a moment, watching the road unfold ahead. Then: "Home."

CHAPTER

13

EVANS TURNED ONTO LAKESIDE DRIVE, following the curve along the golf course. The houses sat back from the road—single-story ranches mostly, some with screened porches, others with boats parked in driveways like lawn ornaments. The street dead-ended. He could see the fairway stretching out beyond the backyards, grass still green despite the heat, bunkers catching the last of the light. Somewhere in the distance, a sprinkler system ticked on, the rhythmic spray carrying on the evening air.

Roan's house sat at the end. Brick front, modest, unshowy. A single palm tree in the yard. The driveway cracked, but it was clean. No decorative touches. No mailbox shaped like a fish. Just a number on the wall—1315—and a door with two deadbolts.

Evans pulled into the driveway and turned off the engine. Sat for a moment. Roan lived here. Came here after the bodies and the interviews and the beach walks. Slept here. Ate here. Existed here between shifts.

Roan opened his door, stepped out, and glanced across the greens. He said, "You play golf?"

Evans shook his head. "Barely. I lose balls faster than I lose patience." He allowed a quick smile. "My son's better. He's on a team."

Roan gave a nod, as if the boy's swing mattered more than his father's.

They walked toward the front door. Roan unlocked it—both deadbolts, as Evans expected—and pushed it open. The air inside was cool, still, untouched. No smell of cooking. No sound of a TV left on—just the hum of the A/C and the faint creak of the door closing behind them.

The living room held little.

A couch. A leather chair, cushion molded to shape. A coffee table with nothing on it. No magazines. No remote left out. Nothing hung on the walls except for one framed print—a black-and-white photo of a pier at night, empty, as if the world was holding its breath.

Case binders lined one wall—thick spines labeled by year, some with names Evans recognized, others he didn't. Morales sat on the end, already thicker than it should be for two days in. Next to the binders: books. Worn paperbacks mostly. Hemingway's The Old Man and the Sea, spine cracked and white. Chandler's The Long Goodbye and Trouble is My Business, pages dog-eared. A Coltrane biography with a receipt still marking a page. Florida history—Land of Sunshine, State of Dreams—margin notes in pen, Roan's tight handwriting commenting on redlining maps and railroad routes.

Below the books: a vintage stereo receiver, a model with vacuum tubes that glowed warm when powered on. Next to it, a stack of vinyl records—Kind of Blue, A Love Supreme, Sketches of Spain. Jazz. All of it. Sleeves were worn soft at the edges.

Evans' gaze drifted to the corner of the room. A small table. On it, a chessboard. Wooden, worn smooth. Pieces set up in the opening of a game—White's pawn stood on e4. Black had yet to respond.

No photos. Nowhere. Not on the shelves, not on the walls, not on the coffee table.

Evans stood in the center of the room, hands in his pockets, taking it in. The absence of photos confirmed what he'd suspected since that first conversation with Norris—whatever Roan had lost, he'd left no visible trace of it behind. The house felt like a hotel room someone had lived in for years without unpacking. Functional. Disciplined. A place to sleep between work.

But the records. The chessboard. The books with notes.

"You want coffee?" Roan asked.

"I'm good."

Roan moved toward the kitchen. Evans followed.

The kitchen was cleaner than Evans'. Counters wiped down. The dish rack was empty. A single coffee mug sat in the sink—rinsed, waiting. The fridge hummed. Roan opened it. Beer, water, takeout containers labeled with dates in marker. Milk. Eggs. The basics.

Evans noticed the coffeemaker—expensive, like one you'd see in specialty shops. Not a Mr. Coffee. The grinder beside it looked used. Roan drank his coffee seriously.

"You've been here long?" Evans asked.

"Twenty years."

Roan pulled a bottle of water from the fridge, cracked it, and drank. Didn't offer Evans one. Just moved past him back toward the hallway.

"Garage is this way."

The garage was immaculate.

Workbench along one wall, tools hung on pegboard—everything in its place, outlines drawn so you knew where each wrench went. Floor swept clean. Oil stains scrubbed out. A metal cabinet in the corner, locked. Roan's handwriting on masking tape: Evidence—Archive.

In the center, under a grey canvas tarp, sat something large. Car-shaped. Evans could see the outline—classic lines, long hood, curved fenders.

Evans' eyes swept the workbench. Next to the organized tools sat a small cluster of modern equipment—an electronic fuel injection controller, still sealed in its box. A Dakota Digital gauge cluster, with its LED displays dark, and a wiring harness coiled beside it. An alternator conversion kit. Parts that didn't belong to the era under that tarp. Upgrades for a classic car. Restomoded old bones with new tech.

"What's under there?" Evans asked.

Roan glanced at it. "Old project."

"What kind?"

"The kind that doesn't get finished."

Evans waited, but Roan didn't move toward it. Didn't pull the tarp back. Just stood there like the car was furniture.

"You work on it?" Evans asked.

"Used to."

"What is it?"

"A classic."

"Why'd you stop?"

Roan's jaw tightened. "Ran out of time."

Evans didn't push. He'd seen enough walls to know when one wasn't coming down. But his eyes lingered on the EFI controller. On the digital gauges. Modern parts waiting to breathe life into something old. A project interrupted. When Roan said he'd run out of time, Evans heard what wasn't said—that some projects required hope, and hope had a shelf life.

Roan walked to a shelf on the far side of the garage and pulled down a white plastic bucket. Inside: golf balls. Dozens of them. Titleist, Callaway, and no-name brands scuffed and grass-stained. He held the bucket out.

"For your son."

Evans blinked. "What?"

"Golf balls. They come over the fence. Every week. I collect them." Roan shook the bucket slightly. "He's on a golf team. He'll use them."

Evans took the bucket. Felt the weight. Looked at Roan, who was already turning back toward the house.

"You didn't have to—"

"I wasn't using them. Much better than the trash."

Evans followed Roan back inside, the bucket handle digging into his palm. Useful and impersonal at once.

But it was something.

They stood in the living room. Evans held the bucket. Roan checked his Seamaster watch.

"I should go," Evans said. "Clara's making dinner."

"Yeah."

"Thanks for this." Evans lifted the bucket slightly.

Roan nodded. "Tell your son to keep his head down through the swing."

Evans almost smiled. "I will."

They walked to the door. Roan opened it. The evening air pushed in—warm, thick, carrying the sound of someone mowing a lawn three houses down. Evans stepped onto the porch and faced Roan once more.

"You good?" he asked.

Roan looked at him. "Always."

"I mean it. You need anything—"

"I'm good, Evans."

Evans nodded. Walked to the Explorer. Set the bucket on the passenger seat. Started the engine. Pulled out of the driveway.

In the rearview mirror, he saw Roan standing in the doorway, hands in his pockets, watching him leave. Then the door closed. The house went still.

Roan locked the door. Both deadbolts. Checked the windows. Pulled the blinds.

The house settled into its familiar hush.

He walked to the kitchen, opened the freezer, and pulled out the Ketel One. Poured two fingers into a rocks glass. No ice. Took a sip. Let it burn.

Then, he walked to his desk.

The laptop was already on—he never shut it off. The screen glowed in the dimness. One new email. No subject line. Sender: an address he recognized, a string of numbers and letters that meant nothing to anyone who wasn't looking for it.

He opened it.

One line:

e5?

The corners of his mouth softened. His shoulders dropped a fraction. For a moment, the weight loosened.

He stared at the screen, rereading the move again. *e5?*

Good. Solid. Expected. But good.

He hit print.

The printer whirred to life and spat out a single sheet. He took it, walked to a filing cabinet beside the desk, unlocked it, and pulled open the top drawer. Inside: a stack of printed emails, each one a single line. Chess notation. Questions and answers. No names. No signatures. Just moves.

He placed the new one on top of the stack. Locked the drawer.

Then he walked to the corner of the living room where the small table sat—the chessboard. White's pawn stood on e4, waiting. Black's pieces sat untouched on the back rank.

Roan reached down, picked up Black's king's pawn, and moved it two squares forward. e5.

He stood there for a moment, looking at the board. Then he picked up White's knight and placed it on f3. Nf3.

The Italian Opening. Classic. Aggressive but not reckless. Control of the center. Development. Pressure.

He studied the position. Thought ahead three moves, four, five. Whoever was on the other end played patiently—played carefully— never rushed.

Roan walked back to the computer. Opened a reply:

Nf3. Your move.

Send.

He closed the laptop. Finished the vodka. Poured another two fingers.

The stereo sat on the shelf beside the Chandler novels. Vintage receiver, he turned it on, let it hum to life. Pulled a record from the stack. "Kind of Blue" by Miles Davis. The cover was faded, with frayed edges. He'd owned it longer than he'd lived in this house.

He set the needle down.

The first notes of "So What" drifted out—slow, languid, the bass walking in like it had nowhere else to be. The piano answered. Then Miles, his trumpet cool and distant, improvised around the tune without ever settling on it.

Roan sank into the leather chair—the only piece of furniture that looked used. The cushion had molded to him over the years. He leaned back, vodka in hand, eyes half-closed.

The music played.

Outside, someone hit a golf ball—he heard the distant crack of club on ball, the rustle of it landing somewhere past the fence. Tomorrow, he'd find it in the yard. Add it to the bucket. The cycle never stopped.

He thought about Evans. About the way he'd looked at the house—trying to read it, trying to understand the man who lived here. But there was nothing to read. Just a place. Just walls, a roof, and a chair that fit.

He thought about the car in the garage. The tarp that hadn't come off in a year. The project that wasn't a project anymore. Just weight. Just a reminder that some things didn't get finished.

He thought about the chessboard. About the invisible opponent who moved pieces in the dark, who never spoke, who only asked questions in notation. e5? A response. An answer. A continuation. The game moved forward. Always forward.

And for reasons he didn't examine, that mattered.

He thought about Camila Morales, twenty-one. Lying on the sand. Seven hours missing. A waitress with eight grand in tuition money. A girl in a black dress that nobody could find. A man in linen who walked out calmly. Moves he couldn't see yet.

But they were there.

The vodka warmed him. The music carried him. The house held him.

Miles played. The bass walked. The piano answered.

Roan's eyes drifted closed.

The world outside kept spinning. Golf balls kept flying over fences. Emails kept arriving in the dark. Cases kept stacking on shelves. But here, in this chair, with the music and the vodka and the silence, he could let it go. Just for a moment. Just until the song ended.

His breathing slowed.

The leather creaked as he shifted, settling deeper.

"So What" played on—no rush, no resolution, the trumpet and bass trading phrases.

And somewhere between one section and the next, Roan slipped under.

Not sleep, exactly. Just in the space between waking and dreaming where the case lived, and the pieces moved, and the invisible opponent waited for a reply.

The record played.

The house kept its secrets.

And Roan, alone in his chair, let the music carry him into the dark.

CHAPTER

14

Neon bled into asphalt on Dixie Highway. Cars drifted past in slow lanes, headlights cutting through the humidity. The broken motel sign above her flickered—AC ANCY—the V and the second A burnt out. She stood beneath it, one hip cocked, phone in hand like she was texting someone who mattered, but she wasn't. She was scouting cars, noting whether their headlights were on, how fast they were going, and, importantly, if the passenger-side window was down.

Three years on this corner had taught her the language. The sedans with families never slowed—tinted windows, car seats in back, voices carrying through cracked glass. Trucks with contractors kept moving —paint-splattered, toolboxes rattling, men too tired to look. The ones that mattered rolled past twice. First pass: checking. Second pass: deciding. Third pass: committed.

A Honda Civic slowed with its window down. Kid driving, maybe twenty-two, backward cap, cologne that caught in her throat. She shook her head before he could speak. Too young, broke, and stupid to know what no meant.

He drove on.

She checked her phone. 12:14 a.m. Slow night. Fridays were usually better—payday, men drinking courage, wallets loose. But tonight the street felt thin. Four cars in two hours. One serious, three just looking.

Rent was due on Friday. Her manager at the motel—the real one six blocks south where she actually lived—had left notes under her door. Yellow slips with numbers underlined twice. Red ink now. She owed $340. Had $190. Needed one more good night. Maybe two.

A Camry rolled past. Older guy, sixties, wedding ring catching streetlight, eyes straight ahead like she didn't exist. The window stayed up. She watched it go. That type never stopped. They thought about it. Circled the block sometimes, but guilt or fear always won.

Then the white car.

It came from the south, cruising smoothly, headlights too bright. She squinted, stepping back. Something clean. The car slowed. Window halfway down. Not all the way—never a good sign—but halfway.

She waited.

The voice came first. Male, flat and polite.

"You working?"

She leaned in, not too close. Never too close until you know. "Depends."

"On what?"

"What you're looking for."

Silence. Then: "Company."

The word hung in the air between them. Clean. Neutral. A word that meant everything and nothing.

She studied what she could see. Clean interior. No fast-food bags. No trash. No air freshener swinging from the mirror. Dash lit blue. She couldn't see his face, just the shadow behind the wheel. Hands on the wheel. Ten and two. Like a driving instructor.

"How much?" she asked.

"Hundred."

She almost laughed. "Hundred fifty."

"Deal."

Too fast. No negotiation. Her stomach tightened. But a hundred fifty was a hundred fifty, and rent was two days past due, and the yellow slips were turning red.

The locks clicked. She opened the door.

The interior smelled clean. Faint aftershave—something woody— and beneath it, smoke. Not cigarettes. Something else she couldn't place. The seats were leather. The dash was spotless—no coffee stains. No dust. Like he'd just detailed it.

She slid into the passenger seat and pulled the door shut. It closed with a solid thud.

"Where to?" she asked.

He didn't answer. Just pulled away from the curb, smooth and controlled. No jerky movements. No revving engine. Just steady acceleration onto Dixie, heading south.

She glanced at him and couldn't make out much in the dark. Just hands on the wheel. Steady. A polo shirt, she thought. Something dark. Tucked in. The type of shirt managers wore. Retail, maybe.

"You from around here?" she asked. Testing. Filling the silence.

"Close enough."

"Work nearby?"

"Yeah."

One-word answers. That was fine. Some guys didn't want to talk. Some wanted a therapist. You learned to read, which was which.

They passed the 7-Eleven, a pawnshop, and the check-cashing place, which had bars on the windows. Dixie at night was a string of fluorescent signs and empty parking lots. She knew every block. Knew which alleys had lights. Knew which gas stations had cameras. Knew where to run if things went sideways.

"I'm not going far," she said. Her standard line. Establishing boundaries. "Thirty minutes, max."

"Won't be long."

His voice was flat. Not angry, not nervous. Just... nothing. Like reading ingredients off a box. She'd heard nervous before—stammering, over-explaining, hands shaking on the wheel. She'd heard angry—clipped words, tight jaw, knuckles white. This was neither. This was blank.

Her pulse quickened.

He turned right off Dixie.

Her stomach dropped.

"Where are we going?" she asked.

"Quieter spot."

"I don't do quiet spots. I told you, I'm not—"

"It's close."

It wasn't. The street got darker—fewer lights. The businesses here were closed—warehouses with roll-down doors, a tile distributor with a chain-link fence, a plumbing supply yard with stacks of PVC pipe catching what little light remained. No pedestrians. No traffic. Just an empty road and the sound of the engine.

She reached for the door handle.

The handle wouldn't budge.

"Unlock the door," she said. Calm. Firm. The voice she used when things started going wrong.

He didn't respond. Just kept driving. Steady. Twenty-five miles an hour. Like he was sightseeing.

"Hey, unlock the door."

Nothing.

Her heart kicked. She pulled the handle again. Nothing. Tried the window button. Dead. Child locks, probably. Or something worse. Something deliberate.

"Let me out."

"Not yet."

She looked at him. His face was calm in profile. Hands still at ten and two. Breathing steady. As if he were driving to the grocery store. Like this was routine.

"Let me the fuck out!"

"We're almost there."

Almost where? There was nothing out here—just warehouses and chain-link and shadows. No cameras. No witnesses. No help.

She fumbled for her phone. He reached over—fast, faster than his calm suggested—and plucked it from her hand. Tossed it onto the dashboard as if it were trash.

"You don't need that."

Panic spiked. She pushed herself against the door, eyes on him. What to do? Jumped—but the door was locked, and they were moving. Fight—but he was bigger, and she was trapped. Scream—but who would hear?

"Please," she said. Hating the word. Hating the sound of it in her mouth. Hating that it was all she had left.

He turned into an alley. Loose dirt crunched under the tires. Slowed. Stopped.

Killed the engine.

Silence.

Just her breathing. And his. Steady as a metronome.

His hand moved to the center console.

She saw it before he pulled it out.

The knife.

Large. The blade caught the faint light from a distant streetlamp—long, tapered, professionally sharp.

"No," she said.

He didn't look at her. Just held the knife, examining it and testing the weight.

"Please don't."

"Won't take long."

She kicked. Hard. Her heel hit the dash, cracked the vent cover, and the plastic split with a snap. She kicked again, aiming for him, for his face, for anything. He blocked it calmly.

She screamed. Raw. Loud. The sound filled the car, bounced off the glass, and died in the gravel and darkness.

He grabbed her hair and yanked her toward him. Her head slammed against the console. Lights popped behind her eyes.

The first stab came fast. Deep. Just below her ribs. She felt the punch of it before the pain—hot, immediate, stealing her breath.

She clawed at his arm. The knife pulled free. She tried to push him away.

The second stab was lower. Abdomen. Deeper. Something inside her tore. She couldn't scream. Couldn't breathe—just a wet gasp.

Her hands found the blade. Grabbed. Her palms split open, trying to stop it.

He pulled the knife free. She slumped forward.

The third was across her throat. Quick. Clean. Precise.

Then nothing.

He sat back. Breathing steady. No heavier than before.

He looked at her. Checked her pulse at the neck with two fingers. Professional. Clinical. Waited. Thirty seconds. A minute.

Nothing.

He wiped the blade on his pant leg. Slipped it back into the console. Closed the lid.

Then he opened the glove box. Pulled out a small packet of restaurant wipes. He tore one open. Cleaned his hands. Each finger. Between the knuckles. Under the nails. Then, the steering wheel. The dash where she'd touched it. The door handle. The gear shift. Methodical. Practiced. Like wiping down a counter after closing.

He checked the time on the dashboard—12:47.

Good. Still early.

He started the engine.

Pulled out of the alley.

Drove.

The neighborhood was quiet.

Single-story houses. Chain-link fences. Cars parked in driveways, some covered with tarps, others baking under porch lights. A basketball hoop leaned in one yard, net torn. Another had a trampoline, but this one had rusted springs. Mailboxes stood crooked at the curbs, numbers faded or missing. Working-class, tired. A neighborhood where people minded their own business because they had enough of their own.

Porch lights burned at some houses while others sat dark. A dog barked two streets over. Somewhere, a TV glowed blue through curtains, late-night infomercials selling things nobody needed.

He turned onto the block. Drove slowly. Ten miles an hour. Looking.

Mid-block, on the left: an empty lot.

Chain-link fence, half collapsed. Weeds growing waist-high through cracked concrete where a house used to stand. Foundation still visible—cinder blocks stacked like broken teeth, rebar jutting from rubble. The city had knocked it down two years ago. Nobody had built anything new.

He pulled onto the curb. Killed the lights. Left the engine running.

Opened his door. Stepped out. The night air was thick and humid, with a faint scent of cut grass and the approaching garbage day.

He walked around to the passenger side. Opened the door.

She slumped forward. He caught her. Lifted her. Lighter than expected. They always were.

He carried her to the fence. Found the gap—chain-link torn back, just wide enough. Stepped through. Weeds brushed his legs. Concrete crunched under his shoes.

He walked to the center of the lot. Set her down on the cracked foundation. Adjusted her arms. Made sure her face was visible from the street. Made sure she'd be seen.

He stepped back. Looked around.

A paper fluttered past his feet. White. Caught in the weeds. Then another. He glanced down.

Flyers.

They were everywhere. Stapled to posts. Taped to streetlights and blown into yards.

One flyer had snagged on the rebar near the body.

He stared at it for a long moment. Then walked back through the fence gap.

Got in the car. Closed the door. Pulled away.

No rush. Just steady. Three blocks south. Left on Dixie. Let the highway carry him north, back toward the lights and the noise and the world that didn't notice.

Silence surrounded a shape curled on the lot of an ordinary street with ordinary mailboxes. The wind scattered loose bits of paper across the asphalt and into the gutter, bearing bold text that read: "The Wages of Sin is Death." Romans 6:23.

CHAPTER

15

ROAN JERKED upright in the leather chair, disoriented, the record still spinning on the turntable—static hiss where music used to be. The vodka glass sat empty on the side table. His neck ached. The house was dark except for the glow of his phone vibrating on the arm of the chair.

He grabbed it. His voice came out steadily. "Roan."

"It's Rocca. We got another one."

Roan's pulse steadied. "Where?"

"Empty lot. Dixie Highway. Knife job." Rocca's voice was tight. Controlled. "Need you to see this."

"Give me twenty."

He stood. Walked to the bathroom. Splashed cold water on his face. Looked at himself in the mirror—eyes bloodshot, jaw tight, the man who didn't sleep enough staring back. He grabbed his holster from the bedroom. Checked his Glock. There are forty-seven rounds in the safe. He loaded a fresh magazine. Seventeen plus one.

Pulled on a jacket. Checked his watch—4:47 a.m.

Called Evans.

Evans pulled up eighteen minutes later in the Explorer, headlights cutting through the pre-dawn grey. Roan climbed in without a word. Evans handed him coffee—black, no sugar, gas station coffee in a paper cup.

"Thanks."

They drove in silence.

The city looked different at this hour. Rain fell overnight, leaving the streets slick and black, their surfaces reflecting the yellow glow of the streetlights. Palm trees bent in the breeze. A garbage truck rumbled past, hydraulics hissing. The sky was the color of ash, not yet pink, not quite night.

Evans kept his hands at ten and two. Jaw set. Roan could see the tension in his shoulders.

"Rocca, say anything else?" Evans asked.

"Knife. Empty lot. That's it."

"Same as Camila?"

"Don't know yet."

Evans nodded. Drove faster. They hit Dixie and turned south. The road was empty except for a delivery truck and a cop car heading in the opposite direction.

Roan sipped the coffee. Tasted like burnt rubber. He drank it anyway.

"Did you get any sleep?" Evans asked.

"Some."

"Clara asked about you last night. Wanted to know if you ate."

Roan glanced at him. "Tell her I'm fine."

"I did. She didn't believe me."

"Smart woman."

They passed the 7-Eleven. The pawn shop. The check-cashing place. Familiar territory now.

Evans slowed. Ahead, red and blue flashers strobed against the grey sky. Yellow crime scene tape stretched across the entrance to an empty lot. News vans had already parked on the shoulder, their cameras setting up, as reporters in rain jackets talked into their microphones.

Roan's stomach tightened.

"Jesus," Evans muttered.

Roan said nothing. Just watched the scene grow larger as they pulled closer.

Evans parked behind a patrol car. They stepped out into the damp air. The smell hit first—wet asphalt, and something underneath.

Uniforms milled near the tape. One Roan didn't know was talking to a reporter, hands up, shaking his head. No comment. Not yet. The reporters pressed on anyway.

Roan ducked under the tape. Evans followed.

Officer Pérez stood near the fence gap, notebook in hand, talking to a uniformed officer. She looked up when they approached. Her face was pale. Tight. Professional mask holding, but barely. Roan recognized the look—she'd seen the body, processed the scene, and was now running on discipline alone.

"Detective," she said.

"Officer." Roan nodded. "What do we have?"

Pérez flipped her notebook. "The victim is Julia Aguilar, mid-twenties. Known to work in Dixie. Vice had contact with her twice last year. A jogger found her at 4:32 a.m. Called it in. First responders confirmed DOA."

"Where's Rocca?"

"With the body."

Roan looked past her. Through the gap in the chain-link fence, he could see movement. Flashlights. The forensic tech's white coveralls. And beyond them, on the cracked concrete foundation, was a shape covered with a tarp.

"Walk me through it," Roan said.

Pérez led them through the fence. The lot was overgrown with weeds, waist-high in places. Concrete slabs jutted up like broken teeth. Rebar stuck out from cinder blocks—the remnants of a house that was knocked down years ago and never rebuilt.

Rocca stood near the body, cigarette between his fingers, talking to a CSI tech. Smoke curled up slowly, caught the breeze, and scattered. He looked up when Roan approached, took a drag, and exhaled before speaking.

"Roan."

"Detective."

They shook hands. Rocca gestured to the tarp with the cigarette. "Brace yourself."

Roan knelt. Pulled back the tarp.

Julia Aguilar stared at nothing. Mid-twenties, like Pérez said. Dark hair, matted with blood. She wore a short skirt, a tank top, and heels —one of which was missing. Her skin was pale, waxy. Three wounds were visible even under the blood.

Chest. Side. Throat.

Roan studied her face. No defensive wounds on her hands that he could see from here. No signs of a prolonged struggle. Just the cuts. Clean. Deliberate. Her clothing had been straightened, skirt pulled down, and tank top adjusted. Someone had arranged her.

He let the tarp fall back.

"Same guy," Rocca said quietly, flicking ash onto the concrete.

Roan stood. Looked around. The body was positioned near the fence, visible from the street, not hidden, not buried. Displayed.

"Who found her?"

"Jogger. Guy runs this route every morning. Saw her through the fence, called 911." Rocca checked his notes. "Name's Mitchell. Works at the post office. Lives two blocks over. Patrol's got his statement."

"He touch anything?"

"Says no. Looked, freaked, called."

"Believe him?"

"Yeah."

Roan walked the perimeter. Evans stayed close, watching, learning. The ground was damp from the rain. Footprints everywhere now—uniforms, CSI, the jogger probably. But near the body, drag marks. Faint. Leading from the fence gap towards where she lay. Heels dragged, suggesting she'd been pulled backward by the shoulders.

"She wasn't killed here," Roan said.

"No," Rocca agreed. "Moved postmortem. Same as Camila."

Roan crouched near the drag marks. Studied the angle—the direction. Someone had carried her through the fence, set her down, and adjusted her position. Made sure she'd be seen.

"What time did the jogger call it in?" Roan asked.

"4:32 a.m.," Pérez said from behind him.

"Sun's not up yet. How'd he see her?"

"Headlamp," Pérez said. "He wears one when he runs. Beam caught her face."

Roan nodded. Stood. Looked at the street beyond the fence. Cars were starting to pass now—early commuters, shift workers heading home. Life was moving on while death sat fifty feet away.

"Cameras?" Roan asked.

Rocca shook his head, taking another drag. Roan noticed his hand was trembling slightly when he wasn't actively smoking. "Motel across the street's got one, but it's been busted for a month. The pawnshop next door closes at six, with no overnight surveillance. The Shell station a block south has exterior cams, but the angle's wrong. We're pulling footage anyway, but I'm not optimistic."

"Witnesses?"

"The Shell's night clerk saw headlights slow around 1:00 a.m. Didn't see a vehicle. Didn't see anyone get out. Just lights."

"That's it?"

"That's it."

Roan walked back to the body. Knelt again. Pulled the tarp back further. Studied the wounds. Two to the torso—one chest, one side. Deep. Precise. The third across the throat. All clean cuts. No hesitation marks. No jagged edges.

Practiced.

"Where's Martin?" Roan asked.

"On his way," Rocca said. "ETA ten minutes." He lit a second cigarette from the butt of the first, flicked the spent one to the ground, then thought better and picked it back up, pocketing it.

Roan let the tarp fall. Stood. Looked at Evans. "Walk the perimeter. Look for anything that doesn't belong. Cigarette butts. Fabric. Footprints that stand out."

Evans nodded. Moved off with Pérez. Roan watched him crouch near a section of disturbed ground, studying it without touching, keeping his observations methodical. Good. The kid was learning.

Rocca stepped closer, exhaling smoke. "It's him, isn't it?"

Roan said nothing. Just looked at the body. At the lot. At the street beyond.

"Yeah," he said finally. "It's him."

Dr. Martin Avery arrived five minutes later in a black SUV, medical bag in hand. He'd been on call, probably grabbed coffee, and driven straight here. He nodded to Roan, said nothing, and went straight to work.

Roan stood a few feet back. Avery, undeterred by the grimness of the task, knelt beside the sprawled body and drew on his gloves. There was something dispassionate, almost automatic, in the way Avery approached it—as though repetition, rather than any inclination, had made this routine. Lividity, rigor, wounds: he moved through each, ticking off observations with clinical precision, calipers glinting as he studied them. Experience had not made him careless, only oddly absent from the moment, as if he might have examined a thousand bodies just like this one, and expected to examine a thousand more.

"Talk to me, Martin," Roan said after a few minutes.

Avery didn't look up. "Three incised wounds. Two to the torso— one punctured the left lung, the other nicked the liver. Third, across the anterior neck, severing the carotid and jugular. Any one of the three could have been fatal, but the neck wound is what killed her. Immediate exsanguination."

"Same blade as Camila?"

"Won't know for certain until I get her on the table, but the wound characteristics are consistent. Clean edges. Uniform depth. Controlled pressure. Whoever did this knows how to use a knife."

"Time of death?"

Avery checked his watch. Looked at the body's temp and the lividity pattern. "Rigor's just starting in the smaller muscles. Lividity is fixed but not fully developed. I'd estimate three to four hours. Puts the TOD somewhere between midnight and 1:00 a.m."

Roan made a mental note. The Shell clerk saw headlights at 1:00 a.m. Lined up.

"Postmortem relocation?" Roan asked.

"Definitely. The lividity pattern is inconsistent with her current position. She was moved after death, probably within thirty minutes to an hour. Lividity hadn't fully set."

"Cause of death?"

"Pending a full autopsy, but I'm confident it's exsanguination from the neck wound."

"Sexual assault?"

"No obvious signs, but I'll check during the post."

"Anything else?"

Avery pulled back the victim's hair to examine her scalp. "Blunt force trauma to the head. It could be from the attack or from being moved. I'll know more later."

He stood, peeling off his gloves. "I'll have a preliminary report by noon. Full post this afternoon."

"Thanks, Doc."

Avery nodded. Walked back to his SUV.

Roan stood there, staring at the body, his mind working the pattern.

Two victims. Both young women. Both stabbed. Both moved postmortem. Both left in public places—Camila on the beach, Julia in an empty lot. Both deliberate.

This wasn't about hiding bodies. This was about displaying them.

Evans returned with Pérez. Both looked tired. Frustrated.

"Anything?" Roan asked.

Evans shook his head. "A couple of cigarette butts, but they look old. Rain washed most of the prints away. Found some tire marks near the curb, but they're partial. CSI's photographing them."

"Shell station footage?"

Pérez checked her phone. "Just got word. The footage is grainy. Shows headlights slowing around 1:08 a.m., but the vehicle is not visible. It could be a sedan. It could be an SUV. Can't tell the color. Clerk didn't get a plate."

Roan nodded. Expected. "Has anyone canvassed the block yet?"

"Uniforms are working it," Pérez said. "Most people were asleep. One guy heard a car door close around 1:30, but he didn't look out the window. Figured it was someone parking."

"That's it?"

"So far."

Roan's eyes moved from the vacant lot to the body, then swept across to the street. Something nagged at his mind—a loose thread he couldn't quite grasp. He crossed to the chain-link fence, found the tear, and slipped through. At the perimeter of the property, he paused, gaze fixed on the opposite side of the road, searching for what his subconscious had already spotted.

The apartment block was two stories high, sunk in beige stucco, the stucco itself faded, peeling at the edges as if worn thin by too many salt-bright days. Above, an iron-railed walkway ran the length of the upper floor; the metal was orange with rust where the sea air had gnawed it raw, a patchwork of neglect showing through what paint remained. Every window was blacked out: the blank stare of empty rooms, save one. On the second floor, at the corner, a unit glowed, the only sign of life in the dull hush.

And then he saw it.

Laundry hanging on a balcony. A child's bike was propped against the wall.

The Morales family.

Roan's stomach dropped.

He pulled his attention back to the lot. To the body. To the fence.

Fifty yards. Maybe less.

"Rocca," he called.

Rocca walked over, cigarette smoke trailing. "Yeah?"

Roan pointed across the street. "That's the Morales apartment. Second floor, corner unit."

Rocca followed his gaze. His face went pale. "Shit."

"Yeah."

Evans joined them, looking confused. "What am I missing?"

Roan turned to him. "The dump site. It's directly across from Camila's family home."

Evans looked. Then looked at the body. Then back at the apartment complex. "That's not a coincidence."

"No," Roan said. "It's not."

They stood in silence for a moment. Rocca's cigarette trembled between his fingers.

"He's sending a message," Rocca said quietly, flicking ash.

"Or taunting us," Evans added.

Roan shook his head. "Both. He's showing us he's not afraid. He's escalating."

He walked back to the body. Stood over it. Studied the positioning again. Arms at her sides. Face up. Visible from the street.

This wasn't sloppy. This wasn't panic. This was practiced. Methodical. Controlled.

"He's done this before," Roan said.

Rocca frowned. "What do you mean?"

"These aren't his first kills. The way he moves them. The way he positions them. The wounds. He's not learning. He's executing a pattern." Roan looked at Rocca. "Run Julia Aguilar's name. Check whether she has a prior record. Known associates. Anything that connects her to Camila—friends, clients, locations they both frequented."

"On it."

"And pull unsolved knife homicides. The last five years. Broward, Miami-Dade, Monroe. Expand if you must. Look for a similar M.O. —postmortem relocation, public dump sites, incised wounds."

Rocca nodded, then dragged his phone from his pocket.

Roan turned to Evans. "Canvass the block again. Talk to everyone. Someone saw something. They always do."

"Got it."

Pérez stepped forward, evidence bags in hand containing what looked like fiber samples and soil specimens. "What do you need from me?"

"Trace evidence. Focus on the drag marks. Fibers. Anything transferred from the killer to the body or the scene. And check for cigarette brands, tire tread patterns, anything that can narrow the vehicle."

"I'm on it."

They dispersed. Roan stayed with the body.

The sun was breaking over the horizon now—pale pink light bleeding into grey. Birds were waking up. Somewhere, a dog barked. Life moved forward while death sat still.

Roan looked at Julia Aguilar's face. Twenty-something. With a whole life ahead of her, now gone. He thought about her last moments. The fear. The pain. The realization that nobody was coming to save her.

He thought about Camila. About the seven hours between the

diner and the pub. About the man in linen, nobody could find anything about him.

And now Julia. Abducted and dumped. Same method. Same result.

But why Julia? Why this victim in this location? Was she connected to Camila, or was the Morales apartment the actual target —a way of showing the family, showing the investigation, that he could strike anywhere?

"Who are you?" Roan muttered.

They bagged the body an hour later. The coroner's van pulled away, followed by half the news crews who'd got what they needed—body bag, detectives with grim faces, the empty lot framed against the rising sun. The rest lingered, hoping for a statement. They wouldn't get one. But word was spreading fast—on social media, police scanners, and morning shows, which were picking up the story. Second body in a week. Same area. Panic was starting to build.

The four of them stood near the fence gap—Roan, Evans, Rocca, Pérez. The crime scene was cleared. Uniforms rolled up tape. CSI packed evidence bags. The lot that had been chaos an hour ago was settling back into silence.

Rocca lit another cigarette. His third since they'd arrived. He took a long drag, exhaled smoke into the damp morning air. "Two in a week. Same M.O., same blade. Same everything."

"Serial," Pérez said quietly. The word hung there.

"Yeah," Rocca said. "Serial."

Evans looked at Roan. "What are we dealing with?"

Roan considered that in silence. He was staring at the apartment complex across the street. Two-story building. Beige stucco. Iron railings on the second floor. Corner unit—the Morales family.

"Someone organized," Roan said finally. "Someone who plans. Who doesn't panic. Who knows how to move a body without leaving evidence."

"Why here?" Pérez asked. "Why dump her across from Camila's family?"

"Because he can," Rocca said. "Because he wants us to know he's in control."

"Or because he's saying something," Evans added.

Roan turned to face them. "Both. He's not just killing. He's communicating. The dumpsites aren't random. They're deliberate. The beach. This lot. Both public. Both were visible. He wants them found."

"Why?" Pérez asked.

"Because the act isn't enough," Roan said. "He needs witnesses. He needs the aftermath. The cameras. The cops. The families grieving." He paused. "He's feeding on it."

Rocca flicked ash. "So what do we do?"

"We work the pattern," Roan said. "Two victims. Both young women. Both knife wounds. Both moved postmortem. That's the signature. Now we find the connection."

"What if there isn't one?" Evans asked. "What if they're targets of opportunity?"

"There's always a connection," Roan said. "Even if it's just geography. Dixie Highway. That's his hunting ground."

Pérez crossed her arms. "So we canvass every motel, every corner, every place these women worked."

"Yeah."

"That's hundreds of hours."

"Then we put in hundreds of hours."

Silence settled over them. The sun was higher now, burning off the last of the pre-dawn grey. The city was waking up. Traffic on Dixie was picking up. Somewhere a siren wailed.

Roan looked at each of them—Rocca, worn and tired, cigarette burning between his fingers. Pérez, young and determined, jaw set. Evans was processing, learning, trying to reconcile the horror with the job.

"This won't be the last," Roan said.

Evans frowned. "What do you mean?"

"He's not going to stop. Not now. He's found a rhythm. A method. And it's working. No witnesses. No physical evidence. No mistakes." Roan's voice was flat. Certain. "He's just getting started."

The humid air felt heavier for a moment.

Rocca took a long drag. Exhaled. Didn't say anything.

Pérez looked at the ground.

Evans' hands curled into fists at his sides. He thought about his son. About the question: Do you catch bad guys? He'd said yes. Now he had to make it true.

Roan looked back at the lot. To the spot where Julia Aguilar had lain. To the drag marks in the dirt. To the fence that hadn't kept her safe.

"Back to the station," Roan said. "We start pulling files—every unsolved knife homicide in South Florida over the last five years. Then we map Dixie Highway—every business, every corner, every camera. We find the pattern."

They walked towards the cars. The scene behind them was empty now—just weeds and concrete and the memory of death.

The city kept moving.

And somewhere, a killer was planning his next move.

CHAPTER

16

Roan stood at the fence gap, staring across the street.

Two-story apartment complex. Beige stucco faded to grey. Iron railings on the second floor. Corner unit—laundry hanging on the balcony, child's bike propped against the wall.

The Morales family.

Fifty yards. Maybe less.

The killer had dumped Julia Aguilar directly across the street from Camila's home.

Evans stepped up beside him and followed Roan's gaze. He saw it too. The proximity. The deliberation.

"Jesus," Evans muttered.

"Yeah." Roan's voice was flat. He surveyed the scene one last time, then looked at Evans. "We're going over there. Now."

Evans nodded.

They left the Explorer in the lot and crossed the street on foot. The morning sun broke through the grey just after eight a.m. Early enough that Ariel's return could be from anywhere—friend's house, night shift, or something else entirely.

Evans' hand tightened on his notepad. Clara would be making coffee. Matthew would be eating his cereal at the table. Emily would be singing already. Safe at home.)

Maria Morales would wake up in that apartment and look out the window, seeing crime scene tape across the street. Another body. Another girl.

"You good?" Roan asked, not looking at him.

"Yeah."

Roan didn't push. Just kept walking.

The apartment complex sat mid-block, two stories of beige stucco faded to grey. Iron railings lined the second-floor walkway, rusted where salt had chewed through the paint. A few units had laundry hanging on the balconies. Others had bicycles propped against walls. The building looked tired—its paint was peeling, the gutters sagged, and cracks spider-webbed through the concrete stairs.

They climbed the exterior stairs to the second floor. The metal steps clanged under their boots. Roan led, Evans a step behind, notepad already in hand.

The corner unit sat at the end of the walkway. Number 2B. Same address from Camila's student records. The door was dented near the bottom, as if someone had kicked it years ago and never bothered to repair it. A child's bike leaned against the railing—pink, streamers frayed. Too small for a teenager. Camila's from years ago, probably. Never thrown away.

Roan knocked.

Waited.

Footsteps inside, slow, hesitant, the door opened a crack. Chain still on.

Maria Morales looked out through the gap. Her face was grey, hollowed out. Hair pulled back, greasy. Eyes clear—sober, Roan noted. Whether from exhaustion or effort, he couldn't tell—but was barely holding together. She wore a faded floral blouse, stained around the collar. Mid-forties, he guessed, but looked older.

"Detective," she said. Her voice was quiet, scraped raw.

"Mrs. Morales." Roan kept his tone even. "Can we come in?"

She stared at him. Then at Evans. Something on her face cracked. She closed the door, unhooked the chain, and opened it wider.

Roan stepped inside. Evans followed.

The apartment was stuffy, the A/C off or broken, the air thick and unmoving. The air smelled stale—cigarette smoke, old food, sweat. The blinds were drawn, allowing light to filter in thinly and grey, making everything look washed out and colorless.

A TV murmured somewhere in the building—otherwise, silence.

The living room was a disaster. Empty bottles clustered on the coffee table—cheap vodka, wine, beer cans crushed flat. A plate sat on the arm of the couch, a sandwich half-eaten, bread curled at the edges. Flies buzzed near the kitchen sink. Dishes piled high. The trash overflowed. A garbage bag sat by the door, half-full—an attempt at cleaning that hadn't made it outside.

Maria stood in the center of the room, arms wrapped around herself.

Roan's gaze moved across the space. He didn't judge. Didn't comment. Just cataloged. Evans stayed near the door, notepad out, pen ready.

Roan's jaw tightened. He'd seen plenty of families break under the weight like this. Grief. Guilt. Poverty. It ground people down until there was nothing left but bottles and silence. The apartment told a story—Maria trying, failing, trying again. Never quite making it.

This wasn't official yet. Just conversation. But it would be.

"Sit," Roan said quietly.

Maria moved to the couch. Sat. Hands folded in her lap, fingers knotted together.

Roan pulled a chair from the small dining table and set it across from her. Evans stayed standing, back against the wall.

"How are you holding up?" Roan asked.

Maria's laugh came out bitter. "How do you think?"

"Fair."

She looked at him then—really looked—and her face crumbled. "There's another girl. They said on the news. Another girl is dead."

"Yes."

"Same as Camila?"

"We're investigating."

Maria's hands tightened. "It's him, isn't it? The one who took Camila. He killed again."

Roan didn't answer. The silence confirmed it.

Maria closed her eyes. Tears slipped down her cheeks. When she opened them again, they were red, wet, and exhausted. "What do you need?"

Roan started slowly. Let the questions settle.

"Did Camila bring friends home?" he asked.

Maria shook her head. "No. Not here."

"Why not?"

"She..." Maria's gaze drifted to the bottles. "She didn't want them to see this. Me."

Roan nodded. No judgment in his expression. Just patience.

"Did she talk about her friends?"

"Sometimes. Not much. She kept that part separate."

"Separate?"

"School. Work. Her life outside." Maria's voice dropped. "She didn't want me in it."

Evans shifted near the wall. Matthew was ten. Still brought friends home. Still wanted his dad to watch him play basketball. Still asked questions at dinner.

What happened when that stopped? When your kids shut you out?

Evans thought about judgment. About how easy it was to see bottles and trash and think you understood. About how much harder it was to see Maria's hands shaking and remember she'd lost everything.

Evans' chest tightened. He pushed the thought away.

"Did she ever mention a girl?" Roan asked. "Asian, early twenties, dark hair?"

Maria frowned. Shook her head. "No. Why?"

"We're trying to identify someone who may have known Camila."

"I don't know her friends." Maria's voice broke. "She didn't bring them around. She shut me out. Months ago."

Roan leaned forward slightly. "Mrs. Morales. Camila paid for school. Tuition. Books. That's not cheap."

Maria's eyes dropped.

"She worked at the diner," Roan continued. "Minimum wage plus tips. That doesn't add up to $4,000 a semester. Where was the money coming from?"

Maria didn't answer.

"Mrs. Morales?"

"I don't know." The words came out choked.

"You never asked?"

"No."

"Why not?"

Maria looked up. Her eyes were wet, red-rimmed. "Because it was safer not to."

The room went still.

"Safer for who?" Roan asked, voice soft.

"For me." Maria's voice cracked. "For all of us. She was paying bills. Keeping the lights on. I didn't ask because I didn't want to know."

Evans' pen stopped moving. Clara. Trust. The rituals that held a family together—dinner at six, bedtime stories, Saturday morning pancakes.

The Morales family had none of that. Just absences. Bottles. Silence.

Maria's words tumbled out, faster now, as if silence might swallow her.

"Her father left before she was born," Maria said. "Never met her. Never called. Just gone."

"Camila's father," Roan said. "You ever hear from him?"

Maria let out a sound that was half a laugh, half a sob. "Never knew him. Not really. I was nineteen. Thought I was in love."

Her voice faltered, then steadied. "I raised her myself. Did the best I could. But it wasn't enough."

Evans didn't write this part down. Some things didn't belong in ink.

"And Ariel's father?" Roan asked.

Maria's shoulders lifted and fell. "Different man. Stuck around longer, but left when Ariel was still in diapers. That one hurt more. I thought he'd stay. He didn't."

Her words hung sour in the air. She stared at the carpet, shaking her head. "Two kids. Two fathers. Neither stayed."

Roan listened. Didn't interrupt.

"You did your best," Roan said quietly.

"Did I?" Maria's voice broke. "Look at this place. Look at me. Camila raised herself. Ariel..." She stopped. Shook her head. "Ariel's gone somewhere I can't reach."

"Where does Ariel go?" Roan asked.

Maria looked at him, eyes unfocused. "I don't know."

"You don't know?"

"He leaves. Comes back. I stopped asking."

"Does he work? Go to school?"

"He dropped out. Sophomore year. Said he'd get his GED. Never did. I don't know what he does all day. He just... leaves."

Roan leaned back. Let the silence stretch. His voice, when it came, was steady. Almost gentle. "You're still here, Mrs. Morales. That counts for something."

Maria looked at him like she didn't believe it.

"Mrs. Morales," Roan said carefully. "The night Camila died. Where was Ariel?"

Maria froze.

"Was he home?"

"I... I don't know."

"You don't know?"

"I passed out. Before nine. I don't remember."

"Did you hear him come in?"

"No."

"Did you see him the next morning?"

Maria shook her head. "He was already gone. Or still gone. I don't know."

Roan kept his voice level. "Where does he go, Mrs. Morales?"

"I don't know." The words came out strangled. "He doesn't tell me. Hasn't for months. He just... leaves."

"At night?"

"Sometimes."

"How often?"

"I don't know. I'm not awake most nights."

Evans made a note. Underlined it.

Roan watched Maria's face. Her hands trembled in her lap. She'd lost control and lost her daughter. And now she was losing her son.

"Mrs. Morales," Roan said quietly. "Ariel still needs you."

Maria laughed. Sharp. Broken. "He doesn't need me."

"He's still your son."

"Is he?" Maria looked at Roan, eyes hollow. "I don't know who he is anymore."

The front door rattled. Keys scraped against the lock—multiple attempts, fumbling. All three turned.

The knob turned slowly, then the door edged open. Ariel stepped in.

CHAPTER

17

"Hello, Ariel," Roan said. "We need to talk."

Ariel shut the door with his heel. His eyes flicked over Roan, then Evans, then back to Maria. He shifted the keys into his pocket. A white bandage wrapped his left wrist, edges damp.

Ariel was nineteen, technically an adult, but his hollowed-out frame made him look younger.

"What happened there?"

Ariel looked down at the bandage like he'd forgotten it. "Cut myself." He hesitated, then added, "Smashed one of mom's bottles last night. Glass caught me."

"Last night," Roan repeated. Not a question.

Ariel nodded. Didn't elaborate.

The apartment felt smaller now, the air tighter. The stuffy apartment made sweat bead at Roan's collar.

Maintained the professional distance. Maria sat frozen on the couch, hands knotted in her lap. Evans stayed against the wall, notepad ready, pen hovering.

Not custodial yet. Voluntary conversation. But it wouldn't be for long.

Roan's gaze moved from the bandage to Ariel's face. The boy was thin, all sharp angles—jaw, shoulders, collarbones pressing through a faded T-shirt. Dark hair stuck up at odd angles like he'd slept wrong, or hadn't slept at all. His eyes caught the light filtering through the blinds, unblinking. Ariel's leg bounced, heel tapping against the floor in a nervous rhythm he didn't seem to notice.

"Sit," Roan said.

Ariel didn't move. "I'd rather stand."

"Sit."

Roan's voice went flat. Ariel hesitated, then moved to the armchair across from his mother. He sat stiffly, back straight, hands on his knees. The bandage caught the dim light filtering through the blinds. Self-applied, wrapped too tightly at the wrist, tape bunching at the edges.

Roan pulled his chair closer. Not crowding, but close enough to read every twitch, every tell.

"Let's start simple," Roan said. "Where were you last night?"

"Here," Ariel said. "Reading."

"Reading what?"

"Scripture."

"Which part?"

Ariel's eyes flicked to the side. "Psalms."

"Which one?"

Ariel blinked. The muscle in his cheek ticked. "All of them," he said, and it landed wrong in the room. He scrambled, voice thinner now. "Twenty-three. Though I walk through the valley—"

"And this morning?" Roan asked.

Roan let the silence stretch. Evans logged it without looking up, catching the tremor in Ariel's voice more than the words.

"Mass."

"Where?"

"Federal Highway." Ariel paused between each word. "They do an early one."

Roan noted his eyes darted to his mother. He filed it away.

"Who saw you there?"

"I don't know. It was still dark. I prayed. I left."

Roan leaned back slightly. "Your mother says she doesn't know where you go. Says you leave for hours. Don't tell her where."

Maria flinched. Ariel's jaw tightened.

"I go where God leads me," Ariel said.

"God led you to smash bottles?"

Ariel's eyes flashed. "Sometimes."

"Sometimes," Roan repeated. His voice stayed calm. "Show me your hands."

Ariel hesitated, then held them up. Cuts showed under the bandage, small nicks along his fingers. Glass cuts, maybe. Or not.

"You smash a lot of bottles?" Roan asked.

Ariel swallowed. "Sometimes. When I'm angry."

"Angry at who?"

Ariel's mouth opened, then shut. He shrugged. "At life."

The boy's shoulders hunched forward. Evans thought of his own son, shoulders still loose, never hunched like this. He tapped his pen against his pad once, then stopped.

Roan didn't move closer. His voice was steady. "We need clear, Ariel. You say you were here last night. Reading. Then, church this morning. That's your story?"

Ariel nodded once. His eyes didn't leave the floor.

Maria spoke up, voice thin. "He tells the truth."

Roan looked at her, then back at Ariel. "We'll check."

Silence pressed in again. The hum of the fridge, the tick of the wall clock. A neighbor's TV murmured through the thin walls. Evans made a note for follow-up, but in his gut, he felt it wasn't enough.

Roan shifted forward, elbows on his knees. "Ariel, those flyers on the pier—Romans 6:23. The wages of sin is death. We know you were out yesterday afternoon, stapling them. You left in your mother's sedan."

Ariel's chin lifted, just a fraction. "People need Scripture. They need to know." His eyes flicked to the bandage as if it pulled at him. "Camila is with God."

Maria flinched. "Mijo—"

Roan's voice stayed even. "So you took your mother's car to spread the Word."

"She wasn't using it," Ariel said. His jaw locked. "She was asleep."

"Keys," Roan asked. "Where'd you get them?"

"On the hook by the door." His answer came quickly. "They're always there."

Maria shook her head, uncertain. "Sometimes I keep them in my purse."

Ariel didn't look at her. "They were on the hook."

The boy's hands hovered near the bandage, fingers flexing against the ache. The tape's edge was stained with a dull brown, caught in the weave. Evans wrote it down without looking at the page.

"You told me you were home reading last night," Roan said. "Then you told me you went to early Mass this morning."

"I did both," Ariel said, too fast. "I read. I prayed. I went to Mass."

"You put up Romans yesterday," Roan said. Not accusing. Not kind. "You wrote judgment across half the pier."

Ariel's stare hardened. "The verse is true."

"Truth isn't the question," Roan said. "Timing is."

The boy's fingers curled into fists. Evans glanced at Maria. She was small on the couch, hands knotted, eyes darting between them like she knew something was slipping out of reach.

"You didn't answer about the car," Roan went on. "What time did you take it yesterday?"

Ariel's mouth opened, then closed. He looked at the floor. "Afternoon."

"You came back when?"

"Before dark." His voice firmed. "I was home all night."

Roan let the quiet stretch. "You drove your mother's car. You stapled flyers about sin and death. You came back with a cut you say came from one of her bottles." His eyes fell to the bandage. "Where's the glass?"

"In the garbage," Ariel said.

"Show me."

Ariel hesitated. "It's… pickup day. The can is at the curb."

Evans pictured the block that morning—cans tipped, lids ajar, rain pooled. A truck had already passed two streets over when they'd rolled in. He kept that thought to himself, but it sat heavily.

Roan's jaw tightened. Garbage pickup on the exact morning after a murder. Too convenient. Or true.

Roan shifted, voice lower. "Ariel, listen to me. I don't care about curfew. I care about your sister. I care about where you were and what you did while the city slept."

"I told you," Ariel said. Ariel's jaw locked. His fingers drummed against his knee. "I prayed. I asked God to see Camila."

Maria's voice cracked. "Why that verse, mijo? Why death?"

Ariel finally looked at her. His face softened and hardened at once. "Because it's what people understand." He swallowed. "Because it's true if you live wrong. Because I wanted them to fear what happened to her."

Roan studied him. "Fear isn't the same as help."

Ariel's eyes flashed. "Neither is this," he said, flicking his gaze at Roan's badge. "You didn't save her."

Maria made a small sound, like the air had cut her. Her mouth opened, closed. No defense came. Just tears. Evans felt it land. He kept his pen still.

Roan didn't rise to it. "We're trying to save the next girl," he said. "That starts with the truth."

The silence held. Ariel's hands clenched on his knees. Maria stared at the floor. Evans could hear the wall clock ticking, each second loud as a hammer.

Roan pushed himself up from the chair. Three steps to the window. His fingers found the edge of the blinds, creating just enough space to view the scene below. Yellow tape caught the breeze, marking off the vacant lot where Julia Aguilar's blood had turned the earth a deeper shade of brown, not even a full city block from their current position.

"You know there's another girl," Roan said, back still to the room.

Ariel didn't answer.

"Another body. Same as Camila." Roan turned. "Dumped across the street from where your sister lived."

Maria's breath hitched.

Ariel's face went pale. "I didn't—"

"Didn't what?" Roan asked.

"I didn't know."

"You didn't know there was another body? Or you didn't know it was across the street?"

Ariel's mouth worked. No sound came out.

Roan crossed back to him. Stood over the chair. "You were out yesterday. Putting up flyers about death. You came home with cuts. You can't account for your time last night. Your mother was passed out. You don't know where the glass is that supposedly cut you." He paused. "And now there's another dead girl fifty yards from your front door."

"I didn't do anything," Ariel said. His voice cracked.

"Then help me understand," Roan said. "Because right now, the only story I have is yours. And it doesn't hold."

Ariel looked at his mother. Maria's eyes were wide, wet, and terrified.

"Mijo," she whispered. "Tell him."

"There's nothing to tell," Ariel said. But his voice was hollow.

Roan sat back down—closer this time. "Let's go through it again. Slow."

Ariel's hands were shaking now. He pressed them flat against his knees.

"Yesterday afternoon. You took your mother's car. You put up flyers at the pier. What time?"

"Three. Maybe four."

"How long did that take?"

"An hour. Maybe more."

"Then what?"

"I came home."

"Straight home?"

Ariel hesitated. "I stopped."

"Where?"

"Gas station. Federal Highway."

Roan made a note. "Which one?"

"Shell."

"You get gas?"

"No. Just… sat in the parking lot."

"For how long?"

"I don't know. An hour?"

"Why?"

Ariel's jaw worked. "I didn't want to come home."

Maria made a small sound.

"Why didn't you want to come home?" Roan asked.

"Because she was drunk," Ariel said, voice bitter. "Because she's always drunk. Because this place—" He gestured at the apartment. "It's hell."

Roan let that sit. "You sat in a Shell station parking lot for an hour. Then what?"

"Then I came home."

"What time?"

"Six. Maybe seven."

"Your mother was passed out?"

"Yeah."

"And you?"

"I went to my room. Read."

"All night?"

"Yeah."

"Smashed the bottle when?"

Ariel's eyes dropped. "Late. Maybe midnight."

"Why?"

"Because I was angry."

"At what?"

"At her! At Camila! At God!" His voice broke. "At everything."

Ariel's face crumpled. His hands covered his eyes. For a moment, he was just a kid. Scared. Lost. Then he breathed, and the mask returned.

Roan leaned back. The bandage was coming loose at one edge, a dark stain spreading across it.

"This morning," Roan said. "Mass. What time?"

"Six."

"You left here when?"

"Five-thirty."

"In your mother's car?"

"Yeah."

"Keys on the hook?"

"Yeah."

"You came back when?"

"Seven. Maybe seven-thirty."

"And went where?"

"Nowhere. I walked."

"Walked where?"

"Around. The block."

"Anyone see you?"

"I don't know."

Roan studied him. "Ariel, I need you to understand something. We're going to check all of this. The gas station. The church. We're going to pull security footage. Talk to priests. Ask if anyone remembers a skinny kid with a bandage on his wrist sitting in a pew at six a.m."

Ariel swallowed.

"And if your story doesn't hold," Roan continued, "if there's one piece that doesn't line up, I'm going to assume you're lying about all of it."

"I'm not lying."

Roan crouched in front of him—eye level. "Ariel, I think you're a smart kid. I think you know exactly how this looks. I think you're scared. And I think you're not telling me everything."

Ariel's eyes were wet now.

"So I'm going to ask you one more time," Roan said. "Where were you last night?"

"Here," Ariel whispered.

"All night?"

"Yes."

"Reading Psalms?"

"Yes."

"Smashing bottles?"

"Yes."

"And this morning? Mass?"

"Yes."

Roan stood. His voice remained level, but the command beneath it was steel. "Ariel, change that bandage. Get a clean one. And no more flyers. Not without talking to me first."

Ariel didn't answer. Just stared at the floor.

Maria's voice came out small. "Detective—"

"Mrs. Morales," Roan said, cutting her off gently. "Keep him here. Don't let him leave without telling you where he's going."

She nodded, hands still knotted in her lap.

Roan moved to the door. Evans followed. They stepped into the walkway, and Roan pulled the door shut behind them.

The metal stairs clanged under their boots as they descended. Neither spoke until they reached the parking lot. The morning sun was higher now, heat pressing down, humidity thick enough to taste. Sweat darkened Evans' collar.

Roan stopped at Maria's white sedan.

The car gleamed. Water still beaded on the hood, chrome catching the light. Too clean. Too perfect. Roan walked around it slowly, eyes cataloguing every detail. He crouched near the driver's side door and looked through the window.

Evans stepped up beside him. "Interior's spotless."

"Yeah."

"Floor mats. Dashboard. Not even dust on the vents."

Roan stood. Ran his hand along the roof. The metal was warm, drying fast in the sun. He opened the driver's door—unlocked—and leaned in. The smell hit him first. Chemical clean. The chemical smell wasn't just detergent. Strong enough to make eyes water when the door first opened. The air freshener was trying too hard to mask it.

He pulled back. Shut the door.

"Too clean for a boy's late-night run," Evans said.

Roan nodded. Didn't need to say it. The car was its own answer.

Evans thought about giving Ariel the benefit of the doubt. Then he thought about Julia Aguilar, fifty yards away. The doubt evaporated.

They walked towards the Explorer. Evans broke the silence. "What do you think?"

Roan's stare didn't move from the apartment building: second floor, corner unit. The blinds twitched. Someone watching. "That boy's hiding something. More than he'll admit. More than his mother even sees."

Evans flipped open his notepad. "The Mass story?"

"We verify it," Roan said. "Names. Sacristan. Security cameras, if they have them. Church on Dixie—Federal Highway was a slip, he corrected himself, but not fast enough." He pulled his phone and scrolled through contacts. "I'll have Rocca pull footage from the Shell station, too. If Ariel sat in that parking lot for an hour like he claims, cameras would show it."

Roan would check more than cameras. Communion records. The priest's memory of regulars. The sign-in sheet some parishes kept.

Evans made a list. "And the car?"

"Warrant for forensics. If there's blood, if there're fibers, the detail won't hide it." Warrant would take hours—Judge's signature. Proper paperwork. The car would sit, secured, until then. Roan pocketed his phone. "But we don't wait on that. Next stop is the diner."

"DeAngelo," Evans said.

Roan's jaw tightened. "Yeah. DeAngelo."

"You don't like him."

"I don't like men who talk about dead girls like they're inconveniences." Roan climbed into the passenger seat.

Evans slid behind the wheel. Started the engine. The A/C kicked on, blasting hot air before it cooled.

"What if Ariel's telling the truth?" Evans asked. "What if he really was home? What if the cuts are from a bottle?"

Evans pulled out of the lot, turning south. Roan stared out the window. "Then his timing's the worst luck I've ever seen. Sister dies. He puts up flyers about death and sin. Another girl dies fifty yards from his front door. And he just happens to wash the car the next morning."

Evans said nothing. Just gripped the wheel, eyes on the road.

Roan's voice came quieter. "No. That boy is hiding something. And we're going to find out what."

They drove in silence for a block. The crime scene tape still fluttered across the empty lot. Patrol had cleared out, but the stain remained—a dark patch in the dirt where Julia Aguilar had bled out.

Roan glanced at it as they passed. "Two girls. Same age. Same wounds. Same killer. And Ariel Morales right in the middle of it— either the unluckiest kid in Lake Worth, or something worse."

Evans thought about Matthew. Ten years old. Still asked his dad for help with his homework. Still slept with the door cracked open because the dark scared him sometimes.

He thought about Ariel. Alone in that apartment. Religious drawings covering his walls like prayers or threats. Angry at his mother. Angry at his sister. Angry at God.

"You think he's capable?" Evans asked.

Traffic thickened as they hit Dixie. Morning commuters, delivery trucks, the city waking up to another day.

Roan drew a slow breath, then answered. "I think anger makes people capable of things they never imagined. I think scripture twisted the wrong way can justify anything. And I think that boy's been twisting for a long time."

CHAPTER

18

THE DENNY'S sat off Dixie, past the pawn shops and check-cashing places, their neon signs dark in the morning rain. The parking lot smelled of wet asphalt, rain dripping steadily off the awning where the gutter had given up. Inside, the place hummed low—truck drivers bent over eggs, retirees nursing endless coffee, a waitress with a tired smile refilling mugs without being asked.

Rocca slid into a booth near the back, coat damp at the shoulders, hair matted where the rain had found him. He ordered without looking at the menu—pancakes, sausage, eggs over easy, hash browns, and extra toast.

Pérez just asked for coffee and oatmeal.

The waitress raised an eyebrow but didn't comment. Just scribbled on her pad and walked off, shoes squeaking against the lino.

They'd left the crime scene twenty minutes ago with orders to file reports, but neither was ready to sit at a desk yet. The Denny's was a habit—Rocca's ritual after bad crime scenes. Roan and Evans were at the other diner by now, squeezing DeAngelo. They'd compare notes later. The second body changed things.

Rocca leaned back against the booth, the vinyl creaking under his weight. "Well," he said, "that was a scene. Aguilar looked too much like Morales to call it a coincidence."

Pérez stirred her coffee, trying not to see Aguilar's face every time she blinked. "Same wounds. Same dump job. Same nothing from the cameras. And right across from the Morales apartment."

"Same area," Rocca added. He rubbed his chin with a tired hand, stubble rasping under his palm. "Guy's making a circuit. Establishing territory." He traced a mental map on the table with one finger. "Dixie

Highway corridor. Both dumps are within three miles. Working-class areas. Victims with limited support systems. The geographic pattern's tightening."

Pérez's spoon clicked against the cup. She set it down carefully. "You think it's the same man?"

"Yeah." Rocca's answer came flat, no hesitation. "Different would be lazy. This felt... practiced. Not his first night."

"The kid—Ariel. Roan likes him for it?"

Rocca shrugged. "Kid's got the anger. Got the opportunity."

Pérez didn't answer straightaway. She looked out the window at the slick street, where a bus hissed past, throwing spray against the glass. The world kept moving. Bodies kept piling up.

The waitress came back with their plates. She slid Rocca's spread down—pancakes stacked three high, eggs bleeding yolk, sausage links glistening with grease. Pérez got her oatmeal, steam curling off the surface. Rocca drowned his eggs in hot sauce without looking.

"You're quiet," he said.

"I'm thinking." Pérez sipped her coffee. It was too hot, but she didn't flinch. "If this is connected, then Camila wasn't random. He's hunting specific types."

Rocca cut into his pancakes. Syrup bled across the plate, pooling at the edges. "Lot of hunters in this city. Few who stick with the same ground." He shoved a bite in, chewed, then pointed at her with his fork. "And none of 'em care who you are. Badge or not."

Pérez pulled out her phone and reviewed the photos from the drag marks. "Same technique. Pulled by the shoulders, heels dragging. He's got a method."

"And he's confident," Rocca added. "Dumps 'em where they'll be found. Wants the attention."

Pérez set her spoon down. "You make it sound hopeless."

He smirked, tired around the edges. "Hopeless keeps me in work."

They ate in silence for a minute—the clink of forks. The buzz of neon came from the sign outside. The low chatter of other tables faded.

"You ever get tired of it?" she asked. "The grind. The dead ends. The faces you can't forget."

Rocca wiped syrup from his beard with a napkin. "Every day."

"Then why stay?"

He grinned, not wide, just enough to crease the corners of his eyes. "Cigarettes. Marina fees. Somebody's gotta keep the rookies from screwing up."

Pérez let out a breath, half a laugh. "You think I'm screwing up?"

"Not yet," Rocca said. He leaned back, fork still in hand. "But you're itching. I can see it. Shield got away from you and went to Evans. That eats at you."

Pérez's jaw tightened. She stared at her oatmeal. "You don't know that."

"I do." Rocca stabbed his fork into his hash browns, breaking the crust. "Because you're better than him. Cleaner. Quicker. You want it more. He's got the family man glow, that's why they gave it to him. Safer bet."

Pérez didn't look at him. "You think I'll get it next time."

Rocca chewed, swallowed, and washed it down with coffee. "Aguilar'll probably be my last. After this, I'm out. Gonna hang a P.I. shingle. Chase cheating husbands, track missing cats. Real work." He smirked. "Slot'll open. Might be yours if you don't piss anyone off."

Pérez sat back in the booth, spoon idle in her coffee. "It should've been me," she said. Quiet, but not soft. "I did the hours. I worked the scenes. I know this job better than Evans. And he gets the shield because he fits the picture."

Rocca leaned an elbow on the table, watching her. "You're not wrong. But let me tell you something—you don't want to fit the picture. Pictures fade. Brass promotes people who look like they'll make good Christmas cards. Half of 'em wash out, half of 'em get desked. You? You'd break the desk before you sat behind it."

Pérez let out a sharp breath, part laugh, part frustration. "That's supposed to be a compliment?"

"Best kind," Rocca said. He tore open another sugar packet and dumped it into his coffee. "Look, kid, the brass don't see straight. They see who won't rock their boat. Evans? He's got the ring, the smile, and the report writing. He looks safe. You? You look like trouble. And that's good. Trouble gets cases solved."

Pérez's eyes narrowed. "Trouble doesn't get you promoted."

Rocca pointed his spoon at her. "Not yet. But it will. You think the city can hide what's out there forever? They need people who bite. Evans is a good cop, don't get me wrong. But you—you've got teeth. That's what the job remembers, even if the brass don't."

Pérez's phone buzzed on the table, screen lighting her face. She saw the name, hesitated, then slid it up with her thumb.

"Hey," she said.

Her tone softened at first, but only momentarily. Her brow pulled tight. "I'm at work... No, I told you—" She glanced at Rocca, who pretended to study the diner's cracked blinds. "Don't start this now."

Her voice climbed sharper. "I don't know when I'll be home. That's the job. You think I can clock out when I want? Because I can't."

She listened, jaw tightening, then fired back. "You always say that. But you don't get it. You've never gotten it."

Rocca dipped another triangle of toast into his eggs, acting like the hum of the place drowned her out. A waitress refilled his coffee without asking. He nodded thanks, eyes fixed anywhere but Pérez.

Pérez's voice dropped, low and final. "Then maybe you should stop calling."

She hit the screen and set the phone down with a hard thud. The silverware rattled. She leaned back, arms crossed, eyes glassy with anger she wouldn't let fall as tears.

Silence held the booth for a stretch.

Rocca broke it with a mouthful of bacon. "Guy sounds like a real prize."

Pérez let out a dry laugh, more air than sound. "Yeah. Hell of a prize."

"You could do better."

"Could I?" she said, biting it off. "Every time I try, the job gets in the way. Nobody wants to wait around while you're chasing corpses."

Rocca shrugged. "Then you don't need somebody who makes you choose. You need somebody who can stand the storm." He set his fork down. "And if they can't, you cut 'em loose. It's that simple."

Pérez shook her head. "You make everything sound simple."

"That's because I've already lived the complicated part." His smile didn't reach his eyes. "Trust me, better to lose a man now than drag dead weight for years."

Pérez exhaled, slowly, steadying herself. The fight drained out, leaving only the ache. "I hate that he makes me feel like I'm the problem."

"You're not," Rocca said. Flat. No room for argument. "He is."

Pérez studied him a moment. The lines on his face, the steadiness in his tone. He wasn't being kind; he was being honest. Somehow, it hit harder than comfort would have.

Rocca stabbed the last sausage link, chewed, then said, "You know I live on a boat, right?"

Pérez blinked. "You don't."

"Do." He sipped his coffee. "Thirty-five footer, tied up down at Riviera. Leaks in the rain, rocks like hell in a storm. But it's mine."

Pérez gave him a look, halfway between disbelief and a smile. "You're telling me you go home to a boat every night?"

"Beats paying rent," Rocca said. "Besides, no neighbors. Just water and seagulls. Peaceful."

Pérez shook her head, finally laughing under her breath. "God, you're serious."

"Serious as cholesterol," he said, patting his stomach.

For the first time that morning, the tightness eased out of her shoulders. She leaned back in the booth, coffee warming her hands, and let the moment sit. Rocca dug into his toast crumbs, unbothered.

He checked his watch. "Paperwork by noon. Then I'm pulling every unsolved knife job in the tri-county. You hit the databases and cross-reference victim profiles. Age, occupation, geographic patterns. See if there's more we're missing."

Pérez nodded, pulling out her notebook. "Looking for what specifically?"

"Knife wounds. Women under thirty. Postmortem movement. Public dump sites." Rocca wiped his mouth. "If this bastard's been at it longer than two bodies, we need to know."

"And if we find more?"

"Then we've got a proper serial," Rocca said. "And a pattern. Patterns are how you catch 'em."

THE RAIN THINNED to mist as they passed Lake Avenue. Evans drove, hands steady at ten and two, while Roan stared out the passenger window at the empty lot across the street.

Evans broke the silence. "I found something."

Roan turned his head. "What?"

"Two things." Evans kept his eyes on the road, but his jaw was tight. "I traced the unknown number from Camila's call log. Came back to a dealership. Auto Exotics. The number appeared three times over two weeks—two outgoing calls from Camila's phone, one incoming."

Roan's brow furrowed. "Auto Exotics."

"High-end dealership. Federal Highway, just north of Belvedere Road." Evans glanced at him. "Sells luxury cars. European imports. Price tags that start at six figures."

Roan leaned back against the seat. "Could be spam. Dealerships— they just robocall everyone."

"Maybe," Evans said. "But why would a diner waitress scraping by for college tuition be calling a luxury car dealership?"

Traffic thickened as they approached Tenth Avenue. Delivery vans and commuters pressed forward. Roan watched the city grind on.

"She wouldn't," Roan said finally.

"No," Evans agreed. "She wouldn't."

"Unless someone else was."

Evans nodded. "That's what I thought. Maybe she wasn't calling about a car. Maybe someone connected to Auto Exotics was connected to her."

Roan turned the idea over in his head. "Customer? Employee?"

"Don't know yet," Evans said. "But it's a thread."

Roan nodded. "Good work. We'll visit Auto Exotics after this. See who she was calling and why." He pulled his phone, made a note, then pocketed it. "What's the second thing?"

Evans took a breath. "The diary. Camila's diary—Maria gave it to us during the initial investigation. There's an entry dated August 15th, six months before she died. She mentions someone. Doesn't name him, just calls him 'the regular.' Older guy. Black hair. Always sat in her section. Always paid cash."

Roan's eyes narrowed. "She say anything else?"

"Not much. Just that he was nice. Tipped well. Asked about her classes." Evans paused. "She wrote that he made her feel seen. Like she mattered."

The words hung in the air.

Roan's voice came quietly. "Grooming." His jaw tightened—an older man and a young girl who is struggling financially. The pattern was textbook. Made him want to break something.

"Yeah," Evans said. "That's what it reads like."

Evans thought about Matthew. About teaching him to recognize predators. About hoping he'd never have to.

"Older. Black hair. Cash payer. Regular at the diner." Roan's jaw tightened. "That's a profile."

"Matches what we're looking for," Evans said.

"If he's real." Roan stared out the window again. "Could be nothing. Could be a customer who was just nice to her. Could be—"

"Or it could be our guy," Evans said.

Roan didn't argue. He just watched the city blur past. Pawn shops. Liquor stores. Check-cashing places with bars on the windows. This was hunting ground. This was where predators found prey.

"We press DeAngelo," Roan said. "Hard. He knows who his regulars are. If there's a guy fitting that description, DeAngelo's seen him."

Evans pulled into the lot behind the Nifty Fifty Diner. The neon sign buzzed "Nifty Fi y," just as before. Same broken letters. Same grease smell hanging in the damp air.

They sat in the Explorer for a moment. Engine ticking. Rain was misting the windshield.

"DeAngelo's not going to want to talk," Evans said.

"He doesn't have a choice."

The diner was half-full. Morning crowd—truck drivers nursing coffee, an old couple picking at eggs, a couple of waitresses moving between tables with pots of burnt sludge and tired smiles. The place smelled like fryer grease and bleach, linoleum sticky under their shoes. The griddle hissed in the back. Someone dropped cutlery. The bell above the door chimed as another customer left.

Frank DeAngelo stood behind the counter, arms crossed, face already set in a scowl. He saw them walk in, and his expression didn't change. Just hardened.

"Detectives," he said. Not a greeting. A warning.

Roan walked straight to him. Evans followed, notepad out.

"Mr. DeAngelo," Roan said. "We need to talk."

"I already talked to you," DeAngelo said. "Talked to your whole department. Answered every question. My staff answered every question. We've got nothing else to say."

"You do now," Roan said.

DeAngelo's eyes whipped to the customers, glancing off them quick as a cue ball before pinging back to Roan. "I run a business here. If you want to interrogate me, do it somewhere else."

Roan's voice came flat and hard. "We can do it here or at the station. Your choice."

DeAngelo's jaw worked. Eyes flicked from Evans to Roan, weighing his options. "Fine. Back office. Five minutes."

Roan didn't shift. "Take as long as it takes."

The back office was stifling—broken A/C and a closed door trapping the heat from the kitchen. DeAngelo slouched into the chair behind the battered desk, arms flopping. Roan stood in front of the desk, motionless. Evans hung back, shoulder against the wall, pen poised over his notebook. The only sound was the scrape of DeAngelo's chair legs on the floor.

Evans' notes would become formal statements later. For now, this was information gathering.

"What do you want?" DeAngelo asked.

"Regulars," Roan said. "Camila had regulars. Customers who came in often. Sat in her section. You know who they are."

DeAngelo shrugged. "Sure. Lot of regulars. We're a diner. People come back."

"Older guy," Roan said. "Black hair. Always paid cash. Always sat in Camila's section."

DeAngelo's face didn't change. "That describes half my customers."

"Don't play games," Roan said. His voice remained level, but the edge was still there. "You know who I'm talking about. You see everyone who walks through that door. You know their faces. You know their orders. You know who they talk to."

DeAngelo leaned back in his chair. "Even if I did, what's that got to do with Camila?"

"He might've been the last person to see her alive," Roan said.

DeAngelo's eyes flicked to Evans, then back. "You saying one of my customers killed her?"

"I'm saying we need to talk to him."

DeAngelo's confusion looked genuine. He honestly didn't track individual customers that closely. Roan filed that away.

Evans flipped a page in his notepad. "Did Camila have another job? Somewhere else she worked?"

DeAngelo frowned. "Not that I know of. She was here five days a week. Plus classes during the day. When would she have time?"

"How was she paying for college?" Roan asked. "Tuition. Books. Living expenses."

DeAngelo's frown deepened. "Hell if I know. We pay minimum wage plus tips. That's not college money."

"So someone was helping her," Roan said.

"I wouldn't know," DeAngelo said. "She didn't talk about her personal business."

"But you wondered," Evans said.

DeAngelo's jaw tightened. "What I wonder isn't your concern."

"It is when two girls are dead," Roan said.

DeAngelo's face went pale. "I don't know who you're talking about."

Roan leaned forward, hands on the desk. "Yes, you do."

DeAngelo held his gaze. "No. I don't."

The quiet settled between them.

"Mr. DeAngelo," Roan said quietly, "there's another girl. Found this morning. Same wounds. Same MO. Same killer. You want a third girl on your conscience because you wouldn't cooperate?"

DeAngelo's face went paler. "That's not fair."

"Fair doesn't matter," Roan said. "Dead girls matter. You know something. Tell me."

DeAngelo looked down at his desk. His hands clenched into fists. "I don't remember every face."

"Yes, you do," Roan said.

"Even if I did," DeAngelo said, voice tight, "I'm not throwing my customers under the bus because you've got a hunch."

Roan straightened. "Then we'll talk to your staff. All of them. One by one. Until someone remembers."

DeAngelo's jaw tightened. "You're wasting your time."

"We'll see," Roan said.

They spent two hours reinterviewing the staff. Same corner booth, improvised interview space. Same questions. Evans was taking notes while Roan asked the same things over and over. Roan's voice had gone hoarse from repeating the same questions. Evans had filled six pages of notes.

Outside the window, the lunch rush was starting. Roan's coffee had gone cold an hour ago.

Older man. Black hair. Paid cash. Sat in Camila's section. You remember him?

Did Camila have another job? How was she paying for college? Was someone giving her money?

Most shook their heads. Didn't remember. Didn't notice. Minded their own business. The cook barely looked up from the grill. The dishwasher just shrugged. No one knew how Camila afforded school. No one asked. The money question kept hitting dead ends.

By the fifth interview, Roan's patience was wearing thin. Evans could see it—the way his jaw clenched, the way his questions came sharper, clipped.

Then they called over the last waitress.

Her name tag said Paola. Early twenties, dark ponytail showing grey roots, she probably couldn't afford to cover. Nervous eyes that wouldn't stay still.

She slid into the booth across from Roan, hands knotted in her lap.

"Paola," Roan said. "How long have you been working here?"

"Two years," she said. Voice quiet.

"You knew Camila?"

"Yeah. We worked some shifts together."

"Did she have another job? Somewhere else she worked?"

Paola shook her head. "Not that I know of. She was here five days a week. I don't know when she would've had time."

"How was she paying for college?" Roan asked. "Tuition at Palm Beach State isn't cheap. Plus books. Living expenses."

Paola's eyes dropped. "I... I don't know. I wondered about that too."

"She ever mention someone helping her?" Evans asked. "Family? A boyfriend? Anyone giving her money?"

"No," Paola said. "Her mom couldn't help—everyone knew that. And she didn't talk about a boyfriend."

Roan leaned forward. "But someone was helping her. Four thousand dollars a semester. That doesn't come from diner wages."

Paola's hands twisted tighter. "I don't know where the money came from."

"She ever talk about her customers?"

Paola hesitated. "Sometimes."

"Anyone in particular?"

Paola's eyes dropped to the table. "I don't know."

"Paola," Roan said, leaning forward over the Formica. "I'm not trying to get you in trouble. That's not why I'm here. Nobody's come to shut the diner down." He glanced at the door. A waitress balanced a tray. "Two girls are dead, and I think someone who came through that door knows why. Maybe you do too."

Paola swallowed. Her hands twisted tighter. She reached for the napkin dispenser. Her hands shook. She twisted it between her fingers until it tore.

"Older man," Roan continued. "Black hair. Paid cash. Sat in Camila's section. You remember him?"

Paola didn't answer.

"Paola," Evans said, voice softer than Roan's. "If you know something, now's the time."

Paola looked up. Her eyes were wet. "I... I remember him."

Roan went still. "Tell me."

"He came in a lot," Paola said. "Maybe once a week. Always at lunch. Always asked for Camila's section." She paused. "He was nice. Polite. Dressed well. Tipped good."

"What'd he look like?" Roan asked.

"Older. Maybe forties. Black hair. Clean-shaven. Nice clothes—not suits, but expensive. Button-down shirts. Nice shoes."

"How'd he pay?"

"Cash. Always cash."

"What'd they talk about?"

Paola shook her head. "I don't know. I didn't listen. But... she smiled when he was there. Like she was happy to see him."

Roan's stomach tightened. "When's the last time you saw him?"

Paola thought. "Two weeks before she died. Maybe three."

"You know his name?"

"No."

"He ever come in with anyone?"

"No. Always alone."

"What'd he drive?"

Paola blinked. "I... I don't know. I never saw him leave. My shift ended at two—before his lunch visits finished."

Roan leaned back. "Anything else? Anything that stood out?"

Paola hesitated. Then: "He had a tan line where a ring used to be."

Roan's eyes narrowed. "Which hand?"

"Left. Ring finger."

Evans stopped writing. The booth felt smaller.

"Married," Roan said quietly. "Or was."

Paola nodded. "That's what I thought. But I never overheard anything."

"Did Camila notice?" Roan asked.

"I don't know. We never talked about it." Paola's voice dropped. "I should've said something. Should've told her to be careful."

"You didn't know," Evans said.

"But I wondered," Paola said. "A guy like that, coming in alone, always asking for her section. Paying cash. No ring but a tan line." She looked up, tears spilling over. "I wondered."

Roan's voice stayed gentle. "Did you ever see them together outside the diner?"

"No."

"Ever see him waiting for her in the parking lot?"

"No. But I always left before she did. Her shift ended at three. Mine ended at two."

Roan made a note. "Anything else you remember? Car he might've driven? Anything he said? Any detail, no matter how small."

Paola wiped her eyes with the back of her hand. "He... he had nice hands. Clean. Like he didn't do hard work. And his watch was expensive. I noticed because my boyfriend—" She stopped. "It was silver. Big face. Like yours." She pointed to Roan's watch. "Looked like it cost more than I make in a month."

"You think he was giving her money?" Roan asked quietly.

Paola's eyes filled again. "I don't know. But... yeah. Maybe. She was happy when he was here. And after he started coming round, she stopped stressing about tuition as much."

"She told you that?"

"Not directly. But I could tell. She was... lighter. Like a weight had come off."

"When did he first start coming round?"

"Maybe six months ago. Maybe longer."

Evans made a note—older man with money. Young girl struggling to pay for school.

Roan nodded. "Thank you, Paola. You did the right thing."

She looked at him, eyes still wet. "Is he... did he kill her?"

"I don't know yet," Roan said. "But you just helped us get closer to finding out."

DeAngelo was waiting when they came out of the booth. Arms crossed. Face tight.

"Find what you were looking for?" he asked.

"Yeah," Roan said. "Now I need your staff rosters. Last six months. I need to verify everyone's schedules, see if anyone else worked when the regular was here."

DeAngelo's eyes narrowed. "What for?"

"To verify schedules. Cross-reference witness statements."

"I already gave you schedules."

"I need them again," Roan said. "And I need your vendor logs. Delivery schedules. Anyone who came through that door in a professional capacity. Might show if the regular had a legitimate business reason to be here—deliveries, maintenance, anything that gave him access."

"That's private business—"

"Two dead girls," Roan said, cutting him off. "You want a warrant, I'll get one. You want to cooperate, hand them over now."

DeAngelo stared at him. Then he turned, walked back to his office, and came out with a manila folder. He shoved it at Roan. "There. Rosters. Vendor logs are on the computer. I'll email them."

"Today," Roan said.

"Today," DeAngelo repeated.

Roan took the folder. "If you think of anything else about that customer—anything—you call me."

DeAngelo didn't answer. Just walked back behind the counter, arms crossed again, watching them.

They walked towards the front door. The morning crowd had thinned. A truck driver paid his bill at the till. A waitress refilled coffee at a corner table. The cook worked the griddle, metal scraping against metal.

Roan stopped at the door. Glanced back.

Paola stood near the counter, watching them. Her eyes were still red, but she'd stopped crying. She gave a slight nod.

Roan nodded back.

Then he pushed through the door into the damp morning air. The bell above the door chimed. Evans followed.

CHAPTER

20

THE BELL above the diner door chimed as it shut behind them. Roan and Evans stood on the sidewalk, midday traffic humming past on Dixie. The rain had stopped, but the air still hung damp, heavy with humidity and exhaust.

Roan's jaw ached from clenching through two hours of interviews. Grooming. The word sat bitter in his throat. An older man with money, a young girl with nothing. Tale as old as predation.

Evans pulled out his notepad and opened it. "So we've got our suspect profile. Older guy. Black hair. Cash payer. Tan line from a wedding ring. Expensive watch. Started coming round six months ago."

"Yeah," Roan said. But his eyes weren't on Evans. They were locked on the street stretching north.

Evans noticed. "What?"

Roan watched cars pass for a moment before replying. "You see where we're standing?"

Evans frowned, glancing around. "Yeah. Pawn shops, payday loans, and grease joints. Same as a dozen other strips on Dixie."

"No." Roan's voice dropped. "This is where Ellen Mills spotted Camila. Right here. A couple of blocks up, her and the Asian girl. Same stretch."

Evans went still. His pen hovered over the notepad.

Roan turned, eyes tracking. "Nifty Fifty. Right here. Where Camila worked. Where the guy came every week for lunch."

He turned south. "Aguilar's dump site. Five miles that way. Across from the Morales apartment."

Evans looked up and down the strip.

"It's all one line," Roan said. "Everything connects on Dixie. One predator, one territory. He's hunted this strip for months, maybe longer, and no one's seen him because he fits."

The traffic kept moving. A bus hissed past, brakes squealing. A truck's air brakes hissed at the light. Someone's stereo pumped bass that rattled windows. The city ground forward, oblivious.

Evans' jaw tightened. "He's hunting on this street."

"Yeah, and nobody's seeing him because he looks like everyone else." Roan gestured at the block. "Ellen said she saw them here. Waiting. Talking. Normal. That means they were comfortable here. This was their territory."

"Or his," Evans said.

"Yeah," Roan said. "Or his."

The Asian girl. Still no name. Still no ID. She was the key to something, and they were missing it.

They walked north on Dixie. Noon sun beat straight down, bleaching the color from everything, turning the strip into an overexposed photograph. The strip told its own story—pawn shops with barred windows, check-cashing joints, a massage parlor with windows tinted black. Heat rose off the asphalt in waves. Exhaust mixed with grease from the diner, motor oil from the gas station, something sour from the gutter where rainwater pooled.

The Marathon station had cameras on the pumps. Nothing else was watched on the street.

Day laborers clustered near the check-cashing place. A woman in tight jeans and a crop top walked slowly along the shoulder, purse swinging, eyes tracking cars.

At the corner, behind the gas station, Lucky's sat with its neon green sign. Door propped open. Music bleeding out—classic rock, the playlist in every dive bar from here to Miami.

Roan stopped. The smell hit him ten feet from the door—stale beer, cigarette smoke that had soaked into wood over decades.

"That's where we'll find answers," Roan said.

Evans looked at the place—the sort of joint that opened at nine a.m. for the graveyard shift workers.

"You think the killer drinks there?" Evans asked.

"No," Roan said. "But people who work this street do. And people who drink in dives talk."

Evans frowned. "You planning to stroll in and order a drink before noon?"

"I'm planning to ask questions," Roan said. "Different crowd. Different rules."

"You want to go in?"

"Yeah," Roan said. "But not dressed like a cop."

He shrugged off his jacket. Handed it to Evans. Rolled up his sleeves. The badge stayed clipped to his belt, but hidden now under his shirt. Midday. The crowd would be thin. Regulars only. Better for conversation.

Evans watched. "You're going alone?"

"You've got work to do," Roan said. "Ariel's alibi. The church. Talk to the priest, the sacristan—anyone who might've seen Ariel at Mass at six o'clock in the morning."

"You think his story's garbage?"

"I think he's got fresh cuts, Scripture on his walls, and a sister in the ground," Roan said. "That's enough to chase until the story holds or breaks."

Evans nodded. Closed his notepad. "What about the mystery man? The one Paola described?"

"That's what I'm here for," Roan said. "Someone in that bar has seen him. Or heard about him."

Evans hesitated, gripping the jacket. "Roan, you're walking into a dive bar at midday. News of Aguilar's body already ran through this strip before sunrise."

"Maybe that's why they'll talk," Roan said. "Scared people spill faster than calm ones." He jerked his chin towards the bar's neon. "If they're still here, I'll find them."

Evans blew out a breath, looking south again. "You're not subtle. You walk in there, half of Dixie'll know before lunch."

"Subtle doesn't get me answers. But if Camila was seen walking this strip, someone saw her."

Evans studied him for a moment. "You sure you want to go alone?"

"I'm sure I don't want you there," Roan said. "Cop in a suit changes the dynamic."

Evans paused, then nodded. "I'll check missing persons, too. Asian female, early twenties, last two months."

"Good," Roan said. "

Evans walked back to the Explorer. Climbed in. Started the engine.

Roan watched him pull out into traffic. The Explorer merged south, heading towards Federal Highway and the church where Ariel claimed he'd prayed at six a.m., while Julia Aguilar lay across the street from his apartment.

The Explorer disappeared into the distance.

Roan pulled his phone. Texted Rocca:

> Need camera footage from the Marathon station on Dixie near Southern. Last two months.

The reply came fast:

> That's a lot of footage.

Roan typed back:

> Focus on late afternoon/evening. Camila or an Asian girl on the street.

Then:

> Got it.

Roan pocketed his phone.

Heat pressed down. His shirt stuck to his back. Sweat beaded at his temples. The asphalt shimmered.

The pattern was there. Visible now. Camila worked in the diner.

The mystery man came for lunch. Ellen saw Camila and the Asian girl walking this same stretch at night. Aguilar dumped down the road.

Everything connected. One street. One hunting ground.

He walked towards Lucky's. The music grew louder—Lynyrd Skynyrd bleeding into the afternoon heat.

Roan pushed open the door and stepped inside.

CHAPTER

21

THE CHURCH SAT BACK from Federal Highway, old stone and stained glass half-hidden by palms that hadn't been trimmed in years. Evans pulled the Explorer into the parking lot—cracked asphalt, faded lines, only three other cars scattered across the spaces. Early afternoon. Quiet. No birds. No traffic. Just the palm fronds rustling.

He climbed out. Heat hit him first, then the smell: jasmine from somewhere nearby, car exhaust from the street, and underneath it all, something older. Incense maybe. Or just the weight of a building that had stood through hurricanes and heat for longer than he'd been alive.

The church was small, Spanish colonial style. White stone darkened by mold and rain. A wooden door stood open, propped with a brick. No sign. No welcome mat. Just the door and the darkness beyond it.

Evans walked towards it. His shoes crunched on gravel. Somewhere a bird called, sharp and high. The palms rustled in a breeze he couldn't feel.

He stepped through the door into cool shadow.

Inside, the air changed. Cooler. Heavier. The smell of incense was more pungent here—something sweet and burnt at the same time. Candles flickered near the altar, small flames that didn't do much against the dimness. Stained glass windows let in colored light—blues and reds and golds that pooled on wooden pews worn smooth by decades of bodies.

Evans felt the weight of the space—conducting a murder investigation in a house of God. The irony wasn't lost on him.

The ceiling arched high. Wooden beams crossed overhead, dark with age. Stations of the cross lined the walls, each one a small painting of suffering. Christ carrying the cross. Christ falling. Christ was nailed to the cross.

Evans stood just inside the door, letting his eyes adjust. The place felt empty but not abandoned. Someone kept the candles lit. Someone swept the floors.

A sound came from the front—soft, rhythmic. Footsteps maybe. Or the scrape of something being moved.

Evans walked forward. His footsteps echoed despite the carpet runner down the center aisle. The pews stood in perfect rows on either side of the aisle—hymnals tucked in the backs. Kneelers folded up.

At the front, near the altar, a man knelt. Old. White hair. Black shirt and collar. Priest.

Evans stopped a few pews back. "Father?"

The man turned. Seventy maybe. Lined face. Pale eyes that had seen a lot and forgotten nothing. He rose slowly, knees creaking, and turned to face Evans fully.

"Can I help you?" His voice was soft. Accented. Cuban maybe. Or Puerto Rican.

Evans pulled his badge. "Detective Evans. Palm Beach Sheriff's Office. I need to ask you some questions."

The priest looked at the badge. Didn't flinch. Didn't look surprised. "About?"

"A young man who may have attended Mass here. Early this morning."

The priest nodded slowly. "Come. We can speak in the sacristy."

The sacristy was small. Stone walls. A wooden table. Shelves lined with vestments—green, white, purple—folded and stacked like they mattered. A sink in the corner. A window that looked out on the parking lot. A clock ticked somewhere. Water dripped from a tap in the corner sink.

The priest gestured to a chair. Evans sat. The priest stayed standing, hands folded in front of him.

"What is this about?" the priest asked.

"I need to verify whether someone was here. Six a.m. Mass. This morning."

"We have six a.m. Mass every day," the priest said. "Sunday is no different."

"How many people attend?"

"At six?" The priest thought. "Five. Maybe ten. The faithful. The ones who come before work. Before the world wakes up."

"Do you remember a young man? Early twenties. Thin build. Dark hair. Bandage on his wrist."

The priest's eyes narrowed.

"Yes," the priest said. "I remember him."

Evans pulled out his notepad. "What do you remember?"

The priest was quiet for a moment. Then: "He came in late after Mass had started. Sat in the back. Didn't take communion. Didn't kneel when the others knelt. Didn't pray. Just sat staring at the crucifix like he was waiting for an answer that wouldn't come."

"What time did he leave?"

"Not straight away. After Mass ended, he went to the confessional."

Evans looked up. "He confessed?"

"He sat in the confessional," the priest said. "I don't know if he confessed."

"What do you mean?"

The priest walked to the window. Looked out at the parking lot. The colored light shifted as clouds moved outside. Blue became shadow, red faded to rust.

"I waited. I sat in my side of the booth. I could hear him breathing. But he didn't speak. After ten minutes, he left."

"Just left?"

"He lit a candle. Then he left."

Evans noted this. "Which candle did he light?"

"The vigil candles. Near Our Lady. He knelt there for several minutes before leaving."

"What time was this?"

"Six-thirty. Maybe six-forty. I'm not certain."

Evans reviewed his notes. Timeline worked. The church was one mile from Ariel's apartment. Walking distance, barely, but doable if he left at five-thirty. If Ariel was here by six, sitting through Mass, then sitting in the confessional—

"You're sure it was him?" Evans asked.

"I'm sure," the priest said.

"How can you be sure?"

The priest turned from the window. Looked at Evans directly. "Young man, early twenties, thin, dark hair. Hollow-eyed. Looked like he hadn't slept." He paused. "Because he sat in that pew like he was waiting for God to strike him down. And when God didn't, he went to the confessional."

"Did you notice anything else about him?"

"He had a bandage on his wrist. Kept touching it."

Evans' pen stopped. "You've seen him before?"

The priest hesitated. "Yes."

"When?"

"Wednesday evening. We have a young adult group. Bible study, fellowship." The priest's mouth tightened. "He came once. About a month ago."

"Just once?"

"Just once."

Evans waited.

The priest sighed. "He arrived early. Stood outside the parish hall for fifteen minutes before he went in. Like he was working up the courage, I was in the church. I could see him through the window."

"What happened?"

"He went inside. Stayed maybe five minutes. Then he left."

"Why?"

The priest's eyes darkened. "The group leader said Ariel had been... unwelcome, that it wasn't the right time for him to join them. Given his family situation." He paused. "I disagreed. I should have stopped him from leaving that night. The youth group. But I thought he'd come back." The priest's eyes went distant. "They rarely do."

Evans' chest tightened. "So he tried to come back to the church community, and they turned him away."

"Yes."

"And this morning?"

"This morning he looked worse." The priest moved back to the table. "Like he'd stopped sleeping. Stopped eating."

Evans underlined something in his notes. "Did he seem dangerous? Violent?"

The priest was quiet. "We're all capable, Detective. Under the right circumstances. But that boy? He seemed capable of breaking. Not of breaking others."

Part of Evans wanted the story to break. Clean suspect, clear motive. But watching the priest's concern, he wasn't sure what he hoped for anymore.

"Do you think he hurt someone?" the priest asked quietly.

Evans didn't answer straight away. "I'm investigating a homicide. His sister."

The priest closed his eyes briefly. "Dios mío."

"So you can see why I need to know if he was here."

"He was here," the priest said. "From six until about six-thirty or six-forty. I'm certain."

"Were there others at Mass who might have seen him?"

"Three or four. Mrs. Rodriguez. Mr. Garcia. The usual morning faithful."

Evans made a final note. "Thank you, Father."

The priest opened his eyes. "Detective. That boy needs help."

The sacristan confirmed the priest's account—she'd seen Ariel lighting a candle around six-thirty.

Evans walked back through the church. The candles still flickered. The stained glass still pooled light on the pews.

Ariel had been here. The timeline checked. He'd sat through Mass. Gone to the confessional but hadn't spoken. Lit a candle. Left.

Proof he was where he said he was.

Sitting in silence. Unable or unwilling to confess. Grief? Guilt? Or just a kid so broken he couldn't find words for what he carried?

Evans stepped out into the sunlight. The heat outside hit like a wall. After the church's cool stone, it felt aggressive, angry. He walked to the Explorer, climbed in. Sat for a moment with the door open and the engine off.

Evans sat in the Explorer, engine off, door open. Let the information settle. Ariel's story held. He didn't lie about being in church. But something about the boy sitting silent in that confessional wouldn't let go.

Ariel's story checks out. He was at church this morning.

Evans pulled out his phone and tapped Roan.

It rang three times before Roan picked up—the background noise was overwhelming, with the sounds of traffic, voices, and music.

"Yeah."

"It's me," Evans said. "Alibi checks out."

"Talk."

"Ariel was at the church. Six a.m. Mass. Priest and sacristan both confirm it. He came in late, sat through Mass, went to the confessional, lit a candle, and left around six-thirty."

Roan paused. "He confess?"

"Sat in the booth. Didn't say anything. Priest said he just sat there breathing for ten minutes, then left."

"Huh."

"Timeline works," Evans said. "He was at church by six."

"Unless he had help," Roan said.

Evans hadn't thought of that. "You think someone else dumped her while he established an alibi?"

"Anything's possible until it isn't," Roan said. "But yeah. Timeline checks out. He was exactly where he said he'd be."

"There's something else," Evans said. "The priest said Ariel looked like he was waiting for lightning to strike. Said the boy tried to join their youth group a month ago, and they turned him away."

Silence on the line.

"So we've got a kid with fresh cuts, Scripture on his walls, a dead sister, and a story that puts him at church."

"Yeah."

"That's a thin win," Roan said. "But it's a win. He was there. Doesn't clear him completely, but at least he's not lying to us about that."

"You want me to bring him back in?"

"Not yet," Roan said. "Let him sit. If he's guilty of something, he'll crack. If he's just a kid drowning in grief, pushing him won't help."

"What do you want me to do?"

"Write it up. Full report. Interview notes. Timeline. Everything the priest said. Then go home."

Evans blinked. "Home?"

"Yeah. Home. To Clara and the kids. You've been running since this morning. Take a break. I've got Dixie covered."

"Any luck on missing persons?"

"Nothing yet. Rocca's still checking."

"You sure?"

"I'm sure," Roan said. "Ariel's not going anywhere. The older guy's still out there. I'm working the street. You go home. Be with your family. We'll regroup tomorrow."

Evans nodded even though Roan couldn't see him. "Yeah. All right."

"Good work today," Roan said. "Alibi's solid. That matters."

"Cheers."

"Now go home."

The line went dead.

Evans sat in the Explorer, phone still in his hand. The church sat behind him, quiet and heavy. The highway hummed ahead.

The highway opened ahead. Evans thought about Ariel in that confessional—ten minutes of silence. And wondered what the boy couldn't bring himself to say.

He started the engine. Pulled out of the parking lot and turned towards home.

In ten minutes, he'd be there. Clara would be in the kitchen.

Matthew would be playing Minecraft or reading about new Scotty Cameron putters. Emily would be reading, tucked into the corner of the sofa.

A different world from Ariel's. A world with people who wanted him there.

He pressed the accelerator, heading home.

CHAPTER

22

THE DOOR to Lucky's was still propped open when Roan stepped inside. Cool air mixed with the funk of old beer and fried onions. A guitar wailed from hidden speakers—Skynyrd maybe, the solo from *Free Bird* stretching on. The light was dim, a yellow hue, everything coated in decades of nicotine residue that no amount of cleaning could remove.

TVs mounted on the walls showed ESPN. One had a Dolphins game on. Miami was down by two touchdowns in the first quarter. A loss you saw coming from kickoff.

Roan stopped just inside, letting his eyes adjust. The bar ran along the right side, scarred wood worn smooth where elbows rested. Five stools, three occupied. Bartender at the far end, thick arms, greying beard, eyes that never stopped moving even when his hands did.

Booths lined the left wall. One had three women, all in their mid-twenties, all dressed as if they had just come from work or were heading there soon. Tight jeans. Low tops. Too much makeup for early afternoon. Afternoon regulars, waiting for their evening trade. They watched Roan walk in. Didn't look away when he looked back.

Two more booths had single occupants. Old man in a Marlins cap. A younger guy in construction gear, with dust still on his jeans.

Pool table in the back. No one was playing.

Roan walked to the bar. Sat two stools down from the nearest patron. The bartender looked up. Didn't smile.

"What do you need?"

"Miller Lite," Roan said.

The bartender pulled one from the cooler. Popped the cap. Set it down without a coaster.

"Four bucks."

Roan dropped a five on the bar. "Keep it."

The bartender took it. Moved back to the far end where he'd been polishing glasses that already looked clean.

Roan sipped the beer. Cold. Cheap. Exactly what it needed to be.

On the TV, the Dolphins threw an interception. Ice rattled in glasses. The TV announcer's voice rose and fell. The bar's soundtrack played on, indifferent. Nobody cared.

An hour passed. Roan watched. Listened. The afternoon crowd thinned slightly, but the regulars stayed put.

He pulled his badge from under his shirt. Let it sit on the bar next to the beer.

The bartender saw it. Kept polishing.

"Two girls dead," Roan said. "One dump near here."

"Heard about it." The bartender set down the glass, picked up another. "Don't know them."

"Older guy. Black hair. Pays cash. Regular."

"That's half the customers."

The bartender stopped polishing. Looked at Roan directly. "You asking if I run that kind of place?"

"I'm asking if you've seen someone like that."

"No," the bartender said. Flat. Final. "I haven't."

Roan held his gaze for a moment. Then nodded. Sat back. Drank his beer.

Then, Roan moved quickly through the other patrons. The old man in the Marlins cap muttered something about happy girls disappearing, then went back to his beer. The construction worker shrugged and said that everyone on the strip was where they shouldn't be. He jerked his chin towards the women. "They know the street better than anyone."

Roan walked to their booth.

They watched him approach. One—blonde, early twenties, heavy eyeliner—smirked. The second—brunette, older, mid twenties—

leaned back, arms crossed. The third—redhead, youngest, nervous hands—just stared.

"Mind if I sit?"

The blonde shrugged. "Depends what you're buying."

Roan slid into the booth across from them. "Just conversation."

"Cops don't usually want conversation," the brunette said. Jersey accent thick on her words.

Roan held out his phone for them to see Camila's photo. Should've brought Aguilar's, too, but her face was all over the news already. If these women had seen her, they'd remember. "You know her?"

The three women looked. The brunette shook her head first. "No."

The redhead glanced at it. Looked away fast. "No." Southern drawl, soft but unmistakable.

The blonde studied it longer. Then shook her head.

Roan pocketed the phone. "How about an older guy? Black hair. Nice clothes. Drives something expensive. Pays cash."

The three women exchanged looks.

"That's a lot of guys," the brunette said.

"This one might've had a thing for college-age girls."

But the redhead shifted. Looked down at her hands. The redhead wanted to talk—Roan could see it in how her hands shook, how her eyes kept darting to the door. Fear and something else are fighting each other. Guilt, maybe. Or grief for someone lost.

"There's... there's talk," the redhead said quietly.

"Talk about what?"

"Girls. Goin' off with a man. And not comin' back."

The brunette cut her eyes to the redhead, then leaned forward. "You don't know what you're talkin' about."

"When did you hear this?" Roan asked the redhead.

"Couple months ago. Maybe longer."

"Did anyone say what he looked like?"

The redhead shook her head. "Just that he was... normal. Like he didn't stand out."

The brunette grabbed the redhead's arm. "Come on."

"Stop asking," the brunette said to Roan. Her eyes were hard, but her voice cracked slightly. "You're not gonna find answers here."

As the redhead passed, Roan let his hand drop low. His card slid between her fingers. She didn't look down, just kept walking. But he saw her palm close round it.

The blonde stayed.

"You want to know where girls go?" she said. "Follow the street." She walked away.

"Follow the street." Do not follow him. Follow the street itself. The geography. Where girls walked, where they worked, where they disappeared.

Roan sat alone in the booth. On the TV, the Dolphins turned the ball over again.

Outside, shadows lengthened. The A/C was losing its battle against the heat. Even inside, with the sun setting, the air felt thick. The light changed. The yellow interior lights looked harsher as daylight faded outside. Shadows in corners deepened.

Roan moved to a booth by the window. Better sight line to the street. The bartender watched him move, but didn't stop him.

Through the window, Roan watched the street change. Afternoon shifting to evening. Traffic was thinning slightly but never stopping.

A dark sedan slowed near Siam Massage and pulled into the small parking lot beside it. A man got out in a suit, briefcase, and looked like he'd come from an office. Didn't look around. Just walked straight to the door. Disappeared inside.

Siam Massage. Roan had driven past it a dozen times this week. Purple neon, tinted windows, always one of those signs advertising "therapeutic massage" that meant something else entirely.

Ten minutes later, a different man left. Older. Jeans and a button-down. He looked around before getting in his truck. Drove away fast.

The purple neon flickered. On. Off. On.

Roan's back ached from the booth. His eyes felt gritty. The beer smell was getting to him. Or maybe it was just the smell of too many hours in one place, watching and waiting.

Roan pulled out his notepad. Flipped back through the pages. Days of notes. Interviews. Timelines. Evidence.

He stopped on a page from yesterday. Pérez's name at the top. Notes from their phone conversation.

School. Tuition. Certificate.

He flipped forward. Back. Looking for context. There. Buried in a note from Pérez.

Massage therapy certificate. Palm Beach State.

Massage therapy certificate—Pérez had mentioned it in passing, just another line item in Camila's background. But they'd never connected it to actual employment.

Roan went still.

He looked up. Through the window. At the purple neon flickering half a block away.

Siam Massage.

Massage therapy certificate. Palm Beach State. The pieces didn't just fall together—they crashed together, loud and obvious. How had he missed it?

Camila wasn't just working at the diner. She had a massage certificate. She could've been working at the parlor. Extra money. Cash under the table.

The timeline fits. Paola said Camila stopped stressing about tuition six months ago, right when she would've finished her certificate, right when she could've started working.

The Asian girl Ellen saw. If Camila worked at Siam, maybe the other girl did too. Maybe that's where they met.

Camila was trying to pay for school. Probably thought massage therapy was legit work. Probably didn't realize until she was in too deep what kind of establishment Siam actually was.

Roan's jaw tightened.

Everything had connected to there—one door with purple neon and tinted windows.

Camila worked there. The older man went there. The money flowed from there.

Roan closed the notepad. His hands were steady, but his pulse kicked up. This was it.

He pulled his phone. Texted Evans:

Might have something. Update tomorrow.

He finished his beer. Left cash on the bar. The bartender took it without acknowledgement.

Roan stood. Walked to the door. Stepped out into the night.

The air was cooler now. Damp. The streetlights buzzed overhead. Traffic hummed on Dixie.

And half a block down, Siam Massage pulsed purple neon into the dark.

Posing as a client, not something he'd done before. Not something he wanted to do. But if Camila had died because of that place, he needed to see inside.

Going in alone was stupid. He knew it. But waiting meant the trail going cold, meant whoever killed Camila and Julia walked free longer, destroying evidence, and meant more girls would turn up dead.

He'd need a story: why he was there and what he wanted. The massage parlor probably had cameras, definitely had someone watching who came and went—one chance to look around before they got suspicious.

Roan started walking towards it. Not as a cop. As a customer.

CHAPTER

23

Evans U-turned on Lucerne, heading back to Lake Avenue; the signal was ticking in the quiet cabin. The Explorer rolled through the turn lane, then cut east toward the beach. He knew he should've kept west, but his gut gnawed. Roan had said it (sometimes you return twice). Evans would handle the site revisit alone—fresh eyes, a new perspective.

Roan's words echoed: sometimes the second visit reveals what the first one missed.

Lake Worth Beach opened up at the end of the causeway. The parking lot's puddles from last night's rain threw back harsh reflections. Families spilled out of vans, dragging coolers and towels, laughter rising over the thud of car doors.

Twenty, maybe thirty families spread across the beach. Not crowded—weekday afternoon. At one in the morning, it would've been deserted.

Evans pulled into the parking lot. The spot where Camila's body had been found two days ago. He hadn't been here for the initial scene processing—that had been Roan and the first responders. But everything looked different in daylight.

Kids ran towards the water. A dog chased a Frisbee. Towels spread across the sand. Waves crashed beyond the beach. Kids shrieked. A radio played somewhere—reggae, incongruously cheerful—the soundtrack of everyday life where death had visited.

Evans climbed out. Heat pressed down. The heat felt thick, humid. Sweat stuck his shirt to his back. At one a.m., it would've been cooler but still warm. Florida never really cooled. The barbecue smoke mixed with salt air and coconut sunscreen. Beach smell. Summer smell. Not the scent of murder.

He walked towards the pavilion. Towards the spot where Camila Morales had been left two nights ago. The yellow tape was gone. Forensics had cleared the scene. Life had moved on.

Last night, he'd gone home to Clara and the kids. Normal life. This morning, back to this. The contrast never stopped being jarring.

He pulled out his phone and started taking photos. The blind spot between cameras. The sight lines. The distances.

Evans stood at the north gate near Lake Avenue. Simple bar gate, never locked. He traced the route with his eyes—a wide curve through the parking lot, avoiding the camera's field of view. Then he walked to the south gate near South Ocean Boulevard. Same approach, reversed.

Evans pulled his notebook. Drew a rough sketch of the gates, the cameras, and the approach routes.

North gate, south gate—mirror images. A delivery truck rumbled past on Lake Avenue. If that had been there two nights ago, the killer would've used the south entrance instead. Options. Alternatives. No single point of failure.

Evans' jaw tightened as he traced the blind spot between the cameras with his finger. A strip of asphalt that neither camera covered. Wide enough to drive through. Wide enough to stop. Wide enough to place a body.

The killer had scouted this. Knew which cameras worked, which didn't. The pier cam had been broken for months—the city knew, and so did he.

Brandon's Barbeque trailer sat near the pavilion, smoke rising from the pit. The pit-boss stood behind the counter—six-three, massive shoulders, cheeks red with heat.

"You're back," the pit-boss said, recognizing Evans.

"Quick question."

The pit-boss pulled a slab of meat from the warming tray. Set it on the cutting board. "This about that girl? The one they pulled off the beach? Not sure I know anything."

"I know. Just want to confirm a few things."

The pit-boss nodded. Picked up his knife—blade chipped and worn thin, handle wrapped in tape that had seen better days. He steadied the meat with his right hand and started slicing. Clean cuts. Rhythmic. An artful motion you didn't think about anymore.

"You were here that night? When the girl was found?" Evans asked.

"I was here. But I don't work nights. Pack up between eight and nine. Head home."

"Every night?"

"Every night." The pit-boss kept cutting. Didn't look up.

"You see anything unusual? Anyone hanging around?"

"Nothing. Place clears out after I leave. Gets quiet."

"No cars? No people?"

"Not that I saw." Slice. Another piece fell away. He arranged them on a fresh sheet of foil. "Oceanside is the only thing open."

A gull landed near the trailer. Hopped closer. The pit-boss ignored it. Kept working.

"You serve a lot of people during the day?" Evans asked.

"Enough. Lunch rush. Afternoon crowd. Regulars."

"Ever notice anyone who seemed... off? Out of place?"

The pit-boss finally looked up. "Detective, I see hundreds of people a week. Tourists. Locals. Families. Teens. Old folks. They all look the same after a while. I'm here to serve food. Not study faces."

Evans nodded. Fair point. "Thanks for your time."

The pit-boss went back to his work. Wrapped the foil. Set it in the warmer. Pulled another slab.

A lifeguard leaned out of the nearby tower. "Detective! The sand rakers combed everything at five this morning. You won't find prints."

Evans waved acknowledgment. The lifeguard added, "Pier cam's still broken. Has been for months."

Evans moved from the gates to the dump site itself, mentally reconstructing the sequence.

He pulled up the crime scene photos on his phone. Compared the angles. The positioning. Everything matched the report, but seeing it in daylight added context.

Evans stood where Camila had been found. Trying to pay for school. He thought about Matthew. About hoping his son never encountered someone like this killer.

Camila Morales. The name deserved more than clinical analysis. She'd been a person. Had hopes. Had been trying to make something of herself. And someone had taken that.

The spot wasn't hidden—visible from the beach, the bathrooms, and the parking lot. But at one a.m., no one would be looking. The killer wanted her found quickly when families arrived in the morning.

Evans walked the route from the blind spot to the dump site. Counted steps. Timed it. Four minutes, twenty seconds. With a body, probably five. Manageable.

Park in the blind spot. Carry the body twenty feet. Position her carefully—not dumped, not thrown. Arranged. Then drive out through the opposite gate.

The asphalt showed nothing. Two days of traffic had erased any tire marks. But the pattern remained—two routes in, two routes out.

The flexibility made the killer harder to predict. He could adapt to conditions, choose his route based on traffic, witnesses, and instinct. That kind of operational awareness came from experience. Probably not his first time working a dump site with multiple exits. At least, that's what the pattern suggested.

Unless he was wrong. Unless this was beginner's luck, not experience. But his gut said otherwise.

Evans walked back to the Explorer, his understanding crystallizing. The killer wasn't just smart—he was practiced. This wasn't his first time working a dump site with multiple exit routes.

Evans climbed into the Explorer and started the engine. The radio crackled with dispatch chatter. He pulled out of the lot, heading west on the causeway.

The beach shrank in his rearview mirror. Orange afternoon light slanted across the water.

The pattern was clear now. Smart, flexible, experienced. They were building a profile now—not just smart, but tactically aware. Adaptable. Experienced. A killer who'd done this before. And would do it again unless they stopped him.

CHAPTER

24

Roan walked south on Dixie. Four beers over two hours at Lucky's had softened the edges but sharpened his focus. Just drunk enough to seem like every other customer. Not drunk enough to miss details. The air hung humid and thick, heavy with the fumes of gasoline from the nearby station.

The strip glowed brighter than it had in daylight. Siam Massage sat a block ahead, its purple neon barely visible through the night. He could make out the drawn curtains, the darkened windows. A place trying to stay invisible.

He'd stopped at an ATM after the bar, pulled two hundred in twenties. Anticipated this.

He passed a phone-repair shop, a dry cleaner with missing letters —D Y LEA ERS—and a check-cashing place with a queue at the ATM. Two men stood too close to each other, shoulders tight. Roan kept moving.

Siam's violet glow washed the sidewalk as he approached. A hand-painted lotus curled in one corner of the window. Plastic bamboo crowded the other. The door had a brass bell on a bent screw, tarnished from years of handling.

Roan stopped at the entrance. He pushed his badge and gun deeper into the small of his back, covered by jacket and sweat-damp shirt. Let his face go neutral. No backup. No wire. No warrant. If this went wrong, no one would know until tomorrow. Stupid. But necessary—just him walking into a massage parlor that might hold the only witness who could ID Camila's killer.

He pulled the door and went in.

The bell jingled, sharp and small.

Inside was dim and surprisingly cool—a window A/C unit rattling somewhere, fighting against the humidity that seeped through every crack. A counter straight ahead. Fake bamboo poles in one corner, dusty. A faded waterfall poster on the wall, edges curling. Another door waited behind the counter, paint chipped near the knob.

The air was thick with cheap jasmine incense and floral perfume that couldn't quite mask the sour smell underneath—old sweat and bleach and something organic.

A fan hummed weakly in the corner.

Roan stood just inside, eyes adjusting. Counter. Bell on the doorframe. Camera dome in the corner—dead or fake, he'd clocked it immediately. Shoe rack with two pairs of worn slippers. Cash box half-hidden under a towel. Details filed away.

After three seconds, the back door opened.

An older woman stepped out. Hair pulled back, dark with silver threads. Plain blouse, sleeves rolled, apron at the waist. Her gaze moved from his shoes to his face in one sweep.

"You look drunk," she said. Accent thick, consonants clipped—Thai, maybe Vietnamese. "You drunk?"

"No. I don't believe so."

Roan kept his voice steady, although it was slightly slurred. Tired man at the end of a long day.

She studied him—his hands for a wedding ring or cop calluses, past him to check he'd come alone, her weight shifting to her back foot.

"You want massage?" she asked. "Half hour? One hour?"

"Half hour."

A clock ticked behind the counter. The fan wheezed. A car passed outside, headlights sweeping yellow across the wall.

His heart kicked up. Sweat that wasn't just from humidity formed under his collar.

"A friend told me there was a Spanish girl here," Roan said. "Camila. Said she was good."

Her expression shifted. She glanced at the back door, then back to him.

"Not here. Not many days now."

Her tone was flat. Rehearsed.

Roan reached into his pocket and pulled out a fifty. Set it on the counter.

The woman's eyes dropped to the bill. Her jaw tightened. She didn't touch it.

She glanced at the back door again, longer this time. Calculating. A customer asking for a specific girl by name—suspicious. But refusing meant attention, questions. The fifty made the choice easier.

When she looked back, something had changed. Not sympathy. Calculation.

Her hand moved towards the fifty, then stopped. "Spanish girl have friend. Asian girl. Very pretty. You like."

Her fingers slid the fifty off the counter and tucked it away.

Roan gave one quick nod. "Sure."

"Seventy."

He laid the bills on the counter—two twenties, three tens. She slid them into an old metal cash box that clicked shut.

She motioned towards the back door.

The hallway was narrow and dim. Faded cream walls with water stains running down from the ceiling. Paint peeling near the ceiling line, showing white, then pink underneath. How many times had this place been painted over?

Doors lined both sides. Behind one, water ran steadily. Behind another, soft instrumental music played. Behind a third, muffled voices—a man's laugh cut short, then a woman speaking Korean or Mandarin.

Male voices through walls—at least two other customers. Maybe more. Mama-san plus however many workers. Numbers weren't in his favor.

The woman led him down the hall, her slippers whispering against worn carpet that showed concrete underneath in the traffic pattern.

At a T-junction, she turned right and stopped at a door near the end. Pushed it open.

Roan glanced left—another hallway, darker, one door at the end with light underneath. He filed it away and followed her.

The room was small. Eight by ten. A massage table in the center with a sheet washed nearly transparent. A folded towel, yellowed at the edges. A wobbly stool. A shelf with bottles—Sweet Almond Oil and others without labels, one with dried residue around the cap.

Worn linoleum, once white, now grey with ground-in dirt that no mopping could remove.

Dim light from a corner lamp—forty watts maybe, shade yellowed, casting everything in sickly amber. A crack ran corner to corner across the ceiling like a river on a map. Above the table, a water stain that looked like dried blood.

"You wait here. She come."

The woman studied him, as if she wanted to say more. She wanted to warn him. Or warn the girl. Or maybe just wanted him gone. Her eyes said something her mouth wouldn't.

Then she stepped back and pulled the door halfway closed.

Her footsteps faded.

Roan stood in the center, taking it in. He positioned himself where he could see the door—one exit. The window is too small to climb through. If things went bad, the only way out was through.

Posing as a customer looking for sexual services. Line he'd crossed before but never got comfortable with—the things we do.

Thin walls—he could hear movement next door, water running, a door closing. A male voice through the wall, muffled.

Roan used the wait. Memorized the layout. Counted sounds. Built a mental map of the building. A professional habit that never stopped.

Through the wall, he tracked a transaction: the door opening, voices negotiating, the door closing, the rhythmic sounds of a professional massage, water running for cleanup, footsteps in the hallway, and the outer bell ringing faintly as someone left.

Ten minutes. Maybe twelve.

Sweat formed on his neck. He was minutes from meeting the

Asian girl who'd been with Camila. Who might know the older man. Who might know where to find him.

Or who might panic when a stranger asked about her dead friend.

Get her talking. Get a name. Get agreement to meet somewhere safe. Then get out before mama-san gets suspicious or someone else shows up.

Footsteps in the hallway. Lighter than before. Coming closer.

Roan let his hands hang loose, face neutral. Not a cop. Not a threat. Just a tired man.

The door pushed open, and Roan had about thirty seconds before she screamed, ran, or called for help. Thirty seconds to convince her he wasn't a threat. Thirty seconds to get the truth about Camila.

CHAPTER

25

THE DOOR UNLOCKED with a soft click. Evans pushed through. It stuck on the swollen frame, then gave with a low groan that carried straight to the kitchen. He set his keys in the bowl by habit.

The mail sat unopened on the side table. Clara's sneakers were by the door, one tipped over—the ordinary debris of ordinary life.

Garlic and pasta. Clara's cooking. The TV was on in the living room. A baseball game, Mets. Matthew's voice came from somewhere deeper in the house.

Evans stepped inside. Closed the door behind him. Locked it.

He rolled his shoulders and loosened his tie. He should've taken off the badge and gun. Gone to the bedroom, locked them in the safe. But what if Roan called? What if they got a break? The badge and gun stayed heavy at his hip. Camila Morales' killer was still out there— another girl fitting the pattern.

"Dad?"

Matthew's voice from the hallway.

Evans turned. "Yeah. I'm home."

Matthew appeared in the doorway. His hair was like Evans', but he had Clara's eyes, green with gold flecks in certain light.

He wore gym shorts and a T-shirt. Barefoot. His shoulders slumped. He didn't meet Evans' eyes.

"How was practice?" Evans hung his jacket by the door.

Matthew shrugged. "Fine." His hands stayed in his pockets.

"Fine good or fine bad?"

Another shrug.

Evans moved into the living room. Matthew followed but didn't sit. Just stood near the couch, hands in his pockets.

"Talk to me," Evans said.

Matthew looked at the floor. "It's nothing."

"Doesn't look like nothing."

Matthew exhaled. Sat on the arm of the couch.

"Some guys were talking," he said. "After practice."

Evans waited.

"They saw my clubs. Said they were old. Hand-me-downs." He looked up. "Which they are. They're cousin Ricky's from ten years ago."

Evans' jaw tightened. He sat down on the couch, leaned forward, elbows on his knees.

"What'd they say exactly?"

Matthew's jaw worked. "That I should get new ones. That mine look like they came from a garage sale. Jake said his dad just bought him a full set. TaylorMade. Two grand."

"Who's Jake?"

"Kid on the team. His dad's a lawyer."

"And he thinks that matters?"

Matthew didn't answer. Just picked at a thread on his shorts.

"What'd you say when they talked about your clubs?"

"Nothing."

"Nothing?"

"What was I supposed to say? 'Actually, my dad's a cop and we can't afford two-thousand-dollar clubs'?"

"You could've."

"Right. Then I'm the poor kid AND the cop's kid."

Evans crossed to Matthew and put a hand on his shoulder. Matthew didn't pull away, but didn't lean in either. The distance between them felt measured in miles.

"You hit the ball straight?" Evans asked. "Your swing. Center of the face?"

"Yeah. Mostly."

"Ball goes further than the other boys?"

"Yeah."

"Then the club doesn't matter. Equipment doesn't make the shot. You do."

Matthew's expression didn't change. Still deflated.

"I know that," he said. "But they don't."

"So?"

"So it's embarrassing."

Evans nodded. "I get that."

"Listen," Evans said. "Next weekend, you and me. We'll hit the range. Work on that swing. And if those kids keep talking, you just keep hitting straight. Eventually, they'll shut up."

Something eased in Matthew's face. Not all the way. But some.

"Yeah?"

"Yeah."

Matthew stood. "Okay."

"Okay."

Matthew started towards the hall, then stopped.

"Dad?"

"Yeah?"

"Thanks."

"Anytime."

Matthew disappeared down the hall. A door closed. Music started playing, bass-heavy.

Evans sat alone in the living room. The TV droned on.

Camila Morales. Julia Aguilar. Girls who didn't come home.

Then Matthew. Golf clubs and locker-room jabs.

Different problems. Both real.

He stood and headed towards the kitchen, but stopped. Emily first.

Her door was cracked open. Light spilled into the hallway. Family photos lined the wall. Matthew's soccer team from three years ago. Emily's school picture—missing front teeth. Their wedding photo, Evans and Clara, young and certain. When had that certainty eroded?

Evans knocked.

"Em?"

"Yeah?"

Evans pushed the door open. She sat cross-legged on her bed, textbook in her lap, highlighter in hand. Eight. Brown hair like Clara's, pulled back in a ponytail.

She looked up. Smiled. "Hey, Daddy."

"Hey. Homework?"

"Social studies. We have a test tomorrow."

"You ready?"

"Think so." She set down the highlighter. "Did Matthew tell you about practice?"

"He did."

"Those guys are jerks."

"They are."

Emily picked at her textbook page. "I told him it doesn't matter. That he's better than them, anyway."

"That was good of you." She shrugged. "He's my brother."

Evans leaned against the doorframe. Eight years old. Growing up.

"How was your day?" he asked.

"Good. We had art. Mrs. Brown let me work on my painting."

"The one with the beach?"

"Yeah."

"Can I see it when you're done?"

"Sure."

Emily looked at him closely.

"You okay, Dad?"

Evans blinked. "Yeah. Why?"

"You look tired."

"Long day."

"Mom says you're working a hard case."

"Yeah. But it's okay."

Emily nodded.

For half a second—Emily on the sand. No. Camila in the sand. Not moving. Blue lips. Hair tangled with seaweed, she'd been someone's daughter, too. Someone had watched her play. Someone had—

He forced the image away, but it clung like a wet cloth.

His hand tightened on the doorframe.

"Dad?" Emily's voice changed. "Why are you looking at me like that?"

"Dad?" Smaller now. "You're scaring me."

He stepped into the room. "Sorry. Em. Sometimes my job gets in my head."

"The dead girl?" Emily asked.

Eight years old. Too smart.

"Yeah."

Emily studied him with dark eyes—his eyes. "Mom says you're not sleeping."

"Mom talks too much."

"She's worried about you."

"I'm okay, Em."

"You don't look okay."

Emily set her textbook aside. Got up. Wrapped her arms around him.

"It's okay to be sad about sad things," she said into his chest. "Mrs. Parker told us that."

Evans held her. "Mrs. Parker's a smart lady."

"She is." Emily pulled back and studied his face. "You'll catch the bad person, right?"

"That's the plan."

"Good." She went back to her bed. "Because bad people should go to jail. And because you look sad all the time now."

Evans pulled the door closed. Not all the way. Just how she liked it.

The kitchen smelled of garlic, butter, and baking bread. Clara stood at the stove, stirring a pot, hair in a loose ponytail. She wore jeans and one of his old T-shirts, sleeves rolled past her elbows.

She looked over when he came in. Her smile faded.

"What?" Evans asked.

"You look exhausted."

"Long day."

Clara continued stirring. "Did you pick up Emily's prescription?"

The prescription. The pharmacy. The sticky note on his dashboard. "Shit."

"Daniel." Clara set down the spoon. "She needed that tonight."

"I'll go now—"

"The pharmacy closes at seven. It's seven-fifteen."

Clara kept stirring, not looking at him.

"She needed her medicine, Daniel. She was coughing all night. I asked you this morning. You said you'd do it."

"I forgot."

"You forgot your daughter."

The floor seemed to shift under him. His hand tightened on the edge of the table.

"I'm sorry," Evans said.

"I know."

"I'll get it first thing tomorrow."

"She has a cough. She needs it tonight."

"I know."

Clara turned off the burner.

"Dinner's ready," she said. "Pasta. Emily ate already."

"I talked to Matthew. About practice."

"Good." She pulled plates from the cabinet. Set them on the table. Two spots.

Evans sat. Clara moved through the kitchen with practiced efficiency.

Rigatoni in red sauce. Garlic bread in a basket, still steaming. Clara had made his favorite. But he could barely taste it.

They ate in silence. Comfortable at first. Then heavier. The pasta was good. Clara was a good cook. But every bite sat heavily. Across from him, she ate mechanically, not looking up.

Clara took a sip of water.

"How's work?" she asked.

Evans didn't look up. "Same."

"Same good or same bad?"

He smiled. Faint. "Same."

Clara watched him.

"You're carrying something," she said.

He set down his fork. "It's fine."

"It's not."

The concern in her eyes. The exhaustion. Ready to catch him if he fell, but not willing to let him drag her down.

"I'll leave it outside," he said.

"Will you? Because you said that last week. And the week before."

"I'm trying."

"I know you're trying. But trying isn't enough anymore."

Clara set down her fork.

"I've been a cop's wife for seven years."

"I know."

"Do you? Because I don't think you know what that costs. What I've given up. The nights alone. The worry. The rescheduled holidays. I made peace with the shifts, the danger, the canceled plans. I made peace with all of it. But this—" She gestured at the space between them. "This is different. I didn't sign up to be married to a ghost."

The floor seemed to shift under him again.

"You're here." She gestured around the kitchen. "Physically here. But not present. You look at Emily—you're seeing that girl. You look at Matthew—you're thinking about the case."

"That's not—"

"You forgot Emily's prescription. You promised Matthew you'd be at his tournament last week. You missed it."

He had promised, looked Matthew in the eye.

But he hadn't shown up.

"Work ran—"

"Work always runs long." Clara's voice didn't rise. Just went dead. "And I understand that. But when you're home, you have to be home. Not halfway between."

"What do you want me to do?"

"Be here. Actually here. Or admit you can't and let me decide what comes next." She reached across the table. Put her hand on his. "Promise me you'll leave it at work. Because if you can't..." She didn't finish.

Evans stared at their hands. Hers soft. His rough.

A killer was out there. Right now. Maybe selecting his next victim. How could Evans stop thinking about it? How could he just turn it off? But Clara was right. If he couldn't, what did that mean for his marriage? For his kids? Was he willing to lose them to save strangers? Was that nobility or selfishness?

"I'll try," he said.

Clara pulled her hand back. "Trying isn't a promise."

She stood. Started clearing plates.

After dinner, Clara wiped the counters. Evans washed dishes—silence between them.

Emily's door was closed, music playing faintly. Matthew's too.

His phone buzzed. Text from Roan:

> Might have something. Update tomorrow.

Evans typed back:

> Good luck.

Then, he silenced the phone. Work could wait. Had to wait.

Technically, he was on call. Technically, he should keep the phone volume up and stay ready. But Clara's eyes said otherwise. He put it on vibrate. Compromise.

Clara hung the towel on the oven handle.

"I'm going to bed," she said.

"It's eight."

"I'm tired."

She walked down the hall. Their bedroom door closed.

Evans stood in the kitchen alone.

The bathroom door locked. Evans turned on the shower.

Hot water. Steam. He stood under the spray, head down.

The door opened. Closed. The lock turned.

The shower curtain pulled back. Clara stepped in. Water beaded on her skin.

She put her hands on his chest.

"Clara—"

Her finger pressed his lips.

She kissed him. Hard. Demanding.

Her hands moved to his face.

"You're slipping away," she said. Water streamed between them. "You're getting lost."

"I'm right here."

"No. You're not." Her thumb traced his jaw. "But I'm going to pull you back."

"I'm not giving up on you," she whispered against his neck. "But you have to meet me halfway."

She kissed him again. Her body pressed against his. Her nails dug into his shoulders.

He tried. Pulled her closer. Kissed her back.

But Evans couldn't turn it off. Camila Morales. Emily died in the sand. Clara's voice: Promise me. The case sat between them like a third person in the shower. And Clara felt it. She always did.

Clara pulled back.

She saw it. The distance. The wall.

Her eyes shifted. Not anger.

Resignation.

She stepped out. Wrapped a towel around herself and left without a word. Evans heard the bedroom door close. Not slam. Close. Quietly. Definitively. Somehow, that was worse.

Evans stood there. Water cascading.

He found her in bed, facing away, back to him like a wall.

"Clara?"

Her breathing was too deliberate. Pretending to sleep.

He lay down. Kept a distance between them. Used to, they'd sleep tangled together. Now there was a foot of empty mattress. Might as well be a canyon.

"I love you," she said. "But I can't do this again. Whatever happened in Wellington—I can't watch that twice."

Wellington. The case that had broken him three years ago. A little boy, six years old, was found in a drainage ditch. Evans had stopped sleeping, stopped eating, and nearly stopped functioning. Clara had pulled him back then. But barely.

"It's not—"

"Promise me you'll leave it at work. Because if you can't…"

Evans stared at the ceiling after her breathing had evened out.

His phone sat on the nightstand. Silent. No updates from Roan. No breaks in the case. Just him and the dark and the growing distance between his side of the bed and Clara's.

A killer was out there. Waiting.

What if there was a third? A fourth?

He couldn't leave it at work. Not when girls were dying.

But he couldn't lose his family either.

The ceiling offered no answers.

Sleep came thin and restless. He dreamed of beaches, blood, and promises he couldn't keep. Matthew's disappointed face and Emily asking, 'If he'd catch the bad person.' Clara's back turned away.

And through it all, Camila Morales. Pale on the sand. Someone's daughter. Someone who'd died while he wasn't looking.

He woke at three a.m., heart pounding. Checked his phone. Nothing.

Beside him, Clara slept. Or pretended to.

Outside, the neighborhood was quiet. Dark. Safe.

But somewhere out there, a killer waited.

And Evans couldn't stop him from here.

CHAPTER

26

A YOUNG WOMAN STEPPED THROUGH. Asian. Early twenties. She wore a black dress, professional but tight. Her hair was still damp, loose around her shoulders. Eyes dark. Makeup was careful but not heavy. She wore flats, not heels. Moved quietly. Lips pressed tight, like she wasn't sure what kind of man was waiting for her.

The lamp's light painted her skin amber. She hesitated when she noticed he hadn't moved to the table. Most men had already taken off their shirts by now, bills folded and ready on the dresser. He hadn't taken off a thing.

"You waited long?" she asked. Her voice was quiet but carried an edge, like she'd learned to harden it when needed. Her accent curled, faint, not heavy enough to tell where it started.

Roan leaned back in the stool, calm. "Not long."

Her eyes cut over him again, careful. Reading him. She narrowed her eyes. Took a half-step back.

He was still dressed. Fully. Jacket on. Shirt buttoned. He hadn't moved to the table, hadn't undressed, hadn't followed the script.

"You want to shower first?" Voice soft, the practiced script. "Half an hour is short."

Roan shook his head once. "Not here for that."

She blinked. Shifted her weight. One hand moved to the doorframe. Ready to leave. Ready to run.

"You paid," she said. "Seventy dollars for half an hour."

"I know."

Silence stretched. The fan hummed in the corner. Water ran somewhere down the hall.

She stood there. Uncertain. Her survival instincts were kicking in.

Something was wrong. Men didn't pay seventy dollars to sit fully dressed in a massage room. Men didn't stay seated. Men didn't look at her the way he was looking—not hungry, not eager, just... waiting.

"You want me to leave?" she asked. "Get a different girl?"

"No," Roan said. Kept his voice steady. Calm. "I want to talk to you."

Her expression changed. She took another half-step back.

"I don't do that," she blurted. "Just massage. Nothing else."

"I know. That's not what I meant."

"Then what do you want?"

Roan watched her. The way her hand gripped the doorframe. The way her weight was on her back foot. One wrong word and she'd bolt. One wrong move and she'd scream.

He needed her to stay. Needed her to listen. Needed her to trust him for just five minutes.

"I need to ask you about a friend of yours," he said.

Her face went blank. Practiced. "I don't know what you mean."

"I think you do."

She shook her head. "I don't have friends. I work. That's all."

"A Spanish girl," Roan said. "About your age. Worked here. You knew her."

Her eyes widened slightly. She gripped the doorframe tighter.

"I don't know a Spanish girl," she said.

"I think you do."

"No. You're wrong." She took another step back. Into the hallway now. "I'm getting the boss. You can talk to her."

"Wait," Roan said.

She stopped. Hand still on the frame. Eyes still on him. Still ready to run.

Roan stayed seated, keeping his hands where she could see them and his voice low.

"I'm not here to get you in trouble," he said. "I'm not here to hurt you. I just need to talk to you. About your friend."

"I don't have a friend."

"Camila," Roan said.

The girl froze.

Just for a second. Her breath caught. Her hand tightened on the frame.

Then she shook her head. "I don't know that name."

But she did. Roan saw it. The way her eyes went wet. The way her throat worked.

"Please," Roan said. "Just listen. For one minute."

The girl stood there. Torn. Half in the room. Half in the hall.

Then she stepped back inside. Pulled the door closed behind her. Not all the way. Just enough.

"One minute," she said.

Roan reached inside his jacket. Deliberate. Watching her eyes.

She tensed. Hand moving towards the door again.

"It's okay," he said. "Just my badge."

He pulled it out. Held it up. Let her see it. The gold shield. The words:

PALM BEACH SHERIFF'S OFFICE. DETECTIVE.

Her eyes went wide. All the color drained from her face.

"You're police," she said.

"Yes."

"Relax," Roan said quickly, palms open where she could see. "I don't care what goes on here. None of my business." He held her eyes until her breathing evened a notch. "I'm not here to shut you down. I'm here for something else."

"You lied. You said you wanted a massage."

"I lied," Roan said. "I'm sorry. But I needed to talk to you. And you wouldn't have talked to a cop."

She backed against the door. Shaking her head. "No. No. I don't talk to the police. I can't. I have to go."

"Wait. Please. Just look at this."

He pulled his phone from his pocket. Opened the photo gallery. Found the picture of Camila—the one from her mother's apartment. The one where she was smiling. Alive.

He held it up. Turned the screen towards her.

"Do you know this girl?"

The girl's eyes dropped to the screen. To Camila's face.

Recognition, clean and raw.

"She's gone," Roan said, voice still low. "Murdered."

And everything broke.

"Camila," she said. Barely audible.

Her hand flew to her mouth. Her eyes filled. Tears spilled over, running down her cheeks, smearing her makeup.

"Camila," she said again. Louder. Like saying it made it real. Made it hurt.

Her knees buckled. She grabbed the door to steady herself.

Roan stood. Non-threatening. Kept his distance but close enough to catch her if she fell.

"When?" she asked. "When did she—"

"Two nights ago."

The girl's face crumpled. She pressed both hands to her mouth. Shoulders shaking.

Roan gave her space. Didn't touch her. Didn't move closer. Just let her cry.

The sobs hit without warning, hard and ugly, bursting out of her. She slid down against the door, dropping to the floor, burying her face in her hands.

Her whole body convulsed with it. Each sob ripped from somewhere deep—chest heaving, shoulders jerking, breath coming in gasps and hiccups.

"No," she kept saying between sobs. "No, no, no."

Her hands pressed so hard against her face that her knuckles went white. Mascara ran in black streaks down her wrists. Her breath hitched—sharp inhales followed by broken exhales.

Roan crouched nearby. Not touching and not speaking. Just present.

The fan kept humming. Water kept running down the hall. Life kept moving while she shattered.

"She was supposed to..." the girl tried. Couldn't finish. Sobbed harder.

The sobs quieted. Not stopping, just softening. The gasps became shuddering breaths.

She wiped her face with the back of her hand, smearing the mascara worse. Attempted to stand. Failed. Tried again. Got halfway up. Slid back down.

"I'm sorry," she said. To Roan. To Camila. To herself.

After another minute, she looked up at him. Eyes red and swollen. Face blotchy. Makeup destroyed.

"How?" she asked.

"I can't tell you that yet."

"Please."

Roan crouched lower. Still keeping distance. Eye level now.

"I need you to come to the station," he said. "Tomorrow morning. District Fourteen. G Street."

She shook her head. "No. I can't."

"You can."

"No. I can't talk to the police. I—"

"Camila can't tell her half of the story anymore," Roan said. Voice gentle but firm. "You can."

The girl's breath hitched. Fresh tears spilled.

Roan pulled a card from his pocket. Set it on the floor between them. His contact card. Name. Number. Address.

"Tomorrow. District Fourteen. G Street. Just come talk. Tell me what you saw. That's all."

The girl stared at the card. Didn't pick it up.

"She was my friend," she said.

"I know."

"She was a good person."

"I know that too."

The girl wiped her face with the back of her hand again. Drew a shaky breath.

She looked at him for a long moment. Searching his face, looking for the lie. For the trap, then she reached out. Picked up the card and held it tight in her fist.

She stood. Roan stood too.

"G Street," he said.

She nodded. Once. Quick. Made no other promise.

Then she pulled the door open and ran. Footsteps fast down the hallway. A door slamming. Then silence.

Roan stood alone in the small room. Card gone. Girl gone.

He didn't know if she'd show.

But he knew she'd known Camila. Knew she'd cared. Knew she was carrying something heavy.

Tomorrow would tell him if that weight was enough to bring her in.

Roan walked back through the hallway. The same doors. The same sounds. Water running. Music playing. Voices were low, but it felt different now. He wasn't pretending anymore. Wasn't playing customer. The mask was off.

He reached the T-junction. Turned left. Walked to the entry room.

The old Chinese woman stood behind the counter. Same spot. Same expression. But her eyes were different. Harder.

"No refunds," she said flatly, hand snapping towards the door. "Maybe you too big for her."

Roan stopped at the counter. "I didn't ask for one."

Roan turned. Walked to the door. The bell jingled when he pulled it open. He stepped through. Into the humid night. Into purple neon bleeding across the cracked sidewalk.

The door closed behind him. The bell went quiet.

He didn't look back.

This late, the strip had shifted into a different gear. The family crowds were gone. The tourists had retreated to hotels. What was left was the night shift. The people who worked in darkness. The people who hunted in it.

Roan walked north. Back towards where he'd come from. Hands in his pockets. Jacket slung over his shoulder again. Too hot to wear it.

The air was thick. Humid. Clinging to his skin like oil.

Cars slid past. Headlights cutting through the dark. A sedan with a busted taillight. An old Civic with primer on the door. An SUV with illegally dark-tinted windows.

He cataloged them all. Filed them. Kept moving.

A woman stood on the corner. Short skirt. High heels. Leaning against a light pole. She looked at him as he passed. He didn't look back.

Two men stood outside a pawn shop. Smoking. Watching the street. One of them said something low. The other laughed. Roan felt their eyes follow him.

He kept walking.

A bus stop. Empty. Graffiti on the bench. A poster for a bail bondsman peeling off the back panel.

Then the movement ahead.

A truck. Hauling a trailer. Bright orange lettering running down the side.

Roan stopped.

The same truck. The same trailer. Same orange letters burning hot against the dark.

He'd seen it earlier. Hours ago. When he'd been walking south towards Siam Massage, and now it was back. Rolling through the strip. Wrong for the block. Wrong for the hour.

The truck passed under a streetlight. Roan tried to read the lettering. But the angle was bad. The light was wrong. He caught shapes. Letters. But not words.

The truck kept going. Turned at the next light. Disappeared.

Roan stood there. Watching the taillights fade.

Twice. He'd seen it twice. Same truck. Same trailer. Same orange lettering.

Could be nothing. It could be a coincidence. Delivery driver working late. A lost trucker looking for the interstate.

Or.

Roan filed it. Deep. The way you filed things that didn't fit but might matter later.

He pulled his phone free, thumb already moving. Dialed.

Three rings. Then a voice. Dispatch.

"I need a cab. Corner of Dixie and..." He looked up at the street sign. "Southern."

"Copy. Five minutes."

Roan hung up. Waited.

The cab pulled up four minutes later. Yellow. Dented bumper. The driver barely looked at him.

Roan climbed in the back. Gave his address. Sat back.

The cab pulled out. Headed south. Away from the strip. Away from the purple neon. Away from Siam Massage and the girl with Camila's name on her lips.

Roan watched the city pass through the window. Neon fading to streetlights. Streetlights that faded to residential dark. The strip gave way to neighborhoods. To homes. To normal.

The girl's face when she'd seen the photo. The way she'd said Camila's name—the tears.

The cab turned onto his street. Quiet. Dark. Trees overhead were blocking the streetlights.

The driver pulled up to his house.

"Twenty-two," the driver said.

Roan handed him thirty. "Keep it."

He climbed out. The cab pulled away. Taillights fading.

Roan stood in the dark. Looked back towards the city. Towards Dixie. Towards the strip where the girl was probably still hiding. Scared. Grieving.

He turned. Key in the lock. Door opening.

Inside was dark. Quiet. He didn't turn on the lights. Just closed the door. Locked it and stood in the dark.

Tomorrow changed everything.

CHAPTER

27

His pen scraped across the notepad, the sound too loud in the empty bullpen. Evans' coffee had gone cold an hour ago. Three days since Camila Morales. Two bodies. Zero suspects.

Church visit - Father Mendez:
Ariel Morales attended confession,
Priest said: <u>guilt-burdened</u>, waiting for God to strike him down
Story verified
Assessment: guilty conscience

Evans underlined "guilt-burdened." Ariel carried something heavy. Beach reconstruction:

Two routes: North to south OR South to north
Both 4-5 minutes
No cameras at gates
Flexible = Smart = Experienced?

Brandon's BBQ:
Pit boss, Potential witness if killer used north route
Follow up when suspect available

Evans set the pen down. Rubbed his eyes. Pieces. Not answers. "Evans."

Rocca stood at his desk with a manila folder.

"Dr. Avery's autopsy report. Aguilar." Rocca pulled up a chair and opened the folder. "Two metal fragments. Embedded in tissue."

"What kind?"

"Blade fragments. High-carbon steel. Commercial grade."

Evans straightened. "Broke off?"

"Broke off during penetration." Rocca flipped pages. "Wound paths are nearly identical between victims. Same entry points—left side, between fifth and sixth ribs—same angles, twenty-three degrees, depth eight point two inches. Dr. Avery's calling it a signature."

"Left-handed," Evans said.

Rocca looked up. "How'd you know?"

"The angles. Right-handed stabbing enters from the victim's left, angles right as the attacker's arm crosses the body. These enter from the right, angle left. Mirror image. Killer's left-handed."

"No sexual assault. No drugs. He's not sedating them or assaulting them."

"So what's he doing?"

"Killing them. That's it."

Evans sat back. Two girls. Both young. Both from Dixie Highway.

"Control?" Evans said.

"Maybe. Or ritual. We won't know until we catch him." Rocca stood and set the folder down. "Two bodies in three days. Not much choice about prioritizing this." He paused. "You think we're looking at a third?"

Evans flipped pages. "This is good work. Thanks for prioritizing it."

"I think we're looking at someone who's getting comfortable."

The casual certainty chilled Evans.

"Roan around?"

"Not yet."

"Brief him when he gets in."

The door opened. Officer Pérez entered, holding a USB drive.

"Got that footage Detective Roan requested. Marathon station."

Evans took the drive. "You watch it?"

"Asian girl. Ten-thirty. Uses the phone. Black dress. Matches the ER nurse's description."

Evans plugged in the drive. The timestamp read **10:28 PM**. Grainy footage showed a girl entering. Asian. Black dress. She picked up the phone, dialed, talked for three minutes, then left.

This was her—Camila's friend.

"This is good," Evans said.

"I'll send it to tech for enhancement."

"Priority."

"Got it."

Roan walked in with two coffees—jacket over his shoulder.

"Morning." He set one coffee on Evans' desk. "What'd I miss?"

"Autopsy report. Same killer. Left-handed. And Pérez brought gas station footage. Asian girl using the phone at ten-thirty."

Evans turned the monitor. Roan watched, expression calm.

"That's her. Camila's friend. If we can ID her—"

"I already found her," Roan said.

Evans froze. "What?"

"Last night. Found her. Talked to her. She's coming in this morning."

"You... where?"

"Siam Massage. Dixie."

Evans stood. "You went to a massage parlor? Alone? Without backup? Without telling me?"

"I went to talk to her."

"You paid for a massage. You solicited. Do you know what defense counsel will do with that?"

"I showed her my badge before anything happened."

"After you lied to get in the room. After you paid the money. That's entrapment. Coercion. Take your pick."

"Seventy dollars. Showed her my badge. Showed her Camila's photo. She broke down. Gave her my card."

"You compromised a witness."

"I secured a witness."

"She's not coming, Roan."

"She is."

"You spooked her."

"She's not running."

"How do you know?"

"Because grief turns to anger. Anger brings witnesses."

Evans' jaw tightened. "You broke protocol."

"I saw an opening. I took it."

"That's not how partnerships work."

"Partnerships work when both people are available. You were home. With your family. Where you should've been, I wasn't going to call you away from that."

This wasn't about procedure. It was about trust. About the silent agreement partners make:

"We do this together. We watch each other's backs. We don't go into dangerous situations alone."

Roan had broken that trust. They stood facing each other.

"If she doesn't show, this is on you," Evans said.

"She'll show."

They prepped the interview room in silence. The room was eight by ten, with cream-colored walls that were fading to grey with age, and fluorescent lights humming overhead like trapped wasps. Two chairs on one side of the scarred table, one on the other. A camera dome in the corner, with a red light indicating it was armed and recording. The air smelled of industrial cleaner and old sweat.

Eight forty-five.

Nine o'clock came. Evans checked his watch.

"She's not here."

"Give it time."

Nine-thirty.

"Thirty minutes, Roan."

"She's coming."

Evans paced. Three steps one way. Three steps back. Through the walls, muffled sounds: a suspect yelling in booking, someone's phone going off with a tinny ringtone, Sergeant Mitchell's distinctive laugh. The station breathed and moved while they sat frozen.

"How long do we wait?" Evans asked.

"As long as it takes."

"That's not an answer."

"It's the only answer I've got."

"Sergeant's going to ask what we're doing."

"Tell him we're waiting for a witness."

"For how long?"

"Until she shows."

"Why are you so sure?"

"Because I saw her face when she looked at Camila's photo. That kind of grief doesn't let you run."

Ten o'clock.

Evans checked his watch for the third time in the past minute. Roan sat perfectly still, his eyes on the door as if he could will it to open. His coffee sat untouched. Outside, the station moved through its rhythms. Phones ringing. Voices in the corridor. Life continued while they waited.

"One hour."

Roan didn't move. Eyes on the door.

Evans sat. Stood. Sat again. The light through the small window had shifted from morning pale to afternoon bright. Dust motes hung in the beam. Evans watched them drift, hypnotic, mind going fuzzy with waiting.

"When she gets here," Evans said carefully, "we'll need a translator. Her English good enough?"

"Good enough to understand Camila was murdered. Good enough to cry. Good enough to take my card."

"That's not the same as good enough for a formal interview."

"We'll see."

"This is what I'm talking about. You make a call alone. Then we wait."

"When she walks through that door, it'll be worth it."

"If she walks through."

"When."

Ten-thirty.

"What do you want from me?" Roan asked.

"Work with me. Not around me."

"I saw an opening—"

"And took it. I know."

Eleven o'clock.

Evans' back ached from the plastic chair. His bladder protested the two coffees he'd drunk. But leaving meant admitting she wasn't coming. And he wasn't ready to give Roan that satisfaction. Or maybe he wasn't ready to admit Roan might be wrong. He couldn't tell anymore.

He thought about Clara. About Matthew's hand-me-down golf clubs. About the promise to be present. And here he sat, three hours into a vigil for a witness who might never show, while his marriage crumbled.

"This is what breaks partnerships," Evans said quietly. "One person doing something the other can't support."

"I'm asking you to trust it works."

"I can't trust what I can't see."

Eleven-thirty.

For the first time, something flickered across Roan's face. It wasn't doubt exactly. Just... weariness. He ran a hand through his hair. Exhaled long and slow.

"She'll come," he said. But it sounded like he was trying to convince himself.

Evans glanced at the camera dome. Red light steady. Everything they said from the moment they'd entered was recorded. Everything the witness would say would be preserved if she came. If.

Evans walked to the door. "I need coffee."

"Go."

When he returned ten minutes later, Roan hadn't moved. Still watching the door. Still certain.

Noon.

"Three hours."

Silence. Just fluorescent buzz. Air conditioning hum.

Then—

The door buzzer.

Evans' eyes snapped open. His coffee nearly slipped from his hand. Roan straightened, every muscle suddenly taut.

The buzzer sounded again. Insistent.

Someone was here. Someone was asking to be let in.

Evans and Roan locked eyes. The moment hung between them. Everything they'd argued about. Everything that had broken. Everything that might be fixed.

"I'll get it," Evans said.

CHAPTER

28

THE BUZZER SOUNDED AGAIN. Long. Insistent.

Evans yanked open the door. Officer Pérez stood in the hallway. Next to her, a young woman. The Asian girl. Jin stood beside Officer Pérez, smaller than she'd looked in the grainy Marathon footage. Five-two, maybe five-three. The Hollister T-shirt hung loosely on the narrow shoulders. Jeans worn at the knees, frayed hems over white sneakers that had seen better days. Dark hair pulled into a ponytail so tight it looked like it hurt. No makeup. Red-rimmed eyes suggesting she'd done her crying before arrival. She clutched Roan's business card in both hands, edges soft from hours of nervous folding and unfolding.

Evans glanced back at Roan. Their eyes met. No words. Just acknowledgment.

"Detectives. This is Jin Shin. She came to the front desk asking for Detective Roan."

"I'm here," she said.

"Thank you, Pérez," Evans said.

Pérez nodded. "I'll be outside if you need anything."

"Come in, Jin," Roan said.

Jin stepped through. Stopped just inside. Her gaze swept the room —the table, the chairs, the camera in the corner.

"Sit," Roan said. Gestured to the chair across from him.

She hesitated. Then moved. Pulled out the chair. Sat. Hands folded on the table.

Evans closed the door. Sat next to Roan.

For a moment, no one spoke.

Jin stared at the table.

"Thank you for coming," Roan said.

She nodded. Once. Quick.

"Can I get you water?" Evans asked.

She shook her head. "I'm okay."

"You sure?"

"Yes."

Evans kept his voice gentle. "Jin, you've taken a big step coming here. I know that wasn't easy."

She nodded, eyes still down.

"We're going to record this interview. That's standard. The camera up there," he gestured to the dome, and the audio equipment. "Everything you say is documented. That protects you and protects us. Understand?"

"Yes."

"If you need to stop at any time, use the restroom, get some air, just say so. Okay?"

"Okay."

"We need to start with your name," Roan said.

"Jin. Jin Shin."

"Thank you, Jin." Roan wrote it down. "Can you spell that for me?"

"J-I-N. S-H-I-N."

"Got it." Roan set the pen down. "Jin, before we start, I want you to know you're not in trouble. You're not being charged with anything. You're here to help us. That's all."

Jin's jaw tightened. "I know."

"Good. And if you need to stop at any point, we can do so. Okay?"

"Okay."

Evans kept his voice calm. Professional. "Jin, we're investigating the death of Camila Morales. You knew her, right?"

Jin blinked. Nodded.

"How did you know her?" Evans asked.

"We worked together."

"Where?"

Jin hesitated. "Siam Massage. On Dixie."

Evans added a note. "How long did you work there?"

"A year. Maybe more."

"And Camila?"

"She started... maybe six months ago."

"Did you become friends?"

"Yes," Jin said.

Roan let the silence sit. Gave her space.

Jin wiped her eyes. "She was a good person. Kind. She tried to help me with English. Told me about school. About... about things."

"What kind of things?" Roan asked.

"Life. America. How to... how to live here."

"Like what?"

"Getting bills paid. How to get aid for my mom. Everything."

Evans nodded. "Tell us about the work. What did you do at Siam Massage?"

Jin's fingers tightened on the table. "Massage. Back, shoulders, feet. Real massage."

"Just massage?" Evans asked.

"For me, yes. Just massage."

"What about the other girls?"

"Some of them... some did other things."

"What other things?"

"Whatever they were paid for."

Evans didn't push. Just waited.

"Some men and women just wanted a massage. But some wanted more. Some girls said yes. Some didn't. It was their choice."

"Did Camila do more?" Roan asked.

Jin's jaw tightened. "I don't think so."

"You don't think so?"

"She said she didn't. She told me she only did massage. But..." Jin trailed off.

"But what?" Evans asked.

"But I don't know for sure. She could have. Some girls don't tell. They keep it private."

Roan nodded. "Did you ever suspect she might be doing more? With anyone?"

"Not at first."

"But later?"

"Maybe. I don't know."

Evans flipped to another page of his notepad. "Jin, we need you to tell us about a man. Someone who came to see Camila. Someone specific."

Jin's jaw tightened. "Him."

"Yes."

She nodded. "I know him."

"Tell us," Roan said.

Jin stared at the table. Her hands unclenched. Fingers spread flat against the surface.

One hand caught the light. A simple silver ring on her index finger, thin enough to bend light rather than reflect it. She twisted it once, unconsciously—then again, faster—as if turning a thought over in her head. Evans noticed. People fidgeted when they lied, or when they tried not to fall apart. Jin wasn't lying. She was holding herself together by rotation and silence.

"He came a lot," she said. "Maybe once a week. Sometimes more. Always asked for Camila."

"Did you ever see him?" Evans asked.

"A few times. When I was in the front. Or in the hall. He never looked at me. Just waited for Camila."

"Describe him," Roan said.

Jin closed her eyes.

"Older," she said. "Not old. But older than us. Maybe... forty? Forty-five?"

Evans continued in his notepad.

"Hair was dark. Black. Always clean. Always styled. Like he took care of it."

"What else?"

"He dressed nice. Not suits. But nice. Clean shirts. Good jeans. Expensive shoes. His watch looked expensive, too."

"What kind of watch?"

"I don't know brands. But it looked expensive. Silver. Heavy."

"Did you notice anything on his hands?" Roan asked.

Jin opened her eyes. "Yes. His finger. Ring finger. Left hand. There was a line."

"A line?"

"Tan line. Like he wore a ring but took it off."

"You think he was married?" Evans asked.

"Yes. I think so. That's why he took it off. So we wouldn't see."

Roan nodded. "What else did you notice about him?"

"He was careful. Always paid cash. Never use a credit card. Never gave a name. The owner didn't ask. He paid, he went back, he left. That's it."

"Did he speak to you? To the owner?"

"A little. Just... 'Is she available?' That kind of thing. Quiet. Not mean. Just... careful."

"Like he didn't want to be remembered," Evans said.

"Yes."

Roan set his pen down. "Jin, we need to ask you something uncomfortable."

She tensed.

"You said Camila told you she only did massage. But with this man specifically—the one with the tan line—do you think their relationship was different?"

Jin's eyes dropped. Silence stretched.

"Jin?" Roan said.

"I don't know," she said.

"But you suspected something."

"Maybe."

"Why do you suspect it?"

Jin's fingers curled into her palms. "Because of how she talked about him. Because of the gifts. Because..." She stopped.

"Because what?"

"Because one time, after he left, she was different. Happy but... different. She wouldn't look at me. She just went to clean up. Took longer than usual."

"What did you think happened?"

"I thought... I thought maybe they did more than massage."

"Did you ask her?"

"Yes."

"What did she say?"

"She said no. She said they just talked, asked about her life. About school. That he was nice."

"But you didn't believe her?"

Jin's eyes welled. "I wanted to. But no. I didn't believe her."

"Why not?"

"Because girls don't act like that after just talking. And men don't give gifts like that for just talking."

Roan nodded. "Did he give her gifts often?"

"Yes."

"What kind of gifts?"

"The perfume came first. Maybe two months after they started. Camila showed everyone. Chanel No. 5. In the box, black with white lettering. She wouldn't even open it. Just held it. Showed the label. Asked if we could smell through the box."

Jin's mouth twitched, almost a smile.

"Next was the bracelet. About a month later. Sterling silver, she said. Delicate chain. Heart charm. She wore it constantly. Even when the clasp broke, she kept wearing it with tape holding it closed."

"And cash?" Roan prompted.

"That came regularly. Every time he visited. Folded bills. Fifties. Sometimes hundreds. Always folded in half, tucked in her hand when they finished. He'd say, 'For school. For books. For things you need.' But it wasn't school money. Not really. We both knew."

Evans itemized on his pad. Gifts. Cash tips. Perfume. Jewelry. Classic grooming behavior.

"Did Camila talk about him?" Roan asked.

"All the time."

"What did she say?"

"That he was different. That he cared about her. That he asked about her life. About her family. About what she wanted."

"Did she believe that? That he cared?"

Jin's fingers tightened. "Yes. She believed it."

"Did you?"

Anger flickered in Jin's eyes. "No."

"Why not?"

"Because men like that don't care. They pretend. They give gifts. They say nice things. But they don't care. They just want what they want."

Roan held her gaze. "Did you tell Camila that?"

"I tried. She didn't listen."

"Why not?"

"Because she was in love with him," Jin said.

The room went quiet.

Evans watched her. Waiting.

Jin wiped her eyes. "Not the pretend kind. Not the transaction kind that some girls did for tips. Real love. The kind that makes you stupid."

"How could you tell?"

"The way she said his name—she never said it out loud, just called him 'he'—but when she talked about him, her voice changed. Went soft. She'd say things like, 'He asked about my mother today, whether she needs anything. Whether I'm sleeping enough.' Small things. Things nobody else asked."

"Why did that matter?"

"Because nobody sees us. At the parlor. They see bodies. Services. Price points. No one else saw her as more than what she did in that back room. He made her feel seen. Feel real. Feel like a person someone could love. That's more powerful than money. That's what you can't buy." Her voice hardened. "That's what he used against her."

Evans and Roan exchanged a glance.

"At work. During breaks. She'd just stare at nothing. Smiling. I'd ask what she was thinking. She'd say, 'He asked about my mom today. Asked if she was doing okay.' Or, 'He said, I'm too smart for this place. Said I deserve better.'" Jin shook her head. "Small things. Ordinary things. But to Camila, they were everything."

She continued, "She said he was going to take her away, that he was going to help her leave the parlor. That they were going to be together."

"Did you believe that?"

"No."

"Why not?"

"Because he was married. Because he hid his ring. Because he paid cash, so no one would know. Because men like that don't leave their wives for girls like us."

"Jin, did Camila know he was married?" Roan asked.

"She knew about the tan line. I showed her. But she said... she said maybe he was divorced. Maybe it was old. Maybe it didn't mean anything."

"But you knew better."

"Yes."

"Did he ever talk about his life? His family? Where he lived?"

Jin shook her head. "No. Never. He kept everything to himself. Just talked about Camila. About her. About what she wanted. What she dreamed. He made her feel special."

"And that's why she fell for him," Roan said.

Jin nodded. Tears spilled. She wiped them fast. "She thought he loved her. She thought he was going to save her."

Evans walked to the corner. Poured water from the pitcher into a cup. Brought it back. Set it in front of Jin.

"Drink," he said.

She picked it up. Drank. Set it down.

"Jin," Roan said. "We need you to tell us about the last night you saw Camila."

Her breath hitched. "The night she died?"

"Yes."

Jin closed her eyes. "I don't want to."

"I know. But we need to hear it."

She sat there. Silent. Breathing.

Then she opened her eyes. "Okay."

Roan nodded. "Take your time."

Jin drank more water.

"That day, Camila was different. Happy. Excited. She could barely focus at work."

"Why?" Evans asked.

"Because he finally said yes."

"Said yes to what?"

"To taking her out. She'd been asking him for weeks. Every time he came to the parlor. 'Take me somewhere. Let me see your life. Take me out with you.' He always said no. Too complicated. But that day... That day, he called her."

"When?" Evans asked.

"During work. Early. Maybe five o'clock. She stepped outside to take the call. When she came back in, her face was different. She was crying. Happy crying. She grabbed my hands. She said, Jin, he said yes. He's taking me out tonight."

"Did she say where?"

"No. Just that he'd pick her up. That we should meet him at ten. On the corner by Dixie."

"We?" Roan asked.

Jin nodded. "She wanted me to come. At first. Said we'd both go. Solidarity, she called it. We should dress up. Look good together." She paused. "I thought I was going with her."

"So you got ready together?"

"We got ready at the parlor, in the back room. After our last clients left, Camila brought extra makeup. Kohl eyeliner. The good kind. She spent twenty minutes on it. Used the cracked mirror by the sink. I watched her. The way her hands shook. The way she kept checking her reflection."

"What was she saying?" Roan asked.

"'Does this look okay? Is it too much?' I told her she looked beautiful. She did. She really did."

"What time did you leave work?"

"Maybe nine forty-five. We walked to the corner she'd told him about."

"What happened when you got there?"

"We waited. Camila kept checking her phone."

"How was she acting?"

"Nervous. Excited. Kept smoothing her jeans, touching her hair."

"How long?"

"Five, ten minutes. I kept saying maybe he forgot. But she said he was coming—traffic, maybe."

"Then?"

"A car came. Not his. A woman was driving." Jin paused. "Maybe fifty. Tired-looking. Scrubs. She rolled down the window and asked if we were okay."

"What did Camila say?"

"Said we were waiting for someone. The woman looked at us, the empty street, and offered us a ride. Camila said, 'No, thank you.' The woman sat there another minute. Like she wanted to say more. Then drove off."

Evans glanced at Roan. Ellen Mills.

"How did Camila react?" Roan asked.

"Checked her phone again. I started to say we should go home." Jin stopped. "Then we heard it."

"Heard what?"

"The engine. Deep. Powerful. Made my chest vibrate. Camila's head snapped up and her whole face changed—fear gone, just this pure light."

"Describe the car."

"White. Low to the ground. Sleek. Sharp headlights. Everything about it screamed money." Jin's voice dropped. "It didn't belong here."

"What happened?"

"The passenger window slid down. I could see inside—dark leather, dashboard glowing blue. The smell... cologne. Cedar. Money has a smell." She wiped her eyes. "Did he get out?"

"No. Camila moved toward the car. Leaned down to look inside."

"What did you see?"

"Nice clothes. The watch."

"Did he speak?"

"Not that I heard. But Camila was nodding. Smiling. The door opened."

"Then?"

"I moved to get in with her. That was the plan." Jin's breath caught. "But the car only had two doors. Two seats. No back seat. No room for me."

Evans tagged it—two-door coupe.

"I got angry," Jin continued. "Not at her. At him. At myself for believing I was part of this. I said something mean and started walking."

"Did Camila call after you?"

"Yes. But I didn't turn around. Didn't stop. I was crying and didn't want her to see."

"How far did you get?"

"Maybe thirty feet. Then I stopped. Turned around." Jin's voice cracked. "I'll be fine. I'll text you. Promise.' Then she smiled. And waved."

"Then?"

"The car pulled away. Fast, and they turned the corner." She stopped. "That was the last time I saw her alive."

The room fell silent.

"What did you do?" Evans asked.

"I walked to Marathon and called a taxi from the payphone. My phone was dying."

"Did the cashier notice you?"

"Asked if I was okay. I said yes."

"Did Camila text?"

Jin shook her head. "I waited. Checked at eleven forty-five. Told myself she was home safe. I woke up with my phone still in my hand. Started calling at nine. Straight to voicemail. Kept trying. That's when I knew. Really knew."

Evans looked at his notes. "The car. Do you know what kind it was?"

"I don't know cars."

"Shape. Sound. Anything."

Jin closed her eyes. "White. Sleek. Low. The front was sharp. Like an arrow. And the sound... deep. Aggressive. Like thunder. The back had two round red lights. They glowed bright when they accelerated."

"Any symbols? Logos?"

Jin thought. "On the front. There was a symbol. A horse."

Evans' pen stopped. "A horse?"

"Yes. Standing up. On its back legs. Like it was jumping."

Evans caught Roan's eye. The detective's face remained a mask, but a flicker of realization passed between them.

"Jin," Roan said. "Was the horse on a yellow background? Yellow shield?"

Jin opened her eyes. "Yes. Yellow. I remember yellow."

Evans set his pen down.

Ferrari.

"Jin, you're sure about this?"

"Yes."

"White car. Horse symbol on yellow."

"Yes."

"Jin, the license plate. Did you see it?"

She shook her head. "No. Sorry. And it all happened so fast. They were already gone before I could see it."

Evans stood. Paced.

Jin's gaze moved between them. "What? What is it?"

"Jin, the car you're describing is a Ferrari. An expensive sports car. Very expensive."

Jin's eyes widened. "How expensive?"

"Hundreds of thousands of dollars."

She stared. "He had that kind of money?"

"Apparently."

Jin's fingers tightened on the table. "And he spent it on a car. While Camila... while she..."

Her voice broke. She couldn't finish.

"Jin, you did the right thing coming here. You helped us. You helped Camila."

"I didn't help her. She's dead."

"You're helping us find who did this to her."

"Will you catch him?"

"Yes."

"Promise?"

Roan held her gaze. "We'll do everything we can."

Jin nodded. Wiped her face. "Okay."

Evans sat back. "Jin, we're going to need you to stay in the station while we run some things. Can you do that?"

Jin nodded. "Yes."

Roan stood. "Thank you, Jin. You were very brave."

She stood too. "I wasn't brave. I was angry."

"Same thing sometimes."

Evans stood. "Jin, we've been talking for over an hour. Do you need a break? Bathroom? Water? Something to eat?"

She considered. "Bathroom. Yes."

"Of course. Officer Pérez is right outside. She'll show you. Take your time." Jin left with Officer Pérez. The door closed. The interview room fell silent.

Evans turned to Roan. "White Ferrari."

Roan nodded. "Yeah."

"That narrows it down."

"A lot."

Evans picked up his notes. "Older man. Black hair. Expensive watch. Removed wedding ring. Cash payments. Careful. Deliberate. And now we know he drives a white Ferrari."

"Which means money. Real money."

"Enough to groom a girl. Buy her gifts. Pay for sex. And kill her when... when what?"

"When she became a problem."

Evans sat down. Stared at the notes. "We need to run Ferrari registrations. Palm Beach County. Maybe wider. White Ferraris can't be common."

"No. But they exist."

"Roan,"

Roan looked up from his phone.

"You were right. About the grief. About her coming in."

Roan nodded. "I know."

"Thank you for saying that."

"Doesn't mean I agree with how you did it."

"I know."

"And we need to talk. Properly. About how we work together."

"When this is over."

"When this is over," Evans agreed.

They stood there. The friction wasn't gone. It hadn't disappeared with Jin's arrival or her testimony. But it had shifted. Become something they could work with rather than work around. That was enough for now.

Roan and Evans spread their notes across the desk. Somewhere in Palm Beach County, a man was going about his day, heading to work and coming home. Kissing his wife, the one whose ring he slipped off before he walked into massage parlors. Sleeping soundly. Convinced he'd walked away clean.

He didn't know they had Jin Shin's testimony. Didn't know they knew the car he drove. Didn't know the net was tightening.

The investigation had shifted. They weren't hunting shadows anymore. They had a profile. A vehicle. A pattern.

And patterns could be traced.

CHAPTER

29

"Twelve names."

Evans angled the screen so Roan could see, a pulsing window under the DMV logo.

Roan pulled up a chair, knees knocking the desk. "Twelve?"

Evans scrolled quickly, finger tapping the mouse. "White Ferraris in Palm Beach County. Registered. Active."

Roan leaned in, reading. "Cross off anyone who doesn't fit Jin's description—male, forty to forty-five, dark hair."

"We want married or recently married. That tan line," Evans murmured. "Cash-only—he's careful. Or hiding."

Evans snagged a pen, drawing lines through three names. "These three are women."

Roan pointed. "Seventy-two old is out. Twenty-eight, too."

Scratches of pen. Names vanishing. Twelve to seven.

Still too many. Roan rubbed his forehead—tension starting behind his eyes.

Evans pawed through the Morales file, flipping pages until he found it. "Camila called Auto Exotics. The day she died." His voice sounded different now—hungry, groping for connection. "Luxury dealership. West Palm."

Roan frowned. "Why call a Ferrari dealership?"

Evans shook his head. "Three-minute call."

Leaning closer, Roan said, "Business records. Who owns it?"

Typing. Waiting.

"Auto Exotics LLC. Mark Vance. Owner for six years."

Roan's jaw shifted. "Mark Vance owns the dealership?"

"Access to any car on the lot—including white Ferraris."

"Check his registration," Roan said, knuckles drumming.

Evans scrolled. "Mark Vance. Forty-one. Palm Beach Gardens. Ferrari F8 Tributo. White. Registered three years ago. Purchased—Auto Exotics. His own dealership."

"So she called him. Or tried."

Evans checked the call log. "The day she died, the main line. Three minutes."

Roan's tone was low. "She was probably asking for him and trying for their date. Five PM call. Married, rich, dealership owner. Reputation to lose."

"Camila becomes a threat. She wants more. Wants to be seen."

Roan drew a slow breath. "He can't have that."

"Check the rest for dealership connections?"

Evans did—a sweep, silence, then: "Nothing."

Roan stared at Mark Vance's name. "He matches Jin's description. Every detail."

Evans nodded quietly. "It's him."

Roan glanced up. "Jin still needs to confirm."

"She'll know."

Jin hunched over a paper cup in the break room. Pérez sat across from her, silent, keeping watch.

Evans appeared at the door. "Jin."

She looked up.

"We need you for a photo ID."

Jin pushed up from her seat and followed Evans and Pérez to a small conference room. Roan was there already, laying out six enlarged driver's license photos, adjusting their order—deliberate, no pattern, spacing them even. His hands lingered over the third image for half a second longer than the rest. Evans stood behind Jin, hands in pockets, notepad pressed flat.

"Take your time," Roan said.

Jin leaned in. Her breath caught. She slid a finger along each photo, left to right, then again—reading not just faces but what she remembered: posture, smile, the set of a jaw. She faltered at the third photo, lips parted, hand hovering. For a second, everything in her stilled. She touched it. "Him."

Evans exchanged a glance with Roan, tension sharp in the room.

Roan's voice—gentler now but with an edge. "You're sure?"

Jin didn't blink. "Yes."

"Look again. All of them."

Jin scanned through once more, then tapped the third again. "It's him. I'm sure."

Evans picked up the photo and checked it. "Mark Vance."

Roan circled the name on his pad, eyes never leaving Jin.

Jin started to sit, but for a breath she just hovered—unmoored, pale.

Evans moved away, phone to his ear, voice low.

Standing beside the table, Roan studied the photo—Mark Vance—nothing remarkable, standard DMV shot, a face designed to slip through crowds. But Jin's fingerprint was still visible, an indentation on glossy paper.

Evans returned. "Rocca's pulling everything. Background, property, finances, employment, marriage records."

"Married," he added. "Wife's Sabine. No kids. Gated estate in Palm Beach Gardens."

Roan jotted notes. Watching Jin, he kept his silence, letting her reclaim the space.

She looked up. "I never knew his name. Now I do." Her hands trembled.

Roan waited, then, softly: "Does it change anything?"

She swallowed. "He's real now. Not just...the man. He's Mark Vance. He has a wife. Camila never knew."

"Does that bother you?"

Jin nodded once, the gesture brittle. "She thought he cared."

Roan just nodded, staying with her through the quiet.

Jin cleared her throat. "What happens now?"

Evans shut his notebook. "We investigate. Build a case."

Jin's eyes returned to the photo, voice low. "He looks normal."

Roan, quietly: "They usually do."

Rocca entered with a manila folder and clapped it down.

"Prelims," he said, nudging the folder open.

Evans fanned through the records. "Vance. Forty-one. Born in Miami. Here, eleven years. Married Sabine Rousseau."

"Employment?" Roan asked, already knowing.

"Owns Auto Exotics, West Palm Beach, for six years."

Evans drew out a marketing printout: Mark Vance, beside a red Ferrari, arms crossed, with a practiced smile. Watch catching the light, all edges and shine.

Roan turned the photo, holding it a moment longer than needed. "This is what Camila saw—money, a way out."

Evans glanced at him, something unspoken in the look.

"Eight-point-five million gross, one-point-two personal income last year." Said Rocca.

Evans gave a low whistle. "He owns three cars—a white Ferrari, a Porsche Cayenne, and a Range Rover for the wife."

Evans skimmed. "Criminal history?"

"Clean," Rocca said. "Ferrari's an F8 Tributo, registered for three years. Dealer transfer. No sale price."

Roan sat back. "He can drive anything off the lot. Impress anyone, anytime."

"Phone records?"

"Camila's log shows a nine-minute call to Auto Exotics at five twelve p.m. on the murder day. He called her back six oh one, two minutes."

Evans scratched notes. "She called for the date. He called to confirm."

Roan moved to the window, hand on the frame. Outside, the lot shimmered in the late light.

"Name, face, car, phone record. Motive," he said.

Evans closed the folder. "She wanted more. He couldn't give it."

Rocca tapped the table. "Next step?"

"Send this picture over to Marge at Oceanside," Roan said, jaw tight. "See if Vance's the guy she saw with Camila as well. Subpoena his personal calls. Doubt he contacted her on his personal line, though."

"On it," Rocca asked.

Rocca left. Silence rushed in behind.

Jin lingered by the table, staring at the photo.

Evans rested a hand on his notebook. "She ID'd him in three seconds."

Roan nodded, an unspoken pain there. "Certainty."

"She's carried his face for weeks."

"The defense will challenge it," Evans muttered.

"Six photos. Standard array. She picked without prompting. Not easily shaken," Roan said.

Evans gave a half-nod.

Roan approached Jin, took the seat across from her, and sat in silence. "We may need you to testify. Identify him in person. Can you stay available?"

Jin's answer: "Yes."

"Do you have a way home?"

Jin nodded. "Four blocks east. On J."

Roan looked to Evans. Without a word, "I'll drive you," he said, already standing.

Evans blinked. Pérez shrugged.

"He never drives," Evans muttered.

Roan brought the Crown Victoria around from the back, idling beside the cracked sidewalk. Jin waited on the passenger side, bag at her feet.

He unlocked the door, opened it for her, a gesture he hadn't used in years. She slid in, shut it, and the bare bones of the car rattled. He dropped behind the wheel. Files and papers were stripped across the dashboard and back seat—evidence of a life lived on the move.

They drove in quiet, city light slanting through grimy glass. Jin stared through her reflection, chin tipped to the side.

"Which way?" Roan asked, eyes steady on the mirror.

She told him, and he navigated. No wasted movement. One hand loose on the wheel.

"You live with someone?" His tone was gentle now, careful not to intrude.

"My mother," she said.

He nodded—space left for her to elaborate.

"She can't work. I work."

He didn't speak, only letting the road hum beneath them.

"At the massage parlor," she finished.

He risked a glance. "That work—hard?"

Jin's mouth flickered, almost a smile. "It's work. I do what I have to. My mother needs medicine, food, and me." She paused. "She's old —seventy-two or seventy-three. Doesn't remember."

He kept his eyes on the road, but every muscle remembered this kind of story: women holding the world together on minimum wage, silent burdens.

"Blind, mostly. Diabetic. Her hands shake. Sometimes she forgets —medicine, kettle, things like that. The clinic says it's her age, but I see her going. Mind and all."

His hands tightened on the wheel, memories surfacing—his father in that last year, drifting room to room until only the form remained.

Jin spoke quietly. "Camila sometimes brought her soup. Sat with her if I was late. My mother liked her. 'The kind girl.'" Her throat closed. "She doesn't know Camila's gone."

Roan let the silence bloom between them.

"No other family?" he murmured.

She shook her head. "Some in Korea, maybe. I don't know them."

The city changed, buildings sagging. Streets rougher.

"Camila helped you," he said—not just for the record, but as recognition.

Jin nodded, voice thin. "Taught me forms, how to get help. How to cope here."

He let that sit.

"She wouldn't listen to me, in the end," Jin finished, so soft it almost vanished.

Roan didn't offer empty words. Something in the set of his jaw told her he understood regret's weight.

They reached her street—narrow, battered brick. Jin pointed word-lessly at the third building up.

Roan braked, engine idling. Jin reached for the handle, hesitated. "Why did you drive me?"

He met her gaze. "Because you needed it. Everyone needs it, some days."

"I do this all the time," she insisted, forcing bravado.

He nodded. "Today's different."

She studied him with a frown. "Evans was surprised."

"He was."

"Why?"

He watched the building. "Because you came in. Told the truth. Faced him. That's rare. I wanted you to know that."

Jin's eyes prickled. "I'm scared. What if Mark Vance finds out?"

Roan turned, face serious. "He won't. And even if he did, he wouldn't get close. Not to you. Not now."

She shook her head. "You can't promise that."

He met her gaze, steady. "I just did."

Her uncertainty lingered, searching his expression for honesty.

He reached into his jacket, sizing up the impulse, and handed her a card. His direct line, number written by hand.

"Only mine. If you need—call."

She stared at the card, holding it carefully.

"We're going to get him," Roan said, voice no louder than before but carrying something new. "I mean it."

"Promise?" she managed.

He covered her hand with his own—fleeting, grounding.

"I promise."

She stepped out, careful not to meet his eye again. Roan watched her walk inside, waited for the security door to clang shut.

He sat there, engine still running, staring at the building as the light faded. Phone buzzed, Evans:

> Where are you?

> Dropped off Jin. Heading back.

> You drove her home?

> Yeah.

Since when do you drive?

Roan didn't reply; he shifted the gear into drive, and the city rolled past as Jin's shape lingered in the rearview, her silhouette holding his promise for both of them.

His phone buzzed again, Norris:

My office.

Back at the station, Roan moved past the main room. Evans looked up.

"Not now," Roan said.

Captain Norris' door opened. "Roan."

Roan paused. Entered. Norris closed the door.

"Sit."

Roan stayed standing. Norris, too, arms crossed by the window.

"You want to tell me what you were thinking?" Norris' voice was soft steel.

"About what?"

"Siam Massage. Last night. Going in alone."

"I got the ID."

"That's not what I asked. No backup. No wire. No text. You walked into a rub and tug without filing a notice. IA will drag us both if something goes wrong."

Roan's mouth tightened. "I told Evans."

"Once you'd already stepped inside." Norris' frustration was obvious, but tired. "Luck worked this time. Luck runs out."

"I know."

Norris studied him. "You're one misstep from desk duty. You keep improvising, you'll be out."

Roan said nothing, neither a denial nor an apology.

Norris' tone softened, unexpected. "What you did got results. Don't make it a habit."

Roan kept his hands in his pockets. "Won't."

"Good. And if you drive witnesses home, note it."

"That it?"
"For now. Get back to work."
Roan left, crossing the squad. Evans watched him pass.
"You good?"
"Yeah."
"What'd Norris say?"
"To do my job."
Roan settled at his desk. "So let's do it."

CHAPTER

30

Evans drove. Roan sat in the passenger seat. Staring out the window. Neither spoke.

"This is reckless," Evans said.

Roan kept his eyes on the passing buildings. "Noted."

"Phone records aren't back yet. Subpoena's still processing."

"We're not arresting him. Just talking."

"You know he's going to lawyer up the second we show our badges."

"Maybe."

"Definitely."

"Jin ID'd him. And Marge ID'd. This is the guy. And we're well within our rights to interview with him. Plus, maybe we can get a look at the car while we're there."

"I'm telling you, he'll have the lawyers so far up our ass—"

"You want to turn around?" Roan whipped around and looked at him.

Evans exhaled. "No. But I want you to know I think this is a bad idea."

"Also noted."

They drove north. Out of West Palm. Into Palm Beach Gardens. The neighborhoods changed. Got cleaner. Wider. Trees planted in perfect rows. Sidewalks that looked like someone actually swept them. SUVs in driveways instead of rust buckets on blocks.

Evans glanced at Roan. "All I'm telling you is we could've waited. Could've waited for the phone records to connect him to Camila. Could've put surveillance on Siam to see if he went back there and brought him in with a tighter case."

"And let more girls get murdered?"

Evans said nothing.

"This is just an interview. He doesn't know we're coming."

"That's what worries me. No heads-up. No lawyer present. If he says anything, defense will shred it."

"Only if we arrest him."

"You think we won't?"

Roan said nothing.

Evans' knuckles whitened on the wheel. "This is about Jin. The promise you made."

"It's about closing the case."

"It's about you being impatient."

Roan turned away. "Drive."

Evans drove in silence.

The gated community appeared on the right, surrounded by high metal walls. Ornate iron gates. A guardhouse with actual guards. A sign:

OCEAN CREST ESTATES

The hiss of automated sprinklers reached them through the open window. Constant. Rhythmic. Water arcing over lawns that didn't need it.

Evans pulled up to the gate. Rolled down the window.

A guard stepped out. Mid-thirties. Clean uniform. Clipboard. "Can I help you?"

Evans held up his badge. "Palm Beach Sheriff's Office. We need to speak with a resident. Mark Vance."

The guard looked at the badge. Wrote something down. "Is Mr. Vance expecting you?"

"No."

"Does he know you're coming?"

"No."

The guard hesitated. "I'll need to call ahead. Community policy."

Roan leaned across from the passenger seat. "This is police business. Open the gate."

The guard looked at Roan. Then at Evans. Evans said nothing. Just sat there.

The guard exhaled. Stepped back. Pressed a button. The gates swung open.

"Vance residence is 447 Via Palacio Way. Take the first right, then left at the fountain. You'll see it."

Evans nodded. Drove through.

"You didn't have to threaten him," Evans said.

"I didn't threaten anyone. I gave him information."

"You gave him an order."

Roan looked out the window. "He opened the gate, didn't he?"

The streets inside were pristine, with manicured lawns. Palm trees swaying. Perfectly uniform terracotta roofs baking in the midday sun —every house the same shade of burnt orange, like someone had color-matched them with a catalog. Driveways with BMWs and Mercedes. Pools that probably cost more than Evans' car.

Three o'clock on a weekday. No kids were playing outside. No dogs barking. No neighbors talking over fences. Just the hiss of sprinklers and the occasional hum of a lawn service truck disappearing around a corner.

He found the fountain. Turned left—counted houses. The street was empty. Not a person was in sight, as if everyone had been evacuated or was hiding.

447 Via Palacio Way.

Two-story Mediterranean. White stucco. Terracotta roof. Circular driveway. A Range Rover was parked out front. Sabine's car from the records. Behind it, a Porsche Cayenne. Vance's daily driver.

No white Ferrari.

Garage.

Evans pulled in. Put the car in park. Turned off the engine.

They sat there. Looking at the house. An upstairs curtain shifted. Then went still.

"Last chance," Evans said. "We can leave. Come back with a warrant—"

Roan opened his door. Got out.

Evans exhaled. Followed.

They walked to the front door. Roan rang the bell. Heard it chime inside. Deep. Expensive.

Footsteps. A shadow moving behind the frosted glass.

The door opened.

A woman stood there, in her late thirties. Blonde hair pulled back —yoga pants. Designer t-shirt. No makeup. Eyes that looked tired but beautiful. Sabine Vance.

She looked at them. Then, at the badge Roan held up. Her hand gripped the doorframe.

"Mrs. Vance?" Roan said. "I'm Detective Roan. This is Detective Evans. PBSO. We need to speak with your husband."

Sabine's hand went to her throat. "What's this about?"

"We just need to ask him a few questions."

"About what?"

"It's better if we talk to him directly."

Her eyes moved between them. Fear there. And something else. Recognition maybe. Like she'd been expecting this. Like she'd known it would come, eventually.

"Is he in trouble?" she asked.

"We just need to talk," Evans said. Voice gently. "That's all."

Sabine stood there. Hand still at her throat. Then she stepped back. "He's in his office. Down the hall. Last door on the right."

Roan nodded. Started to move.

"Wait," Sabine said.

Roan stopped. Looked at her.

"What did he do?"

Roan met her eyes. Said nothing. After a moment, Sabine released the doorframe. She stepped aside. Let them in.

The interior was exactly what Evans expected. High ceilings. Marble floors. Art on the walls that probably cost more than his salary. Everything clean. Perfect. Cold. The air conditioning hummed somewhere overhead—steady, artificial.

Roan moved down the hall. Evans followed. Sabine stayed by the door. Watching.

The office door stood ajar. Light spilling out. A floorboard creaked overhead.

Roan stepped into the doorway. Stopped.

Mark Vance sat behind a desk. Laptop open. Phone to his ear. He looked up. Saw Roan. His expression didn't change. Just raised a finger—*one minute.*

"Yeah, I'll call you back," Vance said into the phone. Hung up. Set it down. Leaned back in his chair. "Can I help you?"

Roan stepped in. Evans followed. He left the door slightly open behind them.

Vance's office was all dark wood and leather. Bookshelves. Framed photos. A window overlooking the backyard. Pool visible. Perfectly blue.

"Mark Vance?" Roan asked.

"That's me."

Roan held up his badge. "Detective Roan. Detective Evans. PBSO."

Vance's expression still didn't change. "What's this about?"

"Camila Morales."

Nothing. No reaction. Vance just sat there. Then smiled. Polite. Professional. "I'm sorry, who?"

"Camila Morales. You knew her."

"I don't think I did."

"You visited her. At Siam Massage. On Dixie Highway."

Vance's smile didn't waver. "I think you have me confused with someone else."

Roan looked at Vance's hands on the desk. Clean. Manicured. No cuts. No bruises. No defensive wounds.

Roan pulled out his phone, pulled up Jin's photo lineup, and showed him. "This is you. Correct?"

Vance glanced at it. "Could be Photoshop."

"You own a white Ferrari F8 Tributo."

"I own a dealership. I own several cars."

"You took Camila Morales out. Picked her up. Took her for a ride."

Vance leaned forward. Folded his hands. "Detective, I don't know who you're talking about. And I don't appreciate you coming into my home, making accusations."

Evans stepped forward. Pulled out his notebook. "We have a witness stating that they saw you, multiple times, at the Siam massage parlor on Dixie Highway, and picking up Camila Morales on Thursday night at ten-twenty in a white Ferrari F8 Tributo. A second witness states they saw you with Camila at Oceanside Pub at ten-thirty to eleven on the same night."

"Then your witnesses are mistaken."

"They're not," Roan said. Voice cold. "One identified you with no hesitation. Pointed right at your face."

Vance's smile faded. "I want my—"

"You're not under arrest." Roan broke the phrase.

"Then what are you doing here?"

"Talking."

"Looks like accusing."

Roan pulled out a chair. Sat. "Camila Morales was murdered three days ago. Found on Lake Worth Beach. Stabbed. Multiple times. Left to bleed out in the sand."

Vance went still. His hands gripped the edge of the desk. "What?"

"She's dead."

"I... I didn't know that."

"But you knew her."

Vance's mouth opened. Closed. He looked at Evans. Then back at Roan. "I want my—"

"We can do this here," Roan said. "Quiet. Private. Or we can do it at the station. With your wife wondering why detectives are taking you away in the middle of the day. Your choice."

Vance stared at him. Then he exhaled. Ran a hand through his hair. "Fuck."

"Tell us," Evans said. Pen poised over the notebook.

Vance looked at the door. Then back at them. "If I talk, this stays between us?"

"Depends on what you say."

Vance stood. Walked to the window. Looked out at the pool. "Look, I don't know anything about a murder."

"But you knew Camila."

"I might have met someone by that name."

"Where?"

"I don't recall."

"Try harder," Roan said.

Vance turned. "Maybe at a business function. I meet a lot of people."

"At Siam Massage."

"No."

"We have a witness."

"Your witness is wrong."

Evans looked up from his notebook. "When was the last time you saw her?"

"I told you, I don't know her."

"You just said you might have met her."

"I said maybe. At a business function."

Roan stood. Walked closer. "Let me help you remember. Six months ago. You walked into Siam Massage. Asked for the new girl. Pretty. Young. Camila."

"No."

"You went back. Week after week."

"You're mistaken."

"Paid cash. Never gave your name."

Vance's hands clenched. "This is harassment."

"This is an investigation. And you're lying."

"I want my lawyer."

"Fine. Call him. We'll wait. And while we wait, we'll ask your wife some questions. About your Thursday nights. Your cash withdrawals. The nights you came home late."

Vance went pale. "Leave my wife out of this."

Roan didn't move. Just watched him.

A creak from above. Footsteps. Then silence.

Vance looked at the ceiling. Then back at them. His shoulders sagged. "I met her six months ago. At the parlor. She was new."

"Go on."

"I went back a few times."

"How many times?"

"I don't know. Several."

"Try harder."

"Once a week. Sometimes twice."

"For massages?" Evans asked.

Vance looked at him. "Yeah. For massages."

"Just massages?"

Vance said nothing.

"Answer the question," Roan said.

"Not always."

"Sex."

"Sometimes."

"How much did you pay her?"

"Cash. A few hundred."

"When did she ask you to take her out?"

Vance walked back to his desk. Sat. "A month ago. She kept asking. I kept saying no."

"But you finally said yes."

"Yes."

"Why?"

"Because she wouldn't stop asking."

"Where did you take her?" Roan asked.

Vance looked at his hands. Still pristine. Still unmarked. "Ocean-side Pub. On the beach."

"What happened?"

"We had drinks. She asked questions."

"What kind of questions?"

"Personal questions."

"Be specific."

"She asked if I was married."

The room went quiet—another creak from above. Somewhere in the house, the air conditioning cycled off.

"What did you say?" Evans asked.

"I told her the truth. I said yes."

"How did she react?"

Vance's hands gripped the desk. "She got upset. Said we were done. I paid the tab. Left."

"You left her there? Alone? At night?"

"She told me to leave."

"She was drunk. Upset."

"She was an adult."

"She was twenty-one."

"Old enough to make her own choices."

Evans looked up from his notebook. "Did you see her leave?"

"No. I left first."

"Did you see anyone else? Anyone watching her?"

"No. I just wanted to get out of there."

Roan leaned forward. "That was the last time you saw her."

"Yes."

"And you never went back."

"No."

"You left her there to die."

"I left her at a bar. What happened after wasn't my fault."

Roan stared at Vance's hands again—the clean, unmarked hands of a man who hadn't been in a knife fight. Hadn't struggled with a victim, hadn't done the killing.

The door pushed open wider.

Sabine Vance stood in the doorway—shotgun in her hands. Barrel pointed at her husband.

Everyone froze.

"Sabine," Vance said. "Put that down."

She stepped into the room. Eyes red. Hands steady. "How long?"

"What?"

"How long have you been fucking her?"

Vance looked at Roan. Then back to his wife. "Sabine, please—"

"HOW LONG?!"

"I don't know."

"You don't know!" Her voice broke. "You don't know how long you've been cheating on me."

"Six months. It didn't mean anything."

"She was twenty-one."

"It was just—"

"Just what? Just a massage? Just sex? Just what you always say?"

Vance went still.

"Three years ago. The receptionist at the dealership. Fort Lauderdale. Two years ago. The girl at the hotel."

"Sabine—"

"You promised. After the last one. You swore on our marriage."

"I meant it."

"LIAR!"

She stepped closer—barrel inches from his chest.

"I forgave you—every time. I believed you. I stayed. But it was never about me, was it?"

"Sabine, listen—"

"You've been doing this our entire marriage! I'm the one who always sits at home. Waiting."

Vance's hands shook. "It wasn't like that."

"IT WAS EXACTLY LIKE THAT!"

Roan raised his hands. Stepped towards her. "Mrs. Vance. Put the gun down."

She swung the barrel towards him. "Stay back!"

Roan stopped. "You don't want to do this."

"You don't know what I want!"

"I know you're angry. I know he hurt you. But this isn't the answer."

"He's been hurting me for years."

"Sabine—"

"But that girl is dead. Because of him."

"I didn't kill her," Vance said.

"You might as well have!"

Sabine's hands tightened on the shotgun. "I heard everything. Every word you said."

Her voice cracked. "I gave you everything! Fifteen years!"

"I'm sorry."

"You're sorry you got caught!"

"I'm sorry I hurt you."

"You killed her."

Vance blinked. "What?"

"You killed that girl!"

"I didn't. Sabine, I swear."

"You're a liar!"

She pressed the barrel against his chest. "I should kill you!"

Roan moved. "Mrs. Vance. Look at me."

She didn't.

"Look at me."

She turned her head. Eyes still on Vance.

"If you pull that trigger," Roan said, "your life is over."

"My life is already over."

"It's not. But it will be. Prison. Trial. Years locked up."

"I want him to suffer."

"He will. We're arresting him."

"No. You're not."

Roan's voice stayed level. Quiet. "Yes. We are."

Sabine's finger moved to the trigger. "He doesn't get to walk away."

"He's not walking away. I promise."

"Your promises don't mean anything."

"They do to me."

Sabine looked at him. Tears running down her face. "He ruined everything."

"I know."

"He doesn't get to just go to prison."

Roan said nothing. Just held her gaze.

Sabine's hands shook. The barrel wavered.

Vance saw it. Lunged. Grabbed the gun.

"NO—" Roan shouted.

Sabine screamed. Pulled the trigger.

The blast was deafening.

Vance flew backward. Crashed into the desk. Blood sprayed. Across the wall. The floor. Evans.

Roan moved. Fast. Grabbed Sabine. Wrenched the shotgun away. Threw her to the ground. Knee in her back. Pulled out his cuffs.

Sabine sobbed. Screamed. "MARK! MARK!"

Evans ran to Vance. Knelt. "SHIT! SHIT! FUCK!"

Vance lay against the desk. What was left of his face hung in pieces. The shotgun blast had obliterated his lower jaw—teeth, bone, tissue gone. Just a gaping cavity where his mouth used to be. His tongue was visible through the carnage. Blood poured from the wound like a faucet. Two fingers on his right hand were stumps. Bone shards jutted from the flesh.

Vance's eyes had gone wide, moon-white, frantic, animal. He jerked upward, thrashing, the only sounds spilling out of him wet and broken and inhuman. Evans moved fast, both hands at Vance's shoulders, bearing down. "NO! Don't move—" Harder now, Evans braced as Vance fought, hands lashing, slick with blood, each pull smearing dark red onto Evans' shirt. Vance gripped him, desperate, some instinct dragging him upward, but the words were gone, ruined by the mess of his jaw: just bubbles and gargling, choking, drowning.

"STAY DOWN!" Evans got him back against the desk, pressing both hands over what was left of Vance's jaw, trying to stem the torrent. It did nothing. Blood came hot and thick, soaking through Evans' fingers, running in sheets down his wrists, over his sleeves, blooming heavy on his shirt and down his legs. The heat of it was everywhere.

Vance bucked under him, eyes rolling, body shuddering as the shock set in.

"He's going into shock—" Evans threw a look at Roan. "CALL THE PARAMEDICS!"

Even then, Vance still clawed at Evans, bloodied hands scrabbling: jacket, arms, whatever he could catch, painting Evans' front and sleeves in it. The jerks became spasms, violent and wild.

Evans bore down, pressing harder. The pressure squeezed blood between his knuckles, down his forearms, the desk slippery beneath all of it. Beneath his palms, bone fragments shifted, slick with exposed tissue. Things no one should ever touch.

"Stay with me. Stay with me. Don't you fucking die—" There was a moment: Vance's eyes caught Evans', staring, pleading, desperate. Then gone. They rolled back. His body went slack.

"NO! NO, NO, NO—" Evans shook him, hard, refusing to let go. "VANCE. MARK. STAY AWAKE."

The blood pooled out, more than Evans thought a body could hold, pooling under the desk and spreading around them. Evans knelt in it, knees darkening, the warmth seeping through and up, everywhere. There was nothing but the wet, the copper, the raw smell.

Still, Vance's chest managed it: rose, fell, trembling. Then again. Ragged, shallow. Evans kept the pressure on, hands slick, body drowning in the mess. The sharp reek of iron and burnt meat filled the room, overwhelming, until nothing else existed but the heat and the blood.

Roan finished cuffing Sabine. Pulled out his phone. Dialed. "This is Detective Roan, badge eleven thirty-eight. Officer needs assistance. Four-forty-seven Via Palacio Way, Ocean Crest Estates. Gunshot victim. Critical. Need paramedics and backup. Now."

The dispatcher's voice crackled. Professional. Calm. "Units en route. ETA three minutes."

Roan hung up. Looked at Sabine. She lay on the floor. Cuffed. Sobbing. "I'm sorry. I'm sorry. I'm sorry."

But Roan had seen Vance's hands. Clean, unmarked hands. Before the shooting. Before the blood. Vance hadn't killed Camila.

They'd had the wrong man all along.

He looked at Evans. Covered in blood. Hands pressed against a man who couldn't speak. Couldn't answer the question that mattered most.

Who killed her?

CHAPTER

31

THE BLOOD HAD GONE tacky between Evans' fingers, pulling at the fine hairs on his knuckles when he flexed his hand. Vance's blood. Dark rust now, almost black in the noon sun. Under his nails. In the creases of his palms. The copper filled his nose, his throat—he could taste it on his tongue, metallic and thick.

Roan stood beside him on the lawn. Watching.

Sirens filled the air. Red and blue lights painted the white stucco. Neighbors were on their porches. Watching. Phones out. Recording.

The front door stood open. Crime scene tape was going up. Uniforms moving in and out. Radios crackling.

Evans looked down at his hands. The blood had dried stiff on his shirt. His pants. It cracked when he moved, little flakes drifting to the grass.

The smell hit him again. Copper. Gunpowder. Something acrid underneath—burnt flesh from the muzzle blast. It stuck to him. In his nose. His throat.

His hands shook. Just slightly. He clenched them. The dried blood cracked. Flaked.

Around them, voices. Radios. Orders were being shouted. A neighbor was crying. The sounds seemed to come from very far away, muffled and strange, as if his ears needed to pop.

"You okay?" Roan asked.

Evans didn't answer. Somewhere down the street, a car door slammed.

"Evans."

He looked up. "Yeah."

"You're not."

"I'm fine."

Roan studied him. Said nothing.

The ambulance pulled up. Doors opened. Paramedics jumped out, grabbed equipment, and moved fast. One of them glanced at Evans. Saw the blood. Kept moving.

They disappeared inside.

Evans watched the open door. Waiting. The sprinklers hissed, still running their programmed cycle.

"He's alive," Roan said.

"For now."

"Yeah. For now."

They stood in silence.

Five minutes later, the paramedics emerged—a gurney between them. Vance strapped down. Oxygen mask over what remained of his face. Bandages wrapped tightly. Blood seeping through. IV lines. Monitors beeping.

One paramedic at the head. One at the feet. Moving fast but controlled.

Evans watched their hands—quick, precise, no wasted movement. They'd done this before. Gunshot wounds. Critical patients. They didn't panic. Didn't slow.

One of them met Evans' eyes as they passed. A look. Cop to first responder. You did what you could. Not your fault if he doesn't make it.

Evans nodded. Didn't know if he believed it.

"Trauma center," one of them shouted. "We're losing pressure."

They loaded him into the ambulance. Doors slammed. Sirens kicked on. The ambulance pulled away. Fast. Lights flashing.

Evans watched it disappear around the fountain. His shirt stuck to his chest where the blood had soaked through.

"He might make it," Roan said.

"Might."

"Tough son of a bitch. Took that blast and stayed conscious."

Evans said nothing. A neighbor's dog barked, high-pitched and frantic.

Roan turned. Looked at him. "He's not our killer."

Evans met his eyes.

"The hands." Roan's voice lowered. "No cuts. No defensive wounds. No scabs. Killer would've slipped on the blade. Blood makes everything slick. You can't stab someone like that without damaging yourself."

Evans nodded. "Aguilar fought back. Forensics said defensive wounds on her hands. If he'd stabbed her, she would've grabbed. Scratched. Left marks."

"But his hands were clean." Roan looked back at the house. "So we got the wrong guy."

"We got a cheating asshole. But not a killer."

"He took her to the pub. Left her there. Someone else found her."

"Someone else killed her."

Roan's jaw tightened. Evans watched a uniform seal off the driveway with more tape.

"I fucked up," Roan said.

"We followed the evidence," Evans said.

"Evidence pointed to him. White Ferrari. Witness ID. Phone records. Motive. Everything fit."

Evans looked down at his hands again. "Except it didn't."

"No. It didn't."

A cruiser pulled up. Officer Pérez got out. Opened the back door.

Two uniforms brought Sabine out. Hands cuffed behind her. Face pale. Eyes red. Hair falling loose from the blonde ponytail.

She walked like a marionette with loose strings, her body moving but her mind somewhere else entirely.

They guided her towards the cruiser.

"Wait," Evans said.

Roan looked at him.

Evans walked over. Stopped in front of Sabine. His shoes left dark prints on the pristine driveway.

She looked up. Saw the blood on him. Her eyes widened.

"Is he—" she started.

"Alive," Evans said. "Critical. But alive."

Her breath caught. "I didn't mean to—"

"I need to ask you two questions."

She stared at him.

"Was your husband home by eleven p.m. last Thursday?"

Sabine's brow furrowed. "What?"

"Last Thursday. The night Camila was murdered. Was Mark home by eleven?"

"I... yes. Yes, he was."

"You're sure."

"I made dinner. He ate. Went to his office. Came to bed around eleven thirty. I was still awake. Reading. He got in bed." She paused, her voice hollow. "He smelled like beer."

Evans nodded. Pulled out his notebook—the pages were spattered with brown drops he hadn't noticed before. "Second question. Is your husband left-handed or right-handed?"

Sabine blinked. "Right-handed. Why?"

"You're certain."

"Yes. He writes right-handed. Eats right-handed. Everything. Why are you asking me this?"

She looked at the house. At the blood on Evans. At the ambulance, now gone. Understanding dawned in her face, slow and terrible.

"You think he killed her?" she said, voice barely there. "You think my husband murdered that girl."

"We're just confirming details," Evans said.

"But you thought he did." Tears started. "You came here thinking he killed someone. And I... I shot him. Oh God."

The uniforms pulled her towards the cruiser. She didn't resist. Just kept crying.

Evans stepped back. "Thank you."

The uniforms guided her to the cruiser. She got in. Door closed. The cruiser pulled away.

Evans walked back to Roan. His notebook stayed open in his hand, pages fluttering in the breeze.

"Well?" Roan asked.

"Home by eleven. Right-handed."

Roan exhaled. "Dr. Avery's report. The killer was left-handed. Angle of the wounds. Downward trajectory from left to right."

"Vance is right-handed."

"Which means he couldn't have done it."

Evans nodded. "His alibi's solid. His wife confirms the time. And he's the wrong hand."

Roan looked at the house. "Cameras."

"What?"

"Guardhouse cameras. Caught us coming in. They'll have time-stamps. Show when Vance came home Thursday night."

Evans followed his gaze. "And the house cameras."

"Yeah. I saw them. Outside. Above the garage. Above the front door. Probably inside too. Rich people love cameras."

"They'll show him arriving. Staying home. All night."

"Yeah."

The weight of it settled over them both—hours wasted, a man in critical condition, a woman headed to prison. And somewhere out there, the real killer is walking free.

"We're back to zero," Evans said.

"Not zero. We know what we know."

"Which is?"

"We know Vance isn't our guy. We know Camila left the pub alone. We know someone found her between eleven and whenever she died."

"Ellen Mills saw her at ten oh-nine. On Dixie with Jin."

"Vance picked her up. Took her to the pub. They fought. He left. She stayed."

"So someone saw her there. At the pub. After Vance left."

"Yeah."

"And that someone killed her."

Roan nodded.

They stood watching the activity. Crime scene techs were moving in now. Lights set up. Cameras flashing. The office was a crime scene. Blood everywhere.

Sabine would go to the county lockup. Booked. Charged. Aggravated assault. Attempted murder if Vance died—murder. Probably get a decent lawyer. Claim years of abuse. Temporary insanity. Might get off light. Might not.

But that wasn't their case anymore.

Their case was still out there. Still killing.

Roan turned. Looked at Evans. Really looked.

"You're covered," he said.

Evans glanced down. The blood had soaked through everything. Shirt. Pants. Jacket. Even his shoes. Dark stains. Drying. Cracking.

"Yeah."

"Your suit's done." Roan's voice, flat. "Get a go-bag and keep it in the trunk. Buy cheap clothes you don't mind burning." He paused. "You learn that the hard way."

Evans looked at his hands. His shirt. Eight hundred dollars. Gone.

Roan checked his watch. "It's noon. You've been here three hours. Go home. Clean up. Come back fresh tomorrow because we're starting over."

"You're staying?"

"Yeah."

"Why?"

"Because this is my mess."

"It's our mess."

"No." Roan's voice went flat. "I pushed this. I wanted to come here. No warrant. No backup. Just us. You said it was reckless. You were right."

"Roan—"

"I made a call. It was wrong. Vance got shot. Sabine's going to prison. And we're back to square one. That's on me."

Evans looked at him. A crime scene tech walked past carrying evidence bags. "We both made the call."

"You followed my lead."

"I could've said no."

"But you didn't."

"No. I didn't. Because you're the senior detective. And I trust your judgement."

Roan said nothing. Turned away towards the house.

"Even when it's reckless," Evans added.

Roan almost smiled. "Go home. Clean up. See your family."

"What are you going to do?"

"Talk to the captain. Explain what happened. Start damage control."

"He's going to be pissed."

"Yeah."

"We interrogated a suspect without a warrant. His wife shot him. He's in critical condition. Media's going to eat this alive."

"I know."

"You want me here for that?"

"No. I want you home. With Clara. With your kids. Because tomorrow we start over. And whoever killed Camila and Aguilar is still out there."

The words hung between them—the real killer, still hunting, still free. How long until another body turned up? Another girl with her throat cut, dumped like trash?

Evans nodded. "Okay."

"One more thing."

"What?"

"Stop at a florist. Buy Clara flowers."

Evans blinked. "Flowers?"

"Yeah. Flowers. Something nice. Roses. Whatever. Tell her you're sorry that the job got messy. That you love her."

"Why?"

"Because this job takes everything. It takes your time. Your energy. Your sanity. And it takes pieces of you. Little by little. Until one day you look up and realize you've got nothing left for the people who matter."

Evans felt something tighten in his chest.

"So you give her flowers," Roan continued. "You tell her she matters. You remind her of why you do this. And you remind yourself."

"You speaking from experience?"

Evans looked at him. Saw something there. Loss maybe. Regret. Something old and deep.

"Okay," Evans said. "I'll stop for flowers."

"Good."

Evans turned, started walking towards his car, then stopped. Looked back.

"Roan."

Roan already had his phone to his ear. "Yeah, I know. Just remember the flowers."

Evans opened his mouth. Closed it. The blood on his hands had started to itch.

Roan's eyes held something dark, old regrets surfacing.

Evans nodded and kept walking, the blood on his hands cracking with each step. Behind him, the crime scene lights flashed red and blue against the white stucco, and somewhere in Palm Beach County, a killer was getting away with murder.

CHAPTER

32

THE HUMID AIR through the open windows burned Evans' face—hot even at speed. Florida in September still felt like summer anywhere else. Steering through traffic, he focused on the road, stretched his neck, fighting the locked tension in his shoulders. The burnt-meat stink of gunpowder lingered in his hair, in his pores.

Every glance at his hands on the wheel, the blood stood out—dried, cracked along the knuckles, dark stains leaching up his forearms, around his wrists. Eight-hundred-dollar suit, ruined. He checked the rearview: his own eyes, blood caked like a mask. A woman in the next car caught sight of him and floored her accelerator when the light changed.

Breathing through his mouth, Evans forced himself into the present. Clara would be collecting the kids about now. He pictured her as calm and focused, not ready for what might walk through their front door. He promised her once that he wouldn't bring the job home —the carnage, the things he saw and smelled and wore on his skin— but some promises became impossible after a day like this.

He skipped the service station and the McDonald's, unwilling to see the fear in a stranger's face, to explain away someone else's blood. Just home. He pictured the routine: slip through the door, straight to the bathroom, burn the evidence, return to normal.

Five minutes later, a flower cart caught his eye—an old man arranging perfect scarlet blooms under a hand-painted sign:

FLORES - $5.

Evans pulled over almost without thinking. The vendor's eyes flitted from the blood to the badge and back. "You need help?"

"No. Just had a hell of a day. Want roses for my wife."

The old man picked out a dozen and wrapped them neatly. Evans pressed the money into his hand and got back in his car. The roses on the passenger seat looked as out of place as he felt—bloodied hands, fresh flowers, dread coiling in his gut.

Roan had been right. Clara deserved to know she mattered—even if he looked like the last thing she'd want at her door.

His street appeared—a tunnel of green, children cycling, parents chatting, homes that signaled safety. He nearly missed the silver CR-V in the drive. Of course, she was home. His plan, such as it was, dissolved.

Clutching the roses, he let himself in quietly. Music wafted from the kitchen—something Spanish, soft percussion, Clara's favorite. He slipped off his shoes, made for the hallway, hoping for a straight run to the bathroom.

"Daniel?"

He froze. "Yeah. I'm home."

"Good, I—" Clara emerged, drying her hands, smile ready. It faltered as she took him in: him frozen, bloodied, clutching roses. Her scream was brief but piercing, breaking the day's brittle calm.

She backed against the wall, hand to her mouth. The blood, the cracked shirt, the ruined jacket—it all landed. Clara took a slow breath, fumbled with the roses, and set them aside before reaching for him. "Are you hurt?"

He shook his head. "Not my blood."

She stepped closer, voice thinner. "Whose?"

He swallowed. "A suspect. I tried to help."

She brushed his cheek—a trembling, gentle touch—then gathered herself, putting her arms around his neck. He tensed. "I'll ruin your clothes."

"I don't care."

He held her tightly, something unwinding inside. For the first time since the sirens, he allowed himself to drop the shield.

Clara pulled back, taking in the whole state of him. "The kids are at soccer practice. Two hours."

"I thought you'd be out."

"I came back early." Her hands stayed on his face. "Go shower. I'll put on coffee."

He nodded, mouth dry. "Clara—thank you. For not… I'm sorry."

She managed a shaky smile. "Later. Go."

Evans stripped in the bathroom, every item a loss, tossing shirt, pants, socks, and pants into a garbage bag—like Roan said, some things you just burned. Under the shower, scalding water ran first red, then pink, then clear. He scrubbed his skin raw, the stench finally surrendering to soap and steam. Only when his hands began to sting did he stop.

Clean, he dressed and came to the kitchen. Clara waited with coffee, the roses now in a vase. She looked him over, wordlessly pushing a mug toward him. "Sit."

He obeyed, feeling the scrape of the old table's wood under his elbows—a quiet anchor. She reached for his hand, fingers resting over his.

"What happened?" She let the question hang.

Evans stared at their joined hands. He answered, not with the whole narrative, but with fragments: the wrong suspect, the confession, the wife and the gun, the failed rescue. Not reliving the scene, just sharing what it left behind—the memory, the guilt, the thousand-yard stare. "I tried to save him. Even though he didn't deserve it."

Clara squeezed his hand, a silent reassurance.

He tried for a smile. "I can't promise it won't happen again. Or that I won't bring it home by accident."

"Don't promise." She held his gaze. "Just come home. However, you are."

Evans blinked. "And the kids?"

"We'll work it out. They need you—all of you. Just come home, Daniel."

He exhaled, tension easing from his chest. "I love you."

"I love you too."

She moved to his lap, arms tight around his shoulders. He buried his face in her hair—vanilla and coffee, the smell of home. The killer was still out there, the case unfinished. But for now, for tonight, it could all wait.

Later, Clara broke the companionable silence, glancing at the vase. "Roan was right about the flowers."

Daniel glanced at the roses. "Yeah."

"Smart man."

Evans managed a genuine smile. "He said the same about you."

He looked at his scrubbed, raw hands, the bagged clothes by the back door—evidence of the day, but for this moment, left behind.

33

Roan stepped into the Oceanside Pub just after six. The sun bled orange into purple over the water. Inside, dim lights cast shadows patterned by diffused spotlights.

The barstool creaked under his weight. He set his keys on the scarred wood, rolled his shoulders against the day's tension. Beer and fried fish hung in the air, salt bleeding through the walls. The jukebox played something old—country, mournful. A dozen patrons scattered across tables and booths, nursing drinks, avoiding home.

Marge appeared from the back. Hair piled high and shellacked against the humidity—grey streaked with stubborn red she refused to dye out. Strong arms from years of hauling kegs. Jeans, tank top, red lipstick, sharp enough to cut.

She saw him. Didn't look surprised.

"Detective."

"Marge."

She grabbed a glass and poured him a Miller Lite from the tap— long pour. Proper head. Set it in front of him without asking.

"On the house."

"You don't have to."

"I know." She leaned against the bar, studying him. "Business or pleasure?"

Roan took a drink. Cold. Bitter. The alcohol spread through his chest, dulling edges. "Honestly? Don't know."

She nodded. Pulled a rag from her back pocket, started wiping down the bar—not because it needed it, just because that's what bartenders did. She knew when to talk and when to shut up.

He took another drink, letting the silence settle. Camila had been here and argued with Vance. Left alone. And then what?

"We found him," Roan said finally.

Marge stopped wiping. "Found who?"

"Mr. Linen Shirt. The one with Camila that night, Mark Vance."

"Case closed, then."

"He didn't kill her."

Her eyebrows went up. She set the rag down, expression shifting—not pity, understanding. "What happened?"

"His wife shot him. Shotgun. To the face." Roan drained half the glass. "My partner tried to save him. Got covered in blood."

"Jesus."

"Heard her husband confess to cheating. Snapped."

Marge shook her head. "Cheating bastards always get what's coming."

The corner of Roan's mouth twitched. Not quite a smile.

The jukebox switched tracks—more country, still sad. Someone laughed at a back table—sharp, then trailing off.

"So you're here," Marge said, "where Camila was last seen."

"Maybe."

"Or maybe you're still working. Even when you think you're not."

She was right. The job never stopped.

Roan drained the rest of his beer. "I need a piss."

"Down the hall. Left."

The bathroom was small and dingy. Tiles that hadn't been white in years. A urinal. A sink. A mirror with a crack running through it.

Roan stepped to the urinal, unzipped.

Then he saw it.

A flyer. Taped to the wall above the urinal. Eye level. White paper. Black text. Block letters, rigid and controlled:

The Wages of Sin is Death
Romans 6:23

Something clicked—that feeling when a piece fits, even if you don't know the picture yet.

He finished, zipped up. Stepped closer. The tape was slightly yellowed at the edges, while the paper remained crisp and white. He touched the corner, felt the texture. Laser printer. Deliberate placement. Eye level. Impossible to miss.

He pulled out his phone and snapped a photo. The lettering was precise—all caps, evenly spaced. Like someone who believed every stroke mattered. Every word carried God's weight.

He washed his hands, dried them on his pants, and went back to the bar.

Marge was pouring drinks for a couple at the other end. Chatting. Smiling.

Roan sat back down. Waited, turning the beer glass in slow circles on the bar top.

When she came back, he pointed toward the hallway. "The flyer. In the men's room. Above the urinal. How long's it been there?"

Marge's expression didn't change. "A while. Days, maybe longer. Why?"

"See anyone put it up?"

She thought about it. Shook her head. "People put stuff up all the time. Bands. AA meetings. Lost dogs. I pull most down, but sometimes I miss one."

"This one's different. Bible verse. Romans 6:23."

"Wages of sin." She tapped the bar. "Twelve years of Catholic school. St. Mary's. Nuns with rulers and God's wrath. Left at sixteen, but the verses stick."

"What's it mean?"

"First half's judgment. Fire and brimstone. You sin, you die." She wiped the bar again. "Second half's about grace. Salvation. God offers a way out."

"The flyer only has the first half."

"Yeah."

"Why?"

She set the rag down. "Maybe they don't know the full verse. Or maybe they only believe in the first part. Judgment, no mercy." Her voice dropped. "That's someone who thinks they're beyond saving. Or that others are."

Ariel. The name surfaced in Roan's mind like a body floating up from deep water. Ariel had judged Camila. Called her a sinner. Said God punished her.

The wages of sin is death.

He pulled up photos on his phone. Scrolled through images from Ariel's bedroom. Charcoal sketches on the walls—biblical scenes, judgment, suffering, hell. Then the flyers Ariel had stapled to the pier. Block letters. All caps. Rigid. Controlled.

Same style. Same message.

"You see who put it up?" Roan asked. "Even vaguely. Young? Old?"

Marge frowned. "Could've been anyone. Beach bar. People wander in and out all night just to use the bathroom."

"Could it have been a kid? Teenager?"

He pushed his phone toward her. Photo of Ariel from the family home. Dark hair. Gaunt face. Eyes that burned.

"Could've been. This about the murder?"

It wasn't a question.

"Maybe."

"That poor girl."

"Yeah."

She nodded. "I'll keep an eye out. Anyone puts up another one, or asks about it, I'll call."

The door opened. Warm air rushed in with the smell of barbecue smoke. Brandon appeared—six-three, four-fifty, belly stretching an apron stained with sauce.

"Marge! You got my usual?"

"Always do, sugar."

She poured a Modelo and wedged a lime on the rim. Brandon wrapped his massive left hand around the glass and walked off. When he laughed, the sound rang out—deep and whole, brightening faces even among those who hadn't caught the joke.

Roan looked back at his empty glass. Ariel. Bible verses. Sin and judgment.

The door opened again.

This time, the man who entered moved differently. Deliberate. Older—sixties, grey hair slicked back. He wore a button-down shirt, sleeves rolled to the elbows, and walked with the confidence of someone who knew exactly where he belonged.

He approached the bar, chose the stool right next to Roan, even though a dozen others sat empty.

Marge came over. "What can I get you?"

"Scotch. Neat. Top shelf."

"Sure thing."

She reached for the Glenfiddich. Amber liquid splashed into the glass. She slid it across.

"Twenty bucks."

The man pulled out his wallet—leather, worn at the edges—and counted out exact change. Crisp bills. No fumbling.

Roan kept his eyes on his beer. But he'd clocked the voice, the posture, the way the man settled onto the stool like he owned it.

Frank DeAngelo. Owner of the Nifty Fifty Diner. Where Camila had worked day shifts. The man who'd said she was trouble, that she brought drama, that he wasn't surprised when she ended up dead.

And now he was here. Sitting next to Roan. In the same bar where Camila had been last seen alive.

CHAPTER

34

Roan kept his eyes on his beer. Foam settling. Waiting.

Sometimes silence was the sharpest tool.

DeAngelo took a sip of his scotch. Neat. Top shelf. A drink a man ordered to show you he could afford it.

Marge reappeared with a fresh rag, wiping down the space between them. Her eyes flicked to DeAngelo. "Tuesday night ritual, Frank?"

DeAngelo lifted his glass. "Come here, it's just scotch."

"Smart man," Marge said. "Your place packed tonight?"

"Was. Left the kids to handle lockup." He took a sip. Swallowed slowly. "Nice to sit somewhere else's place for once."

Marge smirked. "Long as you don't critique my pours."

"Wouldn't dream of it."

She moved on. Left them alone.

"Saw you on the news," DeAngelo said finally.

Roan studied him. Grey hair slicked back with too much product. Expensive watch—silver, catching the dim light. Flowery shirt that probably cost more than Marge made in tips all night.

Roan stared at DeAngelo. Said nothing.

"That shooting with the car dealer." DeAngelo swirled his glass. Ice clinked. "Looked like a bad day. Whole thing on News 5, blood and all."

"News made it look worse than it was."

"That right?" DeAngelo grinned, but there was no warmth. "Looked plenty bad. Partner had red on him from head to toe. Hard to walk that off."

Roan stared into his beer. "You don't walk it off. You just keep walking." And then. "Wife shot him."

DeAngelo made a low sound, halfway between a laugh and a cough. "Shit. Didn't see that coming."

"Most people don't."

"She gonna do time?"

"Probably."

DeAngelo shook his head. Took another drink. "Cheating bastard got what was coming. You play stupid games, you win stupid prizes."

Roan's jaw tightened, molars grinding. The casual dismissal—like a man who nearly died was just another bar story—entertainment for strangers.

He remembered the diner. DeAngelo was behind that greasy desk, talking about Camila as if she were garbage. Like she'd asked for it. *Should've cut her weeks ago. Gave me nothing but grief.*

Fingernails dug half-moons into his palms. His breath came shallow. One twitch away from violence.

"Did you know Vance?"

"Knew of him. Auto Exotics, right? High-end place. Not my scene. I'm more Cadillac than Maserati."

"But you knew Camila."

DeAngelo's expression shifted. Not much. Just enough. The eyes narrowed a fraction. The mouth tightened.

"Yeah. She worked for me."

"Worked." Roan let the word hang. "Past tense."

"She's dead, Detective. What else would I call it?"

Marge reappeared. Wiped down the bar between them. Gave Roan a look—*you okay?*—then moved on. She knew when to leave cops alone.

Roan turned on his stool. Faced DeAngelo full-on. Close enough to smell the whiskey on his breath. His cologne—woody, expensive, trying too hard.

"You talked about her like she was nothing," Roan said. Voice low. Steady. "At the diner. You sat in that office and told me she was trouble that you should've fired her. That she was probably chasing drugs or men."

DeAngelo's face hardened. "I told you the truth."

"You told me your opinion. There's a difference."

"Look, Detective—"

"She was twenty-one years old. Working her ass off to pay for college. And you treated her like garbage."

DeAngelo's hand tightened around his glass. The knuckles went white.

"I run a business. I don't have time to babysit every waitress who shows up late or causes drama with customers. She was a liability. That's not an opinion. That's a fact."

"Liability, how?"

"She had an attitude. Talked back. Made the new girls uncomfortable. Customers tipped her too much because she flirted. That causes problems."

"So you resented her."

DeAngelo's laugh was sharp. Bitter. "Resented? No. I just didn't like the headache. And now she's dead, and I've got cops crawling all over my diner asking questions that make my staff nervous. The girl is dead, and she's still trouble. You want to know what I resent? That."

His throat closed. Evans covered in blood. Julia in the lot. Camila on the sand. The exhaustion pressed behind his eyes like a migraine building. And this man sitting here, drinking expensive whiskey like none of it mattered.

"This your night off?"

The question blindsided DeAngelo. He blinked. Shifted in his seat. "What?"

"You're here. At the bar. On a weeknight. Is this your night off?"

"Yeah. So?"

"So you come here often?"

DeAngelo's eyes flicked to Marge, then back to Roan. "Sometimes. Why does it matter?"

"Just wondering." Roan took a drink. Let the silence stretch, then "Were you here the night Camila was killed?"

DeAngelo went still. The glass stopped halfway to his mouth. "What?"

"Thursday night. Last week. Camila was here at this bar. Then she ended up dead on the beach. Were you here?"

"No."

"You sure?"

"Yeah, I'm sure. I was at the diner. Closing. I didn't leave until midnight."

"Anyone verify that?"

DeAngelo's face flushed. Anger now. Real anger. "What the hell are you implying?"

"I'm not implying anything. I'm asking a question."

"You think I killed her?"

Roan didn't answer. Just watched. Let the accusation hang in the air like a cloud of smoke.

DeAngelo slammed his glass down. Hard enough that Marge looked over. Hard enough that the couple at the end of the bar turned their heads.

"I didn't kill anyone. I run a diner. I serve food. I pay taxes. I go home, watch TV, and go to bed. That's it. I didn't touch that girl."

"Then you've got nothing to worry about."

"Fuck you, Detective."

Roan's mouth twitched. Almost a smile. "Careful, Mr. DeAngelo. Threatening a cop is a bad look."

"I'm not threatening you. I'm telling you to back off. You've got no right to come at me like this."

"I've got every right. Two girls are dead. One of them connected to this bar. And she worked for you." Roan's stare hardened. "And here you are. Drinking whiskey. Acting like it's just another Tuesday."

DeAngelo stood. The stool scraped loudly against the floor. His face was red now. Veins standing out on his neck.

"I'm done talking to you."

"Sit down, Mr. DeAngelo."

"No."

Roan stood too. Slower. Calmer. Temples throbbed, but his hands hung loose at his sides—coiled pythons waiting for the strike order. His eyes locked on the man, pupils contracted to pinpoints, eyes that said *I'm not threatened. I'm just tired of your bullshit.*

They stood there. Two men. Eye to eye. The bar had gone quiet. Everyone was watching now.

Marge came over. Fast. Her voice cut through the tension like a blade.

"Frank. Sit down."

DeAngelo looked at her. Then back at Roan.

"He's accusing me—"

"I don't care. Sit down. Both of you."

Roan sat first. Slow. Deliberate. Kept his eyes on DeAngelo the whole time.

DeAngelo hesitated. Then sat. Jaw tight. Hands clenched on the bar.

Marge poured him another whiskey. Didn't ask. Just poured.

"On the house," she said. Then to Roan, "You too. Behave."

She walked away. Left them there. Two men in a bar. Hating each other in silence.

After a minute, DeAngelo spoke, quieter now. "I didn't kill her."

"Then help me find who did."

DeAngelo took a drink. Long. Hard. Set the glass down empty.

"I don't know anything."

"You knew her. You saw her five, seven days a week. You talked to her. You watched her interact with customers. You must've noticed something."

DeAngelo's shoulders sagged. The fight was bleeding out of him. Replaced by something else. Exhaustion, maybe. Or fear.

"She was nervous, scared maybe," he said finally.

Roan's fingers tightened on the beer glass. "Of what?"

"I don't know. But the last couple of weeks before she died, she was jumpy. Looking over her shoulder. Wouldn't take a break alone. Made one of the other girls come with her when she was out back."

"Did she say why?"

"No. And I didn't ask. Wasn't my business."

"Did anyone follow her? Hang around the diner longer than they should?"

DeAngelo thought about it. Shook his head. "Not that I saw."

Roan brought out his phone. Scrolled to the photo of Ariel again.

"You ever see this kid?"

DeAngelo squinted at the screen. Frowned. "Yeah. Maybe. Looks familiar."

"Where?"

"The diner. He came in a few times. Always alone. Ordered coffee. Sat in the back booth. Didn't talk to anyone."

Roan studied DeAngelo's face. Looking for the lie. The hesitation. But the man just looked tired. Annoyed.

"When was this?"

"Couple months ago? Maybe longer. I don't remember."

"Did he ever talk to Camila?"

"I don't know. I wasn't watching." DeAngelo paused. Rubbed his temple. "Kid gave off a vibe, though. Never blinked. Made the girls uncomfortable. Camila wouldn't serve him after the second time. Made one of the other girls do it."

Connection confirmed. Ariel knew where she worked. Knew where she might've gone after—the loop closing.

Roan put the phone away. The pieces shifted. Not clicking yet, but moving.

Bible verses at the pub. Coffee at the diner. Watching her.

Marge drifted over, towel on her shoulder. "Staying late tonight, Frank?"

"Trying to unwind."

"Long day?"

"They're all long now."

Marge smirked. "Don't tell me BCI let you down again."

"Always. Freezer compressor went out on Tuesday. The fryer thermostat fried itself on Wednesday. Prep table today. I swear half the stuff they install dies inside a year."

"You should see our kitchen," Marge said. "Feels like a museum of BCI scrap metal. I got a guy from their service line on speed dial."

BCI. The name tucked itself away. "BCI handles both your places?"

DeAngelo nodded. "Yeah. Bulk contracts. They're cheap. That's the pitch."

"How cheap?"

"Cheap enough to regret it every time something snaps."

From down the bar, Marge called back, "Don't forget the pans and knives, Frank. You were complaining about those last time."

DeAngelo huffed, rubbed his eyes. "Right. The fucking knives." He looked at Roan. "We buy their kitchen sets—supposed to be high-carbon steel, commercial grade. Half the blades crack. One edge chips clean through the handle. Shouldn't happen with any brand worth a damn."

"They're doing that here, too?" Roan asked Marge.

"Yeah." She leaned in. "Started a couple of months ago. Thought I was crazy till three broke in one week. Same box from BCI."

Julia Aguilar. CSU pulled metal fragments from the wound. High-carbon steel. Commercial grade.

"You throw the broken ones away?"

DeAngelo shrugged. "Dish kids dump 'em. Sometimes I keep a piece to show the rep, but they never follow up."

Roan stood. "Excuse me a second."

He stepped into the hallway—bathrooms to the left. Back door cracked open—cool air bleeding through, carrying salt and the reek of dumpsters. Dart-scarred wall. Muffled laughter from the bar.

He dialed Pérez.

Two rings. "Roan."

"Need a cross-check," Roan said. "That steel fragment CSU pulled from Julia Aguilar, did the lab ever match the manufacturer's alloy?"

Pérez shuffled papers. "Not yet. Preliminary says high-carbon stainless, food-grade. Looks commercial, maybe restaurant stock."

"Get in touch with BCI. See if their knives match that composition."

"BCI? The supplier?" Pérez paused. "You think someone's sourcing murder weapons from restaurant suppliers?"

"Nifty Fifty Diner uses BCI. So does Oceanside Pub." Roan explained. "And I think someone's been using knives that break. Leaving pieces behind."

Silence on the other end, then "How fast do you need this?"

"Yesterday."

"Lab's backed up, but I could push."

"Push."

"Copy. I'll flag the lab."

"Night, Pérez."

"Try to get some sleep."

"Yeah."

He slipped the phone away. Stood there a moment. The cool air felt good. Helped him think.

He came back to the bar.

Sat down. DeAngelo was still there. Quieter now. Drinking slower.

DeAngelo had a guarded smirk crossing his face. "Calling in backup already?"

"Checking something."

"You really think I did it?"

Roan looked at him. Tired. Honest. "No. But I think you're an asshole."

DeAngelo laughed. "Fair enough."

They sat in silence. Two men who didn't like each other. United by the same dead girl.

Roan drained the last dregs of his beer. Stood. Put down a twenty. Looked at Marge.

"Thanks for the beer."

"Anytime, Detective."

He walked to the door. Stopped. Looked back at the bar.

DeAngelo was watching him.

"If you think of anything else," Roan said, "call me. Don't wait."

DeAngelo nodded. "Yeah. I will."

Roan stepped out into the night. The wind hit him—salt, rot, exhaust. Humidity thick enough to coat his tongue. Somewhere beyond the boulevard, waves hammered sand.

He called a cab. Hadn't gotten the hang of Uber yet.

He stood there while headlights blurred past. Thought about Camila. Last two weeks, jumpy, wouldn't walk to her car alone. She knew. She knew someone was watching, but she didn't know how to say it. Didn't know who to trust.

And he'd missed it. Too busy chasing Vance. Too busy looking at the wrong faces.

The cab pulled up—yellow paint peeling. The driver looked half-asleep.

Behind him, the Oceanside Pub glowed warm against the dark. The sign flickered: OCEAN—dark—SIDE—dark—OCEAN. Inside, people drank and laughed, and for a moment, forgot that death was always waiting.

But Roan didn't forget.

CHAPTER

35

THE TAXI PULLED up to Roan's house. He paid the driver. Got out. Watched the taillights disappear down the street.

He walked to his front door. Unlocked it and stepped inside.

The house was dark. Quiet. His keys hit the counter with a dull clank. He shrugged off his jacket, felt its weight leave his shoulders, but the exhaustion stayed. The kitchen smelled of old coffee, dish soap, and the faint metallic tang of tap water. The refrigerator hummed, filling the silence.

He stood there, staring at nothing.

His phone buzzed:

Unknown Number

He let it ring. Kept staring.

It buzzed again—same unknown number.

He picked up. "Roan."

Silence. Then breathing. Fast. Nervous.

"Detective Roan?" A woman's voice. Young. Shaky. Southern edges on the words.

"Yeah. Who's this?"

"You... you came to Lucky's. Few days back. Gave me your card. I'm Mary... Mary Tucker. The one with the red hair?"

Roan straightened. "Thanks for getting back to me, Mary."

"Yeah." A pause. "I shouldn't be callin'. But I saw the news. 'Bout that guy gettin' shot."

"Mark Vance."

"Is he... is he the one? The one killed that girl on the beach?"

"No."

Another pause. Longer. "Then you're still lookin'."

"Yeah."

Mary exhaled. Shaky. "I keep thinkin' about the others."

Roan grabbed a pen from the counter. Found a receipt. "What others?"

"The girls. The ones who disappeared from the street. Dixie Highway. Where girls like me work, there's been at least three in the last year. Just... gone."

"Did you know them?"

"Two of 'em. Verónica Rojas and Ana López. We wasn't friends or nothin'. But I knew 'em. Saw 'em around."

"When did they disappear?"

"Ana was... maybe eight months back? She stopped showin' up. Everyone said she probably just left. Went somewhere else." She trailed off. "Verónica was five months ago. Same thing. Just vanished."

Roan wrote it down. His fingers tightened on the pen. "Did anyone report them missing?"

Mary laughed—bitter, sharp. "Who's gonna report 'em? Cops don't give a shit when a workin' girl don't show up."

"I give a shit."

Silence. Then: "Yeah. Maybe you do."

Roan paced to the window. Looked out at the dark street. "Tell me about them. Ana and Verónica."

"Ana was tough. Been out here longer'n most. Had this scar—said she got it from some asshole when she was sixteen. First week on the street."

"She have family?"

"Dunno. She never talked about 'em. You don't end up out here if you got people lookin' out for you."

Roan knew. "What about Verónica?"

"Younger. Twenty-somethin'. Real pretty. Spoke Spanish mostly. Used to send money back home to her mama."

"Her mother know she's gone?"

"Probably thinks she just stopped sendin' money." Mary's voice dropped. "They all worked Dixie. Same stretch. Between Lake Worth and West Palm. Where it's dark. No cameras. No streetlights half the time."

Roan's throat closed. "You think someone's targeting them?"

"I think someone watches. Someone knows which girls are vulnerable. Which ones won't be missed. Which ones are alone."

"Alone how?"

"Girls without pimps. Girls who work solo. When you got someone, even if he's a piece of shit, at least somebody knows when you don't come home. But girls like Ana? Like Verónica? Nobody's waitin' up for 'em. They just... disappear."

Roan listened. Wrote. The refrigerator hummed behind him.

"Did Ana or Verónica ever mention anyone? Someone who made them nervous?"

"Nah. But we all got johns that make us nervous. You learn to read 'em—the ones who got that look. But sometimes you can't tell. Sometimes they seem normal. And then..." She paused. "Then they ain't."

His pen stopped moving. "Is there anything else you remember?"

"Just that I should've paid attention. Should've asked questions. But I didn't."

"Mary, you're doing the right thing by calling."

She was quiet for a moment. "Detective?"

"Yeah?"

"Do you think the same person killed all of 'em?"

"I don't know yet. But I'm going to find out."

"What if he just keeps goin'?"

"He won't. I'll stop him."

"You promise?"

The dark kitchen. The empty house. "I promise."

Mary exhaled. Long and shaky. "Okay. I hope you're right."

"Mary, I need you to do something for me. If you see anything—anyone—you call me. Day or night. You understand?"

"Yeah."

"And stay alert. This guy's dangerous. He knows how to pick girls who won't be missed."

Mary's voice got small. Scared. "That's what I keep thinkin' about. That I'm next, that one night I'm gonna get in the wrong car and nobody's gonna know."

"I'm looking now."

"One cop. Out of how many?"

"One's enough."

She laughed. Sad. "Maybe. We ain't worth protectin'. Ain't worth lookin' for."

"You're not disposable."

"Tell that to Ana. Tell that to Verónica."

Roan didn't have an answer for that.

"I'm gonna find him," he said. "Whoever did this."

"And then what? Another one takes his place?"

"You do what you can. That's all anybody can do."

"Yeah. A start." She paused. "Detective?"

"Yeah?"

"Thank you for listenin'. Most cops... they don't. But you... You're different."

"I'm just doing my job."

"Nah. You're seein' us. Really seein' us. And that means somethin'."

The line went dead.

Roan stood there. Pen in hand. His pulse was hammering in his ears.

Someone was hunting them and picking them off one by one.

He walked to his laptop. Opened it on the kitchen counter. The screen's glow lit his face in the dark kitchen. He typed the first name into the database.

Ana López

Age: 26

Last arrest: June 2023. Solicitation.

Dixie Highway between Lake Worth and West Palm Beach.

Prior arrests: 4

All solicitation. All in the exact location.

Last seen: June 8.

Never reported missing.

The photo loaded—young, with dark eyes and a small scar above her left eyebrow. She stared at the camera with a defiant expression that didn't quite hide the exhaustion underneath. Gone.

His jaw clenched. He scrolled. Typed the second name.

Verónica Rojas
Age 19
Last arrest: February 2023. Solicitation.
Dixie Highway.
Prior arrests: 3

All solicitation. Same stretch of road as Ana.

Last seen: March 15.

Never reported missing.

Another photo. Another face. Younger than Ana—too young—with makeup that tried to make her look older but only made her look like a child playing dress-up. She'd attempted a smile for the camera and failed. Gone.

Roan leaned back. His eyes burned from staring at the screen. He forced himself to look at the two images side by side.

Same age range. Same location. Same work. Same as Camila and Julia.

The pattern was there. Had been there all along—the stretch of highway. The girls were working alone in the dark. Someone watching. Someone waiting. Someone who knew which ones wouldn't be missed.

How long had this been going on?

He stood. Walked to the back door. Opened it. The night air hit him—salt, humidity, the distant sound of traffic on the boulevard. Somewhere beyond the houses, waves hammered sand in the dark.

The laptop's glow spilled through the doorway behind him, casting his shadow long across the patio. Inside, on the screen, four faces stared at nothing. Ana. Verónica. Camila. Julia.

Four girls nobody had looked for.

Until now.

Roan stood in the doorway between the dark house and the darker night, and somewhere out there, someone was still hunting.

CHAPTER

36

THE CAR PULLED up to the curb. Another john. Another night on Dixie Highway—half the vehicles cruising were looking for something they couldn't get at home.

Her name was Destiny. Not her real name. Her real name was Jessica Torres, but nobody used real names in this business. Twenty-six. Been working the streets for three years. Started after her boyfriend got locked up and left her with rent she couldn't pay and a habit she couldn't kick.

She stood under the flickering streetlight outside a closed laundromat—red tank top. Denim shorts cut high. Heels that hurt after the first hour, but made her legs look longer. Men liked that. Her feet throbbed—four hours in cheap stilettos on a cracked sidewalk. The straps had rubbed blisters on both ankles. She'd learned to ignore it. Pain was part of the uniform.

The heat made her makeup melt, slide down her face, and pool in the creases of her skin. Foundation gathered in the lines around her mouth. Mascara smudged beneath her eyes. Didn't matter. Men didn't care about makeup. They cared about skin. About what they could touch. About what they could take for an hour and forget by morning.

The laundromat's windows were dark. Inside, washing machines sat empty, their doors hanging open like mouths. During the day, this corner was busy—women with kids, men in work boots, the smell of detergent and dryer sheets. At night, it was her spot. Had been for six months. Good visibility from both directions. Streetlight overhead. Close enough to the bars that men drove past looking.

It had been a slow night. Two dates earlier—both quick, both paid. One hundred forty bucks total. Not bad. But not enough. She needed three hundred to make rent. Tiffany was covering utilities this month, but Jessica still owed her from last week. And the week before that. Tiffany never said anything, but Jessica saw it in her face. The tightness around her mouth. The way she counted bills twice.

Her stomach growled. She'd eaten a granola bar around seven—nothing since. The hunger sat hollow in her gut, making her light-headed when she moved too fast.

The street was mostly empty. A drunk stumbled out of the bar two blocks down, grabbed a lamp post, then weaved toward a taxi. Music thumped from inside—bass-heavy, lyrics indistinct. The beat traveled through the sidewalk, up through her aching feet. A cop car cruised past but didn't slow down. They never did unless someone complained. And nobody complained about girls like her. They were invisible until they weren't. Until they were found in ditches, dumpsters, or floating in retention ponds. Then everyone cared. Then the news vans showed up.

She lit a cigarette. Menthol. Three years in Florida hadn't softened her Jersey edges—the accent that made johns either trust her or dismiss her. Some liked it. Said it reminded them of girls back home. Girls they'd known before moving south. Before marriages went sour, mortgages piled up, and Florida stopped being paradise.

The smoke burnt her throat, but gave her something to do with her hands. Kept them from shaking. She'd been clean for four months. Well, mostly clean. Hadn't touched the hard stuff since February. Just weed now. Just enough to take the edge off. Tiffany said she was doing good. Said she looked better. Less hollow. Less ghostly.

Jessica didn't feel better. Felt the same. Felt like she was treading water in the deep end, legs cramping, waiting to go under.

She took another drag. Watched the street. An SUV cruised past—slowed, window down, man leaning over to look—then sped up when he saw her face. Too old, probably. Or not pretty enough. Or maybe he recognized her from last month and remembered she'd charged him extra.

The car slowed. Grey or white—hard to tell in the dim streetlight. Could've been beige. The color didn't matter. What mattered was whether he'd pay. Whether he'd hurt her. Whether he'd drive her somewhere safe or somewhere she'd never come back from.

The car wasn't new, but it was not falling apart either. Clean. Looked like the kind of car someone washed on weekends. Practical. The type of vehicle that blended in. No dents she could see. No bumper stickers. Nothing memorable.

She straightened. Adjusted her top, pulling it down so more skin showed. Put on the smile that wasn't a smile, but close enough. The smile that said she was interested. That said, she wanted this. That said, she wasn't thinking about her feet or her stomach or the rent money or how her mother hadn't called in two years.

The window rolled down. He leaned over. She couldn't see his face clearly—shadows filled the car, dashboard light casting him in silhouette—no interior light. Most johns kept them off. Didn't want to be seen.

"How much?"

Straight to business. She liked that better than the ones who wanted to chat first. Pretend it was something other than what it was. Those who asked her name, where she was from, and what her sign was. Like they were on a date. Like she'd chosen this.

"Depends what ya lookin' faw."

"Company. Half hour."

Company. That's what they all called it. As if she were a therapist or a friend, instead of what she really was. A body. A transaction. For forty-five minutes, they could pretend that it meant something.

"A hunnert," she said.

He hesitated. She heard it in his breathing. Saw his hands shift on the wheel. "Fifty."

She laughed. A snort. "Ya kiddin' me? Ya think I'm runnin' a clearance sawl?"

"Seventy-five."

She studied what she could see of him through the window. Couldn't make out much in the darkness. A shape. Shoulders. Hands on the wheel—no wedding ring, but that didn't mean anything. Most of them took them off. Or never wore them in the first place. The voice sounded tired. Worn down. Like everyone else at two in the morning.

"Deal."

She opened the door. Slid into the passenger seat. The car smelled like fast food and cleaning chemicals. Fries and bleach. And something else. Something woody. Pine or cedar. Air freshener hanging from the rearview mirror. The interior was clean. No trash. No empty bottles rolling in the footwell. No fast food bags stuffed in the door pocket. The seats were worn but vacuumed. Radio playing low—talk radio droning about politics or sports or something she didn't care about.

He pulled away from the curb. Slow. Careful. Like someone who followed traffic laws. Like someone who didn't want to be pulled over. Most johns drove like that. Cautious. Paranoid.

She pulled out her phone.

Texted Tiffany:

> Got a date. Dixie northbound. Back in 30.

Tiffany would wait an hour. If Jessica didn't check in, she'd call. And if Jessica didn't answer, she'd call the cops. That's how it worked. That's how they survived. The buddy system. The only thing keeping them from disappearing completely.

"Ya got a name?" she asked.

"Does it matter?"

His accent. Not local. Not quite. Something flat in the vowels.

"Guess naw."

He drove north on Dixie Highway. Past the bars where music poured out every time someone opened a door. Past the closed storefronts—pawn shop, check cashing place, liquor store with bars on the windows. Past the gas station where she usually bought cigarettes. She watched the street signs. Memorizing. Another safety thing Tiffany taught her. Always know where you are. Always have an exit.

They kept going north. Past her usual drop-off zone. Past the side streets where most dates took her. Past the empty lot where she'd blown a guy in a Lexus last week.

Her stomach tightened. "Hey. Where we goin'?"

"Somewhere quiet."

Wrong. The word landed wrong. They always said that—somewhere quiet, somewhere private—but something in his voice made her skin prickle. Too calm. Too sure.

She shifted in her seat. Glanced at the door handle. Checked the lock. Not engaged. Could open it if she needed to. Could roll out if he didn't stop. She'd done it before. Hit the ground running. Lost a shoe but kept her money.

Then she saw it.

In the back seat. Through the gap between the front seats. A white cloth—no, a towel—bunched up against the door. Stained with something rusty. Brown.

She stared at it. Her brain caught up slowly.

Not rust. Old blood turned the color of dirt.

Her hands went cold. Her breath caught.

She'd seen enough wounds in three years to know the difference. Fresh was red. Bright. Wet. Arterial spray looked like paint. Old was brown. Dried. The color of mud or coffee grounds. Final.

The towel wasn't small. It wasn't a hand towel someone used to wipe up a nosebleed. It was a bath towel. Soaked. Heavy with it.

Her heart slammed. Once. Twice. Too fast. The cigarette smoke in her lungs turned to concrete.

"Let me out."

"We're almost there."

"I said, let me out. Right now!"

His hands tightened on the wheel. She saw it in the shadows. Knuckles had gone white. Tendons standing out.

"Please," she said—voice breaking. The mask slipping. The smile was gone. "I changed my mind. Just—please pull ovah he-ah. I'll walk back. I won't say nothin'. Ya can have the money back."

He didn't stop. Didn't slow. Kept driving north on Dixie. Past the last of the streetlights. Into the stretch where the road got dark. Where girls disappeared.

Her chest seized. She'd been in bad situations before. Men who got rough. Men who didn't want to pay. Men who liked to slap. To choke. One who tried to strangle her. But she'd got out. She'd survived. This felt different.

This felt like death.

Her hand went to her purse. Slow. Trying to look casual. She unzipped it. The sound was too loud in the quiet car. Felt inside for the brass knuckles she'd bought after a john broke her ribs two years ago. Tiffany made her buy them. Made her carry them. Made her practice.

If ya gonna survive aht he-ah, Tiffany had said, ya gotta be ready to fight. Not just fight. Win.

Cold metal. Four finger holes. She worked her fingers through them. Right hand. Thumb outside. The metal rings tight against her knuckles. Heavy. Solid. She kept her hand hidden inside the purse and kept her face neutral.

"Stop the fuckin' car!"

He glanced at her. Dashboard light caught his face for a second. Pale. Thin lips. Eyes that didn't blink. And in that glance, everything changed.

Even in the darkness, the shift was there. The wrongness. His eyes weren't right. Something hollow behind them. Empty. Like looking into a well and seeing nothing at the bottom.

Then he spoke. Quiet. Calm.

"You're all the same."

Four words. But they carried weight. Finality. The voice of someone who'd said them before. Who'd meant them before. Who'd done something about it before?

His hand went under the seat.

She didn't think. Pulled her fist from the purse. The brass knuckles caught dashboard light—dull gold, scratched metal—and she drove it hard into his face.

The impact sent shockwaves up her arm. His head snapped sideways. Bone crunched under metal. The sound was wet. Horrible. Like stepping on a snail. His nose crumpled inward. Cartilage collapsed.

He grabbed his face. No words. A grunt. Wet breathing through broken passages.

She hit him again. Harder. Aiming for where she thought his temple was. Where Tiffany said to aim.

Side of the head. Temple. Ear. Anything soft. Ya want to disorient them. Make them forget the wheel. Forget everything but the pain.

Metal cracked against skull. His head bounced off the window. Glass spider-webbed from the impact. Cracks were spreading like frost.

Again. Don't stop. Never stop.

He screamed. High. Broken. Not so calm now. Not preaching anymore.

The car swerved hard left. Tires screeched. A horn blared as another car swerved past them, the driver's face white with shock.

"Fuck!"

He lunged at her. Both hands left the wheel. Reaching for her throat. For her face. For anything he could grab.

The car veered. Jumped the curb. Sideswiped a parked car. Metal shrieked against metal. Her head slammed into the passenger window. Stars burst—white light behind her eyes. Pain bloomed.

Then he had the knife.

A flash of steel from under his seat. Blade caught sight of the streetlight as they passed under it. He drove it into her side.

The knife sank in. Pressure first. Then burning. Fire spreading through her ribs. She gasped. Couldn't breathe. Couldn't think. Wetness spreading down her side, soaking her tank top.

He pulled the knife out. The sensation of it leaving was worse than going in. Crimson poured. Warm. Too warm. Soaking her shirt, pooling in her lap.

She screamed.

He stabbed again. Shoulder this time. Not as deep. Hitting bone. The blade scraped against it. The sound traveled through her body. Through her skull. A vibration that made her teeth ache.

She twisted away. Her elbow smashed into his face. His already broken nose shifted and moved to one side. He howled. A sound like an animal. Like something dying.

Her fist swung wildly. Brass knuckles connected with his jaw. Hard. Clean. His head snapped back. Something in his face cracked. Cheekbone, maybe. Bone splintering under metal. His eye socket swelled immediately. Darkening. Closing.

The car jumped the curb again. Hit a garbage can. Metal screamed.

Garbage exploded across the hood. Plastic bags. Cans. Something that smelled like rotting food.

She kicked from her position, half-turned in the seat. Boot heel driving into his ribs. Once. Twice. Three times. He grunted. Breath exploding from his lungs. The wet sound of air forced out.

The knife slashed across her forearm. Deep. Deeper than the others. She felt it cut a muscle. Felt it drag. Scarlet sprayed the windshield. Drops hit the rearview mirror. Slid down like rain. Like tears.

"Stop—moving!"

She didn't stop. Couldn't stop. Adrenaline drowned everything. Drowned the pain. Drowned the fear. Left only the animalistic need to survive.

She punched. Again and again. The brass knuckles split skin. His face swelled. One eye was sealed shut from trauma. The other wide. Panicked. Wet pooled from his nose and mouth. His own. Running down his chin, soaking his shirt collar.

Her other hand clawed at his face. Nails raking. He grabbed her hair. Yanked. Her head slammed into the dashboard. Once. Twice. The world tilted. Spun. Her vision went white. Then grey. Then cleared.

The knife came again.

This time across her throat.

Cold steel dragged across skin. Pressure. Burning. Then heat. Wetness. The sensation of something opening that shouldn't.

Too much pouring down her chest. Hot. Sticky. Soaking everything.

She tried to scream. Nothing came out. A wet gurgling sound. Bubbling. Like drowning on dry land.

Then—snap.

The blade broke.

The pressure of it was released mid-slash. The blade caught on something—bone, cartilage, something hard in her throat—and snapped clean.

A metallic ping as the broken tip hit the dashboard. Bounced. Disappeared into darkness somewhere near the vents.

He made a sound. Rage. Frustration. Disbelief. Looked at the knife in his hand. At the jagged metal stub where the blade used to be. Evidence of his failure.

He threw it. The broken knife clattered somewhere in the footwell. Metal on plastic. Rolling.

He shoved his door open. Stumbled out. Breathing hard. Wheezing through his broken nose. A sound like wind through a straw.

She tried to move. Couldn't. Everything hurt. Everything burned. The wounds in her side, her shoulder, her arm, her throat. All of them were pulsing. All of them were pouring.

The door opened. He grabbed her arm. The wounded one. Pain white-hot. He dragged her out. She hit the pavement hard. Knees scraping asphalt. Skin tearing.

During the struggle, the glove box door had been kicked. Not popped—kicked by her boot heel when she'd fought. Now it hung open. Restaurant wipes were scattered everywhere—white packets with green logos. BCI printed across them. Dozens of them. A whole box. They spilled from the car with her. Some landed on the pavement. Some on her lap. Some were already soaked in blood.

She registered it dimly. Packets. Writing. But the meaning wouldn't come.

He stood over her. She couldn't see his face clearly. Swelling. Damage. Crimson covering him. His features were obscured by trauma. By what she'd done to him.

He kicked her. Hard. Ribs. She heard them crack. Felt them give. Felt something inside shift. Breath wouldn't come. Wouldn't go. Trapped in her chest.

She couldn't speak. Couldn't make a sound. The wound in her throat leaked. Bubbling. Choking.

He kicked her again. Stomach this time. She retched. Bile mixed with copper and combined with everything else.

He staggered back to the car. Got in. The engine revved. Tires squealed. He was gone. Swerving. Weaving. The car disappeared north. Taillights fading.

He'd left her, not finished, left her bleeding. Left her dying. But alive enough to know it.

Jessica lay there. Pavement was cold beneath her. Rough concrete against her cheek. So cold compared to the heat pouring out of her.

She couldn't feel her legs. Couldn't breathe right. The cut on her throat pulsed with every heartbeat. Not deep enough to kill fast. The broken blade had saved her from that. But deep enough. Enough that she'd bleed out. Enough that she'd drown in herself.

She turned her head. Saw lights. Neon. Red and white. Bright against the darkness.

Nifty Fifty Diner.

The sign buzzed. People inside. Shadows moving behind glass. Booths. Tables. Someone laughing. Someone eating. Forks on plates. Glasses clinking. Music from a jukebox. Normal life. Twenty feet away. Twenty feet that might as well be twenty miles.

She tried to crawl. Managed two feet. Her arms were shaking. Gave out. Stopped. Too tired. Too much was gone. Too much of her was soaking into the concrete. Spreading. A dark pool in the streetlight.

The restaurant wipes lay scattered around her. White packets. Some clean. Some soaked. Evidence she didn't know she was leaving. Evidence of where he'd been. What he'd cleaned. Who he'd cleaned up after.

Her phone buzzed in her purse. Three feet away. Screen glowing. Lighting up the darkness.

Tiffany calling.

She couldn't reach it. Couldn't move. Her arms wouldn't work anymore. Wouldn't respond to what her brain told them.

The phone kept buzzing. Tiffany's face on the screen. Smiling. A picture from last summer. Before everything got so hard.

Then it stopped. Went to voicemail. The screen went dark.

The lights from the diner blurred. Darkness was creeping in from the edges, closing in like a fist.

First, the legs. Numb. Dead weight. Then the fingers. Tingling. Pins and needles. Then nothing. Cold.

Vision narrowing. Tunnel closing. World shrinking to the diner sign and the pavement and the wetness spreading beneath her.

She could smell food from inside. Burgers. Coffee. Pie. Her

stomach cramped. Empty and dying. Hadn't eaten since the granola bar. Wouldn't eat again.

They'd finish their meal. Pay the check. Walk past her body on their way to the car. See her there. Call someone. But it'd be too late.

She thought about her mother, how she'd find out if she'd find out. If anyone would call her. If she'd care.

Thought about Tiffany. How she'd blame herself. How she'd think she should've called sooner. Should've come looking. Should've known.

Thought about the boyfriend who started all this. Locked up in Raiford. Serving eight years. Wouldn't even know she was dead. Wouldn't care if he did.

Not like this.

But dying didn't care about preferences. Didn't wait for convenient moments or meaningful last words. Didn't let you say goodbye, make peace, or tie up loose ends. It came. Slow when you wanted fast. Inevitable. Cold.

The pavement smelled of oil, rain, and city dirt. Her cheek pressed against it. Rough. Textured. She could see the individual pieces of aggregate. Focus narrowing to that. To the small things. To the details that didn't matter.

The neon sign hummed. Electric. Constant. The world kept moving. Inside the diner, someone ordered pie. The waitress laughed. A car drove past. Didn't stop. Didn't slow. Didn't see.

And Jessica Torres—twenty-six, street name Destiny—bled out on Dixie Highway with restaurant wipes scattered around her like evidence of a life interrupted.

Her last thought was simple. Clear.

Tiffany's gonna be pissed.

Then darkness.

Morning came slowly and inevitably to District 14. Evans sat at his desk, files spread across the scratched metal surface like evidence of an all-nighter he hadn't actually pulled. But he might as well have. Sleep had come in shallow fits, his mind running through timelines and witness statements.

Three names. Three women. Three sets of stab wounds that refused to line up cleanly into a pattern a prosecutor could sell to a jury.

Camila Morales. Julia Aguilar. Jessica Torres.

The fluorescent lights overhead buzzed, one of them flickering in the pulse of a dying heartbeat. The A/C wheezed cold air that smelled faintly of mildew and old takeout someone had left in a drawer two weeks ago and forgotten. Phones rang in waves across the bullpen.

Evans rubbed his eyes. They felt gritty, like someone had poured sand under his eyelids while he slept. His neck ached from the angle he'd held it yesterday, hunched over these same files, looking for connections that kept slipping just out of reach. The coffee in his mug had gone cold an hour ago. He took a sip anyway. Bitter. Thick.

He pulled up the crime scene photo on his phone. The pavement in front of Nifty Fifty was lit by the harsh glare of a camera flash and the red-blue pulse of ambulance lights.

Blood. So much blood. Pooled on the concrete in shapes that looked almost deliberate—dark, arterial red going rust-brown at the edges where it had started to dry, smeared in drag marks where Torres had tried to crawl toward the diner's front door, fingers leaving streaks like something out of a horror film. The wipes were every-where, restaurant-issue packets torn open and left scattered across the floor, white rectangles stamped with the green BCI logo. Each wrapper was soaked through with blood so dark that the stains appeared black.

Evans set the phone down. Stared at the preliminary report on Jessica Torres. Street name Destiny. Twenty-six years old. Three priors—solicitation, possession, trespassing. Three years on the street, by most accounts. Picked up on Dixie Highway sometime after two in the morning. Attacked. Stabbed. Beaten and dumped in front of the Nifty Fifty Diner at half past four.

Victim transported to Good Samaritan Medical Center—critical condition. Surgery is ongoing as of six this morning. Rocca and Pérez were already en route to the hospital, waiting for the doctors to finish piecing her back together enough that she could maybe tell them who'd done this to her—if she lived.

Evans flipped to the Aguilar file. Cross-referenced dates. Locations. Victim profiles. Something was there.

Julia Aguilar. Twenty-three. Found in a vacant lot off Dixie Highway in proximity to the Morales' home. Stabbed. Dumped. High-carbon steel fragments were pulled from the wound—commercial grade. You'd find any of these in any restaurant kitchen.

He pulled the Morales file closer. Crime scene photos he'd looked at so many times he could see them when he closed his eyes. Twenty-one years old. College student. Waitress. Stabbed on Lake Worth Beach, left in the sand like trash. No witnesses. No forensics led anywhere useful—just a body and a family that would never be whole again.

And now Torres. Stabbed. Beaten and dumped at a restaurant.

The pattern was there. Just out of reach, but there. The fragments hovered close, refusing to resolve—not yet.

He'd been reviewing case files since six-forty-five, trying to find the thread that connected all three—trying to see what Roan would see. What Roan always seemed to see before anyone else did.

Behind him, Detective Martinez slammed his phone down. "¡No me jodas!" His chair scraped against the floor—heavy footsteps toward the break room.

Evans barely noticed. His eyes scanned the three files, searching for overlap.

Roan would strip it down to geography. To routine. To the spaces where victims and killers occupied the same square footage without knowing it. Diners. Bars. Gas stations. Laundromats. The invisible infrastructure of working-class life, where nobody looked twice at anyone.

Evans started a new column on his notepad. Overlap - Locations:

Nifty Fifty Diner (Camila worked, Torres dumped)
Dixie Highway corridor (all three)
Lake Worth Beach (Camila, all three?)

The bullpen door opened.

Evans looked up.

Detective Roan walked in carrying a Starbucks cup, looking like he'd slept, which Evans knew was a lie. Roan didn't sleep. He just paused between days long enough to shower, shave, and pretend the last twelve hours hadn't happened. Dark suit, no tie—still crisp enough it looked like he'd just pulled it from the cleaners. Hair still damp, smelling faintly of Irish Spring soap and something else underneath. Coffee. Exhaustion. The chemical tang of adrenaline that never quite washed off. Freshly shaven, but his eyes had that thousand-yard stare Evans was starting to recognize—the look of a man who'd been up all night and hadn't caught anything.

The bullpen didn't go quiet when Roan entered. It never did. But the noise shifted. Conversations became more focused. Typing became more deliberate. Martinez's voice dropped half a register from the break room.

Roan moved through the bullpen like weather. People adjusted without realizing they were doing it.

He stopped at Evans' desk. Set the coffee cup down on the corner —black, no sugar, still warm. Didn't say anything. Just looked at the files spread across the desk, then at Evans.

Roan pulled out the chair across from Evans' desk and sat. Leaned back. Studied the files without touching them. His gaze tracked across the photos, the timelines, the notes Evans had scrawled in margins. Reading the case through Evans' eyes.

"Torres," Roan said. Not a question.

"Yeah." Evans pulled the Torres file closer.

"Walk me through it."

Evans took a breath. Organized his thoughts the way Roan had been teaching him—facts first, speculation later, never mix the two. He tapped the preliminary report. "Dispatch got the call at 4:47 a.m. Female victim, multiple stab wounds, dumped in front of Nifty Fifty Diner on Dixie Highway."

He flipped to the next page. "Caller was Frank DeAngelo—"

Roan's eyes sharpened. "DeAngelo."

"Yeah." Evans watched Roan's reaction, filing it away. "Says he was opening up, heard something outside, found her bleeding on the ground out front. Called 911. Stayed with her until paramedics arrived."

"Where was she before the diner?"

Evans shook his head. "Don't know yet. Patrol's still canvassing. Best guess is she was picked up somewhere on Dixie, maybe near one of the bars or strip malls that stretch down that way. Beaten and stabbed in a vehicle or secondary location, then dumped."

"She alive?"

"Critical. Good Samaritan. Surgery started around six." Evans checked his watch. "Rocca and Pérez are en route now, waiting for doctors to stabilize her enough for questions."

Roan was silent for a moment. His gaze moved across the files, connecting dots Evans couldn't see yet. His fingers drummed once against the desk—a tell Evans had learned meant Roan was three steps ahead and deciding whether to share.

"Priors?" Roan asked.

Evans flipped to the rap sheet. "Three. Solicitation in 2021. Possession—marijuana, misdemeanor—in 2022. Trespassing last year. Street name Destiny. Real name Jessica Torres."

Roan went still. His hand moved to the Torres file, pulled it closer. Opened it. Stared at the booking photo clipped to the inside cover.

Late twenties. Brunette. Heavy eyeliner. Tired eyes that had seen too much too young. Three years on the street showed in the lines around her mouth, the way her smile didn't quite reach her eyes, even in the mugshot. Defiant. Scared. Trying to look harder than she felt.

Roan stared at that photo for a long moment. Too long.

Evans straightened in his chair. "You know her." Not a question.

Roan's jaw tightened. "Yeah."

"From where?"

"Lucky's." Roan's voice went flat. "Few days ago. I was canvassing, trying to get information on Camila. Talked to three women in a booth." He tapped the photo. "She was one of them. The brunette. Sat with a blonde and a redhead. Wouldn't give me her name. Said she didn't know Camila. Said girls like them don't talk to cops."

Evans felt something click into place. The weight of it settled in his chest. "She lied."

"Maybe. Or maybe she really didn't know Camila. But she knew something." Roan leaned back, eyes still on the photo. "She was defensive. Protective. She was the one in charge—kept shutting the others down every time they started to talk."

He paused. His thumb traced the edge of the file. "One of the others called me last night. Redhead. Mary something. I'd given her my card at Lucky's—slipped it to her when Torres wasn't looking."

"What'd she say?" Evans grabbed his pen.

"Nothing solid. Rumors. Said she was scared. Someone had been following her. Thought she might be working the streets, but couldn't confirm it. Just bar talk and worry."

"Think she knew the killer?"

Roan's expression went distant. "I think she knew the street. And people on the street know things they don't say out loud because saying them gets you killed."

Evans pulled his notepad closer. Started writing. His pen moved fast across the paper. "So Torres worked Dixie. Camila worked at the diner on Dixie. Aguilar—" He flipped through the file. "Same area. All three in the same general zone."

"Hunting ground," Roan said quietly.

The word hung between them. Evans stopped writing. Looked up.

Hunting ground. That's what they'd been missing. Not a pattern of victims. A pattern of geography. One predator. One territory. One sick bastard who knew every corner of Dixie Highway like it was his personal game preserve.

Evans kept writing, his pen moving faster now. The pieces were clicking together. "DeAngelo called in the Torres attack. DeAngelo employed Camila. DeAngelo—"

"Was at Oceanside Pub last night," Roan finished.

Evans looked up. His pen stopped mid-word. "What?"

Roan leaned forward, elbows on the desk. His coffee cup sat forgotten between them. "I went to the pub after we wrapped at Vance's place. Needed a drink. Needed to think. Found a Bible verse flyer in the bathroom—same verse Ariel's been using. Romans 6:23. 'The wages of sin is death.' Someone taped it above the urinal where every man who pissed there would see it."

Evans wrote:

Ariel

The pieces were connecting now. Faster than he could process. "Ariel kills Camila. Dumps her on the beach. But why Aguilar? Why Torres?"

"Same profile," Roan said. "Young women. Working the streets or working service jobs that put them in contact with men. Ariel sees them as sinners. Thinks he's doing God's work. Cleansing the world one body at a time."

"But why dump Torres at DeAngelo's diner?"

Roan's eyes went cold. Flat. He'd already worked through this and didn't like the answer. "Because DeAngelo was at the pub last night. Sat down right next to me at the bar. Started talking. Asked about the Vance shooting, talked about Camila. Then we talked about BCI—the supplier that provides kitchen equipment to both the diner and the pub. Knives that break. High-carbon steel blades that crack and leave fragments behind."

Evans stopped writing. Looked up. The weight of it hit him. "You think DeAngelo's involved."

"DeAngelo confirmed a kid matching Ariel's description had been in the diner a few times. Always alone. Always ordered coffee. Made the waitresses uncomfortable. Camila wouldn't serve him after the second visit." Roan's fingers drummed the desk again. Once. Twice. "And I think it's not a coincidence that twelve hours later, a third victim gets dumped right in front of his property."

"Message."

"Or warning."

Evans looked down at the files. Three women. Three attacks. All connected by Dixie Highway, by service work, by men who saw them as disposable. By a God-fearing kid with a knife and a scripture verse that justified murder.

"We need to talk to Torres," Evans said. "If she makes it."

"She'll make it," Roan said. Voice flat. Certain. As if he could will it into being true through sheer stubbornness in refusing to accept the alternative. "She fought. You don't fight that hard just to die on an operating table."

He'd been a cop long enough to know better.

Evans turned his phone toward Roan. The crime scene photo filled the screen. "CSU pulled the brass knuckles off her—one hand. Covered in blood—hers and someone else's. She hit him. Hard. Multiple times. His blood's mixed with hers all over the scene."

Roan leaned closer to the phone. Studied the photo. His expression didn't change, but something in his posture shifted. Satisfaction, maybe. Or vindication. "Good."

"DNA's being processed. Fast-tracked. But it will be six weeks, maybe a month, before we get results."

Behind them, the bullpen churned on. Phones rang. Keyboards clacked. The copier jammed, and someone swore. Life was grinding forward, whether they solved this or not.

"Captain know yet?" Roan asked.

As if summoned, Captain Norris' door opened. He stood in the doorway, tie already loosened, collar unbuttoned, face carrying the weight of a man who'd been awake too long on too little sleep. His eyes found Roan immediately. Locked on.

"Roan," Norris called across the bullpen. "My office. Now."

Roan stood. Didn't look surprised. Didn't look concerned. Just tired—a fatigue that had seeped so deeply into him that it would never be shaken off. The sort of exhaustion that made a home within your bones, settling there for good.

"Keep working the files," Roan said to Evans. "Cross-reference Torres' known associates with Camila's and Aguilar's. Find the overlap. See if someone knew all three of them."

"On it."

Roan walked toward Norris' office. The bullpen watched without watching. Conversations continued, quieter now. Everyone knew what it meant when the Captain called you in after a third body dropped.

Either you were getting pulled off the case.

Or you were getting buried in it.

Evans watched him go. Watched the way Roan moved—steady, controlled, deliberate like a man walking toward something inevitable.

Norris stepped aside to let Roan enter. Their eyes met for half a second. Something passed between them—history, maybe, or understanding, or just the shared exhaustion of men who'd been doing this too long.

The door closed.

CHAPTER

38

THE DOOR CLICKED SHUT behind Roan. That sound cut the bullpen noise to a muffled hum. Solid. Final. Captain Norris' office wrapped around him like a tomb. Dark wood paneling that hadn't seen daylight since the '80s. Venetian blinds half-closed against the morning sun, slicing the room into bands of light and shadow. The air smelled stale —old coffee and older sweat, the accumulated weight of three decades' worth of bad news delivered across that desk.

Roan had been in this office more times than he could count. Commendations that felt like accusations. Reprimands disguised as concern. Conversations that started with "Close the door" and ended with "Watch yourself."

This was one of those.

Norris didn't sit right away. He moved to the window, hands in his pockets, looking down at the parking lot two stories below, watching cars come and go, watching the world spin without needing him to push it. Heavier now than he'd been ten years ago—twenty pounds, maybe thirty. The weight that accumulated when you stopped chasing suspects and started chasing budgets.

Roan stayed standing. Always did. Sitting felt like surrender. Like admitting you were wrong before the conversation started.

Behind Norris' desk sat a chair with armrests polished by two decades of anxious palms. The wood gleamed where countless men had gripped tight, bodies rigid, as they absorbed whatever hammer blow was coming next.

Norris finally turned. Gestured to the chair across from his desk. "Sit."

Roan stayed standing.

Norris' mouth twitched. Not quite a smile. "Stubborn bastard."

"Learned from the best."

Norris moved to his desk. Sat. The chair groaned under his weight —a sound Roan knew well.

"Update," Norris said. Not a question. A command.

Roan's back ached. His knees protested standing. But he stayed upright, shoulders square. He let the silence stretch for half a second before responding. "Three victims. Camila Morales, Julia Aguilar, Jessica Torres. All stabbed."

Norris picked up a pen. Tapped it against the desk. Once.

"All dumped in public locations within a two-mile radius of Dixie Highway," Roan continued. "High-carbon steel fragments in two of the wounds. Commercial grade."

Twice.

"Same supplier—BCI—services multiple restaurants in the area."

"Connection?" Norris asked.

"Working theory: all three women worked or frequented the same geographical zone. Dixie corridor. Bars, diners, street corners. Killer's hunting ground. He knows the area. Knows the routine. Knows when and where these women are vulnerable."

"Suspect?"

Roan's shoulders tightened. This was the part Norris wouldn't like. "Ariel Morales. Brother of the first victim. Nineteen years old. History of religious zealotry. Been stalking his sister. Distributing Bible verse flyers with the same passage—Romans 6:23. 'The wages of sin is death.' Flyers were found at the Oceanside Pub, where Camila was last seen alive. Witnesses confirm a kid matching his description being at where she worked. Made staff uncomfortable. Camila refused to serve him."

Norris set the pen down. Leaned back. The chair creaked as he shifted. "Evidence?"

"Circumstantial. Witness statements. Geographic overlap. Motive."

"DNA?"

"Torres fought back. Brass knuckles. Blood at the scene. Lab's processing. Should have results in a month, but a blood type in an hour."

Norris rubbed his face with both hands. Exhaled slowly through his nose. The venetian blinds shifted slightly in the A/C current, striping his face with light and shadow. When he looked up, his eyes had that flat, tired quality Roan recognized from his own mirror. "You know what happens if this gets out."

"Sir—"

"Panic." Norris leaned forward. Elbows on the desk. "Two or three women dead in a little more than a week. Press gets wind there's a serial killer working Dixie Highway, this city loses its goddamn mind —tourism tanks. Real estate plummets. Mayor starts making calls. Sheriff starts asking questions I can't answer."

Roan's hands flexed at his sides. "We contain it."

"How?" Norris' voice sharpened. "You've got circumstantial evidence on a suspect you haven't even brought in yet. Torres is critical. Aguilar's family is screaming for answers. And the press already made a field day out of the Vance shooting."

There it was. The real reason Norris had called him in.

Roan's chest tightened. Not shame. Not quite. Just the dull ache of knowing he'd been wrong. "Vance was a dead end."

"Vance was a mistake." Norris didn't raise his voice. Didn't need to. "You chased him for three days. Wasted manpower. Wasted time. Could've been working other leads. Could've stopped Torres from getting dumped on a sidewalk bleeding out."

The words hit like fists. Roan's shoulders went rigid, but he didn't argue. Couldn't. Because Norris was right.

"I've caught serial killers before," Roan said. Voice flat. Factual.

"I know your history, Robert." Norris' tone softened. Just barely. "You're good at this. Better than most. But you and I are both well past our expiration date."

The phrase hit hard. Expiration date. Like they were cartons of milk left too long in the fridge.

Roan felt it in his knees. In his back. The way his eyes took longer to focus in dim light. The way the stairs felt steeper than they used to. He was fifty-two. Norris was fifty-nine. Neither of them would see sixty behind a desk if they kept grinding the way they had been. The thought settled into him like cold water—inescapable, numbing. This job would kill them both, eventually. The only question was whether it would be a bullet, a heart attack, or the slow erosion of watching too many bodies pile up while bureaucrats counted budgets.

"I'm not pulling you off the case," Norris continued. "But I'm not covering your ass forever, either. The salacious cases—the ones that make headlines, the ones that get you on the news—those are the ones that get me called into the Sheriff's office at seven in the morning to explain why my best detective let a wife shoot an innocent man's face off."

Roan's hands flexed. "Sabine Vance pulled a shotgun—"

"I know what happened." Norris' voice cut through. "I read the report. I watched the news. I know Evans got covered in blood and bone bits, and you had to call it in while his hands were still shaking. But the press doesn't care about that. They care about clicks. And 'Wife Shoots Husband in the Face' is clickable."

Roan said nothing because there was nothing to say.

Norris stood. Walked to the window again. Arms crossed. The morning light caught the grey in his hair, turning it silver. "I won't be here forever, Robert. Another year, maybe two, and I'm taking my pension and moving to North Carolina, where my son lives. When I'm gone, someone else sits in this chair. Someone who doesn't know you. Someone who doesn't owe you. Someone who won't cover your more questionable judgment calls."

Tread carefully. Your protection has an expiration date.

Roan's exhaustion settled deeper into his bones—the weight of twenty-seven years on the job. The weight of three bodies hadn't stopped. The weight of knowing Norris was right—they were both past their prime, both running on fumes, both one bad case away from being forced into retirement.

But he wasn't done yet.

"We know who the killer might be," Roan said.

Norris turned. "You said Ariel Morales. Circumstantial evidence."

"Correct." Roan's throat tightened. He thought of Vance. Of being wrong. Of wasting three days chasing the wrong man. "Everything points to him. But I'm not making assumptions this time."

"Prove it."

"I'm going to pick him up. Bring him in. Let him sit in an interview room while we check his blood type against the blood type found at the Torres crime scene. If the blood at the Torres scene matches his, we've got him. If it doesn't, we let him walk and keep working."

Norris studied him. Long and hard. A gaze that weighed whether you were confident or desperate. Whether you were chasing the truth or chasing vindication.

The silence stretched. Somewhere beyond the door, a phone rang. Someone laughed.

"Take Evans," Norris said finally.

"Already planned to."

"And Robert?" Norris' voice dropped. Quiet. Almost gentle. "If you're wrong about this—if Ariel Morales walks and the real killer strikes again—I can't protect you from what comes next."

Roan met his eyes. Held them. Nodded once.

Norris nodded back. Slow. Deliberate. "Then go pick him up."

Roan turned toward the door. His hand closed around the knob.

"Robert."

He stopped. Didn't turn around.

"Be careful."

Roan's throat worked. He wanted to say something. Wanted to acknowledge the years between them, the cases they'd worked, the bodies they'd seen, the weight they both carried. But the words wouldn't come.

He opened the door and walked out.

The weight of Norris' words followed him into the bullpen. If you're wrong about this... He'd been wrong before. Vance proved that. But Ariel fit. The pieces lined up. They just needed to confirm the blood type. Or prove him wrong again.

The bullpen noise came like waves. Phones ringing. Keyboards clacking. Martinez arguing. The machine was grinding ever forward.

Evans looked up from his desk. Eyes sharp. Alert. Something in his posture shifted when he saw Roan's face—recognition of a conversation that hadn't gone well, or had gone exactly as badly as expected.

Roan crossed the room. Stopped at Evans' desk. "We're going to pick up Ariel Morales."

Evans stood. Grabbed his jacket from the back of his chair. "Where?"

"We check the Morales apartment first."

"You think it's him?"

Roan's grey eyes stayed flat. Measured. "Most things point to him. We need to bring him in."

"What if you're wrong?"

The question hung between them. Evans' face was open and genuine—not challenging, just seeking clarity, wanting to understand what had happened in that office. What weight was Roan carrying now?

"Then we keep looking," Roan said. "But right now, he's our best lead."

Evans studied him for a moment. Then nodded. "Alright."

"You're driving," Roan continued. "I need to think."

Evans grabbed his keys. "Let's go."

They walked toward the exit. Past Martinez, who was still arguing in Spanish. Past the bulletin board with clearance rates, softball photos, and wanted posters for men who'd been dead or caught years ago.

The morning sun hit them hard when they stepped outside. Bright. Hot. Florida's humidity was already thick enough to choke on.

Evans unlocked the Ford Explorer. Slid into the driver's seat. Roan took shotgun. The engine turned over. Rattled. Settled into a rough idle. Evans pulled out of the parking lot.

CHAPTER

39

SUNLIGHT HIT like a fist when they stepped outside Good Samaritan. White. Brutal. Unrelenting. The hospital doors slid shut behind them, sealing off the antiseptic chill and leaving them to the mercy of midday Florida heat. Pérez squinted against it, fishing sunglasses from her breast pocket while the asphalt shimmered in waves that made the parking lot look liquid. Lunchtime in Florida meant a sidewalk that could fry eggs and air thick enough to chew.

Rocca walked beside her toward the cruiser, shoulders sagging just enough that she noticed. The hospital smell clung to them—disinfectant and floor wax and something that might've been fear or might've been death.

"Well," he said. "That was cheerful."

Pérez unlocked the cruiser. Slid into the driver's seat. The interior was an oven. Leather scorched through her uniform pants. She started the engine and cranked the A/C to maximum. Hot air blasted from the vents.

"Give it a minute," she said.

Rocca dropped into the passenger seat. Closed his eyes. Leaned his head back against the headrest.

Torres was in a coma. The surgeon had used words like 'critical', 'touch-and-go', and 'we'll know more in forty-eight hours'. Translation: her body would decide whether she lived or died. Medicine had done all it could.

Pérez pulled out of the parking lot. Merged onto Flagler. Traffic crawled. Everyone was heading somewhere for lunch. Fast food. Diners. Anywhere with A/C.

"Saw Ellen Mills in the ER," Rocca said.

Pérez glanced at him. "Yeah?"

"Yeah. She gave me that look nurses give cops when they're processing another stabbing victim."

"What look?"

"The 'you people need to figure your shit out' look."

Pérez smiled despite herself. "Ellen's good people."

"She is," Rocca agreed. "Doesn't mean she's wrong."

The A/C finally kicked in cold. Pérez adjusted the vents. Pointed one at her face. The temperature gauge on the dashboard read ninety-four degrees. Felt hotter. Always did when humidity wrapped around you like wet wool.

"Tiffany was a wreck," Pérez said.

Rocca opened his eyes. Looked at her. "The blonde?"

"Yeah. Torres' roommate."

"Friend."

"More than that. They work together."

Rocca nodded. She knew what she meant without saying it. Tiffany wasn't just a friend. She was a colleague. Same profession. Same risks. Torres could've been her.

"She give you anything useful?" Rocca asked.

"Not much, we didn't already have." Pérez changed lanes, cutting around a pickup truck doing fifteen miles per hour under the limit. "She kept twisting her hands together. Couldn't sit still. Said Torres went to work like usual, didn't see her after that." She paused, remembering the way Tiffany's voice had cracked. "Mentioned Torres had been nervous the last few weeks. Jumpy."

"Nervous about what?"

"Wouldn't say. Maybe didn't know."

Rocca's hand went to his jaw, rubbing the stubble there. The motion pulled at his shirt. Made him look older. Tired. He was forty. Looked fifty on bad days. Today qualified.

"Brass knuckles," he said.

"Yeah."

"She fought back."

"Yeah."

"Good for her."

Pérez continued south on Flagler. The cruiser's tires hummed against asphalt. Palm trees blurred past. Strip malls. Gas stations. The same landscape they'd been driving through for days.

"Restaurant wipes at the scene," Rocca said after a minute.

Pérez frowned. "I know."

"What do you think that's about?"

"No idea."

Rocca shifted in his seat, angling toward her. "He's cleaning something, or wiping something down. But what? His prints are already at the scene, and his blood. So why bother?"

"Maybe himself. Blood on his hands, his clothes."

"Maybe." Rocca didn't sound convinced. His finger tapped against the armrest—once, twice, a rhythm that matched his thinking. "But why restaurant wipes specifically? Why not regular paper towels? Or a rag? Hell, why not just wear gloves?"

"Maybe he works at a restaurant."

"Maybe. Or maybe he's careless. Grabbed what was convenient."

"BCI supplies restaurants. Same company that makes the knives."

"Yeah." Rocca's tapping stopped. "That's not a coincidence."

The silence stretched between them as they headed south. Cars disappeared from the highway one by one, replaced by a white-hot glare that bounced off the asphalt. Sweat beaded at Rocca's temples despite the A/C blasting cold air at his face.

Pérez thought about Torres lying in that hospital bed—tubes, monitors, and machines breathing for her. Tiffany was sitting in the waiting room with her arms wrapped around herself, rocking slightly like the motion could ward off what was coming. Ellen Mills was moving through the ER with that brisk efficiency nurses had when they'd seen too much death to let it slow them down.

"You ever wonder if it's worth it?" Pérez asked.

Rocca looked at her. "What?"

"This. The job. Chasing people who do terrible things. Watching people die. Telling families their daughter's in a coma and might not wake up."

"Every day."

"And?"

"And I keep showing up."

"That's not an answer."

"Sure it is."

Pérez shook her head. Smiled. "You're impossible."

"I'm practical." Rocca shifted in his seat. Adjusted his seatbelt. "You do the job or you don't. Wondering if it's worth it doesn't help Torres."

"No," Pérez said. "It doesn't."

But she still wondered.

They drove past a Wendy's. A Subway. A Taco Bell. The lunch crowd packed the parking lots. Pérez's stomach growled. She ignored it.

Rocca watched the road. Palm trees. Gas stations. The same loop they'd been running for a week. Two women were dead—one in a coma. A killer was still out there.

"You got a place yet?" he asked.

Pérez glanced at him. "What?"

"A place. You and Jacob. You moved in together, right?"

"Yeah. Couple months ago."

"How's that going?"

Pérez's hands tightened on the wheel. Just slightly. "Fine."

"Fine?"

"Yeah. Fine."

Rocca raised an eyebrow but said nothing.

"Jacob's out of town," she said after a minute.

"Yeah?"

"His brother's wedding. Up in Long Island."

"When's he back?"

"Monday."

"You miss him?"

Pérez hesitated. That was enough of an answer.

"It's nice," she said finally. "Having the place to myself. Quiet."

Rocca nodded. Didn't say anything. Just looked out the window.

"What?" Pérez asked.

"Nothing."

"You're thinking something."

"I'm always thinking something."

"Rocca."

He turned to her. "You don't have to explain yourself to me, kid."

"I'm not a kid."

"Figure of speech."

"I'm thirty."

"Like I said."

Pérez rolled her eyes. But she smiled. Rocca had that effect. Made you want to punch him and hug him in equal measure.

Pérez's stomach growled again. Louder this time.

Rocca smiled. "Hungry?"

"Yeah."

"Me too."

"You're always hungry."

"Occupational hazard."

"How is hunger an occupational hazard?"

"Stress eating." Rocca patted his stomach. "I'm carrying ten extra pounds of crime-solving anxiety."

"Ten?"

"Fifteen."

Pérez laughed. "You're ridiculous."

"I'm self-aware."

"Where do you want to eat?"

"Anywhere. I don't care."

"That's not helpful."

"I'm a simple man. Give me a sandwich and I'm happy."

"Subway?"

"God no."

"Picky."

"I have standards."

Pérez turned into a Publix parking lot. "Deli?"

"Perfect."

They drove past Bryant Park. Past the library. Past the police station, where they'd spend the rest of the afternoon filing paperwork and waiting for blood typing results.

"Jacob's a good guy," she said.

"I'm sure he is."

Rocca shrugged. "You like having the place to yourself. That's not a crime."

"I didn't say I don't like having him there."

"You didn't say you do, either."

Pérez didn't answer. Because he was right, she hadn't.

The apartment had felt different with Jacob gone. Bigger. Quieter. She'd come home after long shifts and not had to make conversation. Not had to smile when she was too tired to mean it. Not had to be anything except alone.

And that had felt good.

Which worried her.

"You ever think about getting married?" she asked.

Rocca laughed. Actually laughed. "No."

"Never?"

"Never seriously."

"Why not?"

He shrugged. "Never met anyone I wanted to see every day for the rest of my life."

"That's bleak."

"That's honest." He looked at her. "You thinking about it?"

"Jacob's brother just got married. Jacob's been talking about it more lately."

"And?"

"And I don't know."

"That's also an answer."

"Helpful."

"I'm a detective, not a therapist."

Pérez turned into a Publix parking lot. "I like my job."

"I know."

"I'm good at it."

"You are."

"And I don't know if I want to split my focus. Marriage. Kids. All that."

"Then don't."

"It's not that simple."

"Sure it is."

They parked. Climbed out of the cruiser. The heat hit again. Relentless. Pérez's uniform stuck to her back. She tugged at it. Didn't help.

Inside, the store was freezing. A/C cranked to arctic levels. Rocca headed straight for the deli counter. Pérez followed, her skin prickling as it adjusted to the temperature shock. Her phone buzzed. She checked it.

Text from Jacob:

> Wedding was great. Miss you. Home Monday
> morning. Love you.

She stared at the screen. Felt nothing. Felt guilty for feeling nothing.

"You ordering?" Rocca asked.

Pérez looked up. Slipped the phone back into her pocket. "Yeah. Turkey. Wheat. Mustard."

"That's it?"

"I'm not that hungry."

"Liar."

"Fine. Add cheese."

Rocca grinned. Turned to the deli worker. "Two turkey subs. One with cheese, mustard, lettuce. One with everything."

"Everything?" Pérez asked.

"I said I was hungry."

They paid. Took their sandwiches to a table near the window. Ate in comfortable silence. Outside, the sun blazed. People hurried from cars to storefronts. Nobody lingered, not in this heat.

"You think Torres is going to make it?" Pérez asked.

Rocca swallowed. Took a drink of his soda—too sweet, the kind that left your teeth feeling fuzzy. "I don't know."

"Doctor said forty-eight hours."

"Doctors always say that."

"You think she'll wake up?"

"I think her body will decide."

Pérez picked at her sandwich. "Tiffany's scared."

"She should be."

"You think the killer will go after her?"

"If he thinks she knows something, maybe."

"She doesn't know anything."

"We know that. He doesn't."

Pérez nodded. Took another bite. Chewed slowly. "I told her to call if she sees anything suspicious."

"Good."

"I gave her my phone."

"Also good."

They ate in silence again. Rocca finished his sandwich in what felt like three bites. Pérez was still working on hers when he crumpled his wrapper and tossed it in the trash can.

"You don't owe him marriage just because he's a good guy," Rocca said. His knee cracked as he shifted. He winced. "You owe him honesty. If you're not feeling it, say so."

Pérez set her sandwich down. "What if I'm never sure?"

"Then you're never sure." He looked at her. "But lonely's not the same as unhappy."

"You ever regret it? Not getting married?"

Rocca considered. "Sometimes. Mostly no."

"Why mostly?"

"Because I like my life. I do what I want when I want. I don't answer to anyone except Norris, and he doesn't care what I do as long as I close cases."

Pérez nodded. Something loosened in her chest—just a little.

"You're not me," Rocca added. "Maybe you want different things. But you don't have to decide today."

"I know."

"Good."

Pérez finished her sandwich. Stood. Rocca followed her out to the cruiser.

The heat was worse now. Midday sun directly overhead. No shade. No relief. Pérez started the engine. Waited for the A/C to kick in.

"Back to the station?" Rocca asked.

"Yeah."

"Paperwork?"

"Paperwork."

Rocca sighed. "My favorite."

"Mine too."

They drove back through Lake Worth. Past the same palm trees. Same gas stations. Same strip malls. Everything looked the same in Florida. Endless sun. Endless heat. Endless pavement.

Pérez kept her eyes on the road. "Thanks," she said after a minute.

"For what?"

"For not judging."

Rocca shrugged. "I'm the last person who gets to judge anyone's life choices."

"Still."

"Still nothing. You're a good cop, Pérez. That's what matters to me."

She smiled. "You're not so bad yourself."

"High praise."

"Don't let it go to your head."

"Too late."

They pulled into the station parking lot. Climbed out. Headed inside. The A/C was a relief after the cruiser. Pérez's skin prickled as it adjusted to the temperature change.

Norris was waiting by Rocca's desk. Arms crossed. Face set in that expression that meant bad news or bureaucracy. Probably both.

"Rocca. Pérez," he said.

"Captain," Rocca said.

"Blood typing results back yet?"

"Yes, they are ready."

"And Torres?"

"Critical. Coma. Forty-eight hours."

Norris rubbed his temples. "Wonderful."

"Yeah."

"Get your reports done. I want everything documented before you leave today."

"Will do."

Norris walked away. Rocca dropped into his desk chair. Booted up his computer. Stared at the screen like it personally offended him.

"I hate reports," he muttered.

"Everyone hates reports."

"Then why do we do them?"

"Because Norris said so."

"Bureaucracy."

"Welcome to law enforcement."

"That's why I'm going private."

"OK, Mr. Private Dick."

Rocca grunted. Started typing. Slow. Two fingers. Hunting and pecking across the keyboard like a caveman discovering fire.

Pérez sat at her desk. Opened her own report. Stared at the blinking cursor.

She started typing:

Subject: Jessica Torres
Assault. Critical condition. Brass knuckles. Restaurant wipes.

Outside, the sun kept blazing. The heat kept pressing. And somewhere in Lake Worth, a killer kept walking free.

But for now, there was paperwork—and air conditioning—and Rocca muttering curses at his computer.

CHAPTER

40

ROAN KNOCKED three times on the door—flat, official, the sound carrying down the second-floor walkway and echoing off metal railings and concrete. He waited, watching the door's peeling paint, counting seconds. Behind him, Evans shifted his weight. The morning sun was rising quickly, the heat already pressing down. Sweat gathered at Roan's collar. He could smell garbage from the dumpster below, mixed with grease from the diner across the street.

No answer.

Roan knocked again. Louder this time. Knuckles hard against hollow wood, a deliberate rhythm that said police without needing words.

Movement inside. Slow. Stumbling. Something knocked over— glass maybe, or a bottle.

The chain rattled. The door opened a crack.

Maria Morales looked out. Her face was wrong—skin grey, eyes unfocused. She swayed in the doorway, one hand gripping the frame for balance. Her breath came through the gap, sour with alcohol and something chemical underneath. Evans took a half step back, his hand moving unconsciously to cover his nose.

"Mrs. Morales," Roan said. Kept his voice level. "We need to speak with Ariel."

Maria blinked. Didn't answer right away. Her mouth worked like she was trying to remember how words formed. Roan could see past her into the apartment—darkness, shapes of furniture, bottles catching light.

"Is Ariel home?" Roan asked.

"No." The word slurred.

"Where is he?"

"I don't..." She stopped. Frowned. "I don't know."

Roan exchanged a glance with Evans. The younger detective's jaw tightened, notebook already in hand.

"Can we come in?" Roan asked.

Maria stared at him. Then she stepped back, let the door swing wider. The smell hit them full force—cigarette smoke layered thick in the air, old food, something rotting in the kitchen, and underneath it all, the sharp chemical tang of pills or powder.

Maria shuffled toward the living room. Her steps were unsteady, feet catching on the carpet. She wore the same stained blouse from days ago. Hair unwashed, hanging limp. The heat in the apartment was stifling—windows closed, air stagnant.

The living room looked like a war zone.

Empty bottles everywhere—vodka, wine, beer cans crushed flat. More than last time. Way more. They covered the coffee table and lined the floor near the sofa. Some had tipped over, leaving liquid stains on the carpet in dark, sticky patches that had formed in the heat.

The trash overflowed. Flies buzzed near the kitchen, their sound a constant low drone—dishes piled in the sink, water gone grey.

Evans stopped just inside the doorway. His face went tight. Mouth pressed thin. Jaw working. He looked at Roan—a question in his eyes about whether they should even be here, whether this woman was capable of answering anything.

Roan walked slowly through the space, cataloging everything. Maria dropped onto the sofa, head lolling back. Her eyes closed.

"Mrs. Morales," Roan said. "We need to find Ariel."

She didn't open her eyes. "He's not here."

"Where is he?"

"I don't know."

"When's the last time you saw him?"

Maria's face twisted. She tried to think. Her hand moved to her forehead, rubbing at her temples. "I don't... yesterday? Maybe the day before. I don't remember."

Evans wrote it down, though they both knew the information was useless.

Roan crouched in front of her. Eye level. His knees protested—old injury, too many years kneeling on concrete and hardwood. "Mrs. Morales. This is important. We need to bring Ariel in for questioning. If you know where he is—"

"I don't." Her voice broke. Not tears. Just exhaustion. "He comes and goes. I don't ask anymore."

Roan stood. Looked at Evans. "Search the apartment."

Evans moved toward the hallway. Roan stayed with Maria, watching her breath—shallow, irregular, like someone who'd forgotten how.

In the hallway, the air grew heavier as Evans walked—cigarette smoke, unwashed fabric, something rotting. The carpet stuck to his shoes. He pushed open Ariel's door.

The room was small. Single bed against the wall, sheets tucked tight—military corners. The nightstand beside it held a Bible, leather-bound, its pages swollen from handling. Evans opened it—Bookmark at Romans. Verse 6:23 underlined in pen, the ink pressed so hard it had torn through to the next page.

He closed the Bible. Set it back.

The walls were covered in drawings. Religious iconography—cruci-fixions sketched in pencil, but not the sanitized church versions. These were brutal. Bodies twisted, faces contorted in agony. Angels with flaming swords stood over cowering figures. Demons with twisted faces dragged sinners into darkness. Each one meticulous, hours of work in every line. Nothing hurried, every detail precise. One drawing showed a woman with wings being cast down, her face half-beautiful, half-skeletal.

Evans' chest tightened. He thought of his own bedroom at sixteen —band posters, football trophies, pictures of Clara taped to the mirror. Normal teenage things. Arguments about music volume and curfew. His mother made him clean up before his friends came over.

This wasn't normal. This was obsessive. This was someone who'd spent hours alone in this room, drawing the same themes over and over. Judgment. Punishment. Redemption through violence.

"Bed's made," he called out. "Looks like he hasn't slept here."

He checked the closet. A few shirts. Jeans. Work boots gone. Ariel had dressed and left. When? Yesterday? The day before? There was no way to know.

Evans moved to Camila's room. The door stuck—humidity-swollen wood. He pushed it open.

The room was exactly as he remembered. The bed was unmade from the last time she'd slept in it, sheets twisted where she'd thrown them back that final morning. Dresser cluttered with makeup, hair ties, and loose change. Posters on the wall—boy bands, makeup adverts. A stuffed bear on the pillow, faded from years of handling. Its black button eye was loose, hanging by a thread.

Evans stood in the doorway. A dead girl's room: untouched, preserved. No one had set foot here, not since the beginning, not once. They couldn't; they wouldn't. The makeup on the dresser—she'd never finish that tube of mascara. The bear—she'd never hold it again—everything frozen in the moment before her life ended.

He pulled the door shut.

Roan was in the bathroom. Medicine cabinet open. Evans saw him counting pill bottles—Xanax, Ambien, Vicodin. Half of them were empty. Roan's fingers moved across the labels, checking dates, checking names. All prescribed to Maria.

"Nothing new," Evans said. "Room's the same as before."

They moved to the kitchen together. Counters were cluttered with dirty dishes. The sink piled high. Water in the basin had gone grey, scum floating on top. Flies buzzed near the garbage, landing on plates crusted with old food. The fridge hummed, the loud compressor struggling. Roan opened it. The milk carton expired two weeks ago—leftovers in plastic containers, fuzzy with mold. A single can of beer was on the bottom shelf.

Nothing suggested Ariel had been here recently. Nothing suggested anyone had been living here at all.

Maria hadn't moved from the sofa. Her breathing had slowed. Eyes still closed.

"Mrs. Morales," Roan said. His voice remained calm, but steel lay underneath. "Where does Ariel go?"

She shook her head without opening her eyes. "Church. Or... walking. I don't know."

"Does he have friends? Places he stays?"

"No." The word came out flat. "He doesn't have friends."

"Family? Anyone he might go to?"

"No family." Maria's voice cracked. "Just us. Just me and him."

Roan felt frustration tighten in his chest. He forced it down. Kept his face neutral. Evans stood near the door, notepad in hand, though there was nothing left to write. The same frustration was mirrored in his posture—his shoulders were tight, and his jaw was set.

"When he comes back," Roan said, "you call me. Immediately. Do you understand?"

Maria didn't answer.

"Mrs. Morales." Roan's voice sharpened. "Do you understand?"

She nodded. Barely.

Roan turned toward the kitchen. Saw the bottles clustered on the counter. More pills were scattered near the sink. He thought about telling her she needed help. Thought about calling social services. But he didn't have time for that now. He needed to find Ariel.

Maria shifted on the sofa. Her face went pale—a shade beyond the grey, verging on green. She leaned forward suddenly, hand moving to her mouth.

"Bathroom?" she asked, voice thin.

Roan pointed. "Down the hall."

She tried to stand. Her legs buckled.

Evans moved fast and caught her elbow. But Maria was already folding, knees hitting the carpet.

She vomited. Hard. Liquid splattered across the floor—mostly alcohol, some bile.

The smell hit immediately and sharply. Sour-sweet alcohol mixed with bile and stomach acid. Evans' throat tightened reflexively. He swallowed hard, forced down the nausea rising in his own gut. His hand went to his mouth. He stepped back, breathing through his fingers.

The vomit pooled on the carpet—mostly clear liquid, some yellow-brown chunks. The stain spread dark, soaking into fibers already stiff with old spills.

Roan's stomach turned. Not from disgust—he'd seen worse. From the waste of it. From watching a human being dissolve into this.

Evans turned his face away. His jaw locked. Mouth pressed thin. Breathing shallow through his teeth. One hand braced against the doorframe.

Maria collapsed forward. Cheek hit the carpet. Eyes rolled back, whites showing.

Roan knelt fast. His knees hit the floor hard—a jolt of pain up his thighs, old cartilage grinding. He checked her airway. Clear. Checked her pulse. Weak but steady. Her skin was cold. Clammy. Sweat beaded on her forehead.

She was breathing. Shallow. Ragged. But breathing.

"Call an ambulance," Roan said.

Evans pulled his phone. Dialed. His hand shook slightly as he raised it to his ear.

Roan's hands moved automatically—rolling her onto her side, into the recovery position. Made sure she wouldn't choke if she vomited again. Her skin was cold under his fingers, clammy with that particular sweat that came before shock or death. Pulse still faint. He thought about the pills in the bathroom. The empty bottles. The days—maybe weeks—of drinking herself into oblivion. Beyond grief now. Beyond anything recognizable as coping.

Evans finished the call. "Ambulance is on the way."

"Good." Roan stood slowly, his knees protesting again. Looked around the apartment one last time.

Empty bottles. Overflowing trash. Flies buzzing in the kitchen. A woman passed out on the floor in her own vomit.

And somewhere out there, her son was missing.

Roan's hands curled into fists at his sides. He forced them open.

They'd come here to bring Ariel in. To question him. To get answers.

Instead, they had nothing—no Ariel. No answers. Just another victim of Camila's murder, dying in slow motion.

They waited outside on the walkway. The heat was worse now—midmorning sun beating down, metal railing too hot to touch. Roan leaned against the building's wall, arms crossed. Evans stood at the railing, looking down at the parking lot, at the vacant lot across the street.

Neither spoke. There wasn't much to say.

Minutes stretched. Five. Seven. Ten. Somewhere below, a car door slammed. Music thumped from a neighboring apartment. Life was grinding forward, whether they solved this or not.

Finally, the ambulance arrived. Two paramedics—young, efficient. They checked Maria's vitals, loaded her onto a gurney, and wheeled her out. Roan watched them work, watched them lift her like cargo, strapping her down. She didn't wake.

The ambulance pulled away. Red lights flashing. No siren.

Evans broke the silence first. "What now?"

Roan's eyes fixed on the vacant lot opposite. No yellow tape remained, just that darkness in the soil where Julia Aguilar had been found—the last mark she left on this world. He pulled his phone from his pocket.

"Now we put out a BOLO," Roan said. His voice was flat. Controlled. But underneath, the frustration was clear.

He dialed dispatch. Watched the ambulance disappear around the corner as the line connected.

"This is Detective Roan. I need a BOLO issued immediately. Subject is Ariel Morales—male, approximately nineteen years old, thin build, dark hair, last seen wearing unknown clothing. Subject is wanted for questioning in connection with ongoing homicide investigation. Do not approach—call for backup and notify me immediately if located."

He gave the dispatcher the apartment address, then hung up.

"You think he ran?" Evans asked.

"I think he's smart enough to know we're looking for him." Roan glanced over the apartment. The door stood open; the interior was dark. "And I think he's got something to hide."

They walked down the metal stairs. The heat from each step was radiating warmth through their shoe soles.

They climbed into the Explorer. Evans started the engine and cranked the A/C. Hot air blasted from the vents.

For a moment, neither spoke.

Evans pulled out of the parking lot. Turned north on Dixie. His knuckles were white on the steering wheel.

Maria's hollow look—that emptiness behind her eyes when she'd said 'I don't know' over and over—it reminded him of his own mother last Thanksgiving—the same distance. The same flat 'I'm fine' when he'd asked how she was doing. He should call her. He knew he should call her.

"You think he did it?" Evans asked quietly.

The silence stretched. Roan stared out the window. Watched the neighborhood slide past—pawn shops, check-cashing places, motels with hourly rates. When he spoke, his voice was quiet.

"I think he's capable," Roan said at last. "He's got the rage. The righteousness. He had the opportunity. Smart enough to cover his tracks, unstable enough to believe he's doing God's work." He shifted in his seat. "Someone like that, you never see him coming."

The words hung in the air. Roan kept his eyes fixed outside. "But thinking and proving are different things. And right now, we don't have enough to prove anything."

Evans turned onto Lucerne Avenue. The station was ahead.

"So what do we do?" Evans asked.

"We wait for the BOLO to hit," Roan said. "We check his usual spots—church, Shell station, anywhere he's been before. We pull security footage. We talk to anyone who might've seen him."

His voice stayed level, but the frustration underneath was clear.

"And if we don't find him?"

Roan's jaw tightened. "Then we hope he makes a mistake."

CHAPTER

41

THE STATION DOORS hissed shut behind them. Cool air hit immediately—artificial cold that smelled like recycled breath and the faint chemical tang of industrial cleaner. The temperature shock made Evans' skin prickle. His shirt, which had been damp with sweat seconds ago, went cold against his back.

Evans walked beside him. Silent. He rechecked his hands—unconscious gesture, rubbing thumb against palm.

The bullpen opened before them. Keyboards clicking. The fluorescent lights buzzed overhead—one flickering in that irregular pattern that made Roan's temples ache.

Rocca sat at his desk. Pérez beside him, chair pulled close. Both were hunched over paperwork. Hospital visit reports. Witness statements.

Roan stopped at Evans' desk. Pulled out the chair. Sat. His knees protested—a dull ache that lived there now.

Evans stayed standing and staring at the case board. Three photos were already pinned there. Camila Morales. Julia Aguilar. Jessica Torres.

"We need to add Maria," Evans said quietly.

Roan looked up. "What?"

"Maria Morales. To the board. Not as a victim. As context." Evans turned. His eyes were red-rimmed. Tired. "She's in JFK because of this case. Because her daughter's dead and her son's missing and she's drowning. That matters."

Roan considered. The board was for victims and suspects. But Maria was both and neither. Collateral damage. A casualty that never made headlines but destroyed families just the same.

He nodded once. "Do it."

Evans moved to the board. Started reorganizing. Shifting photos. Making space.

Rocca's eyes sharpened—that cop awareness that said something had happened. He stood, manila folder already in hand. Walked over. Pérez followed, carrying a second folder.

"Torres?" Roan asked.

Rocca dropped the folder on Evans' desk. "Several hours in surgery. Multiple stab wounds—abdomen, chest, one that nicked her left lung. They got her stable, but she lost a lot of blood. She's in a coma. Medically induced. Swelling on the brain."

"Timeline on waking her?" Evans asked, still pinning photos.

"Don't know. Could be hours. Could be days. Could be never." Rocca's voice flattened. "We talked to her roommate. Tiffany Carter. She's scared. Thinks whoever got Jessica is coming for her next."

"Is he?" Evans asked.

"Don't know." Rocca looked at the photos Evans was arranging. "But she's not wrong to be scared."

Pérez stepped forward. Held out the second folder. "Brass knuckles recovered from her right hand. Blood on them. A mix of hers and someone else's. Lab's processing DNA."

Roan took the folder, flipped it open. Crime scene photos—brass knuckles in an evidence bag, dark with dried blood. "How long?"

"We have a blood type, but DNA will be a month, maybe six weeks."

Roan's jaw tightened. He closed the folder.

Evans finished reorganizing the board. Four photos now. Top row —Camila Morales, Julia Aguilar, Jessica Torres. Bottom corner— Maria Morales' booking photo from three years ago. Face younger, eyes clearer before grief had hollowed her out.

"What'd you get from the apartment?" Rocca asked.

Roan stood. His knees cracked. He walked to the board. "Maria's at JFK. OD'd on her living room floor. Ariel's gone. Room empty. Bed made—work boots missing. Don't know when. Maria can't remember."

"BOLO?" Pérez asked.

"Out." Roan pointed at Ariel's photo beside Maria's booking shot. "Ariel Morales. Male, eighteen, thin build, dark hair, approximately five-ten. Wanted for questioning. Do not approach."

"You think he did all three?" Rocca asked carefully.

Roan took a moment before answering, exhaustion in every word. "I think he's capable. But capable and guilty aren't the same thing."

"What about Vance?" Pérez asked quietly.

Evans turned from the board. "Vance is a dead end. Solid alibi verified."

Silence settled. Heavy.

Martinez walked past. Kept walking.

"So what now?" Rocca asked.

Roan turned. "Now we wait. BOLO's out for Ariel. Every patrol has its photo, courtesy of Dispatch. We're pulling security footage from his usual haunts—the church down on Federal, the Shell on Dixie, you know the drill. We're talking to anyone who's seen him in the last seventy-two, and hoping the Blood Type off Torres finally gives us something solid to work with. That's where we are."

Evans stared at the board. Four faces. The fluorescent lights buzzed overhead. That flicker was getting worse.

"Evans."

He looked up. Roan stood close. Voice low.

"You good?"

Evans nodded. "Yeah."

"You're not."

"I'm fine."

Nothing shifted in Roan's face. "Go home. See Clara. See your kids. Eat something that isn't vending-machine food."

"We've got work."

"We've got a stalled case and a BOLO that won't hit for hours. Maybe days." Roan's voice stayed gentle. Firm. "Go home."

Evans wanted to argue. But his hands were shaking. Adrenaline crash from the apartment. From watching Maria collapse.

"After we finish here," Evans said.

Roan nodded. Didn't push.

They turned back to the board. Stood there in silence.

Rocca and Pérez had returned to their desks. Back to paperwork. Reports.

Evans pulled out his notepad. Started writing. Connections. Timeline. Everything they knew. Everything they didn't.

His phone buzzed—a text from Clara:

> When are you home?

He stared at the screen. Guilt settled in his chest. He typed:

> Late. Case stalled. Love you.

Sent it.

Rocca called from across the bullpen. "Coffee run. Anyone want?"

"Yeah," Evans said.

"Roan?"

"No."

Rocca walked to the break room. Poured two cups. Returned. Handed one to Evans.

The coffee was burnt. Thick.

Evans drank it anyway.

The bullpen door opened.

Desk Sergeant Morrison stepped through. Behind him—Jin Shin.

Evans recognized her immediately. Jin Shin. Camila's friend. Black jeans. White t-shirt. Hair pulled back. She carried two large paper bags, grease stains spreading across the bottoms.

She looked nervous. Eyes moving between them.

"Detective Roan," Morrison said. "Got a visitor for you."

Roan turned. Jin stood there. Nothing changed in his face—same hard lines, same careful eyes—but the tension across his shoulders eased, almost imperceptibly.

"Jin," he said.

She stepped forward. The smell hit them as she moved—garlic, sesame oil, grilled meat. Korean barbecue. She set the bags on Evans' desk, hands gripping them tight before letting go. "I brought food. I thought—" She stopped. Glanced around the bullpen. Saw Rocca and Pérez watching. Saw Evans. Then her eyes tracked to the case board.

Her face went pale.

Three women stared back at her—all dead or dying.

"Jin," Roan said gently. "You didn't have to do this."

"I know." Her voice was quiet. Controlled. She couldn't look away from the board. "But I wanted to. You've been working. All of you. Long hours. And I thought—I thought maybe you hadn't eaten. And Camila always said—" Her voice cracked. She stopped. Swallowed hard.

Evans looked at the bags. The smell made his stomach clench. He couldn't remember the last time he'd eaten.

"Thank you," he said. Meant it.

Jin nodded. Still staring at the board. At Camila's photo.

Roan stepped forward. "We haven't told you about the Vance incident."

Jin looked up. Her eyes widened. "What incident?"

"Mark Vance. The man you identified. His wife found out about Camila. About the affair. She shot him two days ago. He's at Good Samaritan. Critical condition."

Jin's eyes widened further. "Is he—is he going to—"

"They don't know yet. But he's alive. Surgery went well. He might make it."

"Good," Jin said. Then, seeing their expressions, "Good, he's alive. So he can answer for what he did to Camila."

"He didn't kill her," Roan said. Voice still gentle but firm.

Jin stared. "What?"

"Mark Vance didn't kill Camila. Solid alibi. He was with Camila earlier. But he didn't kill her."

Jin's face went through a range of emotions, from confusion to anger to relief. "Then who—who did—"

"We don't know yet." Roan's voice stayed measured. "But we're working it—all of us. And we're going to find out. I promise you that."

Jin nodded. Slow. As if she were trying to convince herself.

The bags sat on Evans' desk. Steam rising from inside. The smell filled the bullpen now—garlic and sesame and something richer underneath. Kimchi.

"Rocca's going to love this," Roan said.

Rocca looked up from his desk. "What?"

"Korean BBQ. Jin brought it."

Rocca's face transformed. He stood. "Seriously?"

"Seriously."

"Jin, I could kiss you."

Jin's lips curved slightly. "Please don't."

Rocca laughed. Walked to the desk. Opened the first bag. Pulled out containers. Bulgogi. Kimchi. Japchae. White rice. Banchan. Enough food for six people.

"It's from a place on Lake Avenue. Kim's Kitchen," Jin said. Her hands finally unclenched. "They're good."

"You didn't have to," Pérez said, already standing and moving closer.

"I know." Jin's shoulders dropped slightly. "But Camila would've wanted me to. She always said, 'Be good to good people. People who cared.'"

The bullpen went quiet, just for a moment.

"This is too much," Pérez said, reaching for a container.

"I didn't know how many of you there were," Jin said. "So I got extra. Kim's mother—she owns the restaurant—she packed extra when I told her it was for the police. She said 'Thank you. For working on Camila's case. For caring about girls like us.'"

The weight of that settled over them. Girls like us.

"Tell her we appreciate it," Evans said. Throat tight. "Both of you."

Jin nodded. Looked at the board again at Camila. "She was good, you know. Camila. She was really good."

"We know," Roan said.

They ate at their desks. Quiet. Focused. Evans opened a container of bulgogi—the meat glistening with sauce, rice steaming underneath. The first bite hit his tongue. Sweet. Savory. Perfectly seasoned. Garlic, sesame, and something smoky. He hadn't realized how hungry he was.

Rocca made noises that bordered on obscene. Pérez kicked him under the desk. He didn't stop. "This kimchi," he said around a mouthful. "This is the real thing."

Jin stood near the board. Staring at Camila's photo, not eating. Her arms wrapped around herself.

Roan walked over. Stood beside her. "You should eat too."

"I'm not hungry."

"When's the last time you ate?"

Jin didn't answer. Just kept staring at the photo.

Roan pulled a chair over. Gestured. "Sit."

She sat. Slowly. Like her body was too heavy.

He opened a container—bulgogi and rice. Handed it to her with chopsticks. "Eat."

She took it. Stared at the food. Her hands trembled slightly. Finally took a bite. Small. Mechanical.

"She was a good person," Jin said quietly. Not to Roan. To Camila's photo. "She didn't deserve this."

"No one does," Roan said.

Jin took another bite. Chewed. Swallowed. Her eyes never left the photo. "She wanted a degree, a real one. Like an MBA or to be a doctor." Her voice caught. "Did I tell you that?"

Roan shook his head. Evans stopped eating. Listened.

"She was saving money." Jin's chopsticks moved through the rice, not really eating. "Working double shifts at the diner and the parlor. She had brochures in her room. Florida Atlantic. Florida State."

She paused. Set the container down on her lap. Stared at her hands.

"She was interested in social work, too," Jin continued. Her voice went quieter. "She wanted to help people like her. Like me." She looked up at Roan. "She was always helping, always asking if I was okay. If I needed anything. She gave me money once when I couldn't make rent. Wouldn't let me pay her back. Said that's what friends do."

Roan said nothing. Just listened.

"She would've been good at it," Jin said. "Really good."

"The best," Roan said quietly.

Jin picked up the container again. Took another bite. Bigger this time. "Will you find him? Really?"

Roan met her eyes. Held them. "Yes."

"Promise?"

"I promise."

Jin searched his face. Looking for cracks. For doubt.

Whatever she saw, it was enough. She nodded. Took another bite.

By the time they finished, the containers were empty. Scraped clean. The bullpen smelled like garlic, sesame oil, and something warmer. Something human.

Jin stood. Gathered the empty containers. Stacking them carefully. "I should go. I have work tonight."

"I'll walk you," Roan said, already standing.

Evans looked up. "You don't have to—"

"I'm walking her." Roan's tone left zero room for argument.

Jin smiled. Small but real. "It's only four blocks. I walk it all the time."

"Four blocks is four blocks." Roan grabbed his jacket. "Let's go."

They walked to the door. Jin paused. Looked at the board one more time. At Camila. Then at each of them in turn. Evans. Rocca. Pérez.

"Thank you," she said. Simple. Direct. "For working this. For caring about her. About all of them." She gestured to the board. "Most people don't. Most people think girls like us don't matter."

Evans' throat tightened. "You matter. She mattered. They all did."

She believed him.

"We won't stop until we find him," Evans added.

Jin nodded. Then she turned. Walked out. Roan followed, the door closing softly behind them.

The bullpen settled back into its rhythm.

But something had shifted. Some weight had lifted. Not gone— never gone. But lighter.

Rocca leaned back in his chair. Patted his stomach. "That was the best meal I've had all week."

"You say that every time you eat," Pérez said, already back at her paperwork.

"Because it's always true."

Evans smiled. Tired but real.

He focused on the board. Four faces. Three dead or dying. One collateral damage. And somewhere out there in Lake Worth, a killer was still walking free.

But for twenty minutes, they'd stopped. They'd eaten. They'd remembered that even in the darkest investigations, small acts of kind-ness mattered.

That had to count for something.

Evans pulled out his notepad. Started writing:

Priorities.
Non-negotiable.
First, the Shell station security tapes—seventy-two hours' worth.
Second, another conversation with Father Mendez about Ariel's whereabouts.

Third, the tedious work:

Map every connection between Torres and both victims until something clicked.

The kind of detective work that broke cases or broke detectives.

The list grew. Tasks. Leads.

His phone buzzed. Clara:

> I love you too. Drive safe. There's dinner in the
> fridge.

He stared at the screen. Something loosened in his chest. He typed back:

> I'll be home in an hour. Love you.

Hit send. Set the phone down.

Across the bullpen, Pérez stood. Stretched. "I need more coffee. Anyone?"

"Yeah," Rocca said.

"Evans?"

"No. I'm good."

She walked to the break room. Returned with two fresh cups, handed one to Rocca.

They sat. Drank. Worked.

Evans added one more item to his list:

Thank Jin properly. Maybe get a gift certificate? Something.

The work continued. Files opened. Reports typed. Phone calls made.

And somewhere four blocks away, Detective Roan walked a young woman home through Tuesday afternoon heat, keeping a promise that someone still gave a damn.

CHAPTER

42

THEY STEPPED OUT INTO A SAUNA. The heat and humidity hung so thick it felt manufactured for September. There was no wind, not the faintest current of air; nothing but a heavy wall of heat braced against them as they walked, sweat already blooming down Roan's spine, his shirt clinging to his back before they'd even reached the corner. With every step, the weight of the afternoon pressed in, close and suffocating.

Jin walked beside him. Silent. Her ponytail swung with each step, black hair catching sunlight. She carried the empty containers in a plastic bag, handles twisted around her wrist. The plastic dug into her skin, leaving red marks.

They turned onto Lake Avenue. Pavement cracked, weeds pushing through concrete. The street smelled like exhaust and hot asphalt. A car passed, bass thumping loud enough to rattle Roan's chest.

"We have a new suspect," Roan said.

Jin's step faltered. Just slightly. The bag swung at her side. "Who?"

"I can't say much. But we're looking at someone." He kept his voice level. Professional. "Someone who knew the victim."

"Will you catch him?"

"Yes."

She looked at him. Searching. "You promised."

Roan nodded.

Jin's grip tightened on the bag. "Camila deserves that."

They walked in silence. The street opened up—small businesses, apartments above storefronts. A café. A small gym. A tattoo parlor with neon signs flickering in the window.

Kim's Kitchen sat in the middle of a line of shops. A small storefront with a red awning, faded by the sun. Korean characters painted on the window above English letters. The smell of garlic and sesame oil drifted out even with the door closed.

Jin slowed. Stopped. Stared at the restaurant. Her free hand moved to her throat, fingers pressing against the hollow there.

"My mother used to cook like that," she said quietly. "Before."

Roan didn't ask before what. Didn't need to.

They kept walking.

At J Street, they turned right. The neighborhood shifted. Quieter. Trees lining the sidewalk, roots buckling the concrete. A club sat mid-block—rainbow flag hanging limp in the still air. Music already thumping inside, bass heavy enough to feel through the pavement. Too early for a crowd, but someone was testing the sound system.

Jin glanced at the club. Said nothing.

"You work tonight?" Roan asked.

"Yes. Five to ten."

"Siam?"

"Yes."

Roan thought about the massage parlor—the dim hallway. The overpowering smell of incense had covered up what was underneath. The girls who worked there—Jin, others like her—moving through rooms with practiced smiles.

They reached the end of the block. Jin's apartment building stood ahead—four stories, with stucco peeling, metal railings rusted, and looking like the same complex where Maria Morales lived. Different building. Same poverty.

Jin's building was cleaner. Barely. Someone had tried—flowers planted in pots near the entrance, paint touched up around the doorframe. However, the effort couldn't conceal the decay beneath.

Roan followed her up the stairs. Her apartment was on the third floor—3F. She unlocked the door. Hesitated.

"This is me," Jin said. "You want to come in? Just for a moment?"

Roan should've said no. Should've walked away. He'd done his duty—escorted her home, kept his promise. The professional thing was to leave. But something in her voice made him hesitate. Not pleading. Just... alone. The weight of caring for her mother, working nights, grieving Camila—all of it pressing down on someone too young to carry it.

"Sure," he said.

The apartment was small. One bedroom, maybe. Kitchen visible from the entrance—tiny, cramped, dishes drying in a rack. Roan stepped inside. The door closed behind him with a soft click. The living room opened before him—clean, sparse, a sofa that had seen better days positioned against one wall, a TV on a stand opposite—curtains drawn against the afternoon sun, casting everything in amber half-light.

Movement near the window caught his eye—a chair. Someone was sitting in it.

An old woman. Jin's mother. Small, frail, her hair white and pulled back in a bun. She wore a faded housedress, hands folded in her lap. Her eyes moved toward the door when they entered—slow, unfocused —tracking movement but not seeing.

Jin spoke Korean, her voice soft and gentle. The old woman responded, voice thin and high.

Jin set the bag down. Crossed to her mother and helped her stand. The old woman's legs trembled. Jin steadied her, guided her to the bathroom. More Korean. Jin's patient voice, explaining something. The old woman nodded.

Roan stood in the middle of the living room. Hands in his pockets. Not moving, not touching anything, just watching.

The apartment smelled like ginger and something medicinal—ointment, maybe, or prescription cream. The walls were empty save for one photograph in a frame—a family portrait, years old. Jin, as a child, was maybe ten. Her mother, younger, smiling. A man beside them— Jin's father, probably. All of them were standing in front of a house Roan didn't recognize.

Jin emerged from the bathroom. Alone. "She's okay. I'm getting her ready for bed. I won't be long."

She disappeared into the bedroom. The door stayed open. Roan heard drawers opening—fabric rustling.

He turned toward the TV. The old woman had returned to her chair. Remote in her hand. She clicked through channels—images flashing across the screen. News. Adverts. A cooking show. She stopped on a Korean drama. Subtitles scrolling at the bottom.

Roan watched her watch TV. Her eyes followed the shapes on screen. Not really seeing. Just... present.

Movement caught his peripheral vision. He glanced toward the bedroom door.

Jin stood in the doorway with her back to him. White t-shirt pulled over her head. Bare skin visible for a moment—shoulders, spine, the curve of her waist. She reached for something on the bed. A black tank top. Pulled it on.

Roan looked away fast. Faced the TV. His neck burned.

Not his business. Not his place to look.

Jin emerged a minute later, wearing black jeans and a black tank top. Hair still pulled back. She'd changed for work—the massage parlor uniform—practical, anonymous, designed to disappear.

"Tea?" she asked.

"Sure."

She moved to the kitchen. Filled a kettle. Set it on the burner. The gas ignited, caught fire, and burned blue. She pulled two mugs from the cupboard. Opened a tin. Spooned loose tea into both.

Roan stayed in the living room near the sofa. He watched the old woman flip through the channels again. Landing on a game show. Bright lights. Applause. Contestants jumping. The Price is Right.

From where he stood, he could see into the kitchen, see Jin moving with practised efficiency, but the bedroom door was out of his line of sight.

The kettle whistled. Jin poured. Steam rose. She brought both mugs to the living room. Handed one to Roan.

"Green tea," she said. "My mother used to grow it. In Korea."

Roan sipped. The heat spread across his tongue—slightly bitter, clean, with something earthy underneath.

"Thank you."

They stood there. Drinking tea, not talking.

The old woman laughed at something on TV. High-pitched. Delighted.

Jin smiled. Small. Sad. "She doesn't understand what's happening most days," she said quietly. "But she still laughs at TV. That's something."

Roan nodded. "Yeah. That's something."

Jin set her mug down on the TV stand. Looked at him. "Thank you. For walking me home."

"I wanted to."

"I know. But you didn't have to."

"Yeah. I did."

Something passed between them. Brief. Unspoken.

Jin stepped forward. Just slightly. Her eyes on his. Dark. Searching. The space between them narrowed—close enough that Roan could smell her shampoo, something floral mixed with the ginger from the kitchen. Close enough to feel the warmth radiating from her skin in the stifling apartment.

Roan didn't move.

The moment stretched. His pulse quickened. The old woman's laughter from the TV seemed distant and muffled.

Then Jin stepped back. The moment passed.

"I should get ready for work," she said.

"Yeah." Roan set his mug down beside hers. "I should go."

He moved toward the door. Jin followed.

At the threshold, he turned. "You need anything—anything—you call me. Understand?"

"I understand."

"I mean it."

"I know."

Roan nodded. Stepped into the hallway. The door closed behind him. Soft.

He stood there a moment. Breathing. The hallway smelled like cooking oil and old carpet. Someone's TV played Spanish through a closed door.

He walked down the stairs. Each step was deliberate. At the bottom, he pushed through the entrance, and the heat hit him again—

still oppressive, still heavy, but somehow less suffocating than the air inside Jin's apartment.

He walked back toward the station, not thinking about the almost-moment, not thinking about Jin's eyes searching his, not thinking about anything except the case and the work waiting for him and the promise he'd made to find Camila's killer.

CHAPTER

43

ROAN LEFT Jin's building and turned back toward the station. The heat pressed on him like a hand, sweat already pooling at the base of his spine. He wiped his brow. The sidewalk cracked beneath his shoes, weeds pushing through concrete like bones through skin.

Bass heavy enough to rattle his chest hit him as he walked on J Street. A club sat mid-block, rainbow flag limp in the still air. Neon spilled across the pavement—pink, blue, green. The door was closed, but the sound leaked through the cracks, vibrating through the walls and echoing on the street.

He passed the old jazz club. Dark. Closed.

Then he saw the truck.

White. Parked under a streetlamp. Dirt caked on the wheel wells. Orange lettering on the trailer—faded, peeling. And the driver's side window had a spider-webbed crack, radiating from a single impact point.

Roan stopped.

This truck. He'd seen it before. Where? When?

The club door slammed open.

Sound exploded outward—music, voices, laughter. A man stumbled onto the sidewalk. Young. Latino. Bandages wrapped around both forearms, white gauze stained at the edges. His face—Jesus. Black eye, swollen shut. Lip split. Bruises spread across his cheek like spilled ink.

Ariel Morales.

Roan's chest tightened. His pulse hammered in his ears.

Ariel's eyes snapped up. Saw him. Their eyes met.

For one second, neither moved.

Then Ariel ran.

Roan's body moved before his brain caught up. Years of instinct. Muscle memory. He bolted forward, shoes pounding pavement.

"Stop! Police!"

Ariel didn't stop.

He ran hard, taking long strides, eating up the distance. But something was wrong. He favored his right side. Limped slightly. The bandages on his arms flapped as he pumped them, one hand gripping the other.

Roan ran. His lungs burned. His knees ached. He wasn't young anymore. Wasn't fast. But he was steady. Relentless.

Ariel glanced back. His good eye went wide.

Years of foot pursuits. The street ahead curved right. Chain-link fence on the right side. Apartment building on the left. Ariel was running straight—no plan, just panic. The curve would force him to slow or veer left into the building's alcove.

Roan angled right. Cut across the empty lot beside the club. Broken glass crunched under his feet. A shopping cart lay on its side. Discarded lumber. He vaulted over a low wall, his bad knee screaming protest. Hit the sidewalk running on the far side of the lot, emerging onto the street twenty yards ahead of where the curve would force Ariel to slow.

He emerged at the intersection ahead of Ariel.

Ariel saw him. Too late. His eyes went wide. He tried to pivot. His leg buckled.

Roan closed the distance. Three strides. Two.

Ariel threw his hands up—defensive, not aggressive. Roan grabbed his right wrist. Twisted. Used Ariel's momentum against him. Swept his legs.

Ariel went down hard. Shoulder hit first. Then his hip. He gasped —wind knocked out.

Roan dropped, knee driving into Ariel's back. Not hard. Just enough to pin him. Pain shot up his thigh from the impact—old cartilage grinding bone against bone. He grabbed the bandaged wrists— carefully, not crushing—and pulled them together behind Ariel's back. The handcuffs came out smoothly—muscle memory. Click. Click.

Ariel gasped beneath him. Chest heaving. Blood dripped from his split lip onto the asphalt.

A sedan slowed at the stop sign. Driver—old man, white hair—leaned out the window. "You okay? You need me to—"

"I'm a cop," Roan said. Short. Clipped. "Move along."

The old man hesitated. Studied Ariel. Studied Roan. Then rolled up his window and drove away. Slow. Cautious. Taillights disappearing north.

Roan stood slowly, his knees protesting every inch. Pulled Ariel up with him. Not rough. Not gentle. Just professional.

His lungs ached. His shirt clung to his back, soaked through with sweat. Sweat stung his eyes.

Ariel swayed. His legs wobbled. Roan steadied him with a hand on his elbow.

They stood there. Breathing. The club music still thumped in the distance. Bass rattled windows. Someone laughed inside—high, drunk.

Roan studied Ariel's face. The swelling around the eye was fresh—maybe twelve hours old. The bruises were darker on the edges, yellow spreading toward the center where blood had pooled beneath the skin. His lip had been split recently—scabbed over but still raw, weeping at the edges. And his nose sat slightly crooked. Broken, probably. Recently.

"Who did this to you?" Roan asked.

Ariel didn't answer. Just stared at the ground. Blood dripped from his chin onto his shirt—already stained dark with older blood.

"Ariel. Look at me."

Ariel's good eye flicked up. Dark. Wet.

"Who beat you up?"

Nothing.

Roan exhaled through his nose. He wanted to push. Wanted to demand answers. But the kid looked like he'd been through hell already. Whatever had happened to him—whatever had done this—it was recent. Violent. And Ariel was terrified.

"You're under arrest," Roan said. Formal. By the book. "You have the right to remain silent. Anything you say can and will be used against you in a court of law. You have the right to an attorney. If you cannot afford an attorney, one will be provided for you. Do you understand these rights?"

Ariel nodded. Small.

"Say it out loud."

"Yes." Voice hoarse. Cracked.

"Yes, what?"

"Yes, I understand."

Roan nodded. Turned Ariel toward the station. His hand stayed firm on the kid's elbow. "Walk."

They walked in silence. Lake Avenue stretched ahead. A dog barked somewhere. A car alarm went off three blocks over, then stopped. The afternoon sun beat down, heat radiating from the pavement in visible waves.

Ariel limped beside him. Not fighting, not resisting. Just... broken. His shoulders slumped forward. His head hung. The bandages on his arms were soaked through in places—red blooming beneath white gauze. Fresh blood, not old. Whatever injury he had beneath those wrappings, it was still bleeding.

Roan's grip on Ariel's elbow was firm but not cruel. He'd done this a hundred times. A thousand. Walked suspects down streets, through alleys, into stations. But something about this felt different. Wrong.

Ariel was a suspect. Evidence pointed to him. The connection to Camila. The disappearances after the murders. The religious obsession. The motive.

But the kid walking beside him didn't look like a killer. He looked like a victim.

"Where'd you get the bandages?" Roan asked.

Ariel flinched. "Clinic."

"When?"

"Yesterday."

"What happened to your arms?"

Silence.

Roan let it sit. Sometimes silence worked better than questions. Let the suspect's guilt fill the space. Make them talk just to break the quiet.

But Ariel didn't talk. Just kept walking. Head down. Blood was dripping onto the pavement behind them in small dark spots.

They passed a tattoo parlor. A café. A small gym with bars on the windows and a cat sitting in the doorway. The cat watched them pass, yellow eyes unblinking.

At the corner of Dixie and Lake Avenue, they stopped for a red light. No cars were coming. No one around. But Roan waited anyway. Force of habit. His breathing had finally steadied, but his bad knee throbbed with every heartbeat.

Ariel swayed beside him. Breathing shallow. Quick. Like he couldn't pull enough air. His eyes fluttered closed for a moment.

"You gonna pass out on me?" Roan asked.

"No."

"You sure?"

"Yeah."

The light changed. They crossed.

Dixie was busier. Not crowded. But cars passed—a few pedestrians on the sidewalk. A homeless man pushed a shopping cart full of aluminum cans. A woman walked a small dog, some terrier, yapping at nothing. A teenager on a bicycle swerved wide around them, staring.

People stared as they passed. Not openly. Just glances. Quick. Curious. A man in handcuffs always drew attention. A young mother pulled her child closer, hurrying past. An old woman stopped, hand over her mouth, watching them until they turned the corner.

Roan ignored them. Kept walking and kept his hand on Ariel's elbow.

Ariel's pace slowed. Each step took effort. His legs dragged. He stumbled once—just slightly—and Roan caught him before he fell.

"How much further?" Ariel asked. Voice thin. Strained.

"Two blocks."

Ariel nodded. Kept walking.

The station appeared ahead. Concrete. Functional. Ugly. Yellow light spilled from the windows. The flag hung limp on the pole out front. A patrol car sat in the parking lot, empty. Another turned in, the officer behind the wheel glancing their way.

Roan's phone buzzed in his pocket. He ignored it. Whoever it was could wait.

They climbed the steps. Slow. Ariel's legs shook. Roan steadied him, hand firm on his back.

At the door, Roan paused. Looked at Ariel.

The kid's face was destroyed. Swelling distorted his features. Blood crusted at his nostrils. His eyes—both of them, even the swollen one—were wet. Not crying. Just... broken.

"Last chance," Roan said. "You want to tell me what happened?"

Ariel's jaw tightened. His good eye met Roan's. Held it.

"I didn't kill them," Ariel said. Quiet. Firm. "I didn't kill Camila. I didn't kill any of them."

Roan studied him. Searched his face for the lie. For the crack. For the tell that two decades of interrogations had taught him to spot.

He didn't find it. Either Ariel believed what he was saying, or he was better at lying than anyone Roan had ever arrested.

Roan's phone buzzed again. He pulled it out. Glanced at the screen. Evans:

> Where are you?

Roan typed back one-handed:

> Front door. Got him.

Evans responded immediately:

> What? On my way.

Roan pocketed the phone. Looked at Ariel. The kid stared back at him with that one good eye—dark, desperate, pleading for someone to believe him.

"Let's go," Roan said.

He pushed the door open. Led Ariel inside.

The hallway was bright. Fluorescent lights were buzzing overhead. A desk sergeant—Morrison, grey-haired, reading glasses perched on his nose—looked up from his computer. His eyes widened slightly when he saw Ariel's face. He nodded at Roan.

"Need a holding cell," Roan said.

"Number three's open."

"Thanks."

Morrison watched them pass, already reaching for his phone, probably calling for a medic.

Evans appeared from the hallway, moving fast. Eyes sharp. Alert. He looked at Ariel. Took in the bruises. The bandages. The blood. His face went tight.

"Jesus," Evans said.

"Yeah."

"He say anything?"

"Says he didn't do it."

"They all say that."

"I know."

Evans stepped closer. Lowered his voice. His hand rested unconsciously on his belt. "You believe him?"

Roan didn't answer right away. He looked at Ariel. The way the kid's shoulders slumped. There was blood on his shirt. At the fear in his good eye. At the fresh injuries that someone had inflicted recently, violently.

"I don't know," Roan said finally.

Evans nodded. Glanced at Ariel again, his jaw working. "He needs to be checked out. I'll have someone look at his injuries once he's processed. Make sure we're able to talk to him."

"Good."

"Let's get him settled first. Then we'll talk."

Roan led Ariel down the hallway toward the holding cells. The fluorescent lights were flickering. Their footsteps echoed on the linoleum. Martinez passed them going the other way, stopped, stared. Kept walking.

At cell three, Roan stopped. Unlocked the door. Swung it open.

"Inside," he said.

Ariel stepped in. Turned and looked at Roan.

"I didn't do it," he said again. Quieter this time. Almost pleading.

Roan didn't respond. Just closed the door. Locked it. The metal clanged. Final. Absolute.

Ariel sank onto the bench. Put his head in his bandaged hands. His shoulders shook.

Roan stood there a moment. Watching. Thinking. His knee throbbed. His shirt was still soaked. But his breathing had steadied.

Then he turned and walked away.

Evans was waiting at the end of the hall, leaning against the wall with his arms crossed.

"You good?" Evans asked.

"Yeah."

"You sure? You look like hell."

"I'm fine."

Evans studied him. "He really says he didn't do it?"

"Yeah."

"And?"

Roan glanced back toward the cells. Through the small window, he could see Ariel's silhouette—hunched, broken. "And I don't know if I believe him."

Evans pushed off the wall. "Let's get coffee. Then we'll figure this out."

They walked to the bullpen together. Rocca and Pérez looked up from their desks, questions on their faces. Roan shook his head. *Later.*

Roan pulled out his chair. Sat. His body ached—knees, back, shoulders. His head throbbed. He'd been awake for too long. Running on adrenaline and terrible coffee.

But Ariel Morales was in custody. And Roan would get his answers.

CHAPTER

44

AN HOUR after Ariel's arrest, Roan stood in the observation room with his arms crossed. Lights hummed overhead—flat white swallowing shadows.

Through the one-way mirror, Ariel Morales sat at the metal table. Handcuffed. Alone. His head was bowed, as if he were praying or waiting for judgment, or both.

The bandages were gone. Processing had removed them. The forearms were bare now. Visible. Marks covered them—lines, scars—but from this distance, through the glass, he couldn't tell what they were. Could be anything. Defensive wounds. Scratches. Old injuries.

Evans stood beside Roan. Eyes locked on Ariel through the glass.

Pérez leaned against the wall behind them, arms crossed, face unreadable—the professional mask she wore when the case got messy. The tension lived in her shoulders. The way her weight shifted. This case had worn them all thin.

"Look at his face," Evans said quietly.

Roan did. The swelling had worsened since the arrest—bruising deepening, spreading.

"Someone beat the hell out of him," Pérez said.

"Yeah."

"Recently. Look at the pattern—methodical. Personal."

Evans opened his notepad. Read his notes. "DNA results won't be back for a month at least. But we have a blood type."

Roan turned. "And?"

"Jessica Torres' blood was O-positive. Attacker's blood at the scene was AB-negative."

"You're sure?"

"Lab confirmed it twice. AB-negative. Rare type. About one percent of the population."

Roan looked back at Ariel through the glass. Studied the marks on his forearms. The bruises on his face. The slump of his shoulders. "And Ariel?"

"Ariel agreed to a blood test. It's being processed now. Should have results in twenty minutes."

Twenty minutes. Pressure built behind his sternum. Twenty minutes to either put their prime suspect in handcuffs or cross another name off the board.

"Walk me through it," Roan said.

Evans consulted his notes. "Lack of empathy for Camila's death. Religious zealotry. The flyers with Romans 6:23—'wages of sin is death.' No alibi for either murder. His mother's car was detailed right after Julia Aguilar turned up dead."

Pérez nodded. "Plus, look at his forearms. Those marks could be defensive wounds. Jessica Torres fought back with brass knuckles. Blood under her fingernails. Skin tissue. Someone got hurt."

"Could be," Evans said. "Or could be something else. A fight. Street altercation."

Pérez tilted her head. "Maybe someone he knows. Someone angry."

Roan didn't answer. Just kept watching Ariel through the glass.

The kid sat motionless. Not fidgeting, not looking around, not performing innocence or guilt. Just... still. Like someone who'd already given up. Like someone waiting for the world to finish what it started.

"What about his mother?" Roan asked.

Pérez pulled out her phone. Checked her notes. "Maria Morales. Overdose this morning. Pills and alcohol. Paramedics got there in time. She's at JFK Medical Center. Stable condition. Might be released tomorrow morning."

"Does he know?"

"Not yet."

Roan processed that. Maria overdosing. Ariel beaten. Both of them were falling apart while Camila lay dead in the morgue.

Silence settled in the observation room—the tick of the wall clock.

Ariel was sitting motionless on the other side of the glass, head in his hands.

Evans broke it first. "What if he didn't do it?"

Roan glanced at him. "What makes you say that?"

"Look at him. He doesn't look like a killer. He looks like he's been beaten down his whole life."

"Killers can be victims too," Pérez said.

"I know. But..." Evans trailed off. Stared at Ariel. "Something doesn't fit."

Roan studied Ariel's posture. The marks on his forearms. The bruises. The way he sat so still, like movement might shatter him.

His chest tightened. His pulse kicked up. Not nerves. Something else. Recognition settling in his bones—the same stillness he'd seen in a bedroom doorway fifteen years ago.

He pushed the door open.

The interview room closed in—concrete block walls in institutional beige, a metal table bolted to the floor, two chairs facing each other. Camera mounted in the corner, red light blinking. The air smelled stale, recycled through vents too many times.

Roan stepped in. Ariel's head snapped up—his good eye—dark, wet, terrified—locked on Roan.

"Hello, Ariel," Roan said.

Ariel didn't respond. Just stared.

Roan pulled out the chair. Metal scraped against the floor—harsh, final. He sat across from Ariel, the table between them scarred with old gouges. Evans stood near the door. Hands loose at his sides. Ready but not threatening.

Roan set a folder on the table. Opened it. Inside were crime scene photos. Camila. Julia. Jessica. He didn't show them to Ariel. Not yet. Just let them sit there. Visible. Present.

"You know why you're here," Roan said.

"I didn't kill anyone." Ariel's voice was hoarse. Cracked.

"Then help me understand."

"There's nothing to understand. I didn't do it."

Roan leaned back slightly. Let silence fill the space. Let Ariel feel the weight of it pressing down. The camera blinked. Somewhere down the hall, a phone rang.

"Your sister was murdered," Roan said finally. "Stabbed, left on the beach. You put up flyers all over town. Romans 6:23. 'The wages of sin is death.' You told us she deserved it."

"I didn't—" Ariel stopped. Swallowed. His Adam's apple bobbed. "I didn't mean it like that."

"How did you mean it?"

"I was angry. At her. At God. At everything." Tears welled in his good eye. Spilled over. "She was leaving, going away to school, getting out. And I was stuck there with mom. Alone. I was so angry."

Roan watched him. Studied his face. The pain was real. Raw. Unfiltered.

"Where were you the night Camila died?" Roan asked.

Ariel hesitated. His eyes darted to the side, back to Roan. His hands twisted in the cuffs. "I was... out."

"Out where?"

"Just... around."

"That's not an answer."

Ariel's jaw tightened. He looked down at his cuffed hands.

"What about the night Julia Aguilar died?" Roan asked.

Ariel said nothing. His breathing quickened.

"Ariel. Look at me."

Ariel raised his eyes. Met Roan's gaze. Held it.

"Where were you?"

"I don't remember."

"You don't remember."

"No."

Roan let that sit. Then: "What about your mother's car? You had it detailed."

Ariel's face flushed. "Yeah."

"Why?"

"It was dirty."

"Dirty how?"

"Just... dirty."

Roan leaned forward, elbows on the table. "The morning Julia

Aguilar was murdered, you paid ninety dollars to have your mother's car detailed. Interior and exterior. Full service. Why?"

Ariel's hands trembled. The cuffs rattled against the table. "I told you. It was dirty."

"From what?"

"From... from everything. Mom's stuff. Trash. I just wanted it clean."

Roan didn't believe him. Ariel's eyes kept darting away. His breathing was shallow. Quick.

"Why were you following your sister?" Roan asked.

Ariel looked up. "I wasn't following her."

"You were seen at the Nifty Fifty. The diner where she worked."

"I know. I went there to tell her to stop the massage parlor. To beg her to stop."

"Why?"

"Because it was wrong. What she was doing. Selling herself. It was a sin."

"Did you argue?"

"Yeah. She told me to mind my own business. To leave her alone." His voice cracked. "She said she was getting out. That she'd saved enough money to leave Lake Worth and leave our mom, leave me. She was abandoning us."

Roan heard it then. The real pain. Not judgment. Abandonment.

"You were scared," Roan said.

Ariel looked up. Surprised.

"You were scared she'd leave you alone with your mother. Scared you'd have no one."

Ariel nodded. Tears were streaming down his bruised face.

"That's not a sin, Ariel. That's human."

Ariel sobbed harder. His shoulders shook.

Roan reached across the table. Not touching. Just present. "Your mother overdosed this morning."

Ariel's face went white. "What?"

"Pills and alcohol. She's alive at JFK Medical Center. They're keeping her overnight. She might be released tomorrow."

Ariel's mouth opened. Closed. No words came out. His breathing went ragged.

"Did you know she was using?" Roan asked.

"I..." Ariel swallowed. "I thought she might. I could see it. The way she was drinking. The pills. I knew she was close."

"Why didn't you stop her?"

"How?" Ariel's voice broke. "She doesn't listen to me. Hasn't for years. I tried. I tried so hard. But she just... gave up."

Roan nodded. Silence settled between them. Heavy. Weighted. The fluorescent lights hummed.

Then Roan stared at Ariel. Really saw him for the first time.

Tears welled in Ariel's good eye. Not from the bruising. Not from physical pain. Something deeper. Something Roan recognized.

Something clicked. Sharp. Clear. Recognition flooding through him.

He saw Ariel for what he really was. Not a killer. Not a zealot. A scared, emotionally torn-up kid. A kid with a drunk mother and an absent father. A kid whose religious beliefs tied him up in knots. A kid whose sister was on her way out of the family, out of his life, leaving him alone with everything.

Roan's gaze dropped to Ariel's forearms—the marks he'd seen through the glass. Up close now, they were unmistakable. Thin lines. Parallel. Methodical. Self-inflicted.

His chest tightened.

"How long have you been cutting yourself, Ariel?"

Ariel froze. His eyes went wide. His face went blank.

"How did you know?" Ariel whispered.

"Because I was once a father with a child who was hurting on the inside."

The room went silent. The hum of the lights seemed louder.

Behind the one-way mirror, Evans and Pérez stood frozen. Mouths slightly open. Neither had ever heard Roan talk about his past. Not like this. Not so openly.

Ariel stared at Roan. Searching his face, looking for truth.

"A few months," Ariel whispered. "Maybe longer. I don't remember when it started."

"Why?"

"Because it's the only thing I can control. Everything else is falling apart. Mom. Camila. God. Everything. But this?" He lifted his scarred forearms. "This I can control. This I can feel."

Roan nodded. "I understand."

"Do you?"

"More than you know."

They sat there—two damaged people in a blighted room. One was trying to survive. The other was trying to save him.

Silence stretched. Heavy. Comfortable in its weight.

"The verse you quoted," Roan said. "Romans 6:23. Do you know the whole verse?"

Ariel shook his head.

"'For the wages of sin is death, but the gift of God is eternal life in Christ Jesus our Lord.'"

Ariel stared at him.

"You only quoted the first half," Roan said. "The judgment. But the second half is grace. Redemption. You're not beyond saving, Ariel. None of us are."

Ariel broke completely. He had his head in his hands. Body shaking.

Roan waited. Let the moment. Let Ariel cry.

Then Roan shifted. Looked at Ariel's face. The bruises. The split lip.

"Who beat you up?" Roan asked.

Ariel flinched. "Nobody."

"Ariel."

"I said nobody."

"Someone did that to your face. Someone hit you. Hard. Multiple times. Who?"

"It doesn't matter."

"It matters to me."

Ariel's jaw clenched. Tears spilled down his cheeks. "Just leave it alone."

"I can't leave it alone. Look at me." Roan waited until Ariel met his eyes. "Who beat you up?"

Ariel's voice crumpled. "My boyfriend."

Not a breath moved. In the observation room, Evans stopped writing. Pérez's eyes widened slightly.

Roan's face stayed neutral.

Evans' pen stopped. He blinked once, then his face went neutral.

"Your boyfriend," Roan echoed, saying it slowly, letting the word drop between them with the weight of something new.

"Yes."

"What's his name?"

"Marco," Ariel whispered. "Marco Vargas."

Evans took down the name.

"Why did he hit you?"

Ariel sobbed. Shoulders shaking. "Because I told him he was an abomination. I said... I said God would punish us both because we were sinners. That we didn't deserve love." His voice cracked. "And he lost it. Hit me. Over and over. I didn't fight back. I deserved it."

"No," Roan said. "You didn't."

Ariel stared at him. Confused.

"You didn't deserve that," Roan repeated. "Nobody does."

Ariel broke down. His body shook.

Roan waited. Let him cry. Didn't push. Didn't interrupt. The minutes stretched.

When Ariel finally calmed, Roan spoke again. Voice gentler now. "Where were you the nights Camila and Julia died?"

Ariel wiped his face with his cuffed hands. "With Marco. Or at the club."

"Which club?"

"Pulse. On J Street."

Roan knew it—the club. Rainbow flag. Neon lights. Bass thumping through walls.

"Can anyone verify that?"

"Marco can. The doorman. Or the cameras at the club. They record everything."

Roan made a note. "What about the car? The real reason you had it detailed."

Ariel's face flushed darker. "Marco wears lotion. It has glitter in it. Got all over the seats. I needed to clean it before mom noticed."

"Glitter," Roan repeated. Despite everything, the corner of his mouth almost twitched. The mundane reality of it—not blood evidence, not murder cleanup. Just glitter from a boyfriend's lotion.

"Yeah. It's stupid. But I couldn't let mom see it. She doesn't know about Marco. Doesn't know I'm..." He trailed off.

"Gay."

Ariel nodded. Fresh tears spilled.

Roan let that sit. Let Ariel breathe.

The door opened. Evans stepped out briefly. Came back in. Leaned close to Roan. Whispered: "Blood type came back. Ariel's O-positive. Not AB-negative."

Ariel wasn't the killer.

Roan sat back. Looked at Ariel. The beaten kid with cuts on his arms and tears on his face. The kid who'd been carrying too much by himself for too long.

"Once we verify your alibi, you can go," Roan said. "But you need to see your mother. She needs you. And you need help. Professional help. For the cutting. For everything."

Ariel nodded. "Okay."

Roan stood. Unlocked Ariel's cuffs. The kid rubbed his wrists. Red marks where the metal had pressed.

"Wait here," Roan said. "Someone will bring you water. Food if you're hungry. We'll get this sorted. We'll need your boyfriend to come in to make a statement."

Ariel nodded.

Roan left the room.

In the hallway, Evans stood waiting. Pérez emerged from the observation room. Her face was pale.

"I didn't see that coming," Evans said quietly.

Pérez nodded. "None of us did. A boyfriend. The club. That's why he ran—scared, not guilty."

Roan didn't respond. Just walked toward the bullpen.

Evans fell into step beside him. "You really think he's innocent?"

"Blood type confirms it. AB-negative doesn't match. And everything he said?" Roan shook his head. "That's not a killer. That's a kid who's been drowning and nobody noticed."

They reached the bullpen. Roan sat at his desk. Exhaustion pressed down on him like a physical weight. His chest ached. His hands ached.

Evans sat, opened his phone, and started typing. "I'll run Marco Vargas through the system. See what comes up."

Pérez nodded. "I'll call Pulse. Get the manager to pull footage. Compare timestamps with the murders."

Roan leaned back in his chair. Stared at the ceiling. Someone's phone rang. Unanswered.

Another suspect ruled out. The evidence pointed to Ariel, hadn't it? The behavior. The opportunity. The motive. The religious fervor. Even the cleaned car, the neatness of it, and not a shred of an alibi.

But wrong, all of it.

That old monster: confirmation bias. Tunnel vision. The scramble to wrap things up before another girl wound up dead. They'd chased the wrong lead. Again.

Evans looked up from his phone. "Marco Vargas. Twenty-four. Lives on Fifteenth Avenue North. One prior—disorderly conduct two years ago. Charges dropped."

"Address?"

Evans read it off. Roan wrote it down.

Pérez hung up her phone. "Pulse manager's pulling footage now. Says they keep recordings for thirty days. Should have everything we need by morning."

"Good."

Roan stood. His knees ached. His back hurt. Worn down. Running on fumes and bad coffee.

"Evans," Roan said. "Go home. Get some sleep. First thing tomorrow, talk to Marco. Get his statement. Confirm the timeline."

"Got it."

"Pérez, take Ariel home once we're done here. Review the footage when it arrives. Make sure his alibi holds."

"On it."

Roan grabbed his jacket. Headed for the door.

"Where are you going?" Evans asked.

"Home."

"You sure? We might need—"

"Call me if you find something." Roan's voice was flat. Exhausted. "Otherwise, I'm done for the night."

He walked out. Down the hallway. Through the bullpen. Out into the parking lot.

Night air pressed down. Muggy. Thick. Hot even after the sun went down. Asphalt was still radiating heat. Car exhaust hung in the air. Somewhere, a siren wailed. Sweat bloomed on his temples immediately.

Roan stood there. Hands in his pockets. Staring at nothing.

They'd been wrong. So completely, devastatingly wrong.

Ariel wasn't the killer. He was just a scared kid—a victim of circumstances and bad choices and a family that couldn't hold itself together.

He thought about Ariel. The cuts. The pain. The way he'd broken when Roan said he understood.

Tomorrow they'd start over. Go back through everything they had. Find what they'd missed.

But tonight, he needed to go home. Remember that some things could be fixed.

CHAPTER

45

ROAN STOOD in the hallway outside the bathroom. Arms crossed. Everything felt muffled. Distant. Like he was submerged underwater. Like sound traveled through cotton instead of air.

The apartment hallway smelled like mildew and stale smoke. Desperation. An odor that seeped into the walls over the years. Decades. Generations of people trying and failing to escape.

Camera flashes strobed from behind the bathroom door. White light. Sharp. Cutting through the doorframe. Once. Twice. Again. Again. The mechanical click of the shutter. The rhythm of equipment. Voices low. Professional.

The ringing started in Roan's ear. High-pitched. Thin. Like tinnitus after a gunshot. It grew louder. Deeper. Transformed into something else entirely.

Moaning.

Deep. Guttural. Primal. The sound that predated language somewhere in the apartment. Pure grief given voice. Sorrow.

CSU techs moved past him. Three of them. Young. Tired. They'd seen this before. Death was routine. Package it. Document it. Move on to the next one. They nodded to Roan as they passed. He didn't respond. Just stared at the bathroom door.

Evans appeared beside him. Face pale—dark circles under his eyes like bruises.

"You don't have to go in," Evans said quietly.

Roan pushed past him. Stepped into the bathroom.

Small. Cramped. The tile has yellowed with age and hard water stains. The grout was black with mold. A single bare bulb hung from the ceiling. No shade. The harsh light washed everything out.

The tub dominated the space. Old porcelain. Chipped. Rust stains around the drain where the tap had dripped for years. Maybe decades. Impossible to tell.

Ariel Morales lay in it.

The water had drained. Someone had pulled the plug. Protocol. Preserve the body. Document everything. Diluted blood pooled at the bottom. Pink. Thin. Like watercolor paint.

His arms rested on the edges of the tub. Outstretched. Palms up. Wrists slashed deep.

A crucifixion pose.

Deep gashes in his wrists. The cuts were clean. Vertical cuts. Not horizontal. Deliberate. Precise. Down the veins, not across them. Commitment. One on each side. He'd done the left first, had to. Then used his left hand to cut the right. The blade was still there. A razor blade. Single-edge. Resting on the tile beside the tub.

His head tilted back against the tile. Eyes open. Staring at the ceiling. At nothing. Mouth slightly parted like he'd been praying when it happened.

Yellow bruises. Scabbed lip. Swollen eye. Marco's signature. Evidence of a boyfriend who hit when words failed. Proof of a life that hurt too much to continue living.

Nineteen years old.

His throat tightened. His hands were cold despite the Florida heat.

He stood there. Stared. Memorized the scene. Every detail. The way Ariel's fingers curled slightly inward. The way his hair fell across his forehead. The way his chest didn't move. Would never move again. The way the light caught the water. The way death looked when it came quietly. When it was invited in.

Evans stood in the doorway. Held a sheet of paper in a gloved hand. Standard notebook paper. Lined. Blue ink. The handwriting was neat. Deliberate. Like Ariel had taken his time. Made sure every word was legible. Made sure his last message was clear.

"He left a note," Evans said.

Roan didn't look away from Ariel. Just nodded.

Evans cleared his throat. Read aloud:

"'For the wages of sin is death, but the gift of God is eternal life in

Christ Jesus our Lord.' Romans 6:23. Tell my mother I'm sorry. Tell Marco I'm sorry. Tell God I'm ready for redemption. Ariel."

Silence filled the bathroom. Heavy. Suffocating. Like the air had turned to lead.

Roan stared at Ariel's face. The peace there. Or maybe not peace. Maybe just absence. The absence of pain. The absence of struggle. The absence of fear. The absence of everything.

Nineteen years old. A whole life unlived. Choices unmade. Futures erased. All of it, gone because the present hurt too much.

The ringing in Roan's ear returned. Louder now. Insistent. Demanding attention. His pulse echoed in it. Throbbing.

Evans finished reading. Folded the note carefully. Tucked it into an evidence bag. Looked at Roan. Waited.

Roan stood there another moment. Five seconds. Ten. Then he spoke. His voice was flat. Empty. Drained of everything.

"You should send a copy to Father Mendez." He didn't look at Evans. Kept his eyes on Ariel. On the crucifixion pose. On the irony of it. "The Church loves a redemption story. It's good for business."

He turned. Walked out of the bathroom. Past Evans. Down the narrow hallway toward the living room.

The living room was worse than the bathroom.

Maria Morales sat on the sofa. Rocking. Keening. That deep, primal sound that no mother should ever make. The sound of grief, so pure, it had no words. No beginning. No end. Just an endless cycle of agony.

Officer Pérez sat beside her. Hand on Maria's back. Not rubbing, not patting, just resting there. A point of contact. A reminder that she wasn't alone, even though she was. Even though nothing would ever make this better.

Pérez's face was stone. Professional. But her eyes were red. Wet. She'd been crying. Probably in the hallway. Probably where no one could see.

Officer Nichols stood nearby. Young. Tall. Awkward in his uniform, like he still wasn't used to wearing it. Like it still felt like a costume. But his face was soft. Sympathetic. Open in a way most cops learned not to be.

He held a glass of water. Offered it to Maria. She didn't take it. Didn't even look at it. Didn't even register his presence.

He set it on the coffee table. Careful. Gentle. Like he was handling something fragile. Then he knelt in front of her. Eye level. Moved slowly—no sudden movements.

He spoke quietly. Roan couldn't hear the words from across the room. Didn't need to. The tone was enough. Calm. Steady. Reassuring. As if he were talking to a frightened animal. Like he understood that words didn't matter, only presence mattered—only witness.

Maria looked at Nichols. Her sobs quieted. Not stopped. Just… softer. Less violent. Like she'd found an anchor. Something to hold on to in the flood of grief.

Nichols kept talking. Kept his voice low. Soothing. He had that gift—that rare ability to sit with pain. Not to run from it. Not to try to fix it. Just to be there. Just to bear witness.

Remarkably, Nichols could calm Maria. Better than Pérez. Better than anyone. Maybe it was his youth. Maybe it was his gentleness. Maybe it was just dumb luck. But he had it. That thing that made people trust him. Even in their darkest moments.

Evans joined Roan in the doorway. They stood side by side. Watching. Witnesses to grief. Useless. Unnecessary. But present.

"We're not needed here," Evans said quietly.

Roan nodded. Took one last look at Maria. At her bent back. Her shaking shoulders. Her hands were covering her face.

They left the apartment. Walked down the hallway. Took the stairs down. The sunlight hit them hard. Bright. Hot. Unforgiving. Like the world didn't care. Like death was just another Thursday.

Evans pulled the Explorer onto the street. Started driving. The A/C blasted cold air. Too cold. But neither of them adjusted it.

Roan stared out the window. Said nothing.

Evans didn't turn on the radio. Didn't ask questions. Didn't try to fill the silence with useless words. Just drove.

The silence stretched. Comfortable in its weight. Necessary.

The call came at half-past six. Pérez, on the other end, voice stripped of everything but procedure. That careful flatness cops use when the news isn't something you want to hear.

The drive to the apartment. The parking lot. The stairs. The hallway with its smell of death and failure. The bathroom. The camera flashes—the ringing in his ears.

Ariel in the tub. Arms outstretched. Wrists slashed. Eyes open. Staring at nothing.

The note.

His grey eyes fell.

The verse echoed in his mind. The same one he'd quoted. The same words he'd thought might offer hope.

The thought arrived cold. What if showing him grace—telling him there was a way out of judgment—made the other way out easier? What if eternal life sounded better than this one because a cop told him redemption was waiting?

Professional help. The words were ash in his mouth. There was no professional help for a poor gay kid in Lake Worth with a boyfriend who beat him and a mother who couldn't stay sober. There were pamphlets. Hotlines that went to voicemail. Waiting lists that were six months long.

Roan had given him the verse. Told him grace existed. Then he sent him home to an apartment where his sister's ghost still stained the walls.

He'd seen the signs. All of them. The cutting. The self-loathing. The boyfriend who beat him. The mother who'd overdosed. The sister who'd abandoned him. The religious guilt was eating him alive from the inside.

All the warning signs. Flashing red. Impossible to miss.

And Roan had uncuffed him, told him to go home. Told him to see his mother. Told him to get help. Professional help. As if it were that simple. As if saying the words created resources that didn't exist for poor kids in Lake Worth.

Maria had been released from JFK Medical Center that morning. Discharged. Stable. The paperwork said she was fine. Ready to go home. Back to the apartment where her daughter had lived, and her son was planning his suicide.

An Uber took her back, a twenty-dollar ride. The driver probably didn't say a word. Just watched her in the rear-view mirror—another sad story in a city full of them.

She'd opened the apartment door and called out to Ariel. No answer.

She'd checked his room. Empty. The bed was made like he'd never been there. Like he'd already erased himself.

She looked in the bathroom.

Found him.

She knew immediately. Didn't touch him. Didn't try to pull him out of the tub. Didn't check for a pulse. Didn't call 911. She just knew. Mothers always know. That bond that defies logic. That connection that transcends death.

She collapsed. Right there on the bathroom floor. Cried into the fuzzy shower mat. The front door was still open behind her. Anyone could have walked in. No one did.

A neighbor in the next apartment heard. Mrs. Jimenez. Old woman. Lived there for fifteen years. Seen everything. This was nothing new—just another tragedy in a building full of them.

She called 911.

By the time anyone arrived, Ariel had been dead for hours. Body cold. Blood congealed. Rigor mortis was already setting in. Gone.

Evans turned down Lakeside Drive. The name was aspirational. There was no lake—just the Intracoastal with algae and mosquitoes beyond the golf course.

Twilight settled over the neighborhood. Sky bruised purple and orange. Streetlights flickered on one by one. Palm trees swayed in the breeze. Someone was grilling. The smell of charcoal and meat drifted through the open window. Normal life. Continuing. Indifferent to death.

Roan's house seemed to appear almost out of nowhere: low, square, and so nondescript you would be forgiven for blinking and thinking it was never there at all. The house seemed to dare you to try and remember it later. Exactly what Roan intended. A place to disappear, lost behind its clean lines and the soft green of its carefully managed grass.

Evans pulled into the driveway. Put the Explorer in park. Left the engine running.

Evans nodded. "Get some rest. We'll regroup tomorrow."

Roan reached for the door handle. Stopped. His eyes locked on something ahead.

The front door.

Smashed open.

Wood splintered around the lock. The frame cracked. The door hung crooked on its hinges. Darkness beyond. Deep. Impenetrable.

"Roan?" Evans followed his gaze. "Shit."

Everything he touched turned to wreckage.

Roan's hand moved to his holster. Drew his Glock. Aimed it at the doorway. Safety off. Finger resting on the trigger guard. Not touching. Not yet. But ready.

Evans killed the engine. Drew his own weapon. Opened his door. Quiet. Controlled.

Everything sharpened. The world came into focus. Adrenaline kicked in. Heart pounding. Breathing steady. Training took over—muscle memory.

Roan signaled. Two fingers. Clear right. Evans nodded.

They moved forward. Slowly. Quietly. Every sense alert. Evans to the left. Roan to the right. Flanking the entrance. Standard approach. Weapons, low and ready. Pie the doorway. Slice the fatal funnel. Every window was a threat vector.

The house was silent.

They reached the doorstep. Roan peered inside. Darkness. Shadows. His eyes adjusted. He could make out shapes. A lamp on its side illuminated the floor.

Roan entered.

CHAPTER

46

THE LIVING ROOM had been gutted.

Roan moved through it. Weapon raised. Eyes sweeping corners. Shadows. The places where threats hid.

Chairs overturned. Sofa cushions slashed. Foam spilling out like guts. Books were scattered across the floor. Spines broken. Pages torn. His chess set was smashed. Pieces scattered. The white king lay on its side near the skirting board.

Vodka pooled on the hardwood. The bottle shattered, Glass glittering in the dim light from the hallway. The smell sharp. Medicinal. Mixed with something else—sweat, rage, the stale odor of someone else's presence. Violation.

Someone had been here. Someone had torn through his space. His sanctuary.

Evans moved beside him. Silent. Weapon low ready. Breathing controlled. They'd done this before. Not together. But the training was the same. The muscle memory. The tactical instinct.

Roan signaled. Two fingers. Then pointed. Living room clear. Move to the hallway.

Evans nodded.

They advanced. Slow. Methodical. Pie the corners. Check the blind spots. Every doorway was a potential ambush. Every shadow a threat.

The hallway stretched ahead. Three doors. Bathroom on the left. Bedroom on the right. Kitchen at the end. All closed. All dark.

His pulse was steady. Not elevated. Just present. Constant. The rhythm of focus. Of control. Fear didn't control him. It made him sharper.

Roan positioned himself at the bathroom door, on the left side.

Evans took the right—standard entry. Roan reached for the handle. Turned it slowly. No sound. The hinges were well-oiled. He'd made sure of that. The little things mattered. Always.

He pushed the door open. Fast. Committed. Evans moved in. Weapon sweeping. High corners first. Then low. Then the shower.

"Clear," Evans said. Voice barely above a whisper.

The bedroom door opened to chaos. Mattress sliced. Dresser drawers pulled out. Clothes everywhere. His closet door hung open. Hangers scattered. Everything searched. Everything violated.

But empty.

"Clear."

One room left.

The kitchen.

His throat tightened. The air in the hallway felt heavier. Colder. Like the temperature had dropped ten degrees in the last thirty seconds.

They approached the final door.

Roan reached for the handle. His hand was steady. No tremor. No hesitation. But his gut twisted. An instinct. A warning that could have saved lives if you had listened to it.

He turned the handle.

The kitchen light was off. But there was illumination. Pale. Cold. Coming from the fridge. The door hung open. Just slightly. Just enough for the internal light to spill out.

Roan stepped inside. Evans was behind him. They swept the room. Corners first. Then the pantry. Then behind the door.

Empty. But something wrong.

The fridge hummed. Constant. Mechanical. Cold air spilled out. The smell hit him—copper and rot beneath the chemical tang of refrigeration.

The light flickered. Once. Twice. Stabilized.

Roan approached it. His Glock was still raised. Still ready. He reached out. Pulled the door open entirely.

Light flooded the kitchen.

His brain refused to process it. Rejected the input. Insisted the image was wrong. Impossible.

Then comprehension hit.

Jin Shin's head sat on the middle shelf, between a carton of eggs and a half-empty bottle of orange juice. Her eyes were closed. Mouth slightly open—but not peaceful, not sleeping. Just absent. Her head ended at the neck. Ragged. Hacked rather than cut clean.

And there was a card. Stuffed in her mouth. Folded once. White. Official.

Roan's card.

His business card. The one he'd given her at the massage parlor. The one with his name and number. His connection to her. His fault.

"Fuck."

Evans stepped beside him. Looked. Froze.

"Son of a bitch." His voice cracked.

Jin's face. Hair across her forehead. Skin gone pale. She'd been terrified when he'd interviewed her. Shaking. Looking over her shoulder. Worried about what Vance would do if he found out she'd talked.

Now she'd never talk again.

Fire climbed through Roan's chest. His knuckles went white on the Glock. The kitchen sharpened—too bright, too loud, the fridge hum drilling into his skull.

He'd gone to her, asked questions. Pushed for information. Put a target on her back. And whoever killed Camila had followed through, had made an example.

And they'd brought it here. To his home. To the one place that was supposed to be separate from all of it.

"Roan." Evans' voice. Careful. Controlled. As if he were talking to someone standing on a ledge.

Roan didn't respond. Just kept staring at his business card. His name. His connection. His responsibility.

Evans moved away. Started checking the rest of the kitchen. Opening cupboards. Looking in the pantry. Making sure there were no more surprises.

His phone rang.

The sound was sharp. Jarring. Evans fumbled for it. Pulled it from his pocket. Looked at the screen.

His face went white—hand trembling.

"Clara." He answered. Put it to his ear. "Hey, what's—"

He stopped. Listening. His expression shifted. Fear. Pure. Unfiltered.

"What? Slow down. What are you—"

He listened. Five seconds. Ten. His breathing quickened.

"Don't touch it. Don't go near it. Lock the front door. Right now." His voice steadied—forcing control. "Get the kids. Take them to the bedroom. Lock that door. Get the gun from the safe. You remember the combination?"

Pause.

"Yes. That one. Load it like I showed you." His voice cracked slightly. "Keep the kids behind you. Don't open the door for anyone except me or another cop. You understand?"

Another pause. He closed his eyes briefly.

"I'm coming. Right now. Ten minutes. Maybe less. Just stay calm. Stay locked in. Clara—Clara, listen to me. You're going to be fine. Just do exactly what I said."

He kept his phone on. Looked at Roan. His eyes were wide. Panicked. The controlled detective was gone, replaced by a father. A husband. Someone whose family was in danger.

"There's a box," Evans said. Voice shaking. "On my front porch. Bloody. She said it looks like... like it has pieces inside. Body parts."

Roan's anger shifted. Redirected. Focused.

"Go."

"Roan, I can't just—" Evans glanced at Jin's head. At the crime scene. At the protocol, they were violating.

"Get to your family. I'll call Rocca. He'll meet you there. I'll secure this scene and call it in. Go."

Evans hesitated. Torn. Then he nodded. Holstered his weapon. Turned. Ran.

His footsteps echoed through the house. The front door slammed. The Explorer's engine roared to life. Tires squealed on pavement. And then silence.

Roan stood alone in his kitchen. With Jin Shin's head. With the wreckage of his home. With the message that couldn't be clearer.

They knew who he was. Where he lived, and they weren't afraid.

His phone was in his pocket. He pulled it out. Thumb moving on autopilot. Found Rocca's number—pressed call.

It rang twice.

"Roan. What's up?"

"How fast can you get to Evans' house?"

Pause. "Why? What's going on?"

"Someone left a box on his porch. Possibly body parts. His wife and kids are there. He's en route, but he's ten minutes out. I need you there now."

"Jesus. Yeah. I'm five minutes away. I'll light it up."

"Good. And Rocca? Go in hot. Whoever did this is sending a message. They might still be watching."

"Copy that. You good?"

"No. But I will be. Just get to Evans' family."

"On it."

The line went dead.

Roan lowered the phone. Stared at Jin's head. At his business card protruding from her mouth. The rage was still there. Burning. But now it had direction. Purpose.

He dialed again. Dispatch this time.

"Palm Beach Sheriff's Office, what's your emergency?"

"This is Detective Roan—badge eleven thirty-eight. I need CSU and a supervisor at my residence as soon as possible. I have a crime scene. Homicide victim. Partial remains."

"Copy, Detective. What's your address?"

He gave it. Answered the procedural questions. Location. Nature of the scene. Threat assessment. All of it mechanical. Automatic. The part of his brain that functioned when emotion shut down.

"Units are en route. ETA ten minutes."

"Acknowledged."

He hung up.

The house fell quiet—fridge hum. Clock ticking in the bedroom. Floorboards creaked as the house settled. His own breathing. Too loud in the silence.

He looked around the kitchen. At the destruction. The overturned chairs. The broken dishes. The pantry was ransacked. They'd been thorough. Professional. This wasn't random violence. This was calculated. Planned. A message delivered with precision.

His gun safe, located in the bedroom closet, remained untouched. Still locked. They hadn't tried to break into it. They weren't thieves. They were killers. And they only took what served their purpose.

Sirens wailed in the distance. Growing louder. Multiple units. Coming fast.

Roan walked back to the kitchen. Stood in the doorway. Looked at Jin's head one more time.

"I'm sorry," he said quietly. To her. To the memory of her. To the scared woman who'd tried to do the right thing and died for it. For his card in her mouth. For the target he'd painted on her back.

Then he closed the fridge door.

The light went out. The kitchen fell into darkness.

The sirens were close now. Seconds away.

Roan holstered his weapon. Took a breath. Centered himself. Pushed the rage down. Not gone. Just controlled. Contained. Ready for use when the time comes.

The time would come soon.

He walked to the front door. Opened it. Stepped outside into the warm Florida night.

Red and blue lights strobed down the street. Three patrol cars. An ambulance. The CSU van is pulling in behind them.

Neighbors stood on their porches. Watching. Whispering. Pointing.

Roan's hands were steady. Jaw unclenched. Breathing even.

They thought fear would stop him.

They miscalculated.

He stood in his doorway and watched the cavalry arrive, and knew with absolute certainty that he wouldn't stop until they had a needle in their arm or he was in the ground.

CHAPTER

47

Evans slammed his foot down on the accelerator. The Explorer shot forward; the engine rising to a howl, tires screeching over the raw strip of asphalt. In the grille, red and blue lights pulsed—a hidden pattern, undercover, but not exactly subtle. The traffic up ahead peeled aside, cars sliding right, stuttering brake lights dancing as drivers instinctively made way.

His phone was tossed on the dashboard, still on speaker. Clara's voice filled the cab. She sounded scared, shaky, trying to keep it steady for the kids.

"Where are you now?" Evans asked. He gripped the steering wheel hard—the leather digging into his palms, hot and rough.

"In the hallway. Moving to the bedroom."

"Good. Keep moving. Don't stop."

He weaved around a silver sedan. Too slow. Too cautious. The Explorer's engine screamed. Eighty miles per hour on Lucerne. Dangerous. Reckless. He didn't care.

His pulse hammered. Chest tight. Breathing shallow. Fast. Every nerve on fire. Sweat slicked his palms. Made the wheel slip in his hands.

His family. His whole world. Clara. Emily. Matthew. In danger because of him. Because of his job. Because some psychopath wanted to send a message.

"I'm in the bedroom now," Clara said. Her voice cracked. "Kids are with me."

"Lock the door. Right now."

The click came through the phone. Sharp. Final.

"It's locked."

"Good. Now the gun. You remember where it is?"

"Yes. The safe. Top shelf of the closet."

"What's the combination?"

Pause. "Six-two-four-one."

"That's right. Open it. Careful. Don't rush."

He heard her moving. Footsteps on carpet. Listened to the closet door opening. Hangers scraping. Then silence.

"I can't remember which way to turn," Clara said. Panic edging into her voice.

"Right first. Three full turns. Then left to six. Right to two. Left to four. Right to one."

Silence. The phone speaker crackled with her breath. Fast. Shallow. Then a click.

"I got it."

"Good. Take out the Glock. The black one."

"Okay."

Evans swerved around a white pickup truck hauling a trailer with orange letters stamped across the side. Brake lights flaring. Too close. His heart jumped into his throat. He yanked the wheel left. The Explorer fishtailed. Tires screamed. Then straightened.

"Clara, you still there?"

"I'm here." Her voice was steadier now. Having a task. Something to focus on. It helped.

"Magazine should already be loaded. Check it."

Rustling. "It's in."

"Good. Now rack the slide. Pull it all the way back. Let it go. Don't ride it forward."

The metallic snap came through the phone. Loud. Clear. A round chambering.

"Done."

"Safety's on the left side. Push it down. Red dot means it's off. Ready to fire."

"Okay. It's off."

"Turn it back on for now. Keep it on until you need it."

"Okay."

Evans blew through a red light. Cross traffic honked. Headlights flashing. He didn't slow down. Just kept going. The lights on the Explorer cleared the way.

His hands were shaking. He tightened his grip. Focused on the road. On getting there. Metallic taste in his mouth. Adrenaline.

"Where are the kids?" he asked.

"Behind me. On the bed. Emily's crying."

His chest constricted. His daughter. Eight years old. Terrified. He should be there. Should be protecting them. Instead, he was racing through traffic. Miles away. Useless.

"Tell her it's okay. Tell her Dad's coming."

Clara's voice softened. Away from the phone. "Emily, honey. Dad's almost here. Everything's going to be okay."

Muffled crying. Then silence.

"Matthew's quiet," Clara said. "Too quiet."

Matthew. Ten years old. The quiet one. The thinker. When things got bad, he shut down. Went internal. Evans knew that response. Recognized it.

"He's scared," Evans said. "That's normal. Just keep them close."

"I am."

A bang echoed through the phone. Loud. Sharp. Like something hitting wood.

Clara gasped.

"What was that?" Evans demanded.

"The front door. Someone's knocking."

"Don't answer it."

"I'm not."

"It might be Rocca. He's on his way."

"How do I know it's him?"

"He'll identify himself. Loud. Clear. Won't be shy about it."

Another bang. Louder this time.

Then silence.

Evans held his breath. Listening. Waiting.

Nothing.

"It stopped," Clara whispered.

"Good. Stay put. Don't move. Don't make noise."

"Okay."

Evans passed Lake Worth High School. Empty parking lot. Dark windows. The football field lights were off—just shadows and silence.

His neighborhood came into view. Familiar streets. Familiar houses. Palm trees swaying in the breeze. Streetlights cast orange pools on the sidewalk.

Ahead, he saw Rocca's unmarked Taurus. Black. Nondescript. Parked at an angle in front of his house. The driver's door opened, and Rocca stood beside it. Weapon drawn. Eyes on the house.

Evans pulled up behind him. Slammed the brakes. The Explorer rocked forward. He threw it into park. Left the engine running. Grabbed his Glock from the center console.

His door flew open. Feet hit the driveway. He was moving before he thought about it.

Rocca turned. Saw him. Nodded once.

"Your family inside?" Rocca asked.

"Yeah. Bedroom. Locked in."

"Box is on the porch."

Evans looked.

There it was.

Cardboard. Brown. Unremarkable. Except for the dark stains seeping through the bottom. Wet. Fresh. The smell hit him even from the driveway. Copper. Rot. Death. The boiling heat made it worse. Thick. Cloying.

His stomach turned.

"You open it?" Evans asked.

"No. Waiting for you."

Evans moved toward the porch. His weapon raised. Eyes scanning windows. The front door. The bushes. Anywhere someone could hide.

Rocca fell in beside him. Covering his six.

They reached the porch. The box sat directly in front of the door. No note. No marking. Just the box and the blood.

Evans stared at it. His throat was tight. Mouth dry.

He didn't want to know. But he had to.

"Let me get Clara and the kids first," Evans said.

Rocca nodded. "I'll cover you."

Evans approached the front door. Key already in hand. He unlocked it. Slow. Quiet. Pushed it open. Stepped inside.

The house was dark. Silent. Normal.

He moved through the living room. Down the hallway. Past Matthew's room. Past Emily's. To the master bedroom at the end.

He knocked—three quick raps.

"Clara. It's me."

Footsteps. The lock turned. The door opened a crack. Clara's face appeared. Pale. Eyes red. But focused.

"You're here," she said.

"I'm here."

The door opened fully. Clara stepped into his arms. He held her. Tight. Her body trembled against his. The smell of her shampoo mixed with fear-sweat.

"It's okay," he whispered. "I've got you."

Emily ran over. Wrapped her arms around his leg. Face buried in his pants. She was trembling. Small hands gripping tight.

Matthew stood by the bed. Arms crossed. Face blank. But Evans saw it. The fear beneath the surface. The same shutdown response Evans had when he was a kid.

"Everyone okay?" Evans asked.

Clara nodded against his chest. Her hands were still shaking.

"You did good," Evans said. Looking at her. At the Glock still in her hand. Safety on. Finger off the trigger. "Real good."

He took the gun from her. Checked it. Made it safe. Set it on the dresser.

Emily still wouldn't let go of his leg. He knelt. Looked at her. Tears streaked her face. Eyes wide.

"Is the bad man gone?" she asked. Voice small.

Evans' heart broke. She shouldn't have to ask that question. Shouldn't have to know bad men existed.

"I don't know, sweetheart," he said. Honest. "But I'm here now. And I'm not going to let anything happen to you."

She threw her arms around his neck. He held her. Breathing in the smell of her strawberry shampoo.

Matthew stepped forward. Slow. Hesitant.

"Dad," he said. "We heard screaming. From the phone. Before you got here."

Evans looked at Clara. She nodded.

"That was me on the phone with your mom," Evans said. "Helping her. Telling her what to do."

"Was someone trying to get in?"

"Maybe. But they're gone now."

"What if they come back?"

Evans looked at his son. Ten years old. Too young to carry this sort of fear. Too old to be lied to.

"Then I'll handle it," Evans said. "That's my job. To protect you."

Matthew nodded. But the fear didn't leave his eyes.

"Stay in here," Evans said. Standing, looking at all of them. "Lock the door behind me. Rocca's outside. He's going to check the house. Make sure it's clear. Don't open this door until I come back. Understood?"

"Yes."

He pulled back. Looked at Clara, at Emily still clinging to him, at Matthew standing alone.

"I'll be right back," he said.

He stepped into the hallway. The door closed behind him. The lock turned.

He walked back through the house, out the front door. Rocca was on the porch. Staring at the box.

"Family secure?" Rocca asked.

"Yeah. Locked in the bedroom."

"Good. Let's clear the house."

They moved through each room. Methodical. Room by room. Kitchen. Living room. Bathrooms. Matthew's room. Emily's room. The garage. All clear. No signs of forced entry. No threats.

Just the box.

They returned to the porch.

Evans stared at it. His pulse throbbed in his temples. Jaw clenched. Jaw already aching from grinding teeth.

"You want to open it?" Rocca asked.

"No. But I will."

Evans knelt. A momentary pause with his hand poised above the flaps, the old prickle of nerves seeping through, though training pressed against it, dulling the edge. He reached into his pocket, brought out a pair of latex gloves, and snapped them on. The tremor in his fingers eased; the method took hold. Push the fear aside and concentrate: that was the way; let instinct and repetition carry him through the next steps.

He reached for the box. The cardboard was soaked through, damp and sticky, the structure all but gone to pulp under the pressure of his fingers. The wetness had seeped in. Blood, unmistakably, fresh, still oozing, leaking out in slow, syrupy streaks to the outside. He pulled the flaps apart.

The smell came first, a wave of rot so thick that you could nearly taste it, sharp copper and something else, almost clinical—a chemical tang that might be formaldehyde or bleach, layered on to drown out the rest. Not that it could. The warmth of the Florida night had done its work; whatever had been inside the box was rendered unbearable.

He looked. Had to, though the impulse to jerk away was strong. The skin was a remarkable pallor: all blood stripped out, the flesh left pale and empty, as if drained by a methodical hand. The cuts were not clean. Jagged, rough work, torn through as though the blade had dulled or the hand had lost patience. Rage, perhaps, or haste.

A clot of blood gathered in a corner, thick and glistening, refusing to dry, the whole mass of it holding to the last of its life. His stomach flipped; he closed his mouth tight, forced his gaze to stay level.

They were hands, he realized, small and not old. Woman's hands, likely: the bones fine, the fingers slender, nails decorated a glossy red, though chipped down now almost to the cuticle. One finger bore a ring, plain and silver; barely more than a thread, with a faintly scored mark like a scratch on its band.

Jin Shin. He knew it. She'd worn the ring in the interview room—the one at the station. She had spun it on her finger, again and again, nervous, every time she had to speak, and especially when Vance's photo slid across the table. There was no mistaking it now.

Now it was evidence.

She died because they asked her to talk.

"It's her," Evans said. His voice was flat. Hollow.

Rocca knelt beside him. Looked in. His face hardened.

"Rest of Jin Shin," Rocca said.

"Yeah."

They stared at the contents. Silent. Witnesses to brutality.

Evans closed the flaps. Carefully. Preserving evidence. He stood. Pulled off the gloves. His hands were cold despite the heat of being in latex.

"We need CSU," Evans said.

"Already called them. On the way."

Headlights appeared at the end of the street. Multiple vehicles. Moving fast.

The first was a patrol car. Sheriff's cruiser. Lights off. Silent approach. Professional.

Behind it, another unmarked vehicle. Dark blue sedan.

Then a CSU van. White. Palm Beach Sheriff's Office logo on the side.

They pulled up. Parked in a line along the curb.

Doors opened. Officers emerged—Pérez from the first cruiser, face grim. She'd probably just gotten home when the call came—maybe been asleep. But she came.

Metal groaned as the sedan door swung wide. Captain Norris unfolded from the driver's seat, his department polo stretched across his shoulders, jeans dusty at the cuffs. Weekend clothes. Yet he brought with him a static that made the air feel charged, a presence that didn't need a uniform to mark its authority.

He walked forward, gaze dropping to the box before lifting to meet Evans' face.

"Evans," Norris said.

"Captain."

"Your family okay?"

"Yeah. Inside. Safe."

Norris nodded. "Good. What do we have?"

"Box. Body parts. Looks like the rest of Jin Shin. The witness we interviewed."

Norris' jaw tightened. "The one that ID'd Vance?"

"Yeah."

"Where's Roan now?"

"At his place. Someone left Jin Shin's head in his fridge."

Norris' eyes widened. Just slightly. Then the professional mask returned. "Simultaneously?"

"Maybe have been one after the other."

"Two locations. Same victim."

"That's what it looks like."

Norris looked at Rocca. "You were first on scene?"

"Yes, sir."

"Walk me through it."

Rocca explained. The call from Roan. The drive. The box on the porch. Waiting for Evans. Clearing the house, opening the box.

Norris listened. Asked no questions. Just absorbed the information.

When Rocca finished, Norris turned to the CSU van. Techs were unloading equipment. Cameras. Evidence bags. Lights.

"Process everything," Norris said. "I want photos. Prints. DNA. Trace evidence. Everything. This is priority one."

The lead tech nodded. A woman in her forties. Short grey hair. Competent. Professional. She'd seen it all. But even she looked disturbed.

A dark Explorer rolled up, drawing to a stop behind the CSU van, the engine idling. Its windows were tinted black—a mirror for the early streetlights. The passenger door opened. Roan stepped out. He looked like hell. Drawn face, eyes sunk deep. But sharp. He'd pushed past whatever he'd felt at his house. Compartmentalized. Put it in a box. Dealt with later. Evans knew the look—it was how you stayed upright.

Roan walked over, gaze locking with Evans', a hard line from one to the other—a silent question.

Evans nodded back.

Roan's face didn't move, not even a twitch, but something flicked in his eyes, unsettling, black as engine oil.

Norris turned then, saw Roan coming. His features eased for a half-second. "Roan," Norris said.

"Captain."

"I heard what happened. At your place."

"Yeah."

Norris studied him. Then looked at Evans. Back to Roan.

"You're both off this case," Norris said. Voice flat. Final.

His blood turned to ice. Vision tunneled. The edges of his sight were going dark. "What?"

"You heard me. Off. Effective immediately."

Norris looked at Roan. Then at Evans. Something dark passed across his face. Recognition. History.

"2019," Norris said. Voice quiet. "The Ramirez case."

Roan went still. His jaw tightened.

Evans glanced at his partner. Saw something he'd never seen before. Discomfort. Maybe shame.

"Captain—" Roan started.

"No." Norris cut him off. "You need to hear this." He turned to Evans. "Your partner had a witness—key testimony. Ramirez walked because Roan got too close. Pushed too hard. The witness recanted. Said Roan threatened him. Coerced him. The case collapsed."

Evans looked at Roan. "That true?"

Roan's expression was stone. But his silence was answer enough.

"The witness lied," Roan said finally. Voice low. Controlled. "He was scared. Got to. Changed his story."

"Maybe," Norris said. "Or maybe you crossed a line. Maybe you wanted justice so bad you couldn't see straight. Either way, a killer walked." He paused. Let that sink in. "Ramirez killed two more people before we caught him again. Two more. Because of that case."

The humidity seemed to thicken around the words. Heavy. Suffocating.

Norris stepped closer to Roan. "You're the best detective I've got. Sharp. Relentless. But you've got a blind spot. When it gets personal, you push. And when you push, you break things."

He turned to Evans. "And you? You've been a good cop. By the book. Careful. But tonight?" He gestured at the house. At the box.

"Your family was threatened. Your daughter was crying. Your son was terrified. You think you can work this case with that in your head? You think you won't cross lines to protect them?"

Evans wanted to argue. Wanted to say he could handle it. But the words stuck.

"I'm pulling you both," Norris said. "Not because you're bad cops. Because you're too good. Too invested. And that's when mistakes happen. That's when people get hurt."

Evans wanted to argue. Wanted to fight. But the words stuck in his throat.

Norris stepped closer to Evans. Voice dropping. "Go inside. Be with your family. Make sure they're okay. That's your job now. Not this."

"Captain—"

"That's an order, Detective. Not a suggestion."

Evans stood there. Torn between duty and family. Between rage and reason. Between what he wanted and what he knew was right.

Finally, he nodded.

"Good." Norris turned to Roan. "You. Go home. Get some sleep. Take a few days. We'll reassign your active cases. Come back when you're ready."

Roan didn't move. Just stared at Norris—grey eyes, cold as winter.

"Detective Roan," Norris said. Voice harder now. "Go home."

For a moment, Roan would refuse. Would argue. Would push back.

But he didn't.

He just turned. Walked back to the Explorer. Got in. The door closed with finality. The engine started—low rumble.

And the Explorer drove away.

Evans watched him go. Felt something inside him twist. Anger. Helplessness. Frustration. And beneath it all, a cold determination.

Norris put a hand on his shoulder. "Go be with your family, Daniel. That's where you're needed right now."

Evans shifted his weight, uneasy, observing the box quarantined on his own porch. The CSU team hovered, measuring and dusting, their latex-gloved hands mapping the damage. Red and blue lights pulsed against the siding and windows of his house, broadcasting to the neighbors. His neighborhood. Not just the scene now—a spectacle.

He glanced at his front door. Inside, his family waited. Safe, he hoped. Probably terrified. His job crossed the distance between crime scene and sanctuary.

He nodded once, to no one in particular. Turned away from the investigators. Took the steps up, toward the door. Home.

CHAPTER

48

EVANS SAT at the kitchen table. Seething. Jaw clenched so tight his teeth ached. Hands flat on the wood. The grain beneath his palms was cool. Smooth. Real.

His mind ran through the case. Over and over. Names. Faces. Bodies.

Camila Morales. Twenty-one. Found on the beach. Blood soaked into the sand. Dark. Thick.

Julia Aguilar. Stabbed left in an empty lot.

Jessica Torres. Barely alive. Hooked to machines at Good Samaritan. Tubes down her throat. The doctors said even if she woke up, she'd never be the same.

Jin Shin hacked up and delivered in pieces, like a message.

And others.

Ariel Morales. Haunted. Hollow-eyed. Suicide. And Maria Morales. Mother. Trying to hold herself together. A family that would never be whole again.

Mark Vance, with half his face blown off and still breathing.

Victims, in their own way.

All connected. All suffering.

His phone sat on the table. Battery indicator blinking. Useless tonight. No case to work. No calls to make. Just a rectangle of glass and metal reminding him he'd been benched.

Matthew was next to Evans. Arms crossed tight over his chest. Face rigid. Foot tapping against the table leg. Tap. Tap. Tap. Steady. Anxious.

The kitchen smelled like old coffee and something sweeter. Vanilla.

Clara's candle was on the counter. Still burning. The fridge hummed. Low. Constant. The sound of normal life.

Nothing was normal.

"Dad," Matthew said. Voice quiet. Careful. As if he were afraid of the answer.

Evans looked at him. Really looked. Matthew's jaw was set the same way Evans' was. Tight. Tense. The kid was ten, but he already knew how to hide fear behind anger.

"How long do we have to stay in the house?"

The question hung there. Simple. Innocent. The sort of question a ten-year-old should be asking about a grounding or a punishment. Not about being trapped because a killer left body parts on the porch.

"I don't know, buddy."

Matthew's foot stopped tapping. His eyes dropped. "I'll miss my golf tournament Saturday." His voice cracked. "Coach says I can definitely win the trophy. I've been practicing my drive for two months."

Something shifted in his chest. Softened. The rage that had been simmering since Norris pulled him off the case—since the moment he saw Jin Shin's ring on his porch—eased just slightly.

Kids' minds. So innocent. So focused on what mattered to them. Golf tournaments. Trophies. Drives they'd been practicing.

Matthew should be worrying about whether his swing was smooth enough. Whether he'd beat the kid from Boca, who always placed first. Normal things.

Not this.

"You'll make your tournament, buddy," Evans said. He reached over. Squeezed Matthew's shoulder. Felt the tension there. The kid's muscles were coiled tight. "I promise."

Matthew nodded. But the fear didn't leave his eyes.

The front door opened. Rocca stepped in. He carried a large bag in one hand. Grease was already soaking through the bottom.

Buffalo wings. The sharp tang of hot sauce. Vinegar. Butter. Heat radiating from the container. Barbecue. Sweet and smoky. Molasses dark. The sauce pooled at the bottom. Thick. Sticky. Grease stained the polystyrene.

"Best wings in town," Rocca said. Grinning. Trying to lighten the mood. Trying to pretend this was a normal family dinner and not a crime scene with kids present. He set the bag on the counter. "Figured the kids might be hungry. Even if you adults aren't."

Clara looked up. Managed a smile. Weak. Forced. "Thank you."

Evans stared at the bag. Watched Rocca pull out containers. Steam rose when he opened the first one. Buffalo wings. Bright orange. Glistening. The second container held barbecue. Dark. Sticky.

The kids wouldn't eat the buffalo. Too spicy. But maybe the barbecue. Clara liked spicy, though. Always had. She'd ordered Thai food extra hot, and ate jalapeños straight from the jar.

Emily shifted. Uncrossed her arms. Leaned forward slightly. Looking at the wings.

"Can I have the barbecue ones?" she asked. Voice small.

Evans watched her. Eight. Too young to understand why someone would leave body parts on their porch.

"Course, sweetheart," Rocca said. He slid the container toward her. Grabbed a handful of napkins from the bag. Set them on the table.

Matthew didn't move. Just stared at the food as if it were evidence.

Rocca pulled out the burger. Massive. Wrapped in foil. He set it on the table in front of Clara. "Figured you could split that. The thing's like two pounds."

Clara nodded. Unwrapped it slowly. The smell of beef, cheese, and grilled onions filled the kitchen—normal smells. Comforting smells.

His stomach turned.

"CSU should be wrapping up soon," Rocca said. Looking at Evans. "Pérez and I are guarding the place tonight. We'll be outside if you need anything."

He headed back toward the door.

"Rocca," Evans said.

Rocca stopped. Turned.

"Thanks."

Rocca nodded. Then he was gone. The door closed with a soft click.

The kitchen felt smaller. Tighter. Evans could hear Emily chewing. The sound was too loud. Clara was cutting the burger. The knife scraped against the plate. Matthew's foot started tapping again. Tap. Tap. Tap.

Evans stood. Chair scraping against tile. Loud. Harsh. Everyone looked up.

"Be right back," he said.

He walked to the front door. Stepped outside.

The air hit him. Thick. Humid. Heavy. It smelled like rain was coming. Like wet asphalt and cut grass and the ocean somewhere beyond the houses. The sky was dark. No stars. Cloud cover. Heat lightning in the distance. Flickering. Silent. Far off thunder rumbled. Low. Threatening.

Rocca stood near the porch. He held a cigarette between his fingers. Orange glow in the darkness. He turned when Evans came out. Eyebrows raised.

"You alright?"

"Yeah."

Evans walked over. Stood next to him. Close enough to smell the smoke. Close enough to feel the heat from the cigarette.

"You got another one of those?" Evans asked.

Rocca stared at him. Eyebrows still raised. "I thought you didn't smoke?"

"I don't." Evans held out his hand. Palm up. "Or not anymore. Quit a few years back."

Rocca pulled the pack from his jacket pocket. Marlboro Golds. He tapped one out. Handed it over.

Evans took it. Felt the weight of it between his fingers. Light. Fragile. He put it between his lips.

Rocca flicked his lighter. The flame danced. Caught. Evans leaned in. Inhaled. The smoke burned as it went down. Sharp. Acrid. Wrong.

Familiar.

"Yeah," Rocca said. Pocketing the lighter. "Job will do that."

Evans inhaled again. Deep. Let the smoke fill his lungs. The nicotine hit fast. Head rush. Slight dizziness. His fingers remembered the motion. Three years since he quit. Three years since Clara made him promise. The burn felt wrong. Felt right. Let it ground him. He exhaled slowly. Watched the smoke curl up into the dark.

Rocca reached into his pocket again. Pulled something else out. Handful of napkins. No—restaurant wipes. Individually wrapped. Plastic crinkling in his palm. He handed them to Evans.

"Your kids will need these after those wings."

Evans took them. Clenched them in his fist. The plastic crinkled. Loud. Harsh.

"We'll find this guy, Evans," Rocca said. Voice steady. Confident, "Pérez is a block down the street searching the area. Norris has units canvassing. We're on it."

Evans took one last drag. Deep. Long. Held it. Then flicked the cigarette away. It arced through the darkness. Hit the grass. Glowed orange. Faded.

"They're long gone by now," Evans said.

He turned. Walked back inside.

The kitchen was brighter than outside. Harsh light overhead. Too white. Too sharp. Clara stood at the table now. The massive burger in front of her. Knife in her right hand. She held the burger steady with her left hand. Positioned it, lined up the blade.

Evans set the restaurant wipes on the table. But he held one in his hand. Turned it over. Looked at it.

BCI wipes.

The same ones scattered around Torres. Around the blood. Around the body.

Why wipes? What were they cleaning?

His eyes drifted back to Clara. Watched her work. Right hand holding the knife. Blade angled. Precise. She cut down. Clean. Smooth. The burger split. Juice ran onto the plate.

Left-handed.

No. Right-handed. But using her left to steady.

Something pinged in Evans' mind.

The wipes. BCI brand. Industrial strength.

The cuts. Clean. Precise. Camila's throat—single sweep, left to right. Aguilar—two stab wounds, all angled the same direction. Torres —defensive wounds on her right palm. Attacker coming from the left side.

The medical examiner's report. Downward trajectory. Left to right. Consistent with a left-handed attacker.

The angle. The way the killer had worked. Methodical. Precise. Clean. Controlled.

The chipped blade. Forensics found metal fragments in Torres' sternum—blade damage.

Left-handed. Wipes. Chipped blade—

A surge of adrenaline—a drumline in Evans' ribcage. He could feel his own heart, frantic beneath his shirt. The air caught in his throat sped through his lungs.

He knew.

He wrenched his tie straight. Snatched the jacket from the chair-back. Shoved his phone in his pocket, a cold flash of glass and metal.

"Where are you going?" Clara asked. Looking up. Knife still in her hand.

"I have questions to ask."

"Daniel—"

But he was already halfway across the living room, out through the waiting door, pitching himself into the hungry dark—the thickness of the Florida night ready to close over him.

Rocca turned when Evans came out. Saw the jacket—the look on Evans' face.

"Evans—where ya going?"

"To ask some questions."

"You're off the case." Rocca stepped forward. Hand raised. "Norris said—"

"I know what he said."

Evans moved past him. Headed for his car. Silver Honda CR-V parked in the driveway beside Rocca's Taurus. He pulled the keys from his pocket—metal jangling.

"Evans!" Rocca jogged over. Hand on the car door. "You can't—"

Evans opened the door. Slid into the driver's seat. The leather was hot. Sticky. Key in the ignition. His hands shook slightly. Adrenaline. Rage. Purpose.

The engine turned over. Caught. Rumbled. Dashboard lights glowed green. Air conditioning blasted. Hot air first. Then cool.

"You're acting like Roan," Rocca said.

Evans didn't respond. Just shifted into reverse. Backed out. Tires crunching on gravel.

Rocca stepped back. Pulled his phone from his pocket. Thumbs moving. Hit the screen. Brought it to his ear.

The Honda's headlights cut through the dark. Evans shifted into drive. Hit the gas. The car surged forward.

Behind him, in his rear-view mirror, he saw Rocca standing in the driveway. Phone pressed to his ear. Pacing.

The street lights blurred past. Orange pools stretching and fading. The hum of the engine filled the car. Steady. Constant. The dashboard glowed green. Speedometer climbing. Forty-five. Fifty. Fifty-five.

His hands gripped the wheel. White-knuckled. Tight. Sweat on his palms.

He knew where he was going. Knew who he needed to talk to.

Left-handed. The wipes. The blade.

It fit.

Rocca stood in the driveway. Phone pressed to his ear. Waiting. Listening to the ring. Once. Twice. Three times.

Then—

"You've reached Detective Roan. Leave a message."

Beep.

"Damn it."

Rocca ended the call. Stared at the phone. Then, at the empty street where Evans' taillights had disappeared.

He dialed again. Different number this time.

It rang once. Picked up.

"Pérez," Rocca said. "We got a problem."

CHAPTER

49

THE HOUSE LOOKED like a crime scene because it was one.

Roan stood in his front doorway. His legs felt heavy. Lead. The weight of exhaustion pressed into his bones. He surveyed the wreckage. CSU had torn through every room and left their mess. Fingerprint powder dustings were on surfaces. Black. Smudged. Evidence markers still dotted the floor. Yellow plastic triangles. Numbers in bold.

They'd taken what they needed—left everything else.

The living room sofa was overturned. Cushions pulled. Searched. His coffee table sat at an angle. Books were scattered across the floor. Jazz album covers lay torn from their sleeves. Exposed. Vulnerable.

He stepped inside. The door closed behind him.

The silence pressed against his ears. No hum of the fridge. No ticking clock. The air smelled wrong. Chemical. Fingerprint powder and something else. Rubber gloves. Plastic evidence bags. The scent of strangers in his home. Just the hollow emptiness of a violated space.

His body wanted to move. To storm out. Find the bastard who'd done this. Be the grinder—the relentless force in a suit that didn't stop until the case closed.

But he'd been benched.

Off the case. Ordered home, told to stay put while Norris ran the investigation without him.

The weight of it sat heavily in his chest. Failure. Jin Shin's face kept surfacing in his mind. Not the severed head in his fridge. The person. The woman who'd smiled when she talked about her life. Her mom. Who'd walked beside him down J Street just hours before someone took her life.

He'd been right there. Yards away. His fault. He'd chased Ariel and chased the wrong man while Jin walked alone into an ambush. And he'd missed it.

Roan moved through the living room. Stepped over evidence markers. His shoes crunched on broken glass. A picture frame. The glass spider-webbed from impact.

He needed a drink.

The bar cart sat against the wall. Crystal decanters lined the top. Vodka. Bourbon. Scotch. He reached for the Ketel One. Lifted it. The bottle felt wrong. Light.

He held it up to the dim light filtering through the curtains.

Empty.

No. Not empty. Shattered. The bottom half of the bottle was gone. Jagged edges where the glass had broken. Clear liquid pooled inside the metal tray beneath the cart. The scent hit him. Sharp. Medicinal. Alcohol fumes stung his nostrils. Made his eyes water. He could taste it on his tongue. The phantom burn. Like he'd already taken the drink, he couldn't have.

CSU must have knocked it over. Or maybe they'd taken it as evidence. Checking it for prints. For traces of whoever had been in his home.

Roan set the broken bottle down.

His hands were steady. But his palms were damp. Sweat. The back of his neck burned. Tension coiling up his spine. But his mind raced. Spinning. Churning through details. Suspects. Timelines. Evidence that didn't fit. Pieces that refused to connect.

He turned away from the bar. Walked toward the hallway.

His record collection lined the built-in shelves along the wall. Vinyl he'd collected over decades. Miles Davis. John Coltrane. Muddy Waters. B.B. King.

Half of them were gone.

Pulled from the shelves. Some lay on the floor. Sleeves bent. Records exposed. Others were missing entirely. Taken by CSU. Or destroyed.

He knelt. Picked up a copy of "A Love Supreme". The sleeve was torn. Cover bent. John Coltrane's face creased down the middle.

He lifted the vinyl out. Cracked. Clean break. Straight through "Acknowledgement", "Resolution", "Pursuance", and "Psalm" tracks he'd played a thousand times.

His throat tightened. He set it down. Gentle. Like it still mattered. Like treating it with care could undo the damage.

It couldn't.

His jaw tightened. He stood.

His chest felt hollow. Carved out. Everything that made this place his had been gutted. Examined. Cataloged. Destroyed.

He moved down the hallway, toward his office.

The door hung open. Light from the window spilled across the hardwood floor. His desk sat in the center of the room. Papers strewn across the surface. Drawers pulled. Files emptied.

But the laptop was still there.

Sitting on the corner of the desk. Untouched. CSU hadn't taken it, probably because it was department property and was logged into the network. No personal information is stored on the hard drive.

Roan grabbed it. Tucked it under his arm, turned back toward the kitchen.

The kitchen was worse.

Where his fridge had been, there was nothing—just an empty space. Dust and grime outlined where it had once sat. Power cord dangling from the wall socket.

CSU had taken the whole damn thing.

Evidence. They'd found something inside. Blood. DNA. Something that tied Jin Shin's murder to his house.

He thought about it. Imagined the scene—the killer, standing in his kitchen and opening his fridge, leaving trace evidence behind.

It made him sick.

He set the laptop on the kitchen counter. Flipped it open. Pressed the power button.

His phone sat in his jacket pocket. He pulled it out. Checked the screen.

Black.

Dead.

The battery icon showed empty. Red. He'd been running on fumes since this morning. Too many calls. Too many messages. No time to charge.

Roan set the phone down beside the laptop. Found the charging cable in the drawer beneath the counter. Plugged it into the wall. Connected it to the phone.

The screen flickered. White Apple logo. Then nothing.

It would take a few minutes to come back to life.

He turned his attention back to the laptop. The screen lit up. Blue. Then white. The login screen appeared. The laptop hummed. Warm against his palms. The kitchen was dark around him—only the glow of the screen. It's blue light washing his face.

Roan typed his password. Hit enter. The desktop loaded.

Camila Morales.

Her name sat at the top of an open case file on the screen. He'd been reviewing it when the call about Ariel came in before everything went to hell.

Roan forced himself to move on. Opened the case management system. Navigated to the files. Lab reports. Autopsy summaries. Crime scene photos.

All of it.

He started at the beginning. Camila Morales. Twenty-one. Found on the beach. Throat cut. Two stab wounds to the torso. Defensive wounds on her hands. Left-to-right trajectory. Consistent with a left-handed attacker.

Then Julia Aguilar. Stab wounds. Same pattern. Same weapon. Same killer. Dumped in an empty lot.

Jessica Torres. Barely alive. Hooked to machines at Good Samaritan. Possible brain damage.

Jin Shin. Dismembered. Delivered in pieces, her head in his fridge. The rest on Evans' porch. A message. A warning.

His eyes burned. He blinked. Kept reading.

The details blurred together. Blood spatter patterns. Weapon analysis. DNA results. Nothing new. Nothing that moved the case forward.

He closed the case files. Opened his email.

The inbox was full. Unread messages. Department memos. Updates from Pérez. Reports from the lab. One email stood out:

Subject: Security Footage - Pulse Nightclub
From: Pérez, C.
Sent: This Morning, 6:47 AM

Roan opened it.

Roan,
Pulled all security footage from Pulse. Uploaded to the
department server. Link below. I time-stamped the relevant
clips. Ariel Morales was at the club during all the murders.
Solid alibi. Marco confirms.
—Pérez

Below the message was a link. Roan clicked on it. The browser opened.
Loaded the department server. A folder appeared. **Pulse_Security_-**
Footage.

Inside were dozens of files. Video clips. Time-stamped. Organized
by date.

Roan started with the first one. The night Camila Morales died.

The video opened. Black and white. Grainy. The camera pointed at
the main floor of the nightclub. Bodies moved in the frame. Dancing.
Drinking. The timestamp in the corner read: **11:43 PM**.

He scrubbed through the footage. Watched the crowd. Looked for
Ariel.

There. Center of the frame. Dark hair. Slim build. Dancing with a
man. Marco. The boyfriend. Ariel's alibi.

Roan watched. The timestamp moved forward. **11:52 PM**. **12:04**
AM. **12:19 AM**.

Ariel never left the frame.

He moved to the next file. Julia Aguilar's murder. Same result.
Ariel at the club. Dancing. Drinking. Never leaving.

Jessica Torres. Every timeline matched. Ariel had been at Pulse
during all the murders.

Solid alibi.

Roan leaned back. Rubbed his face. His hands smelled like dust and fingerprint powder.

Ariel wasn't the killer. Confirmed.

Relief should have flooded through him. It didn't. Just hollowness. Knowing who it wasn't didn't help. Jin was still dead. Jessica Torres was still hooked to machines, and Camila Morales was still in the ground.

He clicked through the remaining files. More footage. Different angles. Different cameras.

One folder caught his eye: **Entryway_Cam**.

He clicked it.

The video opened—different angle. The camera was pointed at the front entrance of the club. J Street was visible in the frame. Cars were parked along the curb.

The timestamp read: **Yesterday, 2:14 PM**.

Roan watched. People walking in and out of the club. Nothing unusual.

Then he saw it.

A white pickup truck. Corner of the frame. Parked on J Street.

His pulse kicked up.

He leaned closer to the screen. Squinted. The truck was partially obscured. Faded paint. Cracked driver window.

He'd seen that truck.

He scrubbed forward in the video. Watched the timestamp: **2:22 PM**.

Two figures appeared. Walking down the sidewalk, heading toward Jin Shin's apartment.

His breath caught.

It was him. And Jin.

They walked past the truck.

He scrubbed forward more. Watched the timestamp: **3:12 PM**.

He saw himself pause. Look at the cracked window. Then Ariel appeared, looked at Roan, and ran. Roan took off after him.

The video kept running.

The truck sat there. Unmoving. Minutes passed.

Then the driver's door opened.

Roan hit pause. Stared at the screen.

He couldn't see the driver. The angle was wrong. But the door was open. Someone inside.

He hit play.

Hours passed on the screen. The truck sat. Waiting. The video continued: **9:31 PM. 9:44 PM. 9:57 PM.**

The truck didn't move.

Roan scrubbed forward. Faster now. Looking for movement.

There.

10:12 PM.

Jin Shin. Walking alone. Heading home from the massage parlor. She passed in front of the camera. Small. Unaware. One hand in her jacket pocket. The other is holding her phone. The screen glowed blue against her face.

A large figure emerged from the alley. Fast. Purposeful. Arm raised.

Metal bar. Crowbar. Something heavy.

The impact. Jin's head snapped sideways. She dropped. Instant. No scream. No struggle. Just collapse.

The figure bent. Grabbed her under the arms. Dragged her. Her feet scraped the pavement. Limp. Dead weight.

His breath stopped. His hand gripped the counter edge. Knuckles white. He couldn't look away. Couldn't stop the video.

The figure lifted Jin. Carried her toward the truck. Opened the door. Shoved her inside. The door slammed.

Then, seconds later, the truck's headlights flicked on.

His heart hammered.

He watched. The truck pulled away from the curb.

The truck was pulling a trailer. Metal frame. And on the side, in faded orange letters, a name.

Roan hit pause. Zoomed in. The image pixelated. Grainy. But the letters were legible.

He stared at the screen. His mind raced. Connecting pieces. Following the thread.

The truck. The trailer. The orange letters.

He'd seen it before.

Not on J Street. Somewhere else.

Dixie Highway. By Siam Massage. The night he'd gone undercover there and met Jin.

The truck had been pulling the same trailer, faded orange letters. Out of place. Wrong.

Roan leaned back. His hands gripped the edge of the counter. Hard enough to hurt. Hard enough to feel something besides failure.

He knew the truck. Knew the trailer. Knew who owned it.

CHAPTER

50

"Nearly every night after work." She stopped wiping. Rag suspended midair.

Had Marge ever been on the receiving end of this many questions from the police? She couldn't remember. Possibly never.

"So he's a regular?"

"Yeah."

Evans lowered himself onto a barstool opposite her. Voice professional, steady. "Was he here the night Camila was murdered?"

Her jaw clenched—the tiniest movement, almost nothing—but she looked away. Went back to the rag, began scrubbing the same spot again. Once, twice, three times. "Yeah. He slipped out sometime before she was found."

Three older men sat at the far end of the bar—trucker caps. Flannel shirts. Nursing beers. Eyes on the mounted TV. Baseball game. Playoffs. Low volume. The jukebox in the corner played something slow. Blues. Mournful guitar.

Evans reached into his jacket. Pulled out his phone. Scrolled. Found the photos. Held the screen toward Marge.

"Have you seen either of these women in here?"

Marge leaned forward. Squinted at the screen. Two photos. Julia Aguilar. Jessica Torres.

Her expression shifted. Recognition. "Yeah. I've seen them. Both of them."

His pulse kicked up. He kept his voice even. "Recently?"

"This one was here a few weeks ago. The other one, maybe a month back." Marge's fingers twisted the rag. "They're working girls.

Sometimes they brought their johns here. Ordered drinks before heading out."

His jaw tightened. "Did they ever leave with the same guy? The regular you're telling me about?"

Marge hesitated. Long enough for Evans to know the answer.

"Maybe. I don't know. It's hard to keep track." Her voice dropped. "There's a lot of girls like them come through here."

Evans pocketed his phone. Leaned forward. "Was he in the pub tonight?"

Pause. Long. Tense. The air conditioning kicked on—a low hum. Cold air pushed through vents overhead.

Marge put down the rag; her hands lingered, knotted. She looked at Evans with eyes that seemed tired out of all proportion to the rest of her face. "Yeah. He was chatting up one of the girls from Dixie. Dark hair. Brown eyes. Spanish-type. Working girl."

Evans felt his pulse start up. He worked at keeping his tone level. "Dark hair, brown eyes? Like Camila?"

"That's right."

"You know her name?"

"Sofi… or Sofia." Marge's fingers interlaced and broke apart, weaving and undoing, restless. "I've seen her a handful of times. She works mostly on the strip on Dixie Highway."

The bar under Evans' arms was cool, the wood grooved, smoothed by generations of elbows and glass bottoms, but splintery here and there.

"Do you know if he went anywhere after? With her?"

Marge shook her head. "Nah. I mean, probably just back to his place. He lives in a trailer on the grounds of a cinder block yard. Works as a night guard, porter, something like that. They let him keep a fridge container there, too. Or that's what he says, anyway."

A fridge container. His mind jumped to Jin Shin, to the chopped limbs, the cold, the way flesh seemed to last in a box like that.

He curled his hands into fists under the bar, nails digging in sharply. Pain to sharpen the focus.

"Where is it, exactly?"

Marge's fingers went through their routine, lacing, pulling free, lacing. "It's off Southern Boulevard. Benoist Farms. One of the block yards. Out near the warehouses."

He knew the place. Industrial, deserted after dark, one warehouse after another, big gaps of space, and nobody looking in. *Perfect.*

The jukebox switched over to a new song, heavier on drums and harmonica but still blues, still hung in the air like old smoke. Down at the bar's end, a man coughed, wet and thick, then went straight back to his beer.

"Did he leave with her? With Sofia?"

Marge's voice was almost inaudible. "Yeah. They left together."

Evans felt it then, a tightness just under the ribs, a band cinching in. Another girl, another shot at a victim. He didn't have long.

"You actually think he'd do something bad?" Marge said, her voice trembling at the edge.

He looked her in the face, let her see he meant it. "That's what I intend to find out. I'm going to pay him a visit."

Marge's expression shifted; for a second, there was something like regret or maybe worry. "He acts fine in here. But he's got a short fuse if he's been drinking. You be careful, okay?"

"I will."

He stood and shoved the stool back; the scrape was loud in all that hush. He turned and made for the door, shoes hard on the floor, each step solid.

Behind him, the music filled the silence; none of the regulars bothered to glance up, and Marge stayed rooted behind the bar, twisting her fingers.

He pushed through the door, out into the night.

His shirt was soaked the moment he stepped outside. The humidity was increasing as the storm from the west continued to move east.

And then he saw it.

The beach.

The crime scene.

He imagined the spot where Camila Morales had lain.

Where it had started.

Evans stopped. Stared at the sand beyond. Dark now. Empty. But he could still see it. The blood. The body. The way her eyes had stared at nothing.

Twenty-one years old.

His jaw clenched. Teeth grinding. The muscle in his cheek jumped.

He turned away. Walked to his car.

The silver Honda CR-V sat under a streetlight. Evans pulled the keys from his pocket. Metal jangled. He unlocked the door. Slid into the driver's seat.

The interior was hot. Stifling. He started the engine. Cranked the air conditioning. Hot air blasted from the vents. Then slowly cooled.

Evans gripped the steering wheel. Tight. His pulse hammered in his temples. Steady. Fast. Adrenaline.

He pulled his phone from his jacket. Looked at the screen.

Five percent battery.

The low battery warning flashed red in the corner.

He exhaled. Slow. Controlled. He should call for backup. Right now. Before—

The screen went black.

Dead.

Damn it.

Evans set the phone in the cup holder. Stared at it. Useless. Just dead weight now.

He'd call for backup when he got there. Find a payphone. Use the suspect's landline if he had one.

If he needed it.

Evans shifted into drive; the Honda's engine hummed. Quiet. Reliable. He pulled away from the curb. Headlights cutting through the dark.

A1A stretched ahead. Empty. Late enough that traffic had thinned. Just a few cars. Scattered. Moving slowly.

Evans accelerated. Forty-five. Fifty. The speedometer climbed. Too fast.

To his right, the ocean stretched into blackness. Waves crashed against the shore. Rhythmic. Constant. He couldn't see them. Just heard them. Felt their presence.

To his left, the buildings blurred past. Condos. Million Dollar Homes. All dark now. Closed. Sleeping.

Evans took the roundabout onto Southern Boulevard, passing Mar-a-Lago.

The road widened. Four lanes. Streetlights were spaced further apart. Pools of orange separated by long stretches of shadow.

His heart skipped a beat when he realized he had just passed the spot where Ellen Mills saw Camila and Jin.

He passed a gas station. Bright. Fluorescent. A lone clerk was visible through the window. Head down. Staring at a phone.

Then a strip mall. Empty parking lot. Graffiti on the walls. Boarded windows.

Then nothing.

Just a road. And darkness.

His hands were slick on the wheel. Sweat. He wiped them on his pant leg. One at a time. Kept driving.

His foot pressed harder on the accelerator. Sixty. Sixty-five, the Honda's engine whined. Protesting. But it held.

Then industrial lots. Empty. Overgrown. Chain-link fences sagged. Weeds as tall as a man.

Benoist Farms couldn't be far now.

His pulse thundered in his ears. Loud. Insistent. Or was it the sound of the approaching storm?

The headlights swept across fields. Dark. Empty. Then warehouses. Low buildings. Corrugated metal. Some with doors hanging open. Blackness inside.

And then the sign appeared.

Faded. Weathered. Green letters on white. Half the letters were missing. Just "Beno st arms" now.

Evans slowed. Turned onto the access road.

Gravel crunched under the tires. Loud. The Honda bounced over potholes. Deep. Jarring. The headlights swept across more fields. More warehouses.

And somewhere ahead, in the darkness, a trailer at the cinder block company. A fridge container. A man with a mean streak when he'd been drinking. And a girl with dark hair and brown eyes named Sofia, who'd left the pub with the wrong person.

CHAPTER

51

The Grade-A Concrete Block and Ready Mix Company sat at the edge of nowhere. Three acres of industrial wasteland hemmed in by a twelve-foot chain-link fence topped with rusted barbed wire that curled inward like skeletal fingers. The property stretched back from Benoist Farms off of Southern Boulevard in a long rectangle, swallowed by darkness beyond the reach of the nearest streetlight a half-mile west. Concrete block stacks rose like grey monuments throughout the lot, positioned in deliberate rows that formed a maze of narrow corridors and dead ends. Some stacks climbed fifteen feet high, their shadows stretching long and black across cracked asphalt. Others were only waist-level, barely higher than a man. All cast shapes that shifted with the single security light mounted on a weathered wooden pole near the front gate.

The air smelled like dust and diesel. Old rain was trapped in potholes. Engine oil that had seeped into the ground years ago. Weeds pushed through cracks in the asphalt where delivery trucks had worn the surface thin over decades of traffic. The lot was silent except for the distant hum of Southern Boulevard—cars passing on their way somewhere else. Somewhere better.

A rusted front-end loader sat dormant near the eastern fence, its bucket tilted toward the ground like a sleeping beast. The tires were flat. Deflated. The paint had peeled away from the cab, leaving patches of bare metal that gleamed dully under the security light. Behind it, pallets of cinder blocks wrapped in plastic sheeting. The plastic had torn in places. Wind had gotten underneath. Lifted edges. Made them flap weakly when a breeze came through.

Beyond that, the office trailer. Dark. Locked. A single-wide with aluminum siding. Windows covered with metal shutters—a padlock on the door. The company name was stenciled across the side in faded green letters. The place had been abandoned hours ago, at five o'clock. Everyone had gone home. No one was left but the man who lived in the back corner.

Past the last row of block stacks, past the chain-link barrier that separated the work yard from the employee lot, a single mobile home trailer sat on cinder blocks. Light glowed through thin curtains. Yellow. Flickering. The light that came from cheap bulbs that buzzed when you turned them on. A white pickup truck with a trailer hitch was parked beside it. The truck was old. Faded paint. Dents in the tailgate. Florida plates caked with road dust. The trailer attached to the hitch held a large smoker. Custom-built. Welded steel. Both the trailer and the smoker bore peeling orange letters painted across their sides:

BRANDON'S BBQ

The paint had faded over the years from the sun. Cracked, flaked away in patches that left bare metal underneath.

Next to the pickup, a twenty-foot refrigerated shipping container. White. Dented along the bottom edge. The compressor hummed. Loud. Constant. A mechanical drone that filled the silence. The sort of noise that became invisible after a while. Background. Just there. The container door was closed. Whatever was inside stayed cold and stayed fresh.

Inside the trailer, Brandon Scott Lewis sat at a small fold-out table attached to the wall. Six-foot-three. Four hundred fifty pounds. His massive frame overwhelmed the cheap folding chair beneath him. The metal groaned with every shift of his weight. The table was cluttered. Empty beer cans. Crushed. Dented, stacked in uneven piles. A half-empty bottle of Jim Beam sat within reach. Amber liquid. No glass. He drank straight from the bottle. Had been for hours.

His face was a mess. Bruises mottled the right side. Purple. Yellow. Green where the healing had started. His right eye was swollen. Not shut, but close. The lid drooped. The white of the eye was bloodshot, with red veins spider-webbing across the surface. The bruising extended down his cheekbone to his jaw. Dark. Ugly. Damage that came from getting hit hard. Multiple times. His knuckles were scabbed —split skin over thick bone. Fresh cuts layered over older scars.

He wore a stained white beater that stretched tight across his gut. Grease stains. Sweat stains. The fabric yellowed under the arms. Blue jeans worn thin at the knees. Work boots were unlaced. The trailer smelled like cigarette smoke and old food. Stale beer. Body odor. Whiskey on his breath. The air was thick with it.

Across from him sat Sofía Navarro. Twenty. Hard to tell from looking at her. Dark hair pulled back in a ponytail. Loose strands framing her face. Brown eyes. Tired eyes. The tiredness that went bone-deep. She was thin in a way that spoke of missed meals and bad habits. Her arms were rail-thin. Veins were visible beneath pale skin. Track marks on the inside of her left elbow. Old ones. Scabbed over. Faded. But there. She wore a tank top that hung loosely on her frame. No bra underneath. Denim shorts frayed at the hem. Scuffed sneakers with no socks. Her legs were crossed. One foot bouncing. Nervous energy.

She looked small. Fragile. Next to Brandon, she looked like a child.

Brandon had picked her up an hour ago. Oceanside Pub. A bar where some working girls gathered after dark. Where men with cash and bad intentions came looking. Sofía had been leaning against the wall outside. Smoking. Waiting. He'd pulled up in his truck. He brought her drinks inside. Talked her up and made an offer. Two hundred for the whole night. She'd taken it, needed it. Rent was due. Her supplier didn't take IOUs.

They drank together now. Beer for her. A can of Bud Light. Warm. She'd been nursing it for twenty minutes. Whiskey for him. He took long pulls from the bottle. Swallowed. Grimaced. The conversation was normal. Mundane. Small talk. Nothing heavy. She laughed at something he said. A forced laugh. High-pitched. Her eyes darted to the door. Then back to him.

"You're funny," Sofía said. Her voice was scratchy. Raw. Like she'd been shouting. Or smoking too much. Or both. Spanish accent threading through the words. Not heavy. Just there.

"Yeah?" Brandon leaned back. The chair creaked. Protested. The metal legs bent slightly under his weight.

"Yeah." She took a sip of her beer. Looked at him over the rim of the can. Forced a smile.

He reached across the table. Took her hand. His fingers were thick. Massive. Swallowed hers whole. Rough skin. Calluses. She didn't pull away. Just let him hold it.

"You're pretty," he said. His voice was low. Gravelly.

"Thanks." Her smile faltered, just for a second. Then came back. "Remember my price."

"Come here."

Sofía hesitated. Then stood. Moved around the table. Slow. Careful. He pulled her onto his lap. She was light. Weightless against his bulk. His hand went to the back of her neck. Fingers curling into her hair. Gentle at first. Then firmer.

He kissed her. Hard. Possessive. His hand tightened. Held her in place. His other hand went to her waist. Gripped her side.

She kissed back. Moaned softly. A performance. Her hands went to his chest. Then his shoulders. Playing along.

But his grip tightened.

His hand moved from the back of her neck to the front. Fingers wrapping around her throat. Gentle at first. A caress. Then firmer. Squeezing. His thumb pressed against her windpipe. His other hand joined. Both hands. One over the other. Fingers interlocking. Squeezing harder.

Her moan changed. Became a whimper. She squirmed. Tried to pull back. Her hands went from his shoulders to his wrists. Gripping. Pulling.

"You're hurting me," Sofía said. Voice strained. Breathless. Panicked.

He didn't let go. Didn't respond. Just squeezed. His face was blank. Expressionless. Eyes focused on her throat.

"Brandon—"

"Shh."

She struggled. Harder now. Her hands were clawing at his wrists. Nails scraping skin. Drawing blood. Her eyes went wide. Panicked.

Terror flooding in. She couldn't breathe. Couldn't speak. Her mouth opened. Gasped. Nothing. No air.

He squeezed harder. His jaw clenched—muscle jumping. The bruises on his face darkened with the effort.

She brought her fist down. Hard. Fast. Desperation. Caught him square in the groin.

Brandon roared. Released her. Doubled over. His hands went to his crotch. Pain radiated. Sharp. Blinding. White-hot.

Sofía scrambled off his lap. Stumbled. Caught herself on the edge of the table. Beer cans clattered. Fell. The Jim Beam bottle tipped. Rolled. Hit the floor. Didn't break. Just rolled under the table.

She didn't look back. Just ran.

Out the door. Down the metal steps. Three steps. She hit the ground running into the night.

Brandon surged to his feet. The chair tipped. Crashed backward. Hit the floor. He kicked it aside. Metal scraping across lino. He grabbed the doorframe. Steadied himself. Pain radiated from his groin. Sharp. Blinding. But rage overrode it. Hot. Consuming.

He stepped outside. The night air hit him. Cool. Humid. Storm coming.

"Get back here!"

His voice echoed across the lot. Bounced off the concrete block stacks.

Sofía was already fifty feet away. Running hard. Her breath came in ragged gasps. Feet pounding asphalt. She cut left. Around the first stack of concrete blocks. Disappeared into the maze.

Brandon followed. His bulk moved with surprising speed. Heavy footfalls. Each step was a thunderclap. The ground shook beneath him. He wasn't fast. But he was relentless. Unstoppable. A freight train, gathering momentum.

She ran through the maze of block stacks. Left. Right. Another left. The stacks rose on either side. Fifteen feet high in some places. Barely five in others. Narrow corridors. Shadows were swallowing everything beyond arm's reach. The security light didn't reach back here. Just darkness. Just the sound of her breathing. Her heartbeat was hammering in her ears.

Behind her, Brandon's breathing was ragged. Labored. But close. Too close. She could hear him. Feel him—the vibration of his footsteps through the ground.

She took another turn—right this time. Hit a dead end. A stack of blocks fifteen feet high. No way through. No way over.

She spun. Ran back the way she came. Nearly collided with Brandon rounding the corner.

She screamed. Veered left. Squeezed between two stacks. Barely fit. The blocks scraped her shoulders. Tore her tank top. She kept running.

Her lungs burned. Her legs screamed. Muscles on fire. But she kept running. Had to. No choice.

Behind her, Brandon couldn't fit through the gap. Too wide. He roared. Slammed his fist into the blocks. Once. Twice. Blood on his knuckles. He turned. Took the long way around.

Sofía broke free of the maze. Sprinted toward the fence. The chain-link barrier loomed ahead. Twelve feet high. Topped with barbed wire. No way over. Not fast enough.

The industrial zone spread around her. Dark. Empty. Warehouses lined the access road. Metal buildings with roll-up doors. All closed. All locked. No lights. No cars. No people. Just her. Just him.

She turned. Ran along the fence line. Looking for a gap. A tear. Anything. Her hands were trailing along the metal. Fingers caught on the wire. Cutting. Bleeding.

She screamed.

The sound tore from her throat. Raw. Desperate. High-pitched.

"Help! Somebody help me!"

Her voice echoed across the empty lot. Bounced off warehouse walls. Faded into darkness. No one answered. No lights flickered on. No doors opened. Just silence. Just the hum of the refrigerated container. Just Brandon's footsteps getting closer.

She screamed again. Louder. Throat burning.

"Please! Somebody!"

Nothing. The warehouses sat dark. Indifferent. She was alone. Completely alone.

There.

The gate.

She ran for it. Grabbed the metal. Cold beneath her palms. Pulled. Locked.

A heavy padlock hung from the latch. Thick. Solid. Industrial. Unyielding.

She yanked on it. Once. Twice. Three times. It didn't budge. Didn't even rattle.

Her breath came in sobs now. Panic was taking over. Thoughts fragmenting. She couldn't die here. Not like this. Not in this place. Not by his hands.

Time slowed. Everything crystallized. The smell of diesel. The rough metal of the gate. The distant hum of traffic on Southern Boulevard. Too far. Too far to hear her screams.

She spun around.

A fist hit her hard—a flash of light, then dark.

CHAPTER

52

Pain came first. Sharp. Throbbing. The back of her head felt split open. She lifted her hand to touch it. Couldn't move. Zip-ties cut into her wrists. Her ankles. She pulled. Plastic dug deeper. Nothing gave.

Her eyes opened. Darkness. Not complete. Just dim. Grey. Shapes moving. One shape. Big. Massive. Moving toward her.

Memory flooded back. The punch. The knockout. The man. Brandon.

She screamed. The sound came out broken. Hoarse. Her throat was raw from screaming earlier. From running. From begging for help that never came.

"You're awake." His voice. Low. Calm. As if he were commenting on the weather.

Sofía was moving, being dragged. Her back scraped against rough ground. Asphalt. Gravel. Her heels bounced over uneven pavement. She twisted. Pulled. His grip on her wrists didn't loosen—thick fingers. Iron. Unyielding.

"Where—" Her voice cracked. "Where are you taking me?"

He didn't answer. Just kept dragging. Step after step. His breathing labored. Heavy. The weight of her body meant nothing to him. Just cargo. Just meat.

The container loomed ahead. White. Dented. The compressor hummed. That mechanical drone filled the silence. She'd heard it before when she'd run, when she'd tried to escape. Now it grew louder. Closer. A sound that promised cold. Darkness. Death.

Cold air rolled from the open door. Not just cold. Freezing. The kind that bit at exposed skin and turned breath to fog. The smell hit her next. Metal. Blood. Something sweet and rotten underneath. Meat smell. Old meat. She gagged.

The security light threw shadows inside. Hooks. Dozens of them. Hanging from rails that ran the ceiling. Some empty. Some not. Shapes dangling from the hooks. Dark. She couldn't tell what they were. Then one caught the light—white bone, ragged meat still clinging. Ribs. Not beef. Too small.

"No." The word came out weak. Pathetic. "Please. Please don't."

Brandon stopped. Set her wrists down. Not gently. Just dropped them. Her hands hit the ground. Pain shot through her palms. She scrambled backward. Her ankles were still bound. She couldn't get leverage. Couldn't move.

He stood over her. Backlit by the security light. His face in shadow. But she could see his eyes. Dark. Empty. Flat.

"Why?" Her voice broke. Tears were streaming down her face. "Why are you doing this?"

He tilted his head. Studied her. Like she was something curious. Something interesting. Something less than human.

"You want to know why?" His voice was conversational. Matter-of-fact. "I'm going to fuck you. Then I'm going to kill you. In that order."

Sofía stared at him. Horror flooding through her. Cold. Visceral.

"How many?" The question left her lips before she could stop it. "How many have you—"

"Enough." His smile was crooked. The bruises on his face were pulling at the skin. "Enough that I've got good at it."

"You're crazy," she whispered.

"I'm hungry." He reached for her. "And you're dinner."

He grabbed her tank. Pulled. The fabric tore. Sofía thrashed. Kicked. Her bound ankles caught him in the shin. He didn't flinch. Didn't react. Just reached for her shorts.

"No!" She screamed. Kicked again. Harder. Desperation was fueling her. Raw. Primal. She couldn't let this happen. Couldn't.

His weight came down on her. Crushing. Suffocating. Four hundred fifty pounds pressed her into the cold surface. The air left her lungs. She gasped. Couldn't fill them. His hands pinned her wrists above her head. One massive hand holding both. The other went to her waistband.

Sofía bucked. Thrashed. Nothing moved him. He was a mountain. Immovable. Relentless.

Her right hand broke free. Just for a second. Just enough. She swung. Wild. Blind. Connected with his face. Her fist hit something hard. Bone. Cartilage. His nose.

The same nose he'd broken before.

Brandon roared. Jerked back. Blood poured from his nose. Fresh. Dark. Mixing with the bruises. The damage from before. She'd broken it again. Worse this time. The cartilage crunched. Gave. Collapsed inward.

His hands went to his face. Reflexive. Instinct.

Sofía rolled. Scrambled. Her ankles were still bound, but her hands were free. She pulled at the binding. Plastic. The zip-tie. Her fingers clawed at it. Found the locking mechanism. Pulled.

It gave. Just a little. The plastic stretching.

She got to her knees. Stumbled forward in an awkward shuffle. Away from him. Away from the container. Into the maze of concrete block stacks.

Behind her, Brandon bellowed. Rage. Pain. Fury. All of it boiling over.

Sofía didn't look back. Couldn't. Just moved. Her fingers were still working the binding. One shuffle-step. Then another. The plastic stretching. Tearing. She pulled harder. Yanked.

It gave. Snapped. Fell away.

Her ankles were free.

She ran.

Really ran. No more shuffling. No more hobbling. Full sprint. Her bare feet slapped against the pavement. Pain shot through her soles. Gravel. Glass. She didn't care. Didn't feel it. Just ran.

The block stacks rose around her. Maze walls. Six feet high. Eight. Ten. Some higher. Creating corridors. Dead ends. Passages that twisted and turned. She'd been through here before. When she'd first run, she knew some of the layout. Not all. Just enough.

Turn left. Between two stacks. Another left. Then right. Keep moving. Keep a distance.

Behind her, Brandon's footsteps thundered. Close. Too close. She could feel the vibration through the ground. Hear his ragged breathing. Smell the blood. The whiskey. The rage.

He was faster than before. Angrier. The pain fueled him, rather than slowing him.

Sofía risked a glance back. Mistake.

He was there. Twenty feet behind. Closing. Blood covered his face. His shirt. His eyes locked on her. Predator eyes. Hunter eyes.

She faced forward. Ran harder. Her lungs burned. Her legs screamed. She ignored them. Pushed through.

The fence appeared ahead. Chain-link. Eight feet high. Barbed wire coiling along the top. She'd tried it before. Locked. No way through.

But there—

Concrete blocks. Stacked. Rising in uneven steps. Four blocks high. Then three. Then two. Then one. Like a staircase. Ascending toward the top of the fence. Not planned. Just how they'd been stored. But they were there.

A way up.

A way out.

Sofía ran for them. Her bare feet found traction on the rough pavement. The blocks were right there. Ten feet. Five.

Brandon's hand grabbed at her. Missed. His fingers brushed her shoulder. She jerked away. Dove forward.

Hit the first block. Grabbed it. Pulled herself up. Concrete tore her palms. Grit embedded in flesh, bleeding now. She didn't care. Didn't feel it. Just climbed.

One block. Then the next. Her feet found holds. Pushing. Climbing. Ascending.

The fence was right there. The street beyond. Freedom. Life.

"Get back here!"

His voice. Right behind her. She didn't turn. Didn't look. Just climbed. Her hand bled, gripping concrete. Pulling. Her feet were pushing. One more block. Then another.

He grabbed the first block. Started climbing. His weight made the stacks groan. Shift. Concrete grinding against concrete. The whole structure wobbled.

Sofía reached the top block. Level with the fence top. The barbed wire curled inward. Rusted. Sharp. Vicious. Three strands. Coiled tight. The street below looked far. Too far. Twelve feet. Maybe more.

But if she stayed, she died.

Brandon grabbed her ankle.

She screamed. Kicked down. Her heel connected with his face. His already-broken nose. He howled. Let go.

Sofía didn't hesitate. Grabbed the top of the fence. The barbed wire bit into her palms. Sliced through skin. Blood ran hot over her fingers. She didn't feel it. Didn't care.

She swung her legs up. Over. The wire caught her thigh. Tore through skin. She gasped. Pulled harder. Her body cleared the wire. Hanging on the other side.

Below her, pavement. Hard. Unforgiving. The distance looked impossible. If she landed wrong, she'd break something. Ankle. Leg. Hip. Maybe worse.

But Brandon was climbing. Right there. His massive hand was reaching for the fence. For her.

She took a breath. Let go.

For a moment, she hung in the air. Suspended. Weightless. The street was spinning below her. The security light was behind—Brandon's roar fading.

Then gravity took hold.

She fell.

CHAPTER

53

THE FALL WAS NOTHING. A heartbeat. A breath suspended in the night air. Then impact.

Asphalt slammed into her body. Hard. Unforgiving. The shock traveled from her feet through her legs, up her spine. Her left ankle twisted, not snapped, not broken. But wrong. Burning. The joint screamed in protest.

She went down. Knees hit pavement. Hands scraped concrete. Skin tore. Blood welled hot against the cold street.

Behind her, inside the fence, Brandon bellowed. Not words. Just rage. Pure. Primal.

Sofía pushed up. Got her right foot under her. Tried the left. Weight. Pain. White-hot. Shooting up her calf. She gasped. Stumbled. Caught herself.

Couldn't put full weight on it. Couldn't run.

But she had to move.

She looked back. Brandon was at the concrete blocks. Climbing down. Fast. Too fast for someone his size. Rage fueled him. Made him quick. Made him relentless.

The gate was twenty feet behind her. Chain-link. Padlocked. She'd cleared the fence, but Brandon had the keys. He'd be through in seconds.

She turned. Faced the street. Empty. Dark. Warehouses lined both sides—Windows black. No cars. No lights. No people.

This wasn't a neighborhood. This was industry. Dead after five. Abandoned on weekends.

No one would be here. No one would hear.

Sofía took a step. Her ankle buckled. She caught herself. Hopped.

Tried again—another hop. The pain was massive. Consuming. But she moved.

Behind her, Brandon hit the ground. Heavy boots on asphalt. Running.

She screamed.

"Help! Someone! Please!"

Her voice echoed off the warehouse walls. Came back empty. Hollow. Nothing stirred. No doors opened. No lights came on.

She hopped again. Three steps. Four. Her ankle protested every impact. Tears streamed down her face. Blood ran from her palms. From the cuts on her thigh where the barbed wire had torn her.

But she moved.

"Help me! Please!"

Brandon reached the gate. She heard metal rattle. Keys jangling. The padlock clicked. Chain scraped through links.

Sofía was now about thirty feet from the gate. Moving at a hop. A lurch. A stumble.

He'd be on her in seconds.

The street stretched ahead. Dark. Empty. Endless. She couldn't outrun him. Couldn't fight him. Her ankle wouldn't hold. Her body was spent. She had nothing left.

Except survival.

Sofía hopped. Again. Again. Her vision blurred. Tears. Pain. Exhaustion. All of it mixing. Distorting.

Behind her, the gate shrieked open. Brandon was through. Running. His footsteps pounded on the asphalt. Close. Getting closer.

Ahead. In the distance. Moving and getting brighter.

Headlights. Turning onto the street. Slow. Searching.

Sofía saw the headlights accelerate. Coming toward her. Fast. She waved her arms. Screamed louder.

"Stop! Please stop! Help me!"

The car closed the distance. Twenty yards. Ten. Slowed, stopped— ten feet from where she stood, swaying. Engine idling. Headlights illuminated Brandon. Twenty feet back. Blood-covered. Closing in.

The driver's door opened.

A man stepped out. Tall. Lean. Wearing a suit and tie. His face was shadowed by the headlights behind him.

"He's trying to kill me!" Sofía pointed at Brandon. "Please! He's trying to kill me!"

Evans didn't hesitate. His eyes snapped to the gate. To Brandon. Running toward them. Massive. Blood-covered. Rage-fueled.

His hand went to his hip. Drew his service weapon. Glock. Black. Steady in his hand.

He stepped past Sofía. Put himself between her and Brandon. Raised the gun. Two-handed grip. Aimed.

"Police! Stop! Hands up!"

Brandon slowed. Twenty feet out. Then stopped. Chest heaving. Blood dripping from his face. His nose was crushed. Twice-broken. His eyes locked on Evans. On the gun.

"On the ground! Now!"

His eyes flicked to Sofía. To Evans. Back to Sofía. Calculating. Weighing.

Then he moved.

Not toward them. Toward his truck. Parked near the gate. Keys in his pocket.

"Stop!" Evans advanced. Gun up. "I will shoot!"

Brandon grabbed the padlock chain from the ground. Heavy. Three feet of links. Thick metal.

Evans saw it. Saw what was coming.

Brandon wound up. Threw.

The chain flew. Spinning. End-over-end. Right at Evans' head.

Evans ducked. Reflexive. The chain whipped past. Missed by inches. Slammed into the Honda's windshield behind him. Glass spider-webbed. Cracked.

Brandon turned. Ran.

Back through the gate. Toward the compound. Not toward the truck. Into the maze of concrete blocks and shadows.

Evans straightened. Lowered the gun slightly. Looked at Sofía.

"Get in the car. Lock the doors."

She couldn't move. Shock. Terror. Exhaustion. All of it held her frozen.

"Now!" His voice was sharp. Commanding.

Sofía lurched forward. Reached the Honda. Passenger door. Pulled it open. Fell into the seat. Slammed the door. Hit the lock.

Evans had been driving the industrial blocks for fifteen minutes. Marge's directions had been repeating in his head. Benoist Farms. Block yards. Somewhere near the warehouses. He'd passed two. Wrong layouts. Wrong fencing. Not matching what she'd described.

His gut had said keep going. Same instinct that had pulled him away from the home. Away from his family. Toward something he couldn't name but couldn't ignore. One more block. He'd check one more, then turn around. Call from a payphone. Do it right.

Then the movement had caught his eye. In the middle of the road. A figure. Stumbling. Waving. Screaming. Blood. He'd seen it even from fifty yards out. Covering her hands. Her legs. Dark streaks down pale skin.

Evans ran to the driver's side. Reached through the open door and grabbed for his phone.

The cup holder. Just the dead phone sitting there. Black screen. Useless.

It had gone dead in the car on the way here.

"Damn it."

He looked at Sofía. Bloodied. Terrified. Safe. For now.

Then at the gate. At the darkness beyond. Where Brandon had disappeared.

He couldn't leave her. Couldn't drive her away. Not with Brandon loose. Not with a dead phone. No backup. No way to call it in.

But he couldn't let Brandon escape either. Couldn't let him disappear into the night. To kill again. To find another girl. Another victim.

The decision took a second.

He closed the driver's door. Didn't get in. Checked his gun. Full magazine. One in the chamber. Seventeen rounds total.

He looked at Sofía through the window.

"Stay in the car. Keep the doors locked. If I'm not back in ten minutes, lay on the horn. Don't stop until someone comes."

She nodded. Eyes wide. Terrified. But alive.

Evans turned. Faced the gate. The compound beyond. Dark.

Dangerous. A maze designed to hide things. To conceal bodies. To trap the unwary.

He took a breath. Steadied himself. This was reckless. Stupid. Everything Roan would tell him not to do. Going in alone. No backup. Chasing a killer into his own territory.

Roan would go anyway.

But Sofía was alive because he'd come. Because he'd trusted his instinct. Because he'd driven here on nothing but a hunch and Marge's description.

And Brandon was in there. Cornered. Desperate. Dangerous.

But not invincible.

Evans moved forward. Through the gate, into the compound. His gun was up and ready. Finger alongside the trigger guard. Not on the trigger. Not yet. Discipline. Training. Years of it.

The security light cast harsh shadows. Turned the concrete block stacks into walls. Into labyrinths. The ground was packed dirt and gravel. Asphalt in places. Oil stains dark in the dim light. Industrial debris was scattered. Rebar. Pallets. Discarded equipment.

He moved carefully. Deliberate. Checking corners, watching shadows. His breathing was controlled. Measured. His heart was steady. Adrenaline pushed down. Managed.

This was what he'd trained for. What he was good at. The moment between hesitation and action. The space where decisions mattered. Where competence saved lives.

He cleared the first row of blocks. Moved to the second. The maze twisted. Turned. Branched. He took the left path. Then right. Kept moving deeper.

Somewhere ahead, Brandon was moving too. Wounded. Cornered. Desperate.

The most dangerous kind of suspect.

Evans stopped. Listened. The night was quiet. Just wind. The distant hum of the highway. No footsteps. No breathing. No indication of where Brandon had gone.

The compound was three acres. Maze-like. Easy to hide. Easy to circle back. Easy to ambush.

Evans moved right. Cleared another row. Then another. He was forty yards in now. Deep. The gate behind him was no longer visible. Just blocks. Shadows. Darkness.

Then he saw it.

Ahead. Past the stacks. Past the maze. At the far edge of the property.

A mobile home.

Single-wide. Old. Weathered. White siding stained grey with years of exposure. Windows dark. No lights. But there. Real. Standing alone on the edge of the lot.

Brandon's home.

Evans moved toward it. Cautious. Gun up. Eyes scanning, looking for movement. For threats. For Brandon, hiding in the shadows.

Nothing.

Just the mobile home. Silent. Dark. Waiting.

He reached the clearing—thirty feet of open ground between the last block stack and the home. No cover. No concealment. Just dirt and gravel. Exposed.

The mobile home sat on cinder blocks. Three steps leading to a plywood door. Windows on either side. Dark. Curtains drawn. The roof sagged in the middle. Tar paper patching holes.

This was where Brandon lived, where he planned, where he kept his secrets.

Where he might be hiding.

Evans crossed the clearing. Quick. Efficient. His gun tracking. Left. Right. Scanning windows, checking angles.

Nothing moved.

He reached the steps. Paused. Listened.

Silence.

He climbed. One step. Two. Three. Reached the door.

Wood. Old. Warped. A simple handle. No lock visible from the outside.

He tested it.

Unlocked.

The handle turned under his hand. The door cracked open. Darkness inside. Complete. Absolute.

Evans steadied his breathing. Tightened his grip on the gun. This was it. The moment. The choice.

Go in. Find Brandon. End this.

Or wait. Call for backup. Do it right.

But there was no backup. No phone. No way to call.

Just him. The gun. And whatever waited inside.

He pushed the door wider. Peered into the darkness. Saw nothing. Just black. Shapes were barely visible. Furniture. Maybe. Or something else.

The smell hit him.

Blood. Sweat. Booze. Bleach maybe. Covering something worse.

His gut tightened. This was wrong. All of it. The smell. The darkness. The silence.

Brandon was in there. Or had been. Recently.

Evans took a breath. Raised his gun. Stepped forward.

His foot crossed the threshold. Into the mobile home. Into the dark.

Into whatever horror waited inside.

CHAPTER

54

THE PHONE HAD JUST enough charge. Roan held it. Watched the screen flicker to life. Five percent battery. Maybe ten minutes if he was lucky. A voicemail notification appeared:

Rocca.

Roan ignored it.

He dialed—muscle memory. The number for Oceanside Pub was burned into his brain after years of late shifts and cold cases. It rang twice.

"Oceanside." Marge's voice. Familiar. Tired.

"Marge, it's Roan. The barbecue guy… I need to know—"

"Roan." She cut him off. Firm. Not rude. Just done with questions. "Your partner already came through here asking about Brandon."

Roan stopped breathing.

"My partner?"

"Yeah. Evans. Suit and tie. Whole nine yards. Asked about the same guy you're asking about."

Evans.

His heart kicked. Hard. Once. Then again.

"How long ago?"

"Maybe twenty minutes. Half hour tops."

"Did he say where he was going?"

"Yeah." There was a pause, during which he picked up the slight, brittle sound of ice in a glass, and someone off to the side was laughing, along with the ordinary background noises, the colorless wash of them. All normal except for this. "Said he was heading to Brandon's place. Cinder block company. It's off Southern Boulevard, close to Benoist Farms. Brandon lives out there on the property, in a trailer."

Roan didn't say goodbye.

He ended the call. Stared at the phone. The screen was already dimming—battery at four percent.

Roan moved. Fast. Out of the living room. Through the hall. Phone still in hand. He dialed Evans' phone. It rang.

Voicemail.

Roan hung up.

His eyes scanned the yard. The driveway. Looking for a squad car. Something. Anything. Rocca would have sent someone. Should have sent someone. But the lawn was empty. Just grass. Shadows. The oak tree in the corner.

No car. No lift. No way to get to Evans.

His heart pounded. Faster now. Panic rising. Evans was walking into danger. No backup. Alone. And Roan was stuck here. Suspended. Stranded. Powerless.

Then he remembered.

The garage.

Roan turned. Ran. His shoes hit the driveway—concrete solid beneath him. He threw open the garage door, metal screeching from the rusted chains, and landed with a clatter.

Light spilled in from overhead. Dust hung in the air. And there it was.

Covered by a tarp. Grey canvas stretched tight over curves and angles. Hidden. Waiting.

Roan grabbed the edge. Pulled. The tarp slid off. Pooled on the concrete floor.

A 1965 Ford Mustang Shelby GT350 was revealed.

White, with blue racing stripes down the center. Chrome gleamed even in the dim garage light. The car sat low. Aggressive. Every line was built for speed.

Roan's project. His obsession. Restomoded. Rebuilt. Every inch of it was modern under that classic skin. New engine. New suspension. New everything.

He moved to the pegboard on the wall. Keys hung from a hook.

Right where he'd left them. He grabbed them. Felt the weight in his palm. The metal was cold. Real.

The Mustang's door opened with a solid thunk. Roan dropped into the driver's seat. Leather creaked. Tight. The smell of oil, metal, and something older. Something that mattered.

He jammed the key into the ignition. Turned it.

The engine roared.

Not a cough. Not a sputter. A roar. Deep. Metallic. The sound of American muscle brought back from the dead. The garage shook. The car vibrated beneath him. Alive.

Heat washed over him from the vents. The dashboard lit up. Green. Digital. Modern tech wrapped in vintage beauty.

The transmission was custom. Sequential six-speed. Built for response. Roan slammed it into first. The shifter clicked. Precise. No slop. No hesitation. Carbon fiber shaft. Weighted perfectly. His palm knew every millimeter of its throw.

His hands gripped the wheel. Leather wrapped. Custom. His knuckles were already white.

His phone buzzed on the seat beside him—three percent battery.

He dialed. One hand. Eyes forward. The garage door ahead was still open.

Rocca answered on the first ring.

"Roan, where the hell—"

"Listen to me." His voice was steel. "Keep Pérez on Evans' family. Do not move her. Do you understand?"

"What's going on?"

"Evans is at Benoist Farms. Grade-A Concrete Block and Ready Mix. Alone. Send units. Now."

"Roan, you're suspended. You can't—"

"Send them, Rocca!" His voice cracked. Raw. "Evans is walking in there alone. We found the killer. Send every unit you have."

A pause. Then Rocca's voice. Clipped. Professional.

"On it."

Roan dropped the phone.

He punched the accelerator.

The Mustang shot forward. Tires screamed. Rubber burnt. The car cleared the garage clean. Fishtailed into the driveway. Gravel sprayed. The back end swung wide.

Roan corrected. Hands steady. Muscle memory. He'd driven this car a thousand times in his head. Now it was real.

He hit the street—tires bit asphalt. The Mustang straightened. Roan floored it.

Second gear. The shift was instant. Barely a fraction of a second. The clutch—upgraded, ceramic, designed for this type of abuse—grabbed hard in third gear at forty. The tachometer needle climbed. Red line at seven thousand RPM. Modern engine management. Launch control. Traction control disabled. This wasn't a museum piece. This was a weapon.

The engine roared. The car surged. Sixty in four seconds. Seventy in six. The houses blurred past. Streetlights streaked overhead like tracer rounds.

The G-force pressed him back into the seat. His breath caught. Released.

Dixie Highway ahead.

Roan took the turn hard. The Mustang leaned. Tires held. He came out of it clean. Straight shot north now. Clear road. Empty lanes.

His phone buzzed again on the seat. Dying. He ignored it.

Then the lights.

Behind him. Flashing. Red and blue.

A patrol unit. Coming up fast. Siren wailing.

Roan didn't slow down.

The Mustang hit eighty. Ninety. The patrol car tried to keep up. Fell behind. This wasn't some standard old muscle car.

Lightweight carbon-ceramic brakes. Active suspension. Reinforced chassis. Roan had spent three years building it. Not for show. For this. For moments when every second mattered.

The engine was a destroked 427 Windsor with modern fuel injection. Brembo brakes front and rear. Adjustable coilovers. Limited-slip differential. The Mustang could outrun anything on four wheels short of a Hellcat.

The patrol car's siren grew fainter. Then louder again. Catching up, falling back. Roan didn't care.

He grabbed his phone. Two percent. He dialed dispatch.

"This is Detective Robert Roan—badge eleven-thirty-eight. I'm in a white 1965 Mustang GT350 heading north on Dixie. Do not attempt to stop me. Relay to all units: follow me to Grade-A Concrete Block, Benoist Farms. Officer in danger. Repeat: officer in danger."

He ended the call. Dropped the phone.

One percent battery. Then nothing. The screen went black.

His hands tightened on the wheel. His breathing was shallow. Controlled. The way they'd taught him at the academy. Keep your head. Stay sharp.

But Evans was out there. Alone.

Southern Boulevard ahead. The light was red.

His hand dropped to fourth. The shift was mechanical. Smooth. The throw was perfect. He'd rebuilt the transmission himself. Knew every gear tooth. Every synchro. The car responded as if it were an extension of his body.

He didn't touch the brakes.

Traffic cleared. A sedan swerved. Horn blaring. A truck veered right. Roan blew through the intersection. The Mustang didn't waver. Didn't flinch—just speed and steel and desperation.

The patrol car was back. Joined by another. Two sets of lights now. Following. Not pursuing. Understanding.

Roan took the turn. Hard left onto Southern Boulevard. The Mustang drifted. Controlled. Perfect. The rear end swung out. He counter-steered. Straightened out. The tires caught. Held.

Benoist Farms ahead. The industrial stretch. Warehouses. Empty lots. Darkness broken only by scattered security lights.

Grade-A Concrete Block and Ready Mix was out there, somewhere in that maze of chain-link and shadows.

And Evans was already inside.

Roan pushed the Mustang harder.

Fifth gear. The engine screamed. The speedometer climbed. One hundred. One-ten. The suspension absorbed every imperfection. The steering stayed true.

The engine screamed. The speedometer climbed. The world

narrowed. Pavement. Speed. The desperate hope that he wasn't too late.

Behind him, the sirens grew louder. More units were joining. A convoy of lights. All heading to the same place.

All heading to Evans.

His jaw clenched. His heart hammered. Every second counted. Every second, Evans was alone with a killer.

The Mustang ate the distance. Swallowed miles like nothing. And ahead, somewhere in the industrial wasteland, his partner waited.

CHAPTER

55

THE MOBILE HOME door stood open. Evans paused at the threshold. Listened. Nothing. Just the compressor's hum. Just the wind moving through the compound. Through the gaps in the concrete blocks.

He stepped inside, and the smell. Immediate. Overwhelming. Stale beer. The kind that had been sitting too long. Fermenting in cans and bottles left to rot. Old grease. Thick. Clinging to everything. The grease that came from years of cooking. Of not cleaning. Of letting everything build up until it became part of the walls.

Evans held the Glock low. The weight was familiar in his palm. Comforting.

The interior was sparse. Barely furnished. A sofa against one wall. Torn fabric. Springs were visible through the cushions. Stuffing spilling out. Stains everywhere. Dark stains. Brown. Black. Spreading like disease.

Beer cans were scattered across the floor. Crushed. Empty. Some were still standing. Most knocked over. Rolling when his foot nudged them. The sound was hollow. Metallic. Too loud in the silence.

Bottles too. Spirits. Cheap vodka in plastic bottles. Whiskey in a glass. The labels faded. Peeling. Some were still half-full. Most bone dry. The residue at the bottom was thick and sticky.

Evans moved slowly. Each step was deliberate. Calculated. The floor creaked beneath him. Old wood. Thin that gave away every movement. Every shift of weight. That made sneaking impossible.

A kitchenette to his left. No table. No chairs. Just a worktop. Laminate peeling. Exposing particle board underneath. Swollen from water damage. Rotting.

The sink was piled with dishes. Plates. Bowls. Cutlery. All crusted with food. Old food. Rotting food. The smell coming from there was worse than the rest. Putrid. Rancid. Flies buzzed around it. Dozens of them. Black. Fat. Feeding.

The fridge hummed. Struggled. The motor was loud. Straining. The door was slightly ajar. Light spilling out. Faint. Yellow. Evans approached. Looked inside.

Empty. Mostly. Just condiments. Bottles of sauce. Jars of pickles. Things that didn't need refrigeration but had been put there, anyway. Nothing fresh. Nothing new. Just the remnants of someone who ate elsewhere. Who didn't live here. Who just existed here.

Evans closed the door. The light vanished. The kitchen went dark again.

The hallway was narrow. Dark. A single bulb overhead. Flickering. On. Off. On. Off. Never staying steady, casting shadows that moved when nothing did. That danced on the walls. On the ceiling. Creating shapes. Faces. Hands reaching out.

His hand tightened on his weapon. Finger moving closer to the trigger. Not on it. Not yet. But close.

The first door. To his right. He approached. Pushed it open with his foot. Weapon raised. Ready.

Bathroom.

Small. Cramped. A toilet. Stained. The bowl had a dark ring. Brown. Years old. A shower. No tub. Just a stall. No curtain. The tiles were green with mildew. Creeping up the walls. Spreading across the ceiling. The smell of mold. Of decay. Of things left to rot.

Nothing else. Just pipes. Old fixtures. A medicine cabinet hanging crookedly. The mirror cracked. Reflecting Evans in fragments. Multiple versions of himself. All watching. All waiting.

He backed out. Moved to the next door.

Bedroom.

Evans stepped inside. Weapon first. Eyes scanning. Left to right. Top to bottom.

The room was barely furnished—a mattress on the floor. No frame. No box spring. Just a bare mattress with stains he didn't want to identify. Brown. Yellow. Dark red. Spreading like maps across the surface.

No sheets. No blankets. Just the mattress.

Clothes were scattered everywhere. Dirty. Wrinkled. Thrown across the floor. Piled in corners. Shirts. Pants. Underwear. All thrown together. All reeking. The smell of sweat. Of body odor. Of someone who didn't wash. Who didn't care.

But it was the corner that drew his attention.

Restaurant equipment.

Industrial. Professional grade. Not the kind you bought at a shop. The type you ordered from the suppliers. The kind used in commercial kitchens.

Spice containers. Large. Metal. Labeled. Paprika. Cumin. Garlic powder. Onion powder. Cayenne. Black pepper. Salt. Others Evans didn't recognize. All neatly arranged on a cheap plastic shelf. Five shelves. All full. All organized. Alphabetical.

Next to them, knives.

Not kitchen knives. Not the kind used for cooking at home.

Cleavers. Heavy. Thick. Knives for breaking down meat. For chopping through bone.

Boning knives. Thin. Flexible. For separating meat from bone. For getting into joints. For precision work.

Fillet knives. Long. Sharp. For removing skin. For cutting thin slices.

Each one was clean. Polished. Sharp. The metal gleamed even in the dim light. These weren't decorative. These were tools. Used, maintained, cared for.

Restaurant wipes. Industrial. BCI brand. Cases of them. Stacked against the wall. Four cases. Maybe five. Still sealed. Still new. The same brand was found at the Torres scene.

Evans crouched. Examined the knives closely. No rust. No residue. No blood. Nothing to suggest they'd been used for anything other than their intended purpose. But the fact that they were here. In a bedroom. In this place. That told him everything.

He stood. Turned, scanned the rest of the room—a closet. Door open. Empty except for more clothes. A window. Covered with a sheet. Nailed to the frame. Blocking out light.

Nothing else. Just the mattress. The clothes. The equipment.

Evans backed out. Moved down the hallway. One more door at the end. He approached. Pushed it open.

Storage. Boxes. Old junk. Tools. Nothing useful. Nothing that mattered.

Evans exhaled. Long. Slow. Steadying himself. He'd searched the whole place. Brandon wasn't here.

He turned back towards the front of the trailer. Moved through the hallway. Through the living room. Back towards the door.

Then he heard it.

Bang.

Metal on metal. Loud. Sharp. Echoing through the night.

Evans froze. He tightened his hand on his weapon. Listening.

Silence.

Then another bang. Louder this time. Closer. Coming from behind the trailer. Near where the refrigerated container sat.

Evans moved. Quick. Purposeful. Back through the door. Down the steps. His shoes hit dirt. Gravel mixed in. Each step crunched. Too loud. But there was no helping it.

He moved around the side of the trailer. Slow. Careful. Eyes adjusting to the darkness. The security lights from the compound barely reached here. Just shadows. Shapes. The outline of the refrigerated container ahead. Twenty feet long. Eight feet wide. White. Industrial.

Another bang.

Evans stopped. The sound was coming from the container. The door. Swinging. Hitting the side of the trailer. Once. Twice. The wind was catching it and pushing it open, letting it slam back against the wall.

Evans approached. Weapon raised now. Both hands. Proper grip. The way they taught him at the academy. The way that kept you alive.

The container door was wide open. Swinging on its hinges, moving with the wind. The interior was dark. Black. Cold air spilling out. Fog rolling low. Where condensation met the warm night air. Creating mist, creating ghosts that danced in the darkness.

Evans stopped at the entrance. Peered inside.

Shadows. Shapes hanging from hooks. Meat. Large cuts. Ribs.

Shoulders. Quarters. Hanging like in a butcher shop. Like in the back of a restaurant. The hooks gleaming. The chains swaying. Moving with the air circulation.

The smell was blood. Iron. Copper. Cold. Cold that didn't just cool. It preserved. It stopped the decay. It kept things fresh.

But there was something else.

A figure.

In the back. Hanging. Not meat. A person.

His heart kicked. Once. Hard. His breath caught. His finger moved to the trigger.

"Put your hands up!" His voice cut through the silence. Firm. Commanding. The voice of authority. Of someone in control. "Now!"

The figure didn't move.

Evans stepped inside. The cold hit him immediately. Aggressive. Penetrating. Colder than outside. Colder than any air conditioning. The kind of cold that bit through fabric. Through skin. Into bone. His breath misted. Hung in the air. Thick. Visible.

He moved forward. His weapon was trained on the figure. One step. Two. The hanging meat brushed against his shoulder. Cold. Slick. Wet. The sensation made his skin crawl. Making every nerve scream.

Three more steps.

The figure came into focus.

A woman. Young. Hanging from a hook. Wrists bound above her head. Rope cutting into flesh. Deep. The skin was raw. Bleeding. Her head was down. Hair covering her face. Long. Brown. Matted with blood. With dirt. With things Evans didn't want to identify.

Her body was limp. Hanging and not moving, not breathing.

His eyes traveled down.

She was naked. Skin pale. Blue. The color of death. Of cold. Of things left too long.

Her left leg was gone and removed at the hip. The wound was cauterized. Clean. Surgical. Not hacked, not torn. Cut. Precisely. With skill. With knowledge.

His stomach turned. Bile rose in his throat. He swallowed it down. Forced it down. Stayed focused.

He took another step forward. Reached out. His hand was trembling. Just slightly. Just enough to notice.

Then movement. Behind him.Fast.

Evans turned. Too slow. Half a second too slow.

The cleaver came down.

Evans threw his arm up. Instinct. Training. The blade hit his weapon—metal on metal. A deafening clang rang through the container. Through his bones. Through everything. The gun flew from his hand. Knocked free. Skittered across the container floor. Out of reach. Into the darkness.

Brandon.

Massive. Six-three. Maybe six-four. Four hundred fifty pounds. Maybe more. Shoulders wide as the doorway. Arms thick. Corded with muscle. Face twisted. Eyes wild. Pupils dilated. Mouth open. Breathing hard. Fast. Like an animal.

He swung again.

Evans ducked low, the cleaver cut the air just above him—a rush of displaced air that seemed to flatten his hair, graze his scalp, and the sound of it, a wet whisper. The blade slammed into the meat carcass behind, the steel wedged six inches deep and not moving, and stuck there, for the moment, in a dead thing, not in him.

Brandon yanked it free. Hard. The meat swung. The chains rattled. The whole container seemed to shake.

Evans lunged. Grabbed Brandon's wrist. Both hands. Tried to twist the weapon away. Tried to use leverage. Tried to use techniques. But Brandon was strong. Stronger than Evans expected. Stronger than anyone Evans had ever fought. He didn't budge. Didn't yield. Just pulled, yanked Evans forward.

Brandon drove forward. Used his weight. All of it. Slammed Evans backward into the wall. The metal was unforgiving. Cold. Hard. Unyielding. His head snapped back. Hit the wall. Stars exploded. White. Bright. Blinding. Pain radiated from the base of his skull. Down his spine. Through everything.

Brandon swung again.

The cleaver grazed his arm. Fabric tore. His suit jacket. His shirt.

Skin split. A line of fire. Hot. Bright. Blood welled. Hot against the cold air. Running down his arm, dripping onto the floor.

Evans ignored it. Shoved the pain down. Deep. Drove his knee up. Hard. Fast. Connected with Brandon's midsection. Soft. Yielding. Flesh giving way. Brandon grunted. Stepped back. Just one step. Just enough.

Evans followed. He grabbed the cleaver with both hands. Fought for control. Pushed. Pulled. Twisted. But Brandon was too big. Too strong. His grip was like iron. Like a vice. Unbreakable.

Brandon twisted. Threw Evans sideways. Evans hit the hanging meat. The carcasses swung. Chains rattled. Metal screeched. He stumbled. Caught himself. Hands against cold meat. Against bone. Against things that used to be alive.

Evans saw the opening. Brandon's face. Bruised. Swollen. Purple. Black. Yellow. The damage was visible even in the dim light. Nose bandaged. Eyes ringed with discoloration. Cheeks marked. Jaw dark with bruising.

Evans drove his fist forward. Hard. Straight. All his weight behind it. Connected with Brandon's nose. Dead center. Right where the bandage covered the damage.

The sound was wet. Crunching. Cartilage giving way. The bandage split. Blood erupted. Fresh. Hot. Black in the dim light. Mixing with the bruises. With the swelling. Spraying across his hand. Across his suit. Across everything.

Brandon screamed. High. Animalistic. The sound echoed through the container. Through the meat. Through the cold. His hands flew to his face. To his ruined nose. To the pain. The cleaver dropped. Clattered to the floor. Metal on ice. The sound was sharp.

Evans lunged for it. Hands reaching. Fingers stretching. Almost there. Six inches away. Four. Two.

Then Brandon was on him again.

A hand grabbed his collar. Pulled. Lifted. Threw him. Evans hit the opposite wall. Shoulder first. Something cracked. Not bone. The wall. Metal denting. The impact rattled through his entire body. Through every bone. Every joint. Every nerve.

Evans tried to move. Push off. But Brandon was faster. Grabbed

Evans by the suit jacket. Lifted. Actually lifted him off the ground. Slammed him into the wall again.

His vision swam. The container spun. Or maybe he was spinning. He couldn't tell. The lights. The shadows. The meat. All of it blurring together.

Slam. Again.

This time, Evans hit the meat. Face first. The cold carcass swung. Evans bounced off. Fell to his knees. The floor was ice. Slick. Frozen. His hands slipped. Couldn't find anything solid.

Slam.

Brandon grabbed him. Pulled him up. Threw him into the wall. Again. His head hit. The world went white. Then dark. Then white again. Colors. Sounds. Pain. All mixing together. All becoming one.

He fell. Flat. Face down. The cold seeped through his suit. Through his shirt. Into his skin. His cheek pressed against the floor. Ice beneath. Blood pooling. His blood. The woman's blood. Brandon's blood. All mixing. All freezing. Creating patterns on the floor.

He blinked. Tried to focus. Tried to move. His arms. His legs. Nothing responded. Nothing moved.

Then weight. On his back. Heavy. Crushing. A knee. Brandon's knee. Driving into his spine. Between the shoulder blades. Pinning him. A quarter ton pressing down. Crushing vertebrae. Crushing ribs. Making breathing impossible.

Evans tried to push up. Couldn't. His arms wouldn't respond. Wouldn't move. Just lie there. Useless. Dead weight.

Then something around his neck.

Fabric. Silk. His tie.

Brandon wrapped it. Once. Pulled it tight. Crossed it behind his neck. Pulled again. Tighter.

The pressure was immediate. Overwhelming. Absolute. His throat closed. Air stopped. Just pressure. Just crushing force. Just the tie cutting into flesh. Into the windpipe. Into everything that mattered.

Evans thrashed. Tried to twist. Tried to break free. But Brandon was on top of him. Full weight. The knee in his back. The hands pulling the tie. Tighter. Tighter. Never stopping.

His hands clawed at the floor. At the ice. At the frozen blood.

Looking for something. For anything. There was nothing. Just cold. Just metal. Just slick frozen blood that provided no grip. No hope.

The tie dug in. Cut off everything. No air. No sound. Just pressure and the roar of blood in his ears. The pounding of his heart. Slow at first. Then faster. Panic. Pure animal panic.

His vision narrowed. The edges went dark. Black. Creeping in. A tunnel was forming and growing smaller. Smaller. The light at the end dimmed. Fading.

He tried to breathe. Couldn't. Tried to scream. Couldn't. Tried to do anything. Nothing worked. Just the tie. Just the pressure. Just Brandon's weight, crushing him down into the floor.

His thoughts scattered. Fragmented. Breaking apart like glass.

Clara.

Her face. Clear. Bright. The way she looked in the morning. Hair messy. Eyes still half-closed. Smiling. Always smiling. The way she laughed. That sound. That beautiful sound. The way she looked at him. Like he mattered. Like he was worth something.

Matthew.

His son. Ten years old. Too young to lose his father. Too young to understand. Evans saw him. Playing. Running. Smiling. The way he hit a golf ball. The way his face lit up when Evans came home. "Dad!" That word. That perfect word.

Emily.

His daughter. Eight. Still learning, still asking him to read her bedtime stories. Still believing her daddy was invincible. "One more story, Daddy. Please?" Those eyes. Those perfect eyes looking up at him. Trusting. Believing.

And Roan.

The warning. At the beach. Repeated. The concern in his eyes. The knowledge. The experience. Don't leave your phone. Wear cheap suits. Lose the tie.

I hate anything that gives a stranger a handle on your neck, Roan had said.

But Roan had known, had seen this, and had tried to warn him.

His hands stopped clawing. The strength left them. Drained away. They fell. Limp. Against the cold.

The tunnel narrowed more. Just a pinpoint now. A tiny circle of light in an ocean of dark. In an ocean of nothing.

Clara. Her voice. "Come home safe, Daniel."

Matthew. "Love you, Dad."

Emily. "Read me a story?"

Roan. "Lose the tie."

The light flickered.

Dimmed.

The pressure continued. Never stopping, never easing, just pulling. Crushing. Ending.

Evans thought about his family. About his life. About everything he'd never get to do. Never get to say. Never got to finish.

The morning. Clara making coffee. The smell. The taste. The warmth.

This afternoon. Emily asking for ice cream. That smile when he said yes.

Tonight. Matthew asking him about his golf tournament.

He thought about home. But he wouldn't get home.

Not now. Not ever.

The light grew smaller. A pinpoint. A dot.

Clara. Matthew. Emily.

His body went still. Stopped fighting. Stopped moving. Just lay there. On the frozen floor. In the container. In the dark. The cold seeped deeper. Into his bones. Into his blood. Into everything.

Brandon kept pulling. Kept squeezing. Making sure, making certain.

The compressor hummed. Constant. Mechanical. Uncaring. The meat swayed. Chains clinked—metal against metal.

And Evans lay still.

The dot vanished.

Just dark. Complete. Total. Absolute.

Darkness.

CHAPTER
56

Light.

Bright. Piercing. White.

Heaven?

Evans tried to think. Couldn't be. Everything hurt. Everything cold. The cold. It filled his lungs. Sharp. Deep. Like breathing ice.

Not heaven. Hell? But hell burned. Everyone knew that. Fire. Flames. Eternal heat.

This wasn't heat.

This was cold. Bone-deep. Seeping. The kind that made you forget warmth had ever existed.

His body ached. Ribs. Jaw. Skull. The back of his head throbbed with each heartbeat. Pain everywhere. Radiating. Pulsing.

Hell then. Had to be.

But the cold didn't make sense. Unless...

The light grew brighter. Closer. Or maybe his eyes were adjusting. Sound returned.

A pop. Loud. Sharp. Distant but unmistakable.

A gunshot.

Then yelling. Muffled. Like hearing voices underwater.

Struggling. Movement. Weight shifting.

Evans tried to focus. Tried to understand where he was. What was happening?

Memory flickered. Brief. Fragmented.

Metal floor. Cold against his cheek. Pressing into his skin. Brandon's boot. Black leather. Scuffed. Right there. Near his face. The pressure on his neck. The tie. Tightening, cutting off air, cutting off everything. Then nothing.

His vision cleared. Slowly. The white light resolved into overhead fluorescent tubes. Industrial. Harsh. The kind that hummed.

Metal walls surrounded him. Curved. Aluminum or steel. Frost coated the surfaces. His breath came out in clouds.

The refrigerated container.

Memory flooded back. The fight. Brandon. The cleaver. The punch. Then the world tilting. Falling. Darkness.

He wasn't dead.

He was still in the container.

Another sound. Closer now. The unmistakable mechanical click of handcuffs closing.

Evans tried to sit up. His body protested. Every muscle was screaming. But he pushed. Turned his head.

A figure crouched over another body on the floor. Brandon. Face down—blood pooling from his arm. The figure wore a grey suit.

Roan.

"Are you all right?"

The voice came from above. Evans looked up. Roan stood over him now. His eyes went to his neck. Stayed there. The bruising was already visible. Dark. Linear. The unmistakable pattern of a ligature.

His jaw tightened. Almost imperceptible. But Evans saw it.

Behind Roan, uniformed officers moved. Two of them were hauling Brandon to his feet. The suspect's face was a mess. Blood from his nose. The bruises from Sofía. From Evans. From everything.

"Evans." His voice again. Firmer now. "Can you move?"

Evans nodded. Tried to speak. His throat burned with each attempt, feeling like swallowing broken glass. His voice came out wrong. Hoarse. Damaged. "Yeah."

Roan extended a hand. Evans took it. The grip was strong. Steady. Roan pulled him up. Off the floor. Out of the frigid war zone.

Outside. Warm. The temperature shock was immediate against his frozen skin.

Evans stumbled. His vision wavered. The world was tilting slightly before righting itself. Roan caught him. Steadied him.

"Easy," Roan said.

They moved away from the container. Past the mobile home. Out of the compound's gate into the street.

Red and blue lights painted everything. Police cars. EMT vehicles. Officers moving with purpose. Radios crackling.

An ambulance sat with its back doors open. EMTs working. Evans saw her then. Sofía. Sitting on the bumper. Thermal blanket around her shoulders. An EMT was checking her ankle.

She was young. Twenty. Her skin was pale. Too pale. Shock was visible in her posture. The way she held herself. Rigid. Guarded. But she was alive. Breathing. The fear was still visible in her eyes, but mixed now with something else. Relief. The weight of survival.

She looked up as they passed. Her eyes met his. Recognition. Fear. Relief. All there in that single glance.

Evans nodded to her. She nodded back.

Another ambulance was nearby. This one's doors were still closed. Waiting.

"Sit," Roan said. He guided Evans to the back of the open ambulance. Away from Sofía. Giving her space.

Evans sat. The tailgate was cold under him. Metal. Unforgiving. His ribs protested. His head pounded. His throat felt like fire.

An EMT appeared. Young. Maybe mid-twenties. Blonde hair pulled back. She moved with practiced efficiency.

"I'm Sarah," she said. "Let me take a look."

She started checking him. Light in his eyes. Testing his pupils. Asking questions. His name. The date. Where he was.

Evans answered. Mechanically. His voice was rough. Strained.

"Any nausea?" she asked.

"No," Evans said. Speaking hurt.

The EMT noticed. Moved to his throat. "Let me see your neck."

Evans tilted his head back. Exposed his throat.

Her fingers probed. Gentle. Professional. He winced.

"Linear bruising," she said. "Consistent with ligature strangulation. How long were you unconscious?"

"Don't know," Evans managed.

She examined his eyes next. Shone her penlight. "Petechiae. Subconjunctival hemorrhage in your left eye."

"English," Evans said. His voice cracked.

"Burst blood vessels. From the pressure when you were choked. You're going to have a bloodshot eye for about a week. The neck bruising will take longer."

She moved to his ribs. Pressed. Evans winced.

"Bruised," she said. "Probably not broken. But you should get X-rays."

Evans nodded.

"Blurred vision?"

"It's fine."

She stepped back. "You're lucky. Mild concussion. Bruised ribs. Significant trauma to your larynx. Nothing serious. But you need to get checked out at the hospital."

"I'm fine," Evans said.

"Hospital," she repeated. Firm. Professional. "Not a suggestion."

Roan stood nearby. Watching. His grey suit was immaculate despite everything. Not a wrinkle. Not a stain. Like he'd just stepped out of a car rather than subduing a violent suspect, his expression was unreadable.

Evans looked at him. Really looked. Saw the slight narrowing of his eyes.

"Fine," Evans said.

The EMT moved away. Back to her equipment. Preparing paperwork.

Roan stayed. His presence was solid. Grounding.

Across the street, two officers led Brandon towards a patrol car. One was Rocca. The big man's linebacker frame was unmistakable even from a distance. The other officer, Evans, didn't recognize.

Brandon resisted. Tried to pull away. His feet were dragging against the road.

Rocca's hand shot out. Grabbed Brandon's collar. Lifted. Just slightly. Just enough.

Brandon's feet found ground. His struggling stopped.

They moved to the patrol car. Ducked Brandon's head. Shoved him inside.

The door closed. Brandon's face pressed against the window. Blood still fresh on his features. Rage in his eyes.

Evans looked away.

"I was reckless," Evans said.

Roan didn't respond immediately. Just stood there. Expression neutral.

"You should have left your tie at home."

Evans looked down. His shirt was open at the collar. Rumpled. Stained with blood. Not his own.

"Yeah," Evans said.

"Don't wear a tie from now on," Roan said.

It wasn't a question. It wasn't even really advice. Just a statement. Matter-of-fact.

Evans managed a small laugh. It hurt his ribs. "How did you know where I was?"

His expression didn't change. "Security footage from Pulse. Saw Brandon kidnapping Jin Shin. Recognized him from the beach barbecue stand. Orange letters on the smoker trailer. Brandon's BBQ."

"But how—"

"Called Marge at the Oceanside. She told me you'd been asking about him. Told me exactly where you went."

"Lucky," Evans said.

"No," Roan said. "Procedure. Following leads. Same thing you should have done instead of going alone."

"Thank you," Evans said.

Roan nodded once. Brief. Acknowledged but not dwelt upon.

Footsteps approached. Heavy. Authoritative.

Evans looked up.

Captain Norris.

The man moved through the scene like he owned it. Which, technically, he did. District 14's captain. Evans and Roan's superior. The man who'd told them to stay off the Morales case.

His eyes found Evans first. Then Roan. The expression was unreadable. Anger? Concern? Both?

"Detective Evans," Norris said. His voice carried across the street. "Detective Roan."

They both straightened. Evans stood despite the EMT's previous instructions.

"Captain," Evans said.

"Can either of you explain," Norris said, "how it is that you're here? At a crime scene? Apprehending a suspect? When I explicitly told you both to stay off this case?"

Evans opened his mouth. Closed it. What could he say? The truth was simple. He'd disobeyed a direct order, gone rogue, and nearly gotten himself killed.

Before he could formulate an answer, another voice spoke.

"Evans left his house for a drive, Captain."

Rocca. The big detective had approached from the side. His linebacker frame blocked some of the flashing lights.

Norris turned to him. "A drive."

"Yes, sir," Rocca said. "To clear his head. Said he needed to think." He looked at Evans as he spoke. The message was clear in his eyes. Play along.

Evans caught on. "That's right. I needed to clear my head after everything."

"And you just happened," Norris said, "to drive all the way out here? To this specific concrete block company?"

"It was a long drive," Evans said.

His expression didn't change. But something shifted in his eyes. Skepticism mixed with grudging acceptance.

"And then?" Norris asked.

"I saw the girl," Evans said. "Running down the street. Injured. The suspect was chasing her. I intervened. He resisted arrest."

The words were textbook. Procedure. The thing that looked good in a report.

Norris studied him. The silence stretched. Seconds felt like minutes.

Then Norris turned to Roan. "And why are you here, Detective Roan?"

"Evans called for backup," Roan said. "Called me and Rocca."

The lie was smooth. Confident. No hesitation.

Norris looked between them. Evans. Roan. Rocca. His jaw worked. Grinding teeth. Thinking.

Then his expression shifted. The anger was still there. But beneath it, something else. Understanding maybe. Or exhaustion. The knowledge that sometimes rules got bent. Sometimes cases demanded it.

"Fine," Norris said.

Evans felt the tension in his shoulders release. Just slightly.

"But," Norris continued, "since you're both here. Since you've apprehended the suspect. You'll interview him. In connection with the ongoing homicide cases. Rocca can assist."

It wasn't a request. But it also wasn't punishment. It was permission. Grudging. Reluctant. But permission nonetheless.

"Yes, sir," Evans said.

"Yes, sir," Roan echoed.

Norris held their gaze a moment longer. Then turned. Walked away, back towards his car. His posture was stiff. Formal. The captain was doing his duty even when he didn't like it.

Evans exhaled. Didn't realize he'd been holding his breath.

"That went better than expected," Rocca said.

"He knows," Roan said.

"Yeah," Evans agreed. "He knows."

"But he's letting it go," Rocca said.

"For now," Roan said.

Evans looked towards the patrol car where Brandon sat. Through the window, another EMT worked. Checking vitals. Recording injuries. Standard procedure for suspects in custody.

"Medical clearance first," Roan said. Following his gaze. "Both of you. Then the interview."

"How long?" Evans asked.

Roan shrugged. "Couple hours. Maybe more. Depends on what the docs say."

Evans nodded. His ribs ached with the movement.

They stood in silence. The three of them. Watching Norris' car pull away. The red taillights were disappearing down the street.

The EMT returned. Sarah. She had a clipboard now. Forms.

"You still need to go to the hospital," she said to Evans.

"I'll go," Evans said. "But I'll get a lift in a patrol car."

She looked like she wanted to argue. Then saw his expression. The determination that was there.

"Fine," she said. "But if you pass out or start vomiting, it's on you."

"Understood," Evans said.

She walked away. Shaking her head.

Evans looked around. Taking in the scene properly now. The compound. The maze of cinder blocks. The patrol cars. The EMTs were working with Sofía, who'd escaped.

Then his eyes caught something.

A car.

Parked amongst the police vehicles and ambulances. Different from the rest.

A vintage Mustang. White body. Blue stripes running down the center. Chrome gleaming under the streetlights. A car that turned heads and made people stop and stare.

Evans stared.

"Who brought the Mustang?" he asked.

Roan followed his gaze. Looked at the car. Then back at Evans.

The slightest hint of a smile touched his lips. Barely there. But unmistakable.

"I told you it was a classic," Roan said.

CHAPTER
57

Evans stood in the corner. Arms crossed, back against the wall. He'd refused the chair, refused to sit. His body wouldn't allow it, anyway. Too much pain. Too much tension. Too much adrenaline is still coursing through his system.

His throat ached with every breath. Every swallow felt like broken glass sliding down his esophagus. The bruising had darkened. Purple. Black. Yellow at the edges. The pattern of the tie was visible on his neck. Clear. Linear. Unmistakable. The doctors had documented it, photographed it. Measured it. Evidence of attempted murder.

His ribs protested with each inhale. Sharp. Insistent. The EMT had been right. Bruised. Not broken. But painful enough to remind him he'd been seconds from death. That Brandon's hands had nearly succeeded where the meat cleaver had failed.

He touched his neck. Gentle. The skin was tender. Hot. Swollen. The memory of Brandon's weight on his back was still fresh. His tie cutting off air, off blood, off life.

The medical team had cleared him, reluctantly. Concussion protocol. Observation. Rest. No strenuous activity for seventy-two hours minimum. They'd wanted to keep him overnight. Run more tests. Monitor him. He'd refused and signed the forms. Left against medical advice.

A concussion. Moderate. Bruised ribs. Multiple. Strangulation injuries. Severe. Petechial hemorrhaging in the eyes. Broken blood vessels. Damage to the larynx. The trachea. Everything documented. Everything photographed. Everything preserved.

They'd given him pain medication. He'd refused, needed to be sharp. Alert. Present. This was too important.

This interview was happening. He needed to be here. He needed to see this through, needed to look Brandon Scott Lewis in the eyes and hear what he had to say.

Brandon sat across from Roan. Hands cuffed. Wrists secured with steel restraints. A chain running through a loop bolted to the table. Standard procedure for violent offenders. For killers. For men who'd tried to murder law enforcement. His left hand bore a scar. Fresh. Pink. Raised along the palm where a blade might slip during use. From cutting. From stabbing. The wound was still healing. Evans could see scratch marks on the back of his hands and his forearms.

Defensive wounds.

His face was a mess. Worse than Evans remembered. The swelling had increased. His nose was clearly broken. Bent. Misshapen. Blood had dried in dark crusts around his nostrils. His left eye was swollen nearly shut. Purple. Grotesque. The socket was possibly fractured. His cheekbones were bruised. Yellow. Green. Brown. The injuries from Sofía. From Evans. From Roan. From the takedown. From everything.

His lip was split and scabbed over. His jaw was misaligned and probably fractured. He'd need surgery. Reconstruction. But that would come later. After booking. After the arraignment. After he was processed into the system.

The medical team had cleared him and treated him. Documented every injury. Every cut. Every bruise. Every fracture. Standard procedure for suspects in custody. Protection against claims of abuse. Against brutality accusations. Trial evidence. Proof that his injuries came from resisting arrest. From assaulting officers. From attempted murder.

Brandon wore an orange jumpsuit—county issue. The fabric was thin. Cheap. The kind they gave everyone. Murderers. Thieves. Addicts. Everyone. No belt. No shoelaces. Nothing he could use as a weapon. As a noose. Standard suicide prevention protocol.

Roan sat across from Brandon. Grey suit, immaculate. Not a wrinkle. Not a stain. Fresh from a boardroom rather than subduing a violent serial killer. No tie. His posture relaxed. Comfortable. At ease. The chess player was waiting for the perfect move.

His eyes never left Brandon. Sharp. Focused. Assessing every micro-expression. Every twitch. Every tell. Roan had interviewed suspects thousands of times. Killers. Psychopaths. Sociopaths. He knew the game. Knew the rhythms. Knew how to wait.

Brandon stared back. Silent. His jaw set despite the pain. His breathing was steady. Controlled. The predator caught. Caged. But not broken, not defeated. His eyes held something Evans recognized. Pride. Satisfaction. The look of a man who'd accomplished something. Who'd created something.

The A/C vent rattled overhead. Cold air cut through the stale room. Evans shifted his weight. The wall behind him vibrated with the sound of machinery somewhere deep in the building.

Hours had passed since the arrest. Since the compound. Since Evans had nearly died. Hours of processing. Booking. Medical clearance. Miranda rights. Everything by the book. Everything documented. Everything preserved, ready for trial.

The lawyer had arrived first. Public defender. Overworked. Underpaid. Carrying three hundred cases. She'd met with Brandon and explained his rights. His options. The charges he'd face. The evidence against him. The likelihood of conviction. The certainty of it.

She'd recommended silence. Recommended waiting. Recommended letting her build a defense. Insanity. Diminished capacity. Childhood trauma. Something. Anything. The usual strategies for the clearly guilty.

Brandon had declined and waived his right to counsel. Signed the forms. Said he wanted to talk. Wanted to explain. Wanted them to understand.

Red flag. Always a red flag when suspects want to talk without lawyers. Usually meant they thought they were smarter. Thought they could control the narrative. Thought they could manipulate. Thought they could win.

Roan knew better. Evans knew better. They'd seen it before. The arrogance. The hubris. The belief that they could talk their way out. That their intelligence would save them. That their charm would work.

It never did.

The silence stretched. Minutes. Neither detective spoke. Just watched. Waited. Let the weight of everything settle. Let Brandon sit with it. With the knowledge of what was coming. With the reality of his situation. With the finality of it all.

Evans observed Roan work. The waiting. The silence. The psychological pressure. Letting suspects fill the void. Letting them break their own composure. Letting the quiet become unbearable until they had to speak. Had to explain. Had to confess.

Brandon's fingers twitched. Slight. Almost imperceptible. But there. The first crack in the facade. The first sign of discomfort. Of need. Of compulsion.

His breathing changed. Faster. Shallower. His eyes moved. From Roan to Evans. Back to Roan. Assessing and calculating, planning what to say. How to say it. What effect it would have.

Roan leaned back in his chair. Casual. Unhurried. All the time in the world. No rush. No urgency. Just patience. Infinite patience.

The fluorescent lights hummed. The camera blinked. The silence held.

Then Roan spoke.

"You're never leaving prison alive."

The words dropped. Simple. Declarative. No emotion. No inflection. Just a fact. Just truth. Just reality delivered with surgical precision.

Brandon's eyes narrowed. His jaw tightened. But he didn't respond. Didn't argue. Didn't deny. Because they both knew it was true.

Roan pulled a folder from beside him. Manila. Thick. Heavy with documentation. With evidence. With proof. He opened it. Pages inside. Reports. Photographs. Lab results. The weight of everything they had.

He began to read. His voice was steady. Professional. Clinical.

"Brandon Scott Lewis. Four counts of first-degree murder. Camila Morales. Julia Aguilar. Jin Shin. One unidentified female victim." He paused. Let the names hang in the air. Let Brandon hear them. Remember them. Own them.

"One count of attempted murder of a law enforcement officer. Detective Daniel Evans." Roan's eyes flicked to Evans. Brief. Acknowledging. Then back to Brandon.

"One count of attempted murder. Jessica Torres. If she lives."

Another pause. "Two counts of kidnapping. Jin Shin. Sofía Navarro." The names kept coming. Stacking. Building. "One count of aggravated battery. One count of assault on a law enforcement officer. One count of tampering with evidence. One count of abuse of a corpse. So far."

He closed the folder. Leaned forward. "Capital murder. Death penalty eligible. Florida still has the death penalty, Brandon. The State Attorney will push for it. Hard. Multiple victims. Law enforcement assault. Kidnapping. Torture. You check every box. Every single one."

Roan's voice remained even. Matter-of-fact. "Plus multiple consecutive life sentences. Even if they don't execute you, even if some bleeding-heart jury gives you life, you'll never see daylight again. Never breathe free air. Never walk on a beach. Never eat real food. Never touch a woman. Never do anything but rot in a cage until you die."

The words landed. Heavy. Final. Irrevocable.

Sweat beaded on Evans' forehead despite the cold. The room pressed in. Four walls. One table. One killer. Nowhere else to look.

Brandon's jaw worked. Muscles grinding. Tension building. Then he spoke. The first words since medical clearance. Since they'd brought him here. Since the arrest.

"You wanna know why?"

His voice was rough. Damaged. The swelling was affecting his speech. But the words were clear. Intentional.

Roan said nothing. Just watched. The invitation was clear. Silent. Waiting.

Brandon leaned forward as much as the chains would allow. His eyes locked on Roan. Intense. Focused. Alive in a way they hadn't been before.

"I got needs like everybody. But mine itch. Under the skin. Won't stop itching till I scratch. Till I fucking scratch or go crazy."

Evans felt his stomach turn. The justification begins—the twisted logic.

"They were good-looking," Brandon continued. His voice was taking on a dreamy quality. Distant. Remembering. "Every one of 'em. Ripe. You don't leave good meat out to rot. Goes to waste. Falls off the bone and feeds maggots. Better to use it."

Roan's face gave nothing away; still, as it had been, set and unreadable. Professional. Cold. "Did you follow Camila Morales?"

"Yeah." Brandon smiled. Slight. Satisfied. The expression was grotesque on his swollen face. "She was perfect. Everything I wanted. That fat ass. Full tits. Curves. Hips you could grab onto."

He shifted in his seat. The chains rattled—metal on metal. The sound was loud in the small room.

"I followed her for weeks. Watched her. Where she went. What she did. Who she talked to." His eyes grew distant. Remembering. Savoring. "Diner to that massage place. Massage place to home. Sometimes she'd stop at the shop. Gas station. Always the same. People are creatures of habit."

Evans' hands clenched. Nails digging into palms. The casual way Brandon spoke. Describing stalking like watching birds.

"She was never alone," Brandon continued. "Always with someone from that diner. Or that Asian bitch. They were tight. Friends. Made it hard. Made it complicated. I had to wait. Had to be patient. Had to find the right moment."

His smile widened. "Then I saw her at the pub. That night. Late. Fighting with some guy. Boyfriend maybe. Didn't matter. Saw her drinking. Getting upset. Angry. Saw him leave."

The memory clearly pleased him. His eyes brightened despite the swelling. Despite the pain.

"I waited outside. In my truck. Watched her stumble out. She was drunk. Easy pickings. I walked up. Offered to drive her home. Played the nice guy. The good Samaritan."

Brandon's voice dropped. Softer. More intimate. "She almost got in. Almost. So close. If she had, I could've taken my time, brought her to my place. Had days with her. But she wouldn't get in. Started yelling. Making noise. Drawing attention."

His smile faded. Replaced with something darker. Colder. "So I took her right there. In the parking lot. Grabbed her. Covered her mouth. Dragged her to the truck."

He paused. Eyes distant. Remembering. "I wanted more time. Wanted to take it slow. Make it last. But she fought. Kept screaming.

Even drunk, she fought. Strong bitch. Stronger than she looked. So I stabbed her."

The words came easily. Casual. Cutting meat on a grill. Normal. Mundane.

"Felt good when the blade went in. Felt everything let go. The tension. The need. The itch. All of it. Gone. For a while."

Evans' blood ran cold. The casual description. The lack of remorse. The satisfaction in his voice.

The fluorescent lights flickered. Once. Twice. Evans' vision blurred. Concussion symptoms were flaring. He blinked hard. Focused on Brandon's swollen face.

Roan remained still. Professional. "What about Julia Aguilar?"

Brandon's expression shifted. Thoughtful. "Julia." He said the name slowly. Tasting it. "Found her on Dixie. Late. Working her corner. She got in easily. No questions. Just business."

He leaned back. The chain clinked. "I told her I knew a quiet spot. She didn't want to go. Started getting nervous. Tried to get out. But the locks were on. Child safety locks. Works every time."

His voice remained steady. Clinical. "I drove to an industrial area. Quiet. No cameras. No people. She fought when she saw the knife— kicked the dashboard. Broke the vent. Screamed. Clawed. Strong for her size. But not strong enough."

Brandon's eyes grew distant. Reflective. "Three stabs. Ribs. Gut. Then I cut her throat. Deep. Watched her bleed out. Took maybe two minutes. Then I just sat there."

He paused. Drew out the memory. His smile returned. Satisfied. "Then I took her to that lot. The one by the Morales family building. Carried her through the torn fence. Set her down on the foundation. Made sure she'd be seen. Made sure they'd find her. The brother's flyers were everywhere. Blowing around. One landed right near her. Perfect."

Brandon leaned forward. "Smart placement. Right in their neighborhood. Right where that faggot brother put up all his Jesus signs. Thought you'd look at him. Almost worked too."

Evans' throat constricted. Not just from the strangulation damage. The air felt thick. Used up.

Roan's pen moved across the notepad. Taking notes. Recording.

Documenting. "Did you place Ariel's Romans flyer in the bathroom at the Oceanside Pub?"

"Yeah." Brandon smiled again. Pleased with himself. "Saw him posting them everywhere. Lake Worth. The Beach. Hundreds of them. Thought it'd be perfect. Make you think he was involved. Make you look at him instead of me. Misdirection."

His eyes sparkled. Proud. "Figured if you found the flyer at the pub. Same place Camila had been. Same night. You'd connect them. Think the faggot followed her. Killed her. Staged Julia. Perfect."

Roan made another note. "Jessica Torres fought back."

Brandon's face twisted. Anger flashing. Hot. Immediate. "That bitch." He pointed to his face. To the bruises. The swelling. The damage. "She did this. Fought back hard. Fast. Mean. I had her. Had the knife to her throat. Ready. But she twisted. Kicked. Scratched. Bit. Made me lose my grip."

His voice rose. Frustrated. Bitter. "She ruined it. Ruined everything. Should've been easy. Should've been quick. But no. She had to fight. Had to make it hard."

The anger radiated off him. Real. Deep. Personal.

Heat flushed through Evans' chest. The room suddenly felt too small. Too hot. He pushed harder against the wall. Concrete solid behind him.

Roan let it simmer. Let Brandon stew in it. Then spoke. Calm. Measured. Redirecting. "Why Jin Shin? She wasn't your type."

The anger faded. Replaced with something colder. More calculated.

"I thought she knew something." Brandon's voice leveled out. Controlled again. "Saw her with you. Saw you talking. Asking questions. Saw her answering. Remembering. Figured she'd seen me. Maybe remembered something. Couldn't risk it."

He tilted his head. Studying Roan. Assessing. "Besides. Thought you might like a gift. Detective. A message. Fresh meat delivered right to your door. How'd you like finding her? That head? Mouth open? Did it fuck you up? Do you see it when you close your eyes?"

His smile returned. Cruel. Predatory. "She give good head at that massage place, detective? Before I took hers?"

Roan's expression didn't change. Didn't flinch. Didn't react. Stone. Ice. Immovable.

Brandon's attention shifted. Turned to Evans. His smile widened, showing teeth. Bloodstained. Broken.

"And you, detective." His voice dripped mock sympathy. False concern. "Sorry about the tie. But honestly? I figured your kids could use a box of meat. Fresh cuts. Premium. Maybe your wife, too. What's her name? Clara?"

Evans' jaw clenched. Every muscle tensed.

"I love that mulatto skin," Brandon continued. Voice dropping. Intimate. Violating. "Smooth. I came when she saw my gift. Screaming. Standing there with that sweet fuckable ass of hers. Tell me, detective. Does she like it in the—"

"Enough."

Roan's voice cut through. Sharp. Final. Not loud. But commanding. Absolute.

Brandon stopped. Looked back at Roan. The smile was fading. Realizing he'd overplayed his hand.

The camera blinked red in the corner. Recording everything. Evans' ears rang—white noise building. The room tilted slightly. He steadied himself.

"Who was the girl in the refrigeration container?" Roan asked. Voice steady. Professional. Moving forward.

Brandon shrugged. Casual. Dismissive. "Don't know. Some bitch. Picked her up somewhere. Bar maybe. Street. Don't remember. They all start looking the same after a while."

"Where's her leg?"

"Cleaned it." Brandon's voice remained matter-of-fact. "Ground it up. Spiced it. Packaged it. Might be in my freezer still. Or I sold it. Burgers. Mixed it in with the beef. Ground chuck. People loved them. Came back for seconds. Said they were the best they'd ever had."

He laughed. Soft. Bitter. "Funny, right? Eating their own kind. And they didn't even know. Couldn't tell the difference. Beef. Pork. Human. All meat. All the same, once you cook it right."

Evans felt bile rise. The casual admission. The horror of it. People had eaten human flesh. Unknowing. Unsuspecting. Buying burgers from Brandon's stand on the beach. Feeding it to their families. Their children.

Roan's voice remained steady. Unshaken. "We found other remains in your freezer. Body parts. Organs. Tissue. How many victims?"

Brandon thought. Considered. Counting meat inventory. "Couple. Maybe five. Maybe more. Lost track after a while. After you've had enough, they stop being people. Just become meat. Just become product."

His eyes grew distant. Reflective. "Camila's different, though. Wanted to bite those tits right off. Can't forget her. But the others?" He shrugged. "Names fade. Faces blur. Just bodies. Just flesh."

The room fell silent. The weight of it is crushing. Suffocating. Five more victims. At least. Five more families who'd never know. Five more lives erased, reduced to meat in a freezer. To ground beef sold on a beach. To nothing.

Evans' hands shook. Rage. Horror. Disgust. All of it mixing and swirling, threatening to overwhelm him.

Roan closed the folder. Leaned forward. Eyes locked on Brandon. "How did we find you?"

Brandon's confidence wavered. Slight. But there. Visible. "What?"

"How did we connect you to the murders?" Roan repeated. Slower. Clearer. Each word was deliberate.

Brandon hesitated. The question was unexpected. Off-script. Outside the narrative he'd constructed—the story he'd planned to tell.

Evans spoke for the first time. His voice was rough. Damaged. Raw from the strangulation. But clear enough. Strong enough.

"You're left-handed."

Brandon's eyes snapped to him. Wide. Surprised.

"I saw you on the beach," Evans continued. Each word was an effort. Each syllable was painful. "That day at your stand. You held the knife left-handed. The broken blade. From BCI. Same company that makes restaurant wipes. The ones you can't stop using. The ones we found around Jessica Torres. Your calling card. Your signature."

Understanding dawned in Brandon's eyes. The realization. The small detail that had undone everything. The thing he'd never considered, never thought mattered.

Roan continued. Voice steady. Methodical. "The security camera at Pulse nightclub. Caught you on video. Hitting Jin Shin with a blunt object. Putting her in your truck and driving away with her body. Time-stamped. Dated. Clear image of your face. Your number plate. Everything."

Brandon's face paled. Color draining. "I didn't..." His voice faltered. Cracked. "I didn't check for cameras."

"You parked right in front of one," Roan said. Voice almost gentle. Almost sympathetic. "Entrance camera. Street-facing. High-definition. Mounted on the building across from where you hit her. Caught everything. The impact. The abduction. The getaway. All of it."

Roan leaned back. "If you'd left her alone. If you'd just walked away. If you hadn't tried to silence a witness who didn't actually witness anything. Hadn't left your message at our homes. You might have gotten away with everything. Camila. Julia. The unidentified victims. All of it. But you got greedy. Got paranoid. Got sloppy."

The silence returned. Heavier. Final. Brandon sat there—chains rattling as he shifted. The reality of it was sinking in. The magnitude of his mistake. The stupidity of it.

One mistake. One camera. One moment of carelessness. One decision to kill someone who didn't need killing. Who didn't know anything. Who couldn't hurt him.

And now he'd never leave prison alive.

Brandon's shoulders sagged. Deflated. The bravado was gone. The confidence he had shattered. The realization, he'd been caught not by brilliance. Not by superior detective work. But by his own paranoia. His own compulsion. His own need to eliminate a threat that didn't exist.

The interview continued. More questions. More answers. More details. Names. Dates. Locations. Methods. Everything documented. Everything recorded—everything for trial.

Brandon confessed to it all. Described it all. Explained it all. Not out of remorse. Not out of guilt. But out of pride. Out of the need to be understood. To be recognized. To be seen as more than just a killer. As an artist. A craftsman. A professional.

He was none of those things.

He was a monster. Plain. Simple. Undeniable.

The door opened. Air from the hallway rushed in. Fresher. Cooler. Different. Evans breathed it. Felt the difference. Felt freedom from that small space—that confession chamber.

Two hours later, Roan stood. Gathered his folder. Looked down at Brandon. "Interview concluded. Time is twenty-two forty-seven hours."

He turned. Walked to the door. Evans pushed off the wall. Followed. His ribs were protesting. His throat was burning. His head pounded. But satisfaction was settling in his chest. Deep. Warm. Real.

They had him. All of it. Recorded. Documented. Confessed. Everything they needed for the trial. For conviction. For justice.

The door closed behind them. The sound final. A cell locking. Justice served—a chapter ending.

In the hallway, Evans leaned against the wall. Exhausted. Drained. The adrenaline was fading. The pain was returning. Everything was catching up at once.

His legs felt weak. His vision blurred. The concussion was making itself known, demanding attention, demanding rest.

Roan stood beside him. Silent for a moment. Then spoke. Two words. Simple. But from Roan, they meant everything.

"Good work."

Evans nodded. Couldn't speak. His voice was gone. His throat was too damaged. Too raw. But understanding passed between them. Unspoken. Complete. The case was closed. The killer was caught. The victims could rest.

Behind them, through the one-way glass, Brandon sat alone. Hands cuffed. Head down. The predator was caged. The monster was contained. The evil stopped.

Uniformed officers entered. Took him back to holding. To processing. To the system that would consume him. Grind him down. Destroy him slowly over the years. Decades. Until death finally came.

Evans watched him go. Watched the orange jumpsuit disappear down the hallway. Watched the door close. Watched it all end.

And for the first time in weeks, he felt he could breathe.

The air filled his lungs. Clean. Clear. Free of the weight that had pressed down since that first night on the beach. Since Camila Morales. Since everything started.

"Go home," Roan said. Voice quiet. Firm. "See your family. Clara. The kids. Be alive. Be present. This is done."

Evans looked at him. Roan's face showed something rare. Concern. Real concern. For him. For his health. For his recovery.

"You sure?" Evans' voice barely worked. Whisper. Rasp.

"I'm sure." Roan's hand landed on his shoulder. Brief. Gentle. "Paperwork can wait. Reports can wait. Everything can wait. Go home."

Evans nodded. Pushed off the wall. Steadied himself and walked towards the exit. Each step was an effort. Each movement was painful. But forward. Always forward.

His phone buzzed. Text from Clara:

> Kids asleep. Waiting up. Come home.

He typed back:

> On my way.

The drive took ten minutes. Autopilot. Muscle memory. Mind elsewhere. Processing. Reviewing. Remembering.

The street lights blurred past. Orange haloes in the darkness. The city was sleeping. Unaware that a monster had been caught. That evil had been stopped. That justice was coming.

Evans' hands gripped the wheel. The adrenaline finally drained away, leaving exhaustion. Pain. Relief. All of it mixed.

The bruises on his neck throbbed. The ribs ached with each breath. His head pounded. But he was alive. He was going home. He was done.

Home appeared. Lights on. Clara silhouetted in the window. Waiting. Watching.

He parked. Climbed out. Walked to the door.

She opened it before he could knock. Eyes wide. Taking in his appearance. The bruises. The swelling. The damage. Her hand went to her mouth. Tears welling.

"Daniel..."

He wrapped his arms around her. Held her. Let her hold him. Let himself feel it. The relief. The safety. The end.

"It's done," he whispered. Voice broken. Body broken. But spirit intact. "It's over."

She held him tighter. Didn't ask questions. Didn't need to. Just held him. Just let him be there. Be alive. Be home.

Her hands traced his face. Gentle. Careful. Avoiding the worst of the bruising. Her tears wet against his chest. Silent. Grateful.

The weight lifted. Slowly. Gradually. But lifting.

Tomorrow would bring reports. Statements. Debriefings. Media. Trials. All of it.

But tonight, he was home. He was alive. He was done.

And Brandon Scott Lewis would never hurt anyone again.

CHAPTER

58

AFTERNOON SUNLIGHT REVEALED the building's true condition. Four stories of neglect—stucco flaking away like dead skin, railings bleeding rust, entrance door listing to one side as if too tired to stand straight.

Roan stood on the sidewalk, hands in his pockets, and stared at the third-floor window where Jin Shin's mother lived, where Jin had lived —past tense. Everything about Jin was past tense now.

The September heat hung thick, humid, pressing against his skin like hands. Sweat collected at the base of his neck, soaked through his shirt between his shoulder blades. The air smelled like exhaust and hot concrete, and somewhere nearby, someone was frying fish; the smell drifted through open windows.

He should have come sooner. Should have checked on Mrs. Shin days ago. However, the arrest occurred quickly—Brandon Scott Lewis was in custody, charges had been filed, and the case was moving toward trial. And checking on the blind Korean woman whose daughter died became another item on a list that never got shorter.

Roan climbed the stairs to the third floor. The metal railing was hot under his palm. Apartment 3F sat at the end of the hallway—same door, same peeling paint, same silence pressing out from inside.

He knocked. Three times. Firm but not aggressive.

No answer.

He waited. Knocked again. Heard movement inside—slow, shuffling footsteps, the kind that suggested uncertainty. Then the door opened.

Mrs. Shin stood in the gap. Small. Frail. Her white hair was pulled back in a bun, her faded housedress hanging loosely on her thin frame.

Her eyes moved towards him—unfocused, tracking the shape of his presence but not seeing details. Blind. Not completely. But enough.

She spoke in Korean. Sharp syllables, rising at the end. A question he couldn't answer.

His chest tightened.

"Mrs. Shin," he said. Kept his voice gentle. "My name is Detective Roan. I... I knew Jin."

More Korean. The old woman's voice was higher now. Worried. Her hand gripped the doorframe, knuckles white against dark wood.

"I just want to talk for a minute," Roan said. "Can I come in?"

She stared at him—or through him. Her eyes were searching for something they couldn't find. Then she nodded. Stepped back. Let the door swing open.

The apartment hadn't changed. The same cramped kitchen is visible from the entrance. Same sparse living room—sofa worn thin, TV on a stand, curtains drawn against the afternoon sun. It smelled like ginger and medicine, and something else - something stale and sad.

Jin's shoes sat by the door. Black flats, worn at the heels. His breath caught.

Mrs. Shin shuffled to her chair near the window. The same chair where Roan had seen her before, weeks ago, when Jin was alive, changing for work, and making tea. The old woman lowered herself slowly, gripping the armrests, her legs trembling with the effort.

Roan closed the door behind him. Stood in the middle of the living room. His hands didn't know what to do. He shoved them back in his pockets.

"We caught him," Roan said. Knew she couldn't understand. Said it anyway. "The man who killed those girls. Brandon Scott Lewis. He's in prison now."

Mrs. Shin spoke again. Korean words tumbling fast, urgent. The tone was clear—she was asking something, asking about Jin, probably. Asking where her daughter was, why she hadn't come home, and when she would return.

His throat closed.

He'd delivered death notifications before. Knocked on doors, stood in living rooms, watched families collapse under the weight of words. But this was different. This woman couldn't understand him. Couldn't process the explanation. All she knew was that her daughter was gone, and no one had told her why. Or had, and she didn't remember.

"Jin helped us," he said. His voice came out rough. He cleared his throat. Tried again. "Your daughter was brave. Without her, we wouldn't have caught him. She saved lives."

The old woman tilted her head. Listening, not comprehending.

Roan thought about that day in the bullpen. Jin was standing by Camila's photo, asking if he would catch the killer. The determination in her face. The way she'd looked at him when she promised information.

Promise?

I promise.

He'd kept that promise. But Jin wasn't here to know it.

Roan moved to the sofa. Sat down slowly. His knees ached. Everything ached. He leaned forward, elbows on his thighs, and looked at the old woman who couldn't look back.

"I should have protected her," he said. The words came without permission. "I should have seen it. Should have known she was in danger. Should have done something."

Mrs. Shin made a sound. Soft. Maybe an agreement. Maybe confusion.

He remembered walking Jin home. Four blocks. She'd carried empty containers in a plastic bag, talked about her mother's cooking, and said she worked at Siam to pay for medicine. Said she thought about getting out all the time, but had nowhere to go. *I have my mother.*

That's what mattered. That's what kept her trapped in a massage parlor, taking money from men, risking everything to care for a woman who was slowly forgetting her.

The old woman's hands fidgeted in her lap. Fingers trembling slightly. Diabetes, Jin had said. Her hands shake.

Roan swallowed. Tasted guilt. Bitter. Heavy.

"Because of Jin, he's in prison," Roan said. "He'll never hurt anyone again. She stopped him. Your daughter stopped a killer."

More Korean. Faster now. The old woman's voice rising, cracking at the edges. Worried. Frightened. She was asking where Jin was. Had to be. Why wasn't Jin here? Why wasn't Jin translating? Why had this stranger come instead?

Her hands reached out, grasping at air, and Roan realized she was crying. Silent tears tracking down her weathered cheeks.

Roan stood. Crossed to the window and looked out at the parking lot below—cracked asphalt, weeds pushing through, cars baking in the sun. From here, he could see the street where he'd walked Jin home. Four blocks. She'd talked about her mother growing tea in Korea and talked about how her mother's mind was going, little by little. *Sometimes she forgets things.*

Roan turned back. Mrs. Shin was watching him or watching the shape of him. Her eyes followed his movement, but she did not find his face.

"I'm going to take care of you," Roan said. Didn't matter that she couldn't understand. He needed to say it. "I'm going to find you a place. Somewhere safe. Somewhere they'll look after you. I'm not letting you stay here alone."

The old woman spoke again. Quieter now. Resigned. The way people sound when they've asked the same question too many times without getting an answer.

Roan moved to the kitchen. The kettle sat on the stove—old, dented, the handle wrapped in electrical tape. He filled it at the sink and set it on the burner. Found matches in a drawer, lit the gas. The flame caught, burnt blue.

He opened the cupboard above the sink. Found the tin of green tea. The same tin Jin had used. He remembered her hands—small, efficient, as she spooned loose tea into mugs. Remembered the steam rising, the bitter clean smell. *My mother used to grow it in Korea.*

The kettle whistled.

Roan poured water into a mug. Let the tea steep. Watched the color seep into the water, turning it pale green. The steam rose, carrying that familiar scent—sharp, grassy, almost sweet. He carried the mug to Mrs. Shin and set it on the small table beside her chair, where she could reach it.

She felt for it. Found the handle. Lifted it carefully to her lips. Sipped. Made a slight sound. Maybe approval. Maybe just an acknowledgement.

Roan went back to the kitchen. Made another cup for himself. Held the mug in both hands, felt the heat through the ceramic. Too hot. It burned his palms slightly, but he didn't let go.

He pulled out his phone. Opened his contacts. Found the number for Palm Beach County Social Services. Hit dial.

It rang twice.

"Palm Beach County Social Services, this is Angela."

"This is Detective Roan with PBSO," he said. Kept his voice low. "I need to arrange care for someone. Elder care. She's alone. Blind. Has diabetes and possibly dementia. She needs placement somewhere safe."

"I'll need some information," Angela said. Professional. Efficient. "Name, address, current living situation—"

"Jin Shin's mother," Roan said. "Mrs. Shin. I don't have her first name. She's Korean, with limited English. Lives at 224 J Street, Apartment 3F. Her daughter... her daughter was killed. She's been alone for over a week."

Silence on the line.

"I'm sorry," Angela said. Genuine. "I'll expedite the paperwork. We have a facility in West Palm Beach that specializes in elderly Korean residents. Translators on staff. Medical care. It's... It's expensive, though. Without family support—"

"I'll cover it," Roan said. The words came before he'd thought them through. "Whatever it costs. Send me the bills."

"Detective—"

"Just do it. Please."

Another pause.

"All right," Angela said. "I'll have someone out there tomorrow to assess her. We'll move quickly."

"Thank you."

He ended the call. Looked at Mrs. Shin still watching TV, still holding her tea, still waiting for a daughter who would never come home.

Roan crossed back to the sofa. Sat. Drank his tea. Too hot. Bitter. Familiar.

The TV flickered—a Korean drama, voices speaking a language he couldn't understand, music swelling during what looked like an emotional scene. Mrs. Shin's face was blank. Not following the story. Just present. Just existing in the space her daughter had left behind.

Roan finished his tea. Set the mug on the coffee table. Noticed a framed photo he hadn't seen before—Jin as a child, maybe ten, standing between her parents. All of them were smiling. All of them together. All of them were gone now except the old woman in the chair.

"Jin saved people," he said quietly. To the old woman who couldn't hear him. To the apartment that held too much silence. "Because of her, other daughters went home. Other mothers didn't lose their girls."

It didn't balance the scales. Nothing could.

Roan stood. Walked to the door. Opened it. Paused at the threshold.

"Someone will come tomorrow," he said. "They'll take care of you. They'll make sure you're safe."

Mrs. Shin didn't respond. Just sat in her chair, holding her cooling tea, watching shadows move across a television screen.

Roan stepped into the hallway. The door closed behind him with a soft click.

Inside, Mrs. Shin sat alone.

The tea cooled in her hands. Still warm enough to feel through the ceramic. She lifted it again. Sipped. The taste was familiar. The way Jin made it. Strong. A little bitter. Green and clean like spring grass.

She set the mug down. Felt for the remote. Found it wedged between the chair cushion and the armrest. Clicked through channels. News. Commercials. A cooking show. Stopped on the Korean drama. The voices spoke words she understood. Finally. Something she understood.

On screen, a woman was crying. Mrs. Shin didn't know why.

Couldn't follow the story anymore. But she recognized the emotion—recognized loss.

The apartment was quiet except for the television. No footsteps in the hallway. No key in the lock. No Jin calling out that she was home, that she'd brought dinner, that everything was all right.

Mrs. Shin's hands shook slightly. The tea trembled in the mug. She set it down before it spilled.

"Jin-ah," she said. Calling for her daughter the way she had when Jin was small. When Jin would come running. When Jin would answer.

Silence.

The drama continued. The woman on screen kept crying. Music swelled. Someone said something that might have been important, but Mrs. Shin couldn't concentrate enough to follow.

Her daughter's shoes were still by the door. She couldn't see them, but she knew they were there. Black flats. Jin wore them to work. Complained that they hurt her feet, but kept wearing them because they were professional.

Mrs. Shin reached for her tea again. Brought it to her lips. Cold now. Its bitterness was sharper. She drank it anyway. All of it. Down to the last drop. Because Jin had made it, or someone had made it the way Jin did. And that was close enough to having her daughter here.

Close enough to not being alone.

The television voices spoke Korean. The tea sat empty in her hands. The apartment grew darker as the afternoon turned towards evening, shadows lengthening across furniture Jin had arranged, across a life Jin had built to take care of her mother.

And Mrs. Shin sat in her chair by the window, blind eyes watching nothing, waiting for a daughter who was never coming home.

Waiting.

Always waiting.

CHAPTER

59

THE SUN HAMMERED down on the thirteenth green at Lake Worth Municipal, turning the bag strap into a line of fire across Evans' shoulder, where sweat pooled against healing ribs. Each breath pulled at the tender spots, a constant reminder of what had happened two weeks ago.

At ten years old, Matthew stood focused over his ball, putter gripped loosely in both hands the way Coach Miller had shown him—relaxed but controlled. Evans watched from behind in the caddy position, the bag heavy against his side. White with green trim, the Callaway logo had faded from years of use. Inside were clubs Matthew had saved for by mowing lawns and washing cars, earning every dollar himself.

The hollows beneath Evans' eyes had deepened to purple-grey from nights spent waking with a gasp, his hands flying to his throat to check that he could still breathe. The phantom pressure lingered even now in daylight.

The small gallery consisted mainly of parents and other caddies, with a handful of spectators who followed junior tournaments for Saturday entertainment. The only sounds were distant conversations from different holes and the hum of a mower working the back nine. Matthew's ball sat three feet from the cup on a straight uphill line with no break—just distance and speed to judge. Make it, and he'd go three up on his opponent.

Evans shifted the bag and winced as his ribs protested—healing but not healed, sending a dull ache through his torso with every movement. Matthew went through his putting ritual, crouching down to read the line, standing, then crouching again. The kid approached everything with the same obsessive precision, doing nothing halfway.

Matthew set his putter behind the ball, aligned the face, took one practice stroke, and then addressed. The stroke was smooth, accelerating through impact. The ball rolled true on its line, dead center, and dropped with a satisfying rattle of plastic hitting the metal cup before settling on earth.

Matthew walked to the cup without celebration, picked up his ball, and nodded to Evans—three up with five holes to play.

They walked toward the fourteenth tee; the bag bouncing against Evans' shoulder with each step. The weight felt different from carrying a weapon or a case file—these were just clubs, tools for a game his son loved.

His fingers found his neck again—the third time in ten minutes, not that he was counting. The bruising had faded to yellow-green but remained tender to the touch. The habit had become automatic: checking that the swelling was gone and that his airway was clear.

Movement at the edge of a backyard caught Evans' eye. On the far side of the fence separating the golf course from the residential street, a man stood watching with his hands in his pockets.

Roan.

Evans' chest tightened, then released. For two weeks, he'd wondered if Roan was okay, if they were okay after everything that had happened. Seeing him there, just watching from his yard, lifted a weight Evans hadn't realized he'd been carrying.

Evans stopped and touched Matthew's shoulder. "Hold up, bud."

Matthew turned and followed his dad's gaze to where Roan stood by the fence.

"Who's that?" Matthew asked.

"Someone I work with." Evans adjusted the bag, feeling the pull in his ribs. "Come on. I want you to meet him."

They walked across the dry grass, crackling beneath their feet, past the bunker and over to the fence where Roan stood. He hadn't moved, just watched them approach with those grey eyes that gave nothing away.

"Roan," Evans said, his voice rougher than usual from exhaustion.

"Evans." Roan's tone remained flat and professional, though something warmer lurked underneath.

Roan's gaze moved to Evans' neck, taking in the faded bruising and the dark circles under his eyes. His jaw tightened almost imperceptibly —he didn't need to say anything.

Evans set the bag down, relief flooding his shoulder as he gestured to his son. "This is Matthew."

Matthew extended his hand the way Evans had taught him, with a firm grip and direct eye contact. Roan shook it briefly.

"Matthew," Evans said, "this is Detective Roan. The man who gave us those golf balls."

Matthew's face brightened with recognition. "The ones from your yard?"

"Yeah," Roan said.

"Thank you," Matthew said with genuine enthusiasm. "They're really good balls. I've been using them at practice—they spin way better than the cheap ones."

Roan nodded. "You're welcome."

"I watched you chip and putt from here," Roan said, addressing Matthew. "It's the best part of your game."

Matthew's chest puffed slightly, his fingers tightening on his putter grip. "Coach says the same thing."

"Your coach is right."

A comfortable silence settled between them, filled with the ambient sounds of the golf course—the distant thwack of drives from the range, a golf cart rattling past on the path, wind rustling through the palm fronds overhead.

"Where's Clara?" Roan asked.

Evans glanced toward the clubhouse. "She's up there with Emily. Getting snacks."

"How's Matthew doing?" Roan's eyes moved to the boy, then back to Evans, where they lingered with unspoken concern.

"Up by three now," Evans said. "Was up one on the front nine."

Roan's expression didn't change, but something shifted in his posture—the same subtle straightening Evans had seen when someone made an outstanding arrest.

"Keep it up," Roan said to Matthew.

Evans picked up the bag again, the exhaustion weighing on him more than the clubs. "Rocca's going-away breakfast is in a few weeks. You should come."

Roan was quiet for a moment, considering. Then he nodded. "I'll be there."

"Good."

Matthew glanced between them, picking up on the undercurrent of their conversation—the unspoken history that adults carried.

Evans touched Matthew's shoulder. "We should get moving. Fourteenth tee."

"Yeah," Matthew said. He turned to Roan. "It was nice to meet you."

"You too."

They walked back across the rough, Evans slinging the bag over his shoulder and feeling the familiar pull in his ribs. He glanced back once to see Roan already turning toward his house, walking with the same measured pace, hands back in his pockets.

Evans watched him go, then followed his son toward the fourteenth tee. The sun continued its assault from above, and the bag seemed to gain weight with each step, his ribs protesting the movement.

But he kept walking, one step at a time.

Roan secured his house with two turns of the deadbolts and stood for a moment in the entryway. Everything remained in its proper place—he'd replaced the couch and bought new cushions after the incident, but kept the chess set. Some things you don't discard, especially weighted pieces of solid wood that have traveled with you for years.

The vintage receiver hummed quietly in the corner, vacuum tubes glowing amber through the vents. He rarely turned it off anymore, always ready for moments like this. His fingers slid through his record collection until they found Miles Davis' "Kind of Blue". The sleeve had surrendered to years of handling, its corners soft and splitting from its journey from his life before Florida.

When needle met groove, the initial static gave way to the bass line of "So What", unhurried and self-assured in the afternoon quiet.

Roan moved to his desk, where the laptop waited, always on. He checked his email and found one new message with no subject line from a sender identified only by a string of numbers and letters—the same sender as always.

He opened it. One line:

Nc6.

Roan studied the screen. Black's knight to c6—a developing move, controlling the center. His opponent's response to yesterday's gambit. For the first time in days, the tension in his jaw released, and the corners of his mouth softened into something approaching a smile.

He hit print and listened to the printer whir before taking the single sheet to his filing cabinet. After unlocking the top drawer, he added the new move to a stack of printed emails—each one a move in their ongoing game, a conversation conducted entirely in chess notation.

On the chessboard, the game was in progress. White's pieces had advanced aggressively while Black mounted a careful defense—a battle of patience and position conducted over weeks. Roan studied the position, calculating lines and responses, seeing the traps his opponent might be setting.

He picked up Black's knight and moved it two squares forward, one square left. Nc6. The piece landed with a satisfying click.

Then he selected White's bishop and slid it four squares diagonally to c4—the Italian Opening—a classic, aggressive move that controls the center while pressuring the f7 pawn. Everything was balanced and precise.

Miles played on, the trumpet dancing around the melody without quite touching it. Roan returned to his desk and typed a reply:

Bc4.

The email vanished into the digital void, traveling to whoever waited on the other end—someone who understood the value of a good game, who kept him sharp even in isolation.

Roan closed the laptop and walked to the kitchen, where his rocks glass waited. He poured two fingers of Ketel One—no ice, never ice—and let the first sip burn down his throat.

The leather chair had molded to his shape over the years, and he sank into it now with his vodka in hand. The afternoon light slanted through the blinds, painting gold stripes across the floor. Outside, he heard the distant crack of a club hitting a ball, followed by the rustle of something landing in his yard beyond the fence.

Tomorrow, he'd find it and add it to the bucket. The cycle continued.

But today, at this moment, he could rest. The trumpet played, the bass walked, the piano answered in its own time. Another crack echoed from the course—some kid out there learning the game properly, with patience and practice.

Roan took another sip of vodka and allowed himself a genuine smile. The chess game awaited his opponent's response.

CHAPTER

60

"You actually got me a fedora?" Rocca held the hat in both hands, turning it over to examine the silk interior, the grosgrain band. Black felt. Wide brim. Classic—what private eyes wore in old movies. He looked at Pérez across the table.

Pérez smiled, something that started in her eyes before reaching her mouth. "Don't wear it, though. Use it as décor for your new office."

"You think I need décor advice?"

"I think you need *any* advice."

Rocca set the hat on the table beside his plate. "Says the woman who keeps her handcuffs in a Hello Kitty pouch."

"They're organized," Pérez said. "Unlike your desk."

One of the younger detectives—Harris, Roan thought—laughed. The sound cut through the clatter of silverware on plates, through the breakfast smell of eggs and bacon grease. The Casino building's windows gave onto the ocean, and the morning sun blazed through the glass, turning coffee cups into amber pools. Salt tang cut through the smell of bacon grease and burnt toast. Someone had left a window cracked—the ocean breathed into the room, humid and fish-clean. The morning crowd filled half the tables, mostly tourists who didn't know the locals avoided this place for breakfast.

Rocca's fingers tightened on the hat brim. His voice dropped. "Thank you."

Pérez nodded.

The table held six chairs. Rocca sat at one end, Pérez beside him, then Roan, then Harris and Chen from the unit. The sixth chair sat empty, reserved for Evans, but Evans wasn't there.

Pérez glanced toward the window, down the beach where the sand stretched toward the pier, where Oceanside Pub sat diagonally across the street.

"Where's Evans?" Roan asked.

Pérez pointed. "He had to do something."

Roan followed her gesture. Saw Evans near the water's edge, right where Camila had been killed—the exact spot, Roan knew, measuring it in his mind against the crime scene photos he'd reviewed a dozen times. Evans knelt in the sand, took his time positioning something, pressed it deep, making sure it would hold against the tide. He stood slowly, brushed sand from his hands, and looked at the ocean for a long moment before turning back.

A memorial wreath—what you'd see at a roadside shrine. White and yellow flowers, already wilting in the heat, their brightness obscene against the sand where Camila had bled out.

Roan stood, his chair scraping against the floor. He walked outside, found a table on the patio, and sat. Waited.

The ocean spread before him, crystal in the morning light, blue that looked unreal, like glass, like something you could walk across if you had the faith.

He ordered coffee when the waitress appeared. Black. No sugar.

Evans appeared a few minutes later, walking across the sand, up the steps, favoring his left side slightly. The bruising on his neck had faded to yellow, almost gone, the stitches removed. A thin scar ran along his jaw, still healing but clean. He moved more easily now, with less stiffness in his stride, though something remained—a careful way of breathing, of holding himself, like a man who'd learned not to test his limits.

He sat across from Roan and pulled a pack of Marlboro Golds from his jacket pocket. Tapped one out. Lit it. The lighter clicked—the scratch of the wheel. Flame steady. He inhaled, held it, and exhaled slowly.

Roan lifted his cup, watching the smoke drift sideways in the ocean breeze.

"That's a good thing you did," Roan said finally, nodding toward the wreath.

Evans looked at it in the distance, took another drag. "Someone has to."

"Yeah."

"The whole family was wiped out because of one terrible thing."

Roan nodded, felt the weight of it settle in his chest where it had lived since the night Ariel died. "An anonymous donor paid for the funeral arrangements. Camila. Ariel. And now, Maria Morales."

Evans turned and looked at Roan. "Maria?"

"Walked out into traffic on I-95. Apparent suicide."

Evans stared, silent. He brought the cigarette to his lips and inhaled. The ember glowed orange.

"She resigned herself to death long ago," Roan said. His coffee had gone cold in his hand. "Addiction. If not for the highway, she'd have drunk herself to death, anyway."

Evans exhaled slowly, controlled. Smoke drifted on the breeze, dissipating over the railing. "I don't get it. How someone finds the strength to end it but not the strength to keep going."

Roan was quiet, watching a pair of tourists walk past on the beach below, oblivious as they laughed about something. Then he spoke. "That's just it. They don't want to live that life. Suicide is easier."

He paused, his jaw tightening. "Look at Ariel. His religious beliefs conflicted with his natural feelings. His sister wanted out of a life of poverty, away from a drunk mom. She was about to leave. Ariel feared abandonment—a father he's never seen, a drunk mother coming home to that every day, and a sister who was out the door. It was too much for the kid."

The muscle in Roan's jaw worked. He set down his coffee cup harder than he'd intended. "I should've helped him that night at the station. Gotten him help. But I let him go home." His forearm wiped sweat from his brow. "Marco Vargas was arrested for assault. Turns out the kid has a temper. Ariel wasn't the only one who got him angry."

Evans looked down. Ash hung on to the cigarette. He tapped it into the ashtray on the table, the motion deliberate, controlled. "Then there's Camila. A girl making her way out of it all, just to walk out of a bar into a monster's den."

Roan said nothing. There was nothing to say about that.

Evans continued. "You think Mark Vance was the anonymous donor?"

"Only if he grew a heart."

Evans leaned back in his chair, took another pull, let the smoke fill his lungs before releasing it in a thin stream. "I heard you're doing something for Jin's mom."

Roan nodded. "Got her set up in a good place. They'll take good care of her."

He shifted forward, his elbows on the table. The wood was warm from the sun. "Mary Tucker—the redhead who was friends with Jessica Torres—she called me yesterday. Said she recognized Brandon on the news, saw him pick up other girls." The waitress refilled his coffee, and he waited until she'd moved away. "She ID'd Verónica Rojas as the girl found in the refrigerated container. She's helping to see if we can identify more victims."

"And Jessica?" Evans asked. He stubbed out the cigarette—half-smoked—and ground it into the tray with more force than necessary.

"Woke up three days ago. Able to pick out Brandon from a photo lineup. DNA recovered from her fingernails matches Brandon's, and DNA from Brandon's home matches Jin Shin. Evidence is airtight." Roan felt a sense of satisfaction, clean and simple for once. "He's looking at multiple convictions."

Evans looked back at the restaurant, through the windows at Rocca and the others talking, laughing, celebrating. Then he turned back to Roan. "Think Rocca's got what it takes?"

Roan watched the ember die in the ashtray. "He's stubborn. Doesn't listen. Won't follow the rules." He paused. "Yeah. He'll be excellent."

"Will we see him again?"

Roan's mouth curved slightly, almost a smile. "To be an excellent PI, you've got to step on some police toes. We'll see him again."

Evans' phone buzzed. Clara:

> Emily brought home a puppy.

He replied:

> Really? I think we can make that work.

Roan stood and pushed his chair back. "Want a ride home?"

Evans looked up. "You're driving?"

"Yeah."

They walked back inside, passing through the cool, dim restaurant into the warmth of the group's celebration. Rocca stood when he saw them approach, the fedora still sitting on the table beside his empty plate.

"Heading out?" Rocca asked.

"Yeah," Roan said. He extended his hand.

Rocca shook it—firm grip, brief—the handshake of someone who'd learned something. Then he turned to Evans.

Evans took his hand. "You'll do good."

"Thanks for everything," Rocca said, looking at both of them. "Both of you."

"Stay out of trouble," Roan said.

Rocca grinned. "Trouble is my business."

The two detectives walked across the parking lot toward Roan's car, their footsteps crunching on loose gravel. The 1965 Shelby Mustang sat waiting—white with blue stripes, chrome gleaming, paint perfect under the morning sun.

Roan unlocked the doors. They got in. The interior smelled like leather—old, worn, real—a smell that couldn't be faked or bought new.

Roan turned the key. The car roared to life, engine growling deep and powerful, the vibration traveling up through the steering wheel into his hands.

Evans loosened his tie, fingers working at the knot.

Roan glanced at him; one eyebrow raised in almost-reprimand.

Evans took off his tie completely and dropped it out the window.

Roan watched it fall to the pavement, a strip of dark fabric against the grey asphalt. "I could write you up for littering."

Evans smiled.

The car launched down the beach road, engine roaring, the rush of wind muscling through the open windows, loud enough to drown out thought. Around the corner, the palms flashed by, their shapes reduced to mere smears of green against the blue sky. Off toward the beating heart of Lake Worth they drove, leaving the ocean behind them. In the rearview mirror, the sun blazed over the morning horizon, crimson bleeding into white.

AUTHOR'S NOTE

My deepest thanks to everyone who helped bring Crimson Sand to life.

It's been a five-year journey—one filled with late nights, rewrites, doubt, and discovery—and I'm profoundly grateful to everyone who helped see it through.

Thanks to the friends who shared their time, stories, and perspectives from life in South Florida—each conversation helped keep this world authentic, vivid, and alive.

To the early readers who offered encouragement, feedback, and insight along the way—thank you for your honesty and belief in the story. Your words helped shape this book in ways you may never realize.

Endless gratitude to my family for their patience, support, and understanding through countless late nights and early mornings. You've been my grounding force and my reason to keep going when the writing felt impossible.

Lastly, to Loan, Nolan, and Alexander—without you, none of this would matter.

Chris Binnix

ABOUT THE AUTHOR

CHRIS BINNIX is the author of several novels and novellas in the crime and thriller genre, including *Crimson Sand*, *The Interval*, *Digital Grave*, *Give No Quarter*, and *Criminal Fortune*. His writing explores the darker corners of human nature with sharp detail, atmospheric settings, and characters that stay with readers long after the final page.

Long before he ever sat down to write a novel, he spent more than twenty years in marketing, training, and education, careers built on understanding people: what motivates them, what scares them, and what they're willing to do when the stakes are high enough. Those years of observation would eventually find their way into every character he created.

A lifelong admirer of noir detective stories, true crime, and tightly wound thrillers, Chris grew up on the kinds of books and films where shadows meant something, and no one was exactly who they appeared to be. When he finally turned to fiction writing, he brought that same sensibility to the page—stories where character complexity and tension converge, and where the line between right and wrong isn't always easy to find.

When he isn't writing, Chris can usually be found on a golf course or spending time with his family and friends.